Those who touch

the stars are

marked to die...

I0696703

"*Atlantis*, on glidescope, on centerline."

Sweat beaded on Steve Banke's forehead and lips. Ordinarily, landings were the favorite part of any shuttle commander's flight. But after what had happened four hours earlier, the word "ordinary" no longer applied.

"*Atlantis*, right of centerline and diverging."

Banke swore softly as he moved the stick to the left. In eighty-seven combat missions, nothing he had seen compared to that single, horrible moment a few short hours ago. One instant the man was breathing, talking; the next, he was gone, his life boiling away into nothingness.

At fifteen knots, both nose wheels finally blew, and *Atlantis* screeched to a halt, riding on the alloy rims. For a few moments, no one said anything.

"Congratulations, *Atlantis*, on a job well done."

A job well done? Banke shook his head. Halvorson had already opened the flask of Old Bushmills, and Banke peeled off his gloves and lifted his helmet to accept it. The whole planet had seen it! Banke had been at the aft windows when it happened, and the memory left him queasy. "To a job well done," he mocked and tipped the flask to his lips.

Avon Books are available at special quantity discounts for bulk purchases for sales promotions, premiums, fund raising or educational use. Special books, or book excerpts, can also be created to fit specific needs.

For details write or telephone the office of the Director of Special Markets, Avon Books, Dept. FP, 1350 Avenue of the Americas, New York, New York 10019, 1-800-238-0658.

FINAL ORBIT

S.V. DATE

AVON BOOKS NEW YORK

This is a work of fiction. Names, characters, places, and incidents either are the product of the author's imagination or are used fictitiously. Any resemblance to actual events, locales, organizations, or persons, living or dead, is entirely coincidental and beyond the intent of either the author or the publisher.

AVON BOOKS
A division of
The Hearst Corporation
1350 Avenue of the Americas
New York, New York 10019

Copyright © 1997 by Shirish V. Date
Published by arrangement with the author
Visit our website at **http://www.AvonBooks.com**
Library of Congress Catalog Card Number: 97-93743
ISBN: 0-380-79625-2

All rights reserved, which includes the right to reproduce this book or portions thereof in any form whatsoever except as provided by the U.S. Copyright Law. For information address Knox Burger Associates, 39½ Washington Square South, New York, New York 10012.

First Avon Books Printing: December 1997

AVON TRADEMARK REG. U.S. PAT. OFF. AND IN OTHER COUNTRIES, MARCA REGISTRADA, HECHO EN U.S.A.

Printed in the U.S.A.

WCD 10 9 8 7 6 5 4 3 2 1

If you purchased this book without a cover, you should be aware that this book is stolen property. It was reported as "unsold and destroyed" to the publisher, and neither the author nor the publisher has received any payment for this "stripped book."

To Mary Beth

Thanks to Craig, Ned, Lynn, Donna, Jackie and, of course, Mary Beth, for kind words and gentle suggestions; to my friends at NASA for their help with the technical details and their forbearance for those that aren't *just* right; and to Knox for making it real.

1

Even by garage sale standards, the set tucked in the corner of the living room at 463 Gulfbreeze Terrace was a piece of junk. The whole picture curved inward, bands of red, green and blue glowing at the edges. A beige converter box with a coaxial-to-rabbit-ears splice sat on top: the cable company's attempt to drag its handful of stone-age customers into the twenty-first century. There wasn't even a remote control.

The Dean of American Astronauts didn't care. He rarely turned it on, and on those occasions he did, it showed him all he needed. On this particular night, the ancient machine painted a fuzzy image of two stocky figures, both clad in white, one with a dark stripe encircling each leg. Two hours earlier their movements had been awkward—legs bumping and bouncing, arms pinwheeling fruitlessly. With practice, though, the pair had improved, moving slowly but deliberately along the walls of the cavernous cargo bay. Wrenches, screwdrivers and other, more specialized gadgets dangled from their waists, as Striped Pants unbolted a white metal box from the minivan-size satellite nestled in the bay while Plain Pants held his legs to keep him from spinning in the opposite direction around the power tool. Occasionally a Donald Duck voice broke the static to tell Mission Control that he had completed Step 7-Echo, or that a particular bolt had needed twelve inch-pounds of torque to loosen it, not the eight the engineers had expected.

Santiago Santich watched with as much interest as he could muster. He inverted the green bottle to drain the remaining drops and set the empty Heineken on the coaster atop the end table. He smiled wistfully; it had taken his wife fifteen years to train him to use one. She had been gone four now, and still he kept the habit. He contemplated another beer, remembered there wasn't any more, and settled back into the right-hand side of the love seat—the copilot's side; the pilot's side was Emily's—in front of the TV. It had taken her ten years to make him abandon the easy chair in the corner and sit with her instead.

Striped Pants and Plain Pants succeeded in detaching the microwave-size box and floated it to a locker mounted on the wall. They had already removed the replacement unit from the locker, and the failed module off the satellite fit the bracket exactly for the ride home.

Santich suppressed a sigh and watched with mild envy. A free-floating space walk was something, the only thing, that he hadn't done. Through two flights on Gemini, one on Apollo and three aboard space shuttle, he had never stepped outside in the weightlessness of orbit. True, his was a far loftier accomplishment: one of twelve humans in history, quite possibly for all time to come, to step on another world. But the moon had gravity, though a fraction of Earth's, and Santich wanted to taste the complete freedom that the others, too numerous now to name offhand, had described: the solitude, the fleeting vertigo as one imagined the plummet back into a spinning mass of green forest, white cloud, brown mountain, and blue, blue water.

The thought pricked at Santich's insides, albeit only for a moment. Even a few years back, he would sigh whenever he contemplated that he would never again fly where the sky was star-flecked black. Now the knowledge eased into his consciousness without undue fuss. The Dean of American Astronauts. That's what *Time* magazine had called him back in 1985, after his third trip on the shuttle. Norm Thagard, then Shannon Lucid had broken the final Skylab crew's record for most time in space by an American, but no one—neither American nor Russian—had been up and back as often as Santiago Santich.

And though he wouldn't have traded the moon for anything, he loved flying the shuttle more than the Gemini and Apollo capsules put together. True, the shuttle was almost completely automated and could lift off and land without so much as a cockroach aboard. But Santich and the other Apollo-era astronauts had successfully lobbied the designers to omit the autoland program from the computers, leaving the deployment of the landing gear, the touchdown and the braking of the just-landed ship in human hands. By tradition, one that Santich began with STS-1, the pilot took the stick away from the computers just as the shuttle began its final turn around the field to line up on the landing strip, giving him full control for the last five minutes of a week or two-week flight.

But what a five minutes it was! Before the shuttle, American astronauts splashed home, cannonballing into the water like drunken fraternity boys—certainly no way for a trained naval aviator to end a mission. The shuttle was something else entirely: the steep, fifty-degree bank around the runway, the free fall to the strip, the quick flare-up, and finally the rumble of rubber rolling across concrete. That first landing aboard *Columbia* had been the best. No one knew how many of the thermal tiles on the ship's belly would be lost during ascent; if too many fell off, the superhot plasma flowing around the descending shuttle would burn a hole right through. And even if Santich and Forrester did make it past reentry, would the navigation system work? With no engines on the trip home, the shuttle's computers had to balance speed against altitude to deplete both by the time it arrived at the landing strip. There could be no waving off for a second chance. And what of the tires and brakes? The shuttle weighed as much as a small jetliner, but the demands of getting into orbit made redundant landing gear too heavy a luxury. Had two of the rear tires blown, or one of the front ones, it would have meant military funerals for both men.

As it was, the engineers had been right, and the landing had gone like the simulator said it would. Santich had celebrated by sharing a flask of Old Bushmills with Forrester before the ground crew could unbolt the orbiter's hatch. That, too, had become a tradition that, as far as Santich knew, had continued through all seventy-five landings to date. Santich's next two missions had been routine. He had hoped for one final trip—lucky number seven. And as chief of the astronaut corps, he'd been in a position to take it.

Then *Challenger* blew up, destroying the American psyche like nothing since Kennedy. In the subsequent frenzy of media interest, two of Santich's memos to his bosses criticizing decisions that sacrificed safety margins to save a little money found their way into the newspapers. In the ensuing recriminations, the National Aeronautics and Space Administration underwent a public housecleaning to show the world that safety would now come first. It also relegated the Dean of American Astronauts to a harmless sinecure at Johnson Space Center. They couldn't prove he had blown the whistle, but they didn't have to. After all, he never should have written them in the first place. As if to mock his transgression, they made him special assistant to the center director for safety. The title meant nothing: He was not part of Safety, Reliability, and Quality Assurance, the agency department with enough institutional clout to ground the shuttle fleet if it so deemed. Santich reported to no one, and no one reported to him.

At first he laughed at the snub. They couldn't possibly get away with it. The press that not long ago had deified him, the public that for three decades had stood in awe of his exploits, the president who just two years earlier had given him a medal, *they* wouldn't allow it. He would ride it out until the usurpers in shuttle management were purged, and then assume his rightful place at the top of the pyramid. Santich played his new role straight, attending every SRQA meeting, digging into the gritty technical issues that for two decades he'd largely ignored, and in general trying to prove that they wouldn't break him so easily.

But months passed, then years. Five men aboard *Discovery* got America back in space, the shuttle program resumed a slow but steady pace, and Capt. Santiago "Santy" Santich, USN, Ret., was all but forgotten. His cohorts in the corps, those astronauts chosen at the tail end of Apollo, had retired. The younger ones still quietly admired him as a legend and a moonwalker, but they shared the nearly unanimous sentiment that he'd violated the brotherhood's code, recklessly risked the sacred mission, and, ultimately, deserved what he got. Besides, he was no longer chief astronaut and no longer doled out the all-important flight assignments. Publicly or even privately taking his side meant jeopardizing their own chances of getting into orbit. Why risk that for someone who'd already flown six times? They knew on which side their bread was buttered, and took care to avoid his very name.

And though Santich had never thought much of the press, he had assumed that at least one of them would expose the injustice. After all, whistle-blowers at nuclear power plants, oil companies and even the Department of Energy were deemed heroes, the stuff on which the awards that Santich thought were the journalist's reason for existence were based. But he soon learned that the print and television reporters who hungered after glory and fame quickly lost interest in space after the finger-pointing for *Challenger* and the grand adventure of *Discovery* were finished. The only media left covering space were the same sniveling sycophants who had covered the program in the years before *Challenger*. Why interview Santich and lose access to those astronauts who actually flew?

Pride fermented into anger, anger into resentment, and resentment, finally, into bitterness. Emily tolerated the first two, but not the third. What do you have to prove? she had asked. You've had more opportunity and good fortune than just about anyone who has ever lived. She suggested, then pleaded with him to leave Houston and return to Florida.

If not for himself then for his grandchildren, who were growing up without him, just as his children had done. Four years earlier she decided she'd waited enough, and went home without him.

Over the past months, he'd realized she had been right, and it was time to give up. They'd started talking again, but he didn't yet know whether she'd have him back. The occasional cards and letters they had exchanged told him she was no longer Mrs. Ninth Man on the Moon, but had grown into Emily Pembroke Santich, self-confident, self-sufficient, adult woman. This May 18, six more weeks, would be their thirty-sixth wedding anniversary. He would return to her then, or would try to, anyway. It was a good time to leave NASA. In June he would turn fifty-nine. That was early retirement for most jobs; it would be good enough for him. Unlike his pals who had left NASA soon after their flights for cushy consulting jobs in the aerospace industry, he would never be rich. But with the Navy and civil service pensions—twenty-nine years in one; thirty-five years in the other—he would do okay. More than okay. The kids were out of school, the house was paid for, and he wouldn't be around for more than ten or fifteen years anyway.

It would be nice, finally, to take the rotting canvas cover off that old but nearly new Boston Whaler, put her in the water, get out in the Gulf. Not the dirty, brown Gulf off Galveston but the sparkling green Gulf off Naples, or even further south in the Ten Thousand Islands, or further still off the Keys. Just sit, all day long, with nothing to do but wait for the Big One to strike. Just him, and maybe a grandchild or two, to sit and fish. Something he hadn't had time for, or rather, hadn't *made* time for, in half a century.

The more he thought about leaving, the more he couldn't wait to walk into Bruce's office and tell him to take his assistant to the directorship and stick it up his tight ass. April 12: That would be the day to do it. The sixteenth anniversary of his first flight, when Bruce was still a snotty, stuck-up rookie just two years in the corps and still four years away from flying. The tenth anniversary had been a big deal, with ceremonies and picnics at Johnson, Kennedy, Marshall and Dryden. The seventeenth would be nothing like that, but it would be something. People would sit up and notice, if only to realize they didn't have Santy Santich to feel sorry for anymore.

He permitted himself a sigh and stretched back into the sofa, letting his eyes drop shut for a moment before snapping them open. NASA Select, the agency's in-house television channel, was again showing the inside of the Mission Control room, which it did whenever the crew was asleep or otherwise wanted privacy or, as was often the case, the radio link between the orbiter and the satellites degraded to the point where microwave transmission needed for TV downlink was impossible. The screen showed a dozen or so ground controllers at their monitors, chatting with one another or milling about. In the second row down, along the right-hand side of the aisle just in front of the flight surgeon, sat the capcom, the capsule communicator. Back in the days of Mercury, the astronauts had decreed that only other astronauts were worthy enough to talk to the men in orbit. Successive astronauts had kept the tradition alive, so that to this day, the only voice heard on NASA Select speaking with orbiting astronauts was that of another astronaut.

And as Santich laid his head back against the love seat's cushion, capcom Mike Farina answered one of the Donald Duck voices that, yes, the customer wanted to study the satellite's health check for a few more minutes before giving the go-ahead to start Step 27-Lima.

While waiting, the other Donald Duck voice started humming "Rocket Man," to which Donald Duck Number One answered with "Space Oddity." Farina advised the spacewalkers not to give up their day jobs just yet.

Santich missed the hijinks. He wouldn't have recognized the songs anyway. They weren't of his generation. Instead his eyes stayed closed for ever longer periods before reopening. He had intended to watch all six hours of the space walk, as well as the second one the following night, even though they wouldn't end until 3:00 A.M. Houston time.

NASA Select returned to live video from *Atlantis*'s cargo bay, where the two spacewalkers hovered against the starboard rail beside the satellite they were working on. Within seconds the picture returned to the Mission Control room. And a few moments later, in the lower right-hand corner of Santich's set, where the image was both tinted blue and warped into a convex curve, the flight surgeon quickly reached forward to his monitor, and the broadcast picture was replaced with a test pattern.

Whether anyone noticed or linked the two was impossible to say. Certainly no one at 463 Gulfbreeze Terrace did. The Dean of American Astronauts had fallen asleep.

2

Her normally black belly aglow, *Atlantis* hurtled through the night sky, fifteen times faster than an airliner. To manage her great speed, the four cross-linked computers swerved the ship first left, then right, then left again. Each roll of her wings made *Atlantis* even less aerodynamically efficient than her stubby features dictated, making her lose both speed and altitude all the more rapidly.

Soon she had fallen to 200,000 feet and slowed to only six times the speed of sound. Heavy clouds blanketing both the Midwest and the eastern seaboard kept anyone still awake from seeing the ionized trail she left behind, like a ship sailing through phosphorescent water. Apart from that shimmering wake, which had disappeared by the time she was over Georgia, *Atlantis* was completely dark. Only television spaceships carried port and starboard running lights.

By the time she was over Jacksonville, she was down to 150,000 feet—low enough for her twin sonic booms to rouse light sleepers. By Saint Augustine, even heavy sleepers were awakened by the rumbles, and those space shuttle aficionados among them wondered why the shuttle was coming home five days early.

As *Atlantis* slowed to Mach 1 and dropped below 50,000 feet over Titusville, she wasn't awakening space fans anymore. They had spent the past hour phoning one another: Have you heard? *Atlantis* is coming back tonight! A friend

9

on the convoy team was called in an hour ago!

At 4:17 A.M., *Atlantis* commander Steve Banke took control of the shuttle from the computers and began a large right-hand turn that would take him over the launch pads, out over the ocean, and back over shore north of Cocoa Beach before lining him up on the three-mile slab of concrete tucked amid marsh and drainage canals. But with a thick overcast at 5,000 feet, all Banke could see was a uniform whitish glow beneath him.

"*Atlantis*, we have you low on energy at the one-eighty."

"Roger, low at the one-eighty," Banke answered, nudging the stick ever so slightly forward.

Atlantis's computers instantly translated the movement into minute downward adjustments of the elevons—the wing flaps. The ship's nose pitched down, and the airspeed indicator on the panels in front of Banke and his pilot, Robert Halvorson, began rising. Satisfied, Banke let the stick move back to its neutral position.

"*Atlantis*, on energy at the ninety," came Roy Honeycutt's voice from Houston.

"Roger, on energy."

"*Atlantis*, here's your final weather. At three thousand: two-three-zero at four-zero knots; two thousand, two-three-five at three-zero; one thousand, two-four-zero at two-eight; five hundred, two-three-five at two-zero, peak two-seven; and surface winds at two-three-five, one-two, peak one-niner. How copy?"

"Roger, Houston. Two-three-five at one-two, peak one-niner."

· Sweat beaded on Banke's forehead and lips, dribbling down onto the radio mouthpiece. With helmet in place, there was nothing he could do about it. Ordinarily landings were the favorite part of any shuttle commander's flight— actually the only part where he did any real flying. But after what had happened four hours earlier, the word "ordinary" no longer applied. In eighty-seven combat missions, he'd seen buddies' planes disappear in balls of fire, had seen his share of ugly, torn-open guts on returning pilots. Nothing compared to that single horrible moment. For that's how long it had taken. One instant he was breathing, talking; the next, he was gone, his life boiling away into nothingness. For a few seconds, he'd actually thought they could save him, if only they could get him inside fast enough. Then he got a better look and knew it was already too late.

To cap it off, he did *not* need to be landing through a low cloud deck in twenty knots of crosswind. He was only seven miles away but still couldn't see a thing.

"*Atlantis*, on centerline, low on energy."

"Shit," Banke muttered, twenty-seven years of military radio protocol flying out the window. Arriving "low on energy" meant arriving in the swamp. The landing gear would snap off. The nose would bury itself in the muck. The residual hydrazine and nitrogen tetroxide in the forward tanks would either leak out, killing everyone within two miles, or ignite, killing everyone within two miles. Then alligators would eat his and crewmates' corpses.

The shuttle during landing was an engineless glider with the flight characteristics of a winged brick. Banke had but finite quantities of speed and altitude. To gain one he had to give up the other. Gingerly he again pushed the stick away from him, pointing *Atlantis*'s nose down and speeding her up. When the small circle on the CRT predicting where *Atlantis* would be in thirty seconds moved back into the target corridor, he eased back.

"*Atlantis*, on glide slope, on centerline."

Banke let out a breath of relief but took it in sharply as the approach lights finally punctured the gloom, drifting slowly to the left as the altimeter dropped rapidly through 500 feet.

"*Atlantis*, right of centerline and diverging."

Yes, he could see he was fucking diverging—it wasn't *his* brain-dead idea to land here. He looked at the altimeter: 380 feet. If he rolled left, he'd drop too quickly and wouldn't even make the underrun. Two hundred ninety feet. It was now or never.

"Motherfuck," he swore softly as he moved the stick to the left. "Houston, this is a fuck of a lot more than twenty knots."

Atlantis dropped her left wing, raised her right, and sank even more quickly. Two hundred feet, 160, 120, 80, Banke waited for 50 to roll up on the meter before pulling back on the stick. "Gear down!"

Halvorson flipped the remaining switch to blow open three sets of doors, letting the nose and main landing gear fall out of their recessed compartments as *Atlantis*'s nose pitched upward, bringing the shuttle out of her dive and into a gentle flare. Banke watched the rough but usable underrun approach ever so slowly as *Atlantis* again slipped off the centerline because of the crosswind. There was nothing more he could do; he had used all the altitude he dared to get back to the middle. If he rolled any further, he'd drop all eighty-five tons into the marsh and dig a furrow right to the lip of the runway.

No one said a word, not even the radio. Houston was finished calling. It was all in Banke's hands now.

The runway came to him ever more slowly while *Atlantis*'s lateral movement to the right continued apace. With 300 yards to go, he was nearly at the edge of the strip. With 200 yards left, Banke realized he had to roll the dice. Again his hands pushed the stick to the left, rolling *Atlantis* till her left gear was within feet of the marsh.

With a sudden lurch, the wheels slammed onto rough concrete; *Atlantis* tore through the mist, twin helices trailing off her wingtips, with her left wheels down and right wheels held high above the runway. Still the crosswind pushed her, until her right wheels hovered not over concrete but over soft grass and mud lining the runway's edge.

"Drag chute," Banke said softly, giving Halvorson his cue to flip two final switches.

With a cannon shot, the chute's housing blew off *Atlantis*'s rear, pulling out a small drogue. It pulled out the main red-white-and-blue chute, which filled instantly, giving the unrelenting crosswind a new target.

Immediately the billowing nylon was pushed downwind, pivoting *Atlantis*'s nose sharply upwind—back toward the center of the runway—before exploding into a flurry of cloth. Banke worked the rudder pedals to slow the turn and moved the stick back to its rest position to get the right-hand main gear down. With a sickening lurch, the sluggish ship began a wobble toward the left as a new rumble joined the cacophony enveloping the flight deck.

"Hang on!" Banke called as he jerked the stick forward to bring the nosewheels down—the only way to regain steerage after what he knew must be a blown tire on the left-hand main gear.

The flight computers responded instantly, for a moment transferring much of *Atlantis*'s 171,000 pounds onto her front two tires. The terrific load burned through plies of rubber, overheated the wheels, made steering even more skittish. Banke knew that if the nosewheels blew at that speed, they were finished. He slammed on the brakes; if they melted, they would die. If he didn't try, they would die anyway.

With half of the three-mile runway behind her, *Atlantis* still raced through the mist at more than 120 knots, her tires disintegrating, the shredded remnants of the drag chute shaking the frame hard enough to send flying through the cabin the pens and notebooks that, in the crew's haste, had been left attached to the walls with Velcro. Banke clenched his teeth to keep from biting his tongue as he watched the centerline lights slip beneath the nose. Mist obscured the lights marking the end of the runway, which he knew must be less than a mile away.

Gradually, though, the spaceship's rumble deepened and softened as her speed dropped through one hundred knots, then eighty, then fifty. At fifteen knots both nosewheels finally blew, and *Atlantis* screeched to a halt riding on the alloy rims. For a few moments, no one said a word. Banke gripped the stick with both hands, as if afraid she would start rolling toward the end of the runway if he let go.

Finally Halvorson managed the words that were Banke's to say: "Houston, *Atlantis*. Wheels stopped."

"Roger, *Atlantis*. Wheels stopped." Honeycutt had been dragged from bed just two hours earlier to handle *Atlantis*'s early return and fumbled through the made-for-TV welcoming line. "Congratulations on returning the Gamma Ray Observatory to fully operational condition, to let humankind continue its exploration of the high-energy universe. A job well done."

A job well done? Banke shook his head. The whole planet had seen it! He'd been at the aft windows when it happened, and the memory left him queasy.

Halvorson had already opened the flask of Old Bushmills, and Banke peeled off his gloves and lifted his helmet to accept it. "To a job well done," he mocked, and tipped the flask to his lips.

3

Twice Santich had read through the morning briefing, and twice it made no sense. He tossed the pages on his desk, flipped off the reading glasses, and turned to the now tepid coffee. Why in God's name had he drank that third beer last night? Like most astronauts, Santich had a slight build—five foot eight, 150 pounds—and he'd never been able to handle more than two drinks without a hangover the next morning.

Others in his flight school class, then in his group at Pax River and later in Gemini and Apollo could all drink like fish, even though none had been that much heftier. The height and weight restrictions the military had for fighter and high-performance test pilots meant all their fliers were fairly small. But it had been a point of honor for the others to get piss drunk each evening, stay that way well past midnight, and then get out on the flight line by dawn. He himself had never felt the need to conform, and so had never developed the others' alcohol tolerance.

Any new group he found himself in at first delighted in ridiculing his moderation. Santypuss, they called him. At first it bothered him, but he soon discovered he was always slightly better than the others. Whenever a new engine arrived for flight test or the choice assignments were handed out, Santich would be at the top of the list, and the mockery would become a grudging respect.

In recent years there had been no mockery at all because he had nothing left to prove. He'd walk into the Outpost, where the latest class of astronauts would congregate each day, drinking Lone Star or Dos Equis to fit in, and order his Heineken, drink it, and leave. Often he'd speak to nobody but the barkeep. Occasionally he would meet Hoop and go so far as to have a second Heineken while chatting with his buddy.

In the past year, though, he'd largely stopped going to the Outpost at all and instead drank at home—a change that, when he thought about it, disturbed him. In fact, now that he thought about it, the previous evening had been the fourth, no, the fifth night this month he'd had a third beer. He shook his head, swallowed the rest of the bitter coffee to mask the foul taste in his mouth and began for a third time on the briefing.

It had been prepared by Mission Operations for the mission management team, and distributed only to senior managers within Mission Ops, Crew Branch, Orbiter Flight Project, and, of course, program management at Huntsville and the Cape.

In typical NASA-ese, it described the events of the previous night in a series of bulleted paragraphs, starting with the discovery of a failed logic assembly on the Gamma Ray Observatory's sun sensor, to the failure of fuel cell number three, to the "anomalous readings" on fuel cell number one and the subsequent decision to deorbit next rev, to the landing at Kennedy earlier that morning. And to think he'd slept through it all! Based on the mission elapsed times listed, all the fun must have started just a few minutes after he'd nodded off.

But whatever had possessed them to come back to Florida? He'd seen the weather outlooks the previous day, and the entire East Coast had been socked in, from Portland right down to Key West, while Southern California was completely clear. And how the hell could they have lost two fuel cells in the span of one hour? What were the chances of that?

Santich leaned back in his chair to stretch his arms just in time to see Ned Marsh look down at a sheet of paper and silently open his mouth. Santich jumped forward, shuffling aside papers till he found the remote control for the Sony in the corner.

"At four days, twenty-one hours mission elapsed time, that's about one A.M. central daylight time, EGIL—that's the Electrical Generation and Illumination officer, for those of you new to our program and all its wonderful acronyms—noticed a funny on fuel cell one. It was a brief transient, but our concern was that its primary oxygen valve was exhibiting the same behavior that had shut down fuel cell three."

Poor Marsh, Santich thought. The guy had been up all night and now, as chief of Mission Operations Directorate, had the responsibility of explaining to the world how NASA had screwed it up again. His thinning hair was disheveled, and the harsh TV lights highlighted the deep circles under his eyes. He looked like hell. To make it worse, he sat next to Marty Bruce, who also must have been awake all night, except he looked like he always did: a predator on full alert. A falcon perhaps, or a shark. Every time the camera pulled back for a wide angle, there he was, his beady eyes scanning the press room.

Marsh took a sip of water from a glass and continued. "Rather than risk leaving the crew with just a single source of electricity if fuel cell number one were to fail, the MMT, sorry, the Mission Management Team, decided at four days, twenty-one hours, and thirty minutes to go ahead and de-orbit on the next revolution. As many of you know, the flight software is constantly updated with a possible landing site for every moment of each orbit, in case of a major malfunction that requires an immediate de-orbit.

"We weren't quite so desperate as that. Instead, given our orbital parameters and our ground track, we were able to delay for twenty-five minutes, letting us return to the primary end-of-mission landing site, the Kennedy Space

Center in Florida. Now I know y'all will ask me, so, let me find it . . .''

Marsh searched through a sheaf of papers on the dais while Bruce continued scanning the half-dozen Houston reporters who'd managed to wake up in time to make the press conference.

''. . . okay. The TIG, that's time of ignition—sorry—was at four days, twenty-one hours, fifty-seven minutes and one-point-zero-four seconds''—a slight titter went through the press room—''with a touchdown on KSC runway thirty-three at MET four days, twenty-three hours, six minutes and thirty-four-point-five-six seconds, or three-twenty-one A.M. central daylight time.

''Colonel Banke brought Orbiter Vehicle 104 down safely, and the flight crew is resting at the Operations and Checkout Building at Kennedy, and will be flown back to Ellington Field later this afternoon.''

Marsh looked up from his papers and turned toward Bruce, then the other way, toward Len Concord, the public affairs officer moderating the conference. ''That's all I had, so I guess we can open it up for questions,'' Marsh told Concord.

''Okay,'' Concord said, stopping to listen to his earpiece. ''We'll follow the standard format, starting here and then going around to the other centers. Please wait for the mike and state your name and affiliation.''

Santich leaned forward, spellbound. What bullshit! They could have landed at Edwards Air Force Base that very same orbit, if they'd wanted. No, they landed in Florida for some other reason. . . .

The camera moved to a pretty brunette wearing too much makeup, particularly for such an early morning. ''Hi, this is Sandy Appleton from KHST, and I just wondered what time the astronauts would be returning. My station wants to send a crew out.''

Marsh managed a smile, the pale lips turning upward. ''Well, Sandy, we'll be sure to get that to you. We're in no rush, just waiting for the crew to wake up. Then we'll

put 'em on the STA—uh, the Shuttle Training Aircraft—
sorry again—and bring 'em home.''

Sandy smiled back, teeth glistening perfectly, and the
camera followed the boom to the next reporter.

"Tony Birch from the *Houston Herald*. I was wondering
if one of you could walk me through the decision-making
process you used for deciding to bring *Atlantis* home instead of maybe waiting an extra orbit or two to get smarter
about fuel cell one. And also if you could describe what
the problem was with NASA Select and if that had anything
to do with 104's anomalies.''

Problem with Select? Santich hadn't heard about this,
and leaned even closer toward the set.

"Tony, I apologize; I'd meant to cover that in my opening because I knew y'all would be interested in that. I have
to find my sheet here. . . .'' Marsh shuffled some more papers and settled on a single page. "Here. At MET four
days, twenty hours, twenty-three minutes, NASA lost its
ability to transmit NASA Select television because of an
electrical surge at Goddard Space Flight Center in Green-
belt, Maryland. As most of you are probably aware, the
East Coast has had unsettled weather for the past several
days, and we most likely suffered from a nearby lightning
strike.

"Whatever the exact cause, which we are currently investigating, we were unable to receive the feed from White
Sands. And even if we had, we would have been unable to
retransmit it out to SATCOM 7. The damaged equipment
was replaced about two hours ago, and went back on-line
about an hour ago.''

Lightning strike . . . Couldn't Goddard afford surge pro-
tectors and arresters and whatever the hell other gadgets
were out there? Santich fumbled with the remote control to
turn on the built-in recorder to tape the rest of the conference.

"None of the equipment at White Sands was affected,
and Mission Control's ability to communicate with 104 and
its crew on UHF, S-Band and Ku-Band was never im-

pacted. In fact, like I mentioned, the entire incident was completely transparent to everyone in the MOCR, or Mission Operations Control Room, and we carried on as if nothing had happened. PAO even continued commentary after we were notified we weren't broadcasting. Isn't that right, Len?''

Concord's look became even more officious as he nodded slowly. He turned toward Birch, the TV lights glinting off round, wire-rimmed glasses.

"Yes, Ned, I continued commentary because I didn't know if Select would come back up before touchdown or not." Concord puffed out his pudgy cheeks before continuing. "As deputy news chief here, I'd like to emphasize that we take very seriously our obligation to provide the public and the press a timely and accurate report of all our activities in human spaceflight, and we will study exactly what happened to ensure it doesn't happen again."

Concord turned to Marsh with a back-to-you look he'd gotten from watching television news, and Santich snorted. He hated Concord, a one-time radio reporter who idolized the space program and, at age forty-three, finally got his dream job: NASA flack, getting to talk with real astronauts each and every day. Every time the man opened his mouth, out popped the pronoun "we," as if what Concord did was somehow every bit as important as what the software engineers or flight controllers did.

If Marsh shared Santich's disdain, he hid it and continued with Birch's question.

"And as to why we deorbited; well, we did what we thought best given the circumstances. I don't think anyone in the program would have recommended keeping *Atlantis* up given the chance of only one good fuel cell, and our flight rules are quite clear about the required level of redundancy on Criticality-1R items."

Crit-1R: hardware with redundant backups that if lost, would result in loss of vehicle and crew. How was it that two of three fuel cells had failed within an hour of each other? And how convenient that a storm should simultaneously knock the public access off the air. . . . Santich poured himself a second cup from the pot behind him and heard the all-too-familiar voice of Space Slut.

"This is Jo Pointer with WNS. Do you worry that the early landing will overshadow in the press the successful repair of the GRO?"

Santich rolled his eyes. Another softball blow-job question. He wondered when she would jump back over to NASA, like Concord had. At one time, back when shuttles began flying, she'd been a NASA flack at Kennedy but had become a reporter to become eligible for the Journalist-in-Space Program. When that idea had died along with Teacher-in-Space Christa McAuliffe aboard *Challenger*, her only reason for leaving NASA had disappeared, and she'd been angling to get back for the past five years.

Bruce fielded her question, arms folded across his chest. "Well, Jo, I guess how the press portrays Space Transportation System flight 74 is up to you all." A native midwesterner, Bruce hadn't quite mastered the southernism, giving it the same clipped pronunciation he gave everything. "The whole shuttle team performed in a professional and exemplary manner, and I personally am proud of our achievement. Also, we repaired all that we set out to on the GRO, and I'm proud of the two EVA crew members, Sam Torrington and Alexis Orlov; the rest of the flight crew; and the hundreds of flight controllers on the ground who made it happen. It takes thousands of hours of preparation to make a space shuttle mission happen, and we here at NASA do it six and seven times a year."

The camera moved to Space Slut, who sat with a self-satisfied smirk, and moved back to a wide-angle shot of all three men on the dais.

"Okay, we'll move to the Kennedy Space Center for some questions from there. We have to wrap this up in fifteen minutes, so limit yourselves to one question each, please," Concord announced.

Santich almost turned off the set; the reporters from Florida were even bigger ass-kissers than those from Houston.

But as he hunted for the remote again, his ears perked at the slightly distorted, disembodied voice booming over the picture of Bruce, Marsh and Concord.

"This is Robert Lawrence from *Cocoa Beach Today*, and I have a three-part question. We out here at Kennedy have been hearing all kinds of rumors about the last few hours, and I'd like you guys to set the record straight. First, I understand that the GRO was *not* boosted to the proper orbit prior to redeploy and another repair mission will be needed. Second, the weather here last night seems, to the untrained eye anyway, to have violated flight rules, while the weather at Edwards was calm and clear. And third, we've heard that 104 may have suffered some tire damage, brake damage and possibly some structural damage to the landing gear, and that the drag chute was torn beyond repair."

Marsh and Bruce looked at each other before Bruce nodded.

"I'll try to answer them, Bob, if I can remember them all." Bruce wore the confused look he affected whenever he was particularly irritated with someone. "Let's see. About the GRO. I suppose you all missed the discussion and resolution among the project scientists because Select was down. But, yes, during last night's EVA—that is, for you laymen, extravehicular activity, or space walk—we found a control module for a sun sensor that looked like it had suffered oxidation. The crew relayed this to the GRO scientists, and they ran a health check and decided the module, which is the backup, was indeed failed. The primary unit was examined, and it appeared to have a lesser amount of corrosion. A health check was also done, and it was working properly.

"But to make a long story short, the project team decided that to make it easier for a second repair flight to change out the sensors, it was best to leave it at the lower orbit, which if you will remember from your prelaunch briefings is a perfectly acceptable orbit for science operations."

Bruce licked his lips, a wolf preparing for the kill. "So

in answer to your implication, no the repair was not a failure. Second, I'll guess that few of you in the media are trained meteorologists. It's very easy to play Monday-morning quarterback, and we were faced with one, quite possibly two failed fuel cells. Would you rather that we have left *Atlantis* in orbit, and if the third cell had failed, with the crew stranded? There used to be a saying: Any port in a storm, and early this morning, Florida in marginal weather was a better port than California ninety minutes later.''

That's their story, and they're sticking to it. Santich bit his lip. *What the hell really happened up there?*

''And as to your third question, we haven't had time to study the orbiter in much detail yet. And as it's getting late, if you kids will excuse us, Ned and I have some work to do.''

As Concord looked on, mouth agape, Bruce, followed a moment later by a perplexed Marsh, rose, pushed in his chair and walked away. Santich stared at the Sony in his office, awestruck. He normally loved it when someone thumbed his nose at the press, but his dislike of Bruce and his intense curiosity about the Florida newspaperman's questions left him conflicted.

The abrupt end to the conference equally confused both the cameraman and the producer, as the television picture first followed the two men as they strode out the back entrance to the briefing room, lingered for a moment on the closed door, then panned back to the still-shocked Concord.

''I guess we'll call this to a close,'' Concord managed finally.

4

The figure slumped forward over the steering wheel, arms carelessly on the dashboard. The sun shone brightly, so the top was down: a great morning for a drive. There wouldn't be any traffic. There rarely was. The beach road long ago had been made superfluous by the completion of State Road 3. No one would notice the golden wings on the breast pocket—the mark of a spaceflight veteran—or the dark stain that spread toward them down the ubiquitous blue flight suit.

Quickly, nervously, for the third time, the door handles were wiped clean, inside and out. The transmission lever was pushed from N into D, and the lever on the cruise control flicked to RESUME. With a lurch, the car started rolling forward, slowly at first, then faster.

The first time, the car had sped up solely under the weight of the foot on the accelerator pedal. It had barely damaged the plastic bumper. The second time, the cruise control had been set, and the convertible's hood had begun to crumple, but no fuel spilled out.

The third time, the convertible was still only doing about thirty miles per hour at impact, but because the valve on the tanker was already open and leaking, it was fast enough. Aviation-grade kerosene poured onto the hood, where the still-hot engine easily ignited it.

A quarter mile down the road, a light-blue Chevrolet

with white government license plates pulled onto the asphalt and headed slowly northward. An overall-clad figure leaned head and shoulders out the passenger window, far enough to make sure vomit didn't dribble down the side of the door.

The car was well clear of the area by the time the smoky yellow flames crept backward through the convertible's passenger compartment, found the small leak in the fuel line and detonated the nearly empty gas tank like a bomb.

5

Typing had never been a job requirement for fighter pilots and moonwalkers. So only occasionally did the keyboard chatter as Santich spent much of his time hunting the elusive letters with the index finger of each hand. Like a half-dozen other astronauts in quasi-management roles who retained offices in Building 4, Santich had his own secretary, but he didn't want word of his departure out until he was ready. Telling Lynnette guaranteed that Millie, the office's secretary, would know within fifteen minutes, the rest of the corps would know inside the hour, and the whole of JSC would know by the end of the day.

The letter Q had once again moved to a new spot on the keyboard when one of the handful of people he permitted to barge into his office unannounced did so, a photocopied page thrust out before him. Santich fished out his reading glasses and scanned the five paragraphs while Butch Grieve paced beneath photos of Santich in orbit, Santich on the moon, Santich in the Rose Garden with three different presidents. Cloth patches from six NASA spaceflights, two Navy fighter groups and the flight test school at Patuxent River hung in a row, each behind glass in a square frame. Above them was a single diploma: bachelor of science in aeronautical engineering, United States Naval Academy, Annapolis, Maryland.

"Was anyone else in the car?"

Grieve dropped his stocky frame in the padded steel chair opposite the steel desk, both standard Government Services Administration grade-11 gray, that, along with some filing cabinets and some bookshelves, furnished the small office.

"No. He was alone. I know; the release doesn't say shit. Can you believe that's how they told us? With a fucking news release?"

Santich nodded, read through the sheet a third time: U.S. Army Capt. Samuel James Torrington, veteran of two NASA space shuttle missions, including the just completed STS-74, died from injuries sustained in an automobile accident, declared dead at the scene by Kennedy Space Center paramedics. Entered astronaut corps in class of '89; B.S. from University of Southern California, 1973; U.S. Army from 1973 to 1985; M.S. from University of Alabama, Huntsville, 1982; survived by two sons, Christopher Scott, age 11, and James Wilfred, age 8.

"Why was he driving so soon after landing? Where was he going?"

Grieve shrugged. "The *official* story is that he was going for a run on the beach before coming home. He quote lost control of the vehicle unquote and ran it into a fuel truck by the side of the road, the vehicle became quote engulfed in flames unquote, and he was burned beyond recognition by the time rescue crews arrived."

Santich raised an eyebrow at one of his few friends in the corps and looked at him over his spectacles. The fuel cells, the crazy landing, now this. . . . "And the unofficial story?"

"Who knows? With Sam, a bimbo or booze or some combination would be a pretty safe bet. That's what the rumor mill is already saying."

"What do you think?"

"Come on, Santy!" Grieve stood and began pacing, his arms folded over his chest. "Does any of this make sense? Everything's going along fine, NASA showing its can-do spirit, just like The Old Days, when in the span of three hours, they deep-six GRO, run home with their tails between their legs, and in the process almost crash and burn! And now Torrington's dead!"

Grieve joined the program just after Apollo-Soyuz but before shuttle. He wasn't quite old enough to talk authoritatively about The Old Days, but Santich excused the transgression.

"Crash and burn? How bad was it?"

"Jesus, Santy! What have you been doing in here all morning, playing with yourself? They did ten million dollars' worth of damage to the nose gear and left main. They shredded all six tires and they blew up the chute." Grieve shook his head. "Halvorson went to jettison it at the end of rollout, and there was nothing left but the risers."

Santich raised his eyebrows wearily. The queasy feeling that had come to him that morning returned. Yes, there was something wrong, something a little too pat. . . . But, no more. It wasn't his fight. After the morning press conference, he'd barricaded himself in his office: He could make his resignation effective the end of June and burn his accumulated sick leave. Tomorrow, hell, *today,* could be his last day. Whatever had happened to Orbiter Vehicle 104 was interesting, a nice discussion topic to while away an afternoon, but not his problem anymore.

"Cabin leak?" he asked gamely.

"Cabin leak, meteorite strike, who knows? I guess that's the most likely explanation. If they were bleeding air, that would explain coming back at dark-fucking-thirty in the middle of a gale."

Santich had already come to the same conclusion. "So why lie? Why not just say, 'We were hit by a micrometeoroid and had to come home immediately'?"

"You know damn well why!" Grieve shot Santich an irritated look, sat back down, flinging one blue-jeaned leg over the narrow armrest. "After Wembley-Scott, Headquarters doesn't even want to *hear* the word 'meteor,' not after all the lying those Station pinheads did about how low earth orbit is *self-cleansing* and how the estimates were off by three or four orders of magnitude." Grieve allowed himself a snicker. "I'd love to see those guys go back up Capitol Hill and explain *this*!"

Santich nodded slowly. Mark Wembley and Hannah Scott had been two astronauts who were also mathematicians. Just before leaving the corps the previous year, they finished a paper concluding that a space station like the one NASA wanted to build would have a one-in-ninety-six chance each year of suffering life-threatening damage from orbital debris or meteorite impact. So, over the course of the twenty years it was supposed to stay in orbit, there was a one-in-five chance of a crew getting killed. That argument brought the Station within seventeen votes of cancellation the previous year in the U.S. House of Representatives.

"Okay. Say they were hit and sprang a leak. That would explain why they'd come back on the next rev. But the whole damn thing was on TV: How could they keep a meteor strike secret? You know Banke of all people would have called down the instant it happened."

Grieve seemed amused. "But there *was* no NASA Select, remember?"

"Okay, in this particular case they got lucky. But that's not the sort of thing you plan on, is it?"

"Goddamn, Santy." Grieve shook his head, amazed. "What have you been doing these last two years, playing with yourself?"

Santich looked at him blankly.

"You've never heard of Procedure 2601?"

Six months earlier he'd overheard the phrase as he walked into the Outpost. He'd made a mental note to look into it but then had let it slide. He shrugged helplessly.

Grieve looked for a hint of recognition, saw none, continued. "Dammit, what's happened to you? You used to be on top of everything! Not a single waiver, problem report, procedure even got *written* without your knowing about it. Now *this* happens, and you can't even see what's going on!"

Santich knew that if his friend could sense this, others

could also, and that irritated him beyond the mere fact of its truth. "So what's 2601?" he snapped.

"Okay." Grieve leaned forward conspiratorially. "Now, I don't know this firsthand, but then again, I don't think anyone outside of Bruce's little star chamber does. You remember two summers ago, when the turbine-blade fuckup grounded us for three months? And that Senate committee almost killed Station because we couldn't be trusted to keep the shuttles flying long enough to build the damn thing?"

"I think I might have read something about it," Santich said dryly.

"Well, Bruce got to worrying that if Congress could pitch a fit over something that *might* have happened but didn't, then they'd really scream for blood if we *did* have a bad day. So he cooked up a plan to cover it up."

"Cover up a bad day?" Santich laughed, partly at the in-house euphemism for catastrophe. "How do you hide it when a shuttle blows up in front of twenty thousand tourists at Kennedy?"

"Not *that* bad a day. No, I think everybody accepts that if anyone else dies during ascent, that's the end of the show. What he had in mind was something like what happened this morning. A cabin leak, say, or a fire or something that forced a contingency landing."

"Why? Things break. I think people would understand that, don't you?"

"Look, you want me to explain this or not? This isn't my harebrained scheme, it's Bruce's. I'm just telling it to you." Grieve paused a moment, licked his chubby lips. "All right. Here's what they did: They set up a circuit to take down NASA Select's Goddard transmitter, and kept the proper excuse ready to go at a moment's notice. Like last night, with all the storms around the area, a lightning strike was a natural.

"They wired the flight director's station in Mission Control with a switch that cuts off the feed and also trips a breaker in Goddard that allows the transmitter circuits to overload and blow. If the emergency is cleared up, Goddard techs go about their normal business, fix the transmitter, and get back on the air. But if a longer delay is needed, like, I bet, last night, then someone on Bruce's staff makes sure that repairs take long enough.''

Santich cocked his silver crew cut, squinting his bright blue eyes slightly. ''No. There's no way. . . . He rigged all that just for a cover-up? And people went along with him?''

Grieve shook his head. ''I admit it sounds nuts. I thought so, too, when I first heard it. But trust me. Bruce is dead serious. And you know the atmosphere around here. We'd rather lie about something to the world and leave it broken than get a black eye and fix it. Every single person's livelihood here depends on the shuttle taking off and landing six or seven times a year. Hell, you don't have to take my word. Look at last night! What are the odds that Goddard would take a lightning strike at the same time a meteor hit 104?''

If Grieve was right, he realized with a chill, it had all happened right under his damned nose. What *had* he been doing the past two years? Impatiently he shook his head.

''All right, say that the whole Goddard thing was rigged. The whole thing falls apart if anyone on board says the wrong thing on the radio. And look who you had on 104! I'll grant you most of these new ones are spineless yesmen, but Banke? At the first sign of a cabin leak, he'd have called down, fucking this, piece of shit that. How do you cover *that* up, or does the flight director sit with his finger over the panic button the whole mission?''

Grieve grinned. ''Next time you're in the control room during a flight, go in the back and take a look at PAO's console. He has a NASA Select monitor that gets the Goddard feed rather than the JSC mix. Watch and you'll see.''

Santich thought a moment. ''Tape delay?''

Grieve nodded. ''Five seconds. Everything but launch, landing and the PAO events, you know, interviews, in-flight news conferences, and the other Headquarters bullshit. All that stuff goes out real time.''

It was technically possible, Santich allowed. But how could Bruce expect to pull it off without someone blowing the whistle? NASA was a huge bureaucracy, filled with jealous ideologues and conflicting agendas. If *anybody* in planetary science or astronomy or aeronautics or any of the other offices whose funding was getting slashed to feed the Station-Shuttle beast got wind of this, the game would be up.

"What about Headquarters? How much do they know about all this?"

Grieve shrugged, then stood to resume his pacing. "I haven't the foggiest. I would guess none. You know the kind of latitude they give Bruce: Get the job done, and we'll ask you no questions. How else do you think he could've turned this place into his personal fiefdom? Near as I can tell, this whole thing was supposed to stay within Johnson. Although I have no idea what happens when they roll 104 into the hangar at Kennedy, and instead of a failed fuel cell they find a hole in the crew cabin. You watch. Within two days, some Florida paper will say there was no fuel cell problem, but there *was* a cabin leak, according to anonymous space shuttle sources."

Santich leaned back, rubbing his temples and eyes with his knuckles. On the face of it, the whole thing was ridiculous. But . . . He'd felt funny about it right from the start. It hadn't made sense. What if Torrington . . .

"And Sam? Did the car wreck have something to do with this?"

Grieve was looking at a group shot of the Apollo astronauts, one taken early enough to include Grissom, White and Chaffee. Again he shrugged.

"I don't know. It's just like Sam to go tearing off to blow off some steam. Maybe it was his fault they had to come home early, or that GRO is still broken. Maybe, as you guys used to say, he screwed the pooch."

Screwed the pooch. Santich tried to remember whether they had actually said it, or if it had become common lingo at NASA only after they turned Tom Wolfe's book into a

movie. After that all the new astronauts had loved slipping
it into their everyday speech. Each one thought he was the
first to revive an old standby—sort of pay homage to the
early explorers.

"Besides," Grieve continued, sitting down again,
"whether the wreck had anything to do with the early landing or not doesn't matter. The whole world *thinks* it does.
That's the important thing. Here."

Grieve picked up the remote control and switched it to
CNN, where a hastily spliced piece of film showed the
video highlights of veteran astronaut Sam Torrington's life
and times, from still shots of Sam the high school wide
receiver in Billings, Montana, to ROTC at Southern Cal, to
research in the Army in materials processing, to his first
spaceflight three years earlier, and finally his first space
walk—last night. A true American hero, dead at age forty-
three.

The anchorman went on to read how his just-revealed
death followed NASA's most bizarre space shuttle mission
to date, the first to end in virtual secrecy because of a com-
munications problem, and with a still-unanswered question
about how badly the vehicle may have been damaged. Reports said the amount could exceed $150 million. The clip
ended with the snippet of Bruce insulting the assembled
media, standing up and walking away.

"Can you believe that? Sam's a fucking hero now. Pure
as driven snow." Grieve laughed. "Had he lived through
the month, they would have indicted his ass, and then the
TV would be full of his lousy grades in college, how he
was nearly expelled for cheating, how he diddled the neighbor's dog."

It was common knowledge within Building 4 that the
FBI was nearly finished with Operation Bedbug, a two-year
probe into bid-rigging in the Space Station contracts at
Johnson and that an astronaut would be indicted. That Torrington was the target was a given. Even he had known it
and had hired a criminal lawyer to get off as lightly as he
could.

"You know," Santich mused aloud, "that guy was here,

what, five years? And I don't think anybody in the place is the least bit sorry he's dead.''

Grieve pushed the mute button on the remote. ''Yeah, well, why should we be? He's either fucked, or tried to fuck, half our wives, and probably *has* fucked ninety percent of our girlfriends.''

Grieve had had two extramarital affairs that Santich knew of. The first had ended when the woman, a junior flight controller in the mechanical systems branch, began something with Torrington while she was still seeing Grieve. Santich wondered whether Torrington had moved in on the second mistress, too.

''What about Banke and the rest?'' Santich said, wondering whether they'd stay at the Cape longer now because of Torrington's death.

''They're on their way back.'' Grieve bit his lower lip. ''Funny thing about that. At first they wanted to ship Torrington's body back on the Shuttle Training Aircraft with the crew, but Banke told 'em to stuff it. So they're flying out the second STA special, just to haul him back tonight. I don't know. Maybe he was so falling-down drunk they're trying to hide him from the medical examiner down there. I mean, how would it look for the Great American Hero to have bought it with enough alcohol in his blood to embalm him?''

Probably no worse than if it got out that the commander and pilot chugged a flask of good Irish whiskey after every landing, Santich thought. He glanced at his computer screen, looked up at Grieve, and sighed.

''Well, amigo, whatever's at the bottom of this mess, I'm sure you and the other brave lads and lasses here in Building 4 will sort it out, reward the good, punish the wrongdoers and uphold the American Way.''

It was Grieve's turn to stare blankly. ''What? That's it? The biggest fuckup since *Challenger*, and you're not interested?''

The queasy feeling wrenched his gut. *No!* No

more. "Why? How much interest *should* I have in something that's so clearly not my problem?"

Grieve's dark brown eyes blinked twice. "Not your problem! Santy, you *live* for this! Come on! Why do you think I'm here? I've got it figured out. When all this gets out, they're gonna can Bruce and his minions, including Garvey. And when that happens, they'll need a new program director, and a new chief astronaut. And, yea, the meek shall inherit the Earth!"

"What are you talking about?" Santich sighed. "Bruce isn't going anywhere. Even if *all this* gets out, you forget one important thing: Nobody cares. And if anybody takes the fall for it, it'll be Banke."

Grieve gasped again, stood to relieve his consternation. "Yes! Absolutely! If *we* do nothing, then Bruce rides this out and people like Banke get screwed! But, *but*, if we grab the bull by the horns, we can push things the right way. If Bruce lies about something, like this morning, we make sure the truth gets out."

"Truth? You keep talking like somebody out there cares what happens here."

"They do! Space is still the last page, the final frontier! People care about this. I think they'd get pretty steamed if they found out someone rigged the whole system to cover his ass."

Santich sighed a much practiced, well-worn sigh. "No. They don't care. Nobody in the rest of NASA, nobody in Congress, nobody in the quote unquote public has any interest whatsoever in who runs this country's manned spaceflight program. Look. With a flight every other month, seven slots per flight, we send forty-two people into orbit every year—forty-two out of a quarter billion. All this hierarchy here at Johnson is about one thing: Who gets to ride the go-cart. Sure, we're a seven-billion-dollar-a-year jobs program, but no one outside our little club cares who rides it, so long as *somebody* does, seven times a year, ad infinitum, ad nauseam."

Grieve nodded. "Okay, fine. I admit it: That's the only

reason *I* came here, to go into space. I guess most of us in the corps feel that way. But there are others who believe there's something *to* all of this. Like you, for instance, or like you used to be." Grieve paused, got no response, continued. "And there are people out there who think the whole thing is a waste of money, and others who think there's something to be learned from it all. But one thing they got in common, I think, is that they think it's *their* go-cart, not Bruce's. And if he can't take care of it, then maybe he shouldn't be in charge."

Santich sighed again, turned his computer monitor toward Grieve and motioned for him to read it. "As you can see, while I appreciate your interest and enthusiasm, I really can't help you."

He waited for his friend to finish reading the four and a half paragraphs he'd managed in as many hours. "I'm not part of this anymore. I haven't been for a while. You know it; so does everyone else. It's time I admitted it, too."

Grieve looked bewildered. "This is because of this morning?"

"You mean 104?" Santich waved his hand and snorted. "Hell, no. This has been coming awhile. I've been thinking hard about things. I've only got so many years left. I'd be an idiot to keep banging my head against the wall here.

"No, I'll go back to Emily, if she'll have me, and spend some real time with the kids, and *their* kids." He leaned back, arms stretched overhead. "So I think maybe before I leave today, I'll zip this over to Bruce and make Friday my last day. No, I take that back: I'll make today my last day."

Grieve shook his head. "No! You can't! Come on, Santiago. I know you've been unlucky for eighty days, or ninety days, or whatever the hell it was. But you're on the verge of catching a big one."

Santich smiled. *The Old Man and the Sea* had been his father's favorite book, and that his only boy—named after his grandfather—shared the hero's name had made it that much more special. In recent years Santich had begun to liken his inability to fly again with Santiago's eighty-four days without a fish.

"Why? So the sharks can eat it?"

"Santy, if I get Bruce's job, I can make you chief astronaut again. Which means *you can fly!*"

All the old emotions, packed away for years, returned, unbidden. The practiced, methodical climb into the left-hand chair, the tedious run through the checklists, the endless wait, and, finally, the low rumble, the sudden push on the chest, and a mad, terrible, wonderful headlong rush into an ever darkening sky. A chill flashed up and down his spine, bringing goose bumps.

"Come on, Santy! You've been waiting around a dozen years for this. You can hang on another six months."

Santich kept a poker face. "You've obviously thought this out. What would I have to do? I'm not agreeing, mind you. I just want to hear you out."

Grieve rubbed his hands together. "Piece of cake. Just be yourself. The press will still listen to you, especially after this morning. Anything you say, they'll eat up. And your title allows you access to all the reports, right?"

"In theory. Usually I have to hold my breath and turn blue before they give something to me."

"I bet if you announced that you're forming a committee to investigate STS-74, you'd open all kinds of doors. People will see the writing on the wall. They can either help you, or cast their lot with Bruce. Why go down with a sinking ship?"

"And your role?"

"I'll help you. You're the senior astronaut here; I'm second. Between us, we've got more than fifty years at NASA. If that doesn't bring respect, I don't know what will. Each week we hold a press conference to announce our findings. I think if we can point those pinheads in the right direction, they'll start smelling a Pulitzer Prize and go off on their own. They'll make a much bigger deal out of 2601 if they uncover it themselves than if we hand it to them on a plate."

Santich thought about it, trying to guess how long something like that would take. "How would we start?"

"*Big*, that's how! We'll tell 'em the fleet ought to be grounded until we determine why it was that *Atlantis* had to do such a dangerous, costly landing. That alone will get great publicity, and if we follow up by saying there may have been a cover-up, they'll be eating out of our hands!"

"And then? Bruce up and resigns, like Nixon?"

"He resigns, or becomes enough of an embarrassment that Headquarters has to fire him. Doesn't matter. The point is, if all this comes out, he can't possibly stay. No way."

Again Santich leaned back, his fingertips joined together in a steeple. Grieve let him think for a minute, then could no longer contain his impatience.

"Come on! I don't claim I have this all worked out, but I absolutely guarantee that in six months, Bruce will be finished—*if* we move quickly and stay ahead of this." Grieve studied Santich, decided he needed more. "You know you've been aching for one more trip up. *This* is your last chance, and I think it's a pretty good one. Six months, Santy, that's all I ask."

Santich's body gently rocked back and forth in the vinyl-upholstered office chair, but his mind was twelve years and a thousand miles away. Unlike the slow nudge in the back of the old Saturn 5s, the shuttle boosters were a kick in the pants. A bone-rattling, two-minute rush to the top of the roller coaster. Then the solids burned out and fell away, leaving only the main engines, whisper-quiet and silky-smooth in comparison. And in another six minutes, when those, too, fell silent, nothing. Absolute quiet and total freedom—the most perfect peace he had ever known. How he'd dreamed of it over the last decade. . . .

Santich flicked his eyes up to find his friend staring at him, grinning like he knew he'd get what he'd come for.

"I'll tell you what: Give me a few days to think about it."

Grieve's grin hardened into a thin line. "No! The time to act on this is right now. Look at the TV!"

For the umpteenth time in a few hours, CNN was broadcasting its blurb about the landing. The muted image shifted from the anchor, now a pretty former model, to that morning's press conference. Once again, Bruce silently mouthed his final answer and, once again, silently stood up and walked out. The clip lingered on the closed door for a split second before returning to the ex-model.

"These people have an attention span about this long." Grieve held his thumb and index finger a quarter inch apart. "They're like hunting dogs: basically pretty dumb, but persistent for a while. It's four o'clock. We should fax out notice of our press conference in the next half hour and set it for five. If we do, *we'll* be the major story on the evening news. If we wait three or four days, we don't even rate two paragraphs in the local rag."

Santich smiled. "Where did you learn all this? What are you, interning in PAO?"

Grieve rolled his eyes. "Come on, Santy! I can't do this myself. You're the great hero, not me."

"That's the other thing I was meaning to ask. What's in this for you?"

Grieve shrugged. "The usual for an aging astronaut with college-age kids. More money. I'm grade fourteen. Bruce is SES: one hundred ten grand minimum. If I stay for three years, that's fourteen grand a year more when I get out. I guess I should have cashed in with Hulling-McGee or Spartan Acrospace like everybody else."

"You still could. You're, what, fifty-one, fifty-two?"

Grieve stood, walked to the group photo of the Apollo astronauts. "Yeah. I guess so. Maybe, though, if you were head of the office, and I was your boss, maybe I could manage one last flight, too." He turned to Santich with a grin. "What do you think?"

Santich leaned back, arms folded. "I think I need to think about it."

The grin disappeared. "*Goddammit*, Santy. Today's the day!"

"Tomorrow. I'll decide tonight, and let you know first

thing in the morning.'' Santich raised his eyebrows but kept his arms folded.

Grieve shook his head. ''Goddamn stubborn son of a bitch. All right, tomorrow. But tomorrow morning. No later.'' He turned to leave, then stuck his head back through the doorway. ''Tomorrow morning!''

Santich waved his friend away, waited for the door to click shut. He stood, stretched and walked over to the row of photos, stopping at the one taken in front of the Descartes Mountains. Santich, completely unrecognizable in the bulky white suit and reflective sun visor, stood on a steep ledge overlooking the plain where the lander had touched down. In the background, a gibbous Earth hung in the heavens.

During his three subsequent trips to space, Santich always found time to stare at the moon. He'd pull out the Zeiss binocs and focus in on the familiar pattern of craters, hoping to catch a glint off the car-size mound of metal they'd left behind.

He moved on to the close-up of *Columbia* leaving Kennedy's Launch Complex 39 on her maiden voyage. Again Santich's face was not visible through the multilayered flight deck windows. Nor was it in the photo of *Columbia* about to land on the baked clay desert at Edwards. Only the photo of Santich and Forrester, still dressed in orange pressure suits, helmets under their arms, standing in front of *Columbia*'s nosewheels, proved that he had been in the cockpit.

So how badly did he want it back? He thought about Grieve's proposal, tried hard to avoid wishful thinking. He gave the plan a fair to middling chance of success. He marveled again at the audacity of Bruce's cover-up. He had known since STS-1 that the PAO console in Mission Control had a panic button that immediately cut off the NASA Select feed. Its purpose had been to protect the crew's privacy in the event of a catastrophic accident, like a sudden cabin leak or a smoky fire. It was agreed that no one should have to die on national TV, with final curses and screams broadcast for all to hear. But no one had dreamed of manipulating it like Bruce seemed to have.

So what the hell was Bruce covering up? Was it just a cabin leak? It seemed crazy to risk landing like they did just for that. According to the mission elapsed times they'd given, whatever it was had happened just after the space walk. But what if those times were lies as well? What if whatever disaster happened actually took place during the space walk? Maybe Torrington's death *did* have something to do with whatever happened in orbit. An air embolism maybe . . . Yeah, that was it; a meteor hits *Atlantis* while Torrington and Orlov are outside. They rush to get back in to deorbit. They come home. Torrington suffers an embolism in the brain while driving down the road. . . .

Sure, he had it all figured out. Why bother with an investigation? Besides, none of that was really the point. Grieve was right. If the press got wind of 2601, that was the end of Bruce. True, the realization was self-serving, mercenary almost. He hated the press. They were, with rare exceptions, stupid, sloppy opportunists.

How badly did he want it?

To rid himself of Bruce and go *there* one last time, he would have to cozy up to them for God-only-knew how long. The thought tied a knot in his stomach as he turned to face the still-on, still-muted Sony. Within a minute the blue-and-red NASA logo popped up behind the anchorwoman. This time they included clips from the early part of the space walk, then spliced in footage from one of *Atlantis*'s earlier landings, then finished with the snippet of Bruce leaving the press conference.

Santich sat back down and stared at the television, which had moved on to a stock market update. The dollar was down slightly against the yen but up against the deutsche mark. Short-term interest rates had risen slightly. Santich found the remote and flicked off the set.

He turned the chair ninety degrees to face the computer screen and studied the still-embryonic resignation letter. His right index finger moved over the keyboard, hovered for a moment, then came down with a solid click. A line at the bottom queried whether he wished to exit the document without saving it. He typed the letter Y and gave himself a fresh screen. Letter by letter, he began typing a memo:

> FROM: S. Santich, CB
> TO: MOD, SRQA, OFP
> RE: STS-74
>
> Please CC all IFA data, PRs, backup material to S. Santich, E. Grieve, until further notice. Advise as to all mtgs., telecons, etc.

Santich hit the print button, then started a new page:

> As senior astronaut, I feel duty-bound to safeguard the integrity of the human spaceflight program, which I have been honored to have been part of for these 30 years. It is for this reason that I have joined Butch in this inquiry. As you know, I have always been a staunch believer in program safety, and therefore feel compelled

Compelled to do what? Suck up to you lazy half-wits? Destroy the careers of a half-dozen coworkers so I can get my rocks off one more time?

Getting Bruce fired gave him no moral qualms. The man's ruthless authoritarian streak had been necessary once, when the program was threatening to spin apart. Now it was merely paranoid megalomania, a menace to the program. But there were others around him, like Marsh, who were honest, hardworking people who would fall along with Bruce if 2601 turned out to be true.

An inadvertent glance at his watch showed Santich he was late. He stood, picked his jacket off a hook on the wall, and hit the light switch on his way out.

6

"They're gonna fuckin' crucify him."

Santich took another sip of Heineken and looked up and down the bar. Apart from a few clumps of engineers, there were only the usual handful of groupies and tourists. The tourists wouldn't recognize him, and the groupies knew better.

"Are you listening? I said they're going to crucify him."

Dusty Hooper took a deep gulp of his Lone Star and grabbed a handful of popcorn. He still wore the contractor's badge over the breast pocket of his striped, short-sleeved dress shirt. That, the jeans, and the cowboy boots made up a work uniform that only eccentric researchers and ex-astronauts, even ex-astronauts who had never flown, could get away with.

Santich looked up at the TV over the rows of tequilas, whiskeys and rums. It was the early local newscast, not CNN, so it devoted the first ten minutes to *Atlantis*'s landing and Torrington's death.

"Bruce has crucified people in the past." Santich turned toward his best friend. "He'll crucify others in the future." He, too, reached for the bowl. "Remember when this place gave free potato chips with the beer? Now it's popcorn."

Hooper returned the look, green eyes moist beneath wispy silver hair. "Banke's a good man. He deserves better."

43

Santich looked back up at the TV. They were parading still picture after still picture of Torrington, year by year, it seemed. He wondered how many photos they had stashed away for Santiago Santich's obituary. Or would they even notice?

"What's the big deal? So Banke never flies again. Welcome to the club. Anyhow, I thought he was talking about hanging it up after this flight."

Hooper sat speechless for a moment. "Why are you being such an asshole? I thought you *liked* Banke."

Santich snorted. "Why are *you* being such a puss? Anyway, Banke's still alive. How come you're not broken up about Torrington, American Hero?"

"Torrington." Hooper turned, glassy-eyed, toward the old-fashioned swinging saloon doors that separated the Outpost's real front door from the rest of the bar. "Here come three more of his girlfriends."

Santich looked over his shoulder to see three secretaries, their legs still a winter white beneath their miniskirts. He recognized one of them, a petite bleached blonde, from the SAIL office. Her mascara was smeared.

"I know it's bad to speak ill of the dead and all," Hooper continued, "but if anyone in the corps ever deserved what he got, it was that son of a bitch. What really gets me is that if he'd had the decency to die in orbit, at least the program would have gotten something out of it."

A shiver ran through Santich, and he silently studied Hooper. The two had been part of the original Gemini Nine, but a middle-ear ailment began causing nausea and blackouts just weeks before Hoop's first flight, grounding him. He'd hung on, hoping for a miracle, and had spent a decade running the Astronaut Office before it became clear that if surgery couldn't fix it, then no amount of dogged perseverance was going to either.

"Okay, I give up," Santich conceded finally. "How would Torrington's dying in orbit have helped the program?"

Hooper shrugged, stared into his beer. "He would have

died a martyr, instead of an asshole. People love martyrs. Look at *Challenger*. Who outside the Star Trek geeks would know any of their names if they hadn't blown up?''

Santich shook his head and lifted the empty bottle toward the barkeep. ''You certainly have a unique outlook, I'll give you that much. Anyway, *Challenger* was a once-in-a-lifetime thing. You can't blow up a shuttle every few years to revive interest in the space program.''

Hooper sipped his beer, staring disgustedly at yet another replay of that morning's press conference. ''Look at him! He's the worst thing that ever happened to us!''

Santich turned his head in time to catch Bruce once again getting up and walking out.

''He's really screwed things up good. The landing, Torrington, none of that was such a big deal, until Bruce flipped those guys the bird and ticked 'em off. For all his genius, he sure does some bonehead things once in a while.''

Out of the corner of his eye, Santich saw the smeary-eyed secretary sobbing on her girlfriend's shoulder. ''Let me ask you something,'' he said.

Hooper spun his stool to face Santich. ''Shoot.''

''You've got a pretty good handle on Headquarters politics: How safe is Bruce?'' Santich got a puzzled look. ''I mean, if somehow all this fell on his head, would they stand by him? Or cut him loose?''

Puzzlement turned to wariness. ''Why? What's going on?''

''Just hypothetically. How sacred is he?''

Hooper thought for a moment. ''They like him, as well they should. He's kept the trains running on time. Budget cuts, reductions in force, hardware screwups. Nothing fazes the guy, and Washington gives him a pretty long leash. Hell, he's been in his job a lot longer than anyone at Headquarters.'' He took a sip of beer. ''But safe? I don't think he's got a guardian angel, if that's what you mean. With another Station vote in the House in two more months, I think no one below the level of associate administrator is sacred anymore. At least that's our position on the matter.''

Santich knew "our" meant the battalion of aerospace corporations whose bottom lines rose and fell with NASA's annual budgets. He also knew that if *they* thought some middle- or upper-level agency manager was on thin ice, then he was.

"All things being equal, the best way out of this mess is to pretend it never happened," Hooper continued. "Wave it off, say it wasn't a big deal and get on with it. That's what he should have done, not slapped the media in the face."

"So you think that if the heat's turned up under him, they'll just wash their hands of him."

Again Hooper turned a suspicious eye. "Why? Who's turning up the heat?"

Santich shrugged. "Some of the guys in the office were talking about it today. They think there's more to it than Bruce is letting on. You know, the fuel cells, the hush-hush landing, the fact that Select went down right at the same time. . . . Let's face it. You don't have to believe in the shot from the grassy knoll to think there's something strange going on here." He shrugged again. "They asked me to join them."

Hooper shook his head sadly. "Don't. This has been enough of a nightmare without it going public. I mean, I know you hate Bruce. Hell, who doesn't? He's an asshole. But face it: The guy's good for the program. Ever since he got that job, shuttle has been on time and on budget. Anyway, what's in it for you if he's out?"

Santich knew they were edging a perennially touchy subject. "Same as it's always been."

"Who?" Hooper demanded. "Who's promised you another flight?"

There was no skirting it now. "Grieve. He thinks he can get Bruce's job. He says he'll give me Garvey's."

Hooper turned toward the television and took a long swig. For a minute that seemed an hour, he said nothing. "You know, between the two of you, y'all have been up nine times." He took another swig. "Isn't that enough?"

Santich also kept his eyes locked on the TV. "That's not fair. I'm not doing this to spite you. You *know* I did everything I could to get you up short of stowing you on board."

"That's not the point. Some of those others, I can understand. All they ever wanted to do was fly fast. So if they had to napalm some babies, well, somebody had to do it. But you! I thought you believed in the new manifest destiny, mankind's mission, the survival of the species, all that shit!"

Once in, there was no easy way out. Santich shrugged. "I didn't mean to come argue this with you again. I've tried to explain this to you before." He sighed. "I never . . . none of us ever . . . started out wanting to be spacemen; you know that. It's just . . . I don't know. I can't describe it. Maybe this is what a drunk goes through when he finally accepts that he has to quit, but there's one last glassful left in the bottle." He saw Hooper's unsympathetic eyes. "Maybe it's not like that at all. I don't know."

Hooper sipped his beer. "If you really believe it's man's fate to reach the stars," he said softly, "then you'll help put this fuckup behind us, not make it worse."

Santich tapped his bottle for the barkeep. Once again, it was a three-beer night, and it was only six o'clock. "You think it's such a hot idea to put mankind's destiny in Bruce's hands?" he asked defensively.

"There are worse hands, yes. Look, I know it's hard to swallow, but that son of a bitch believes in that shit, too. Why else would he have stayed where he is all these years? He could be making three, four times as much working for us. But really: Bruce, the pope, the Easter bunny. It doesn't make much difference." Hooper set his glass down to gesture with both hands. "As long as our best and brightest stay together as a team, continue to solve those problems of long-term exposure to the harsh environment of space, of how to live and work there for months on end, then we as a species move closer to leaving planet Earth."

"Jesus, Hoop. Take it easy. This isn't some chamber-of-commerce yahoo you're talking to."

Hooper blushed, turned back to the bar. "Exactly," he continued, voice lowered. "I know it sounds corny, but I also know it's true."

Santich shrugged again, promised himself this would be his last beer, and took that first ice-cold sip. "Sometimes I wonder. It took us eight years to get Apollo to the moon, we spent less than three years there, and for the last twenty-two years we've been holding our dicks in low Earth orbit."

"Well, maybe those of you lucky enough to get to LEO have held their dicks. The rest of us have busted our asses to make getting you there a routine thing." Hooper stopped, turned back to the bar. "You know the rest. Seriously, Santy. I'm asking you as a friend: Let it go. If you take Bruce down right now, Washington cancels the whole enchilada this summer. We can't afford any embarrassments until we have some Station hardware in orbit."

Santich shook his head slowly. "If you guys hadn't low-balled the thing to start with, and maybe had met a deadline or a budget once in a while, maybe we wouldn't be on such thin ice all the time."

"Don't start with me, all right? Just think about what I said, and what you believe in. You think the idiots on Capitol Hill bother themselves about what we do when the interglacial ends or the sun goes red giant? They're just getting even with the Texas delegation, or the California delegation, or just trying to make headlines. Remember that: They don't care, all right?"

Santich started to detail the peculiarities of *Atlantis*'s midnight landing, his conversation with Grieve, his suspicions of Torrington's death, then thought better of it. It would be no use. He nodded, finished his bottle and dug a ten-dollar bill from his wallet to leave on the bar. "I'll keep that in mind."

"Please, Santy. You've had your moment, hell, your *moments* of glory. Is it worth risking the whole program for one more shot?'' Hooper picked up the ten, handed it back to Santich, and replaced it with a twenty. "Keep it. It's on Celestial Data Systems.''

Santich snorted, knowing the contractors all found ways to bill NASA for their lobbying and entertainment expenses. "Oh, so eventually it's on me, my kids, my neighbors?" He put the ten back on the deeply varnished length of mahogany.

Hooper shrugged and looked for a ten in his billfold. "Those are the rules of the game. I didn't make them.''

Santich stood, tried to let his irritation subside and then turned back to his friend. "Have you ever heard of 2601?''

Hooper blinked once, shook his head. "What's that?''

"Some new mals procedure." He turned for the door. "Just wondering.''

7

As usual, Santich had to flick on the lights as he made his way through Building 4's hallways at 5:30 A.M. Even the most eager rookies wouldn't get in until six, giving him a good half hour of quiet time. He wished, though, that he had three hours or four or six before the phones started ringing. He figured he'd need them to finish his one-page statement demanding that NASA suspend all shuttle missions until it had thoroughly investigated STS-74.

He'd known even before meeting with Hooper that his old friend would try to talk him out of it. Perversely, the litany of tired arguments had pushed him the other way. He didn't think he was being contrary, even though Hooper's messianic fervor about spaceflight had, over the years, worn thin. Not that he'd ever really understood it. Of the Gemini Nine, only Hooper and Chaffee had never flown, and Chaffee had been preparing for his first when he perished in the Apollo 1 launch-pad fire. The natural response would have been to turn against the institution that, to cover its butt, had grounded him for a malady that, properly medicated, never showed symptoms.

Santich pushed the matter from his head, thinking instead of calling Grieve at home with his decision, and how it had come just after the ten o'clock news had told him that the space shuttle *Atlantis* was badly damaged during landing due to pilot error, according to anonymous NASA sources.

The sons of bitches *were* going to pin it all on Banke, and they weren't wasting any time.

The first thing Santich noticed when he turned his doorknob was his lighted desk lamp. The second was the chief son of a bitch himself studying Santich's photos.

On hearing the door, Marty Bruce turned with a thin smile. "Good morning. It's gratifying to see that the Dean of American Astronauts still keeps such rigorous hours."

Almost everyone at JSC, particularly the astronauts, looked lost in their seldom-worn, off-the-rack suits. Bruce was the exception. The tailored beige wool fit glovelike over the slender frame, giving the one-time Air Force fighter pilot the incongruous look of a pricy lawyer.

Santich hung his own wrinkled brown jacket on the rack by the door and walked to his desk. Immediately he noticed the computer monitor was on and displaying the press statement he had begun the previous afternoon. On his blotter, the memo he'd printed had been spun around so it could be read from the opposite side of the desk.

He looked up and glared at Bruce. "You finding everything all right?"

Dark beady eyes gazed back, emotionless. The thin, delicate nose twitched once. "I would have thought *you,* of all people, would've learned to put sensitive memos under lock and key, away from prying eyes," Bruce needled.

Santich refused to take the bait and sat down. "Well, you've seen everything here. You've got one hundred seven more desks to root through before eight A.M. You'd best get started."

Again the thin lips curled into a bloodless smile. "Only a few interest me. Anyway, I came to see you. I want you to join me at a press conference at oh-eight-hundred."

Santich blinked, turned toward the computer screen, then back to Bruce. "Sorry, but I've got my own little presentation to make this morning."

"Yes, I've seen. Quite a speech. Would you like to see mine?" Bruce reached under his lapel and pulled out a stack of three-by-five note cards. He leafed through, pulled one out and dropped it on the desk.

Santich didn't touch it but bent down to the tiny block letters arranged in three lines, each prefaced by a black circle. When he looked up, suspicion and anger had darkened his face.

"The fuck do you think you're doing?"

Bruce grinned his vampire's grin. "That's the thanks I get for returning America's Most Experienced Astronaut to space? Very well. You're welcome."

Santich's heart fluttered, raced. Another flight! Not just the conditional promise of one six months away, but here and now! But at what cost? This devil would certainly want his due.

"Let's just be straight with each other." Santich held Bruce's gaze as he spoke. "You don't like me, and you *know* how I feel about you. So what's going on?"

Still the grin. "I guess you don't believe in that expression 'Never look a gift horse in the mouth'?"

Santich realized Bruce was awaiting an answer. "How about 'Beware Greeks bearing gifts'?"

"*Touché.*" The grin vanished. "All right. No, Captain Santich, I've never liked you. Don't take it personally. I like very few people. Consequently, very few people like me. No matter. I don't like you because for all your talent and good fortune, you've never given this program the respect it deserves."

Bruce turned toward the Apollo group portrait. "You see, these men here, and the men and women in our office, are a fraternity. A fraternity of the finest, those chosen to lead the planet. Unfortunately, not all of our *elected* leaders think our task is that important. Of course, the year the glaciers start advancing south across Canada, and the planet has too many people to survive the ice age, *then* what we do will be considered vital. They'll ask why we haven't done more. Until that day, we toil in obscurity, demanding obscene amounts of money for things whose value we can't begin to explain. Which means that each and every year, our mission is placed in jeopardy, subject to the collected wisdom of Congress and the budget office. Therefore, it is up to our fraternity to safeguard the faith. Providing aid and comfort to our enemies, when you're lucky enough to have been here''—he jabbed a finger at the photo of the moon's Descartes Mountains—''is not safeguarding the faith.''

He turned back toward Santich, finished. ''Is that the speech you give all the new astronaut candidates?'' Santich asked.

''I don't need to. You see, they want to be like us, at any cost. Nevertheless, let me explain why, despite my personal feelings, I'm here this morning. Simply, I need you. With the budget in committee right now, we need to recover from yesterday's fiasco—quickly.

''I've learned through the last couple of years that nothing takes the media's attention off a failure more quickly than a success. They have such a superficial understanding of technical matters, and such a childish awe of whatever's new. If we don't want them to write about the last mission, then we need to give them a new one.

''So, to demonstrate the ever advancing maturity of the shuttle program, I'm launching another flight next month to finish the work on Gamma Ray Observatory. You see, the editorial page whiners are already saying, 'If they can't even fix a satellite properly, how can they possibly build a space station?' Well, this nips that right in the bud, and shows how NASA responds to unexpected challenges.''

The adrenaline that charged through Santich when Grieve had dangled the prospect of flying returned. He tried to speak in measured tones. ''The pilot pool's got twenty-six guys qualified to command a mission. I still don't know why you're here.''

The malevolent grin returned. ''I'll tell the press that you're the best, that you still have the best simulator scores for rendezvous, retrieval, entry, landing—not to mention contingency scenarios. You have more total flights than anyone in the corps, and have landed the shuttle as many times as any active astronaut. But they'll know the real reason. Sending you legitimizes the whole thing. If Santiago Santich says it's safe, then it must be.''

The vibration, the push downward on the chest—the horizon growing ever more distant—the sensations returned in a rush, and Santich struggled to push them from his mind. ''Something happened to 104, didn't it?''

Bruce sat in the little chair, crossed his legs, picked a piece of lint off his trousers, and dropped it into the wastepaper basket. ''I'm glad you asked, because there's something I need you to do before you fly. It falls under your official title here, so it dovetails nicely with this mission.''

Santich stiffened, knowing there had to be a catch.

''You see, when I called yesterday's events a fiasco, I didn't tell you the half of it. I'm trusting you with a great deal of sensitive information, on the assumption that even you realize how absolutely devastating its public release would be. This is my big gamble: I believe that deep down, you truly believe in this, as I do, and won't jeopardize losing it all. I think it's fair to say that if this ever gets out, it would be the end of Station, the end of shuttle, the end of NASA. Period.''

Bruce paused to lick his lips. ''As you've no doubt heard on the grapevine, the early landing at KSC was part of a contingency scenario I developed to manage just such an eventuality as the one we encountered last night at MET four days, twenty hours, and thirteen minutes.''

''A cabin leak,'' Santich offered.

''No, somewhat worse.'' Bruce ran a finger through his thinning brown hair, then stared at it, as if looking for dandruff. ''A cabin leak is the sort of thing I'd envisioned, especially after Wembley-Scott and the program's response to it. Last night was a bit more dramatic.'' He stopped grooming himself and stared into Santich's eyes. ''We lost Torrington.''

Santich blinked. ''Lost him. Up there?''

Bruce nodded. ''The seal on his helmet gave way, explosively. Within a second, his suit pressure dropped from four-point-seven psi down to zero. Bravo camera was trained right on him in a close-up. If I hadn't planned for this sort of thing, everyone watching NASA Select would have seen his head explode, live and in color."

Santich's shoulders slumped as he fell back into his seat. "Mary, mother of God."

"Alex saw it happen. He said Sam's face just disappeared. Surprisingly, there was no blood, at least on the walls of the orbiter. I assume it must have frozen instantaneously and dissipated. There was a bit on the inside of the suit, though. The crew wiped it up before entry."

Santich felt his stomach quaver. "Wiped it up?"

"Standard operating procedure. Every crew for the last year and a half has signed off on 2601 as a condition of flight. That's part of it."

"And the car wreck?"

"That convertible he always rented out at the Cape? We arranged an accident with a jet fuel tanker parked by the side of the road. It was a lot easier than I'd feared out at the Cape, despite the emergency landing screwing up all the normal procedures. Only one person saw Torrington's body taken out of the orbiter, and that was the flight surgeon. We flew him out to meet *Atlantis*. He accompanied the body back here for the autopsy. We did have a measure of good fortune in that it was Torrington. His ex-wife dislikes him, his children are young, and he has no surviving family pressing for an investigation."

For a moment both men looked at each other: Bruce calmly, Santich with a flat stare.

"You've lost your mind," Santich said incredulously. "You think you can cover this up."

Bruce shrugged. "This was a bit ambitious, I'll grant you. Procedure 2601 was never really designed for crew death. It was an interesting stretch, though."

"Interesting? For Christ's sake, Marty, a man was killed!"

Bruce stared at Santich for a long moment. "Do you know how many workers the Department of Agriculture loses on the job each year? Ten-point-two. More than ten people dead, every year, doing their jobs. But does Congress suspend the slaughterhouse inspection program pending a blue-ribbon investigation? No. We, on the other hand, have lost ten people in almost forty years, eleven now. And every incident can potentially shut us down forever. And as for Sam Torrington? Spare me. Don't *you* start on how wonderful he was. Did you know the president ordered flags at half-staff today? Ironic, no? In another month he would have been indicted.'' Bruce laughed. ''This is the best thing that could have happened to his career.''

''This can't work,'' Santich said, softly now.

Again Bruce shrugged. ''Without your help, probably not. That's why I'm here. I know this is as hard for you as it was for me. Harder maybe. You think I'm psychotic. So be it. It's an impression I've cultivated over the years. Call it my management style. But I'm asking you now to set that aside, not for your benefit or mine, but for the human species. Right here, this morning, Captain Santich. This is where it's determined whether mankind has a prosperous existence among the stars or winks out without even trying.''

He paused, studied Santich's guarded reaction, licked his lips. ''Look at it this way. The people who most want this thing investigated so it never happens again are right here in this office. Whether the world finds out or it doesn't, *we'll* figure out how and why Sam Torrington died. The only difference is this: If we keep this within the office, the program stays alive. If it gets out, well, then, the whole kingdom is lost.''

''Everyone on console in the control room and the back rooms knows! How can you keep a hundred people quiet about something like this?''

''They don't all know. Flight director, capcom, flight surgeon, EVA and a couple of others know. In fact, the surgeon set everything in motion when he saw the suit pressure drop. That took air-to-ground two off-line, shorted out Goddard's NASA Select transmitter, and triggered the

in-house subroutine that gave us our cover story for the
benefit of EGIL.''

These were details Grieve hadn't known. Santich nodded
for Bruce to continue.

"That's why fuel cells one and three seemed to act up.
In the confusion, Orlov got Torrington's body into the air
lock, and the story was set. One-oh-four had to come home
ASAP.''

Santich's breath caught in his throat. "You guys screwed
with ground control software?''

"It was a relatively simple patch. In a pinch we could
have overridden the changes and returned to nominal electrical status.''

Santich leaned back in his chair, studying the man across
the desk. He had been an Air Force pilot during Vietnam
who'd been shot down behind lines and spent more than a
year in a POW camp before escaping and making his way
to Thailand. That was the official version, anyway. The
unofficial version that had become gospel at JSC was that
Bruce had been with the CIA, and that his low-altitude
bailout was an expensive way to get him somewhere he
wasn't supposed to be. At NASA Bruce had been a boy-
wonder recruit, a master of whatever technical system they
turned him loose upon. After *Challenger*, it was Marty
Bruce who reengineered the disastrous solid rocket motor
program, turned it around, personally pushed through the
new design on schedule. He got no official promotion but
was universally regarded as the corps' first among equals.
In '90, when fuel leaks kept shuttles on the ground all summer, it was Marty Bruce who finally got the situation under
control. When software glitches threatened to ground the
fleet in '92, Marty Bruce had been set free on SAIL, the
Shuttle Avionics Integration Laboratory, and he quietly put
out the fire. He won his big promotion the following year,
and had quickly adopted a low-key, ruthlessly efficient
atmosphere, reminiscent of a "black" military R and D
program, instead of an open, civilian bureaucracy. When
budget cuts came, he shed what he thought were redundant

layers of oversight. His personal risk-management calculus dictated which corners would be cut, and how severely.

Through it all, though, Santich had seen nothing so reckless as he had just heard, and he shook his head in amazement. Ground control software was nearly as sacred as shuttle software. Even the slightest, most innocuous change was supposed to go through two completely independent reviews and countless simulations to look for bugs. Certainly, the very essence of Bruce's 2601 meant none of that would have been possible.

"I'm not here to ask your approval," Bruce said, breaking the brief silence. "I frankly don't care what you think. The fact is, it's done. So far, Station and, therefore, all of manned spaceflight is still alive. I'm asking whether you want to fly next month to help keep it that way."

He felt the ache in his belly, and he couldn't believe what he was doing. Over the years, he'd come to loathe the ends-justifies-the-means way Bruce had run the program. Yet where had his opposition gotten him? Bruce still ran the show and Santich had become a nonentity. Who would it help if he told Bruce to piss off? He would easily find someone else to fly the mission.

Bruce's manipulations had also instantly altered the playing field. If he went to the media with Grieve, there was a good chance that what Bruce predicted would happen: the end of shuttle, the end of NASA. Bruce had almost made that a certainty by turning an accidental death into a massive conspiracy.

"Why 2601?" he asked suddenly.

Bruce shrugged. "I figured the next catastrophe would cause as much damage as the *Challenger* mess squared. *Challenger* was flight 51-L, and fifty-one squared is—"

"Two thousand six hundred and one," Santich finished with a sigh. "Well, I've got to hand it to you. You've really shot your wad, haven't you? I mean, we could have recovered from a faulty helmet. But this? Never. You've blackmailed anyone who gives a rat's ass about the program into going along with you."

Bruce didn't quite smile but did turn his lips upward perceptibly. "I think you underestimate the level of righteous indignation the death of a spacewalking astronaut would cause. And I think I've been quite open about my public-relations philosophy: What they don't know can't come back to bite us. Our biggest mistake with *Challenger* was letting ourselves get nailed to the cross. We should have had the funerals, told them that sometimes people get killed in the space business, and gotten on with it. But like I said, I'm not here to ask your approval. I am, however, asking for your help. The press conference starts at eight. I need your decision right now."

He would let down his only real friend in the corps, yet he knew that Grieve would also jump at the chance to fly on such short notice. Normally a shuttle flight meant twelve to eighteen months of training, much of it boring and repetitive. To fly in just one month meant all of the fun and none of the drudgery.

"Well? What's it going to be?"

A mere twenty-four hours earlier, he'd been composing his resignation letter. His good name, thirty-five years of honorable service to his country, for what? One more ride. One final thrill.

How badly did he want it?

"You knew what the answer would be when you walked in here," Santich said softly.

Bruce allowed himself a smile. "Yes, I did. That's what makes you an astronaut." He turned to leave, then spun back around. "Meet me at oh-seven-fifty at Building Two. You'll be up on the podium with me, but I'll answer all the substantive questions."

"Can I at least know the mission profile?"

"Certainly. Rendezvous with Gamma Ray Observatory, change out the two sun sensors, reboost GRO thirty nautical miles and separate. However, before you fly, you'll prepare a report saying the fuel cell problem on 104 was bad instrumentation, and cannot possibly recur on your flight. That's the task I mentioned earlier."

"So I'm whitewashing it."

"There was no real fuel cell problem, remember? Therefore it's not a whitewash."

"And the helmet problem?"

"I'll take care of it."

"You'll take care of it? How?"

Bruce stared at him blankly. "I'm assigning a tiger team."

"A tiger team? No one's supposed to know about this. How are you going to put a tiger team on it?"

"Whatever the problem, we'll fix it. Believe me, no one wants to go through *this* again. The contractor knows we had a problem, and they're already working on it. They want the Station contract, so you can be sure *they* won't let it happen again." Bruce grinned. "Besides, the safest launch is the one right after one blows, right? These will be the finest space suits the world has ever seen. Anyway, what are you so worried about? *You're* not the one going outside."

"I may be selling my soul to do this, but I won't sell my crew's lives."

The corners of Bruce's lips turned upward slightly. "Bravo. By the way, I'll be telling the media that we won't finalize a crew until next week."

"But you already have, haven't you?"

Again the grin, and a nod. "Orlov, O'Day and Anderson."

"O'Day and Anderson? Two rookies?"

"Go ahead and say it: two rookie *women*. And an African American at that. The new NASA isn't an old boys' club anymore, Santy."

Santich knew Anderson was probably the best pure pilot to come along since some of the Project Mercury guys, but still. "How the hell are you going to justify two rookies on this kind of flight?"

Bruce pulled open the door, and Santich heard the faint echoes of footsteps as some of the hungrier astronaut candidates began arriving.

"I don't have to justify it. They're both qualified; they're both in pilot pool. Plus Headquarters told me that Anderson *would* fly as soon as possible. I figure next month should satisfy them. See you in a couple of hours."

The door clicked shut, and for a few moments Santich eyed it closely, half expecting Bruce to burst in and tell him he was only joking. The coffee machine began to gurgle as its timer switched on. Santich reached into the bottom drawer for his mug and realized his hands were shaking. Slowly he raised them to his eyes, watching the rapid quiver. He clenched and unclenched the fingers, and still they shook.

Thirty years earlier, when he had applied to NASA, few humans had even been in space. More than a few of his cohorts thought him crazy to leave one of the Navy's most prestigious assignments for such a dubious program. But it had been understandable, even laudable, and it had earned him a nation's adulation. This would be different. There was no scientific value, no engineering value, not even any cold war symbolism. It was a tired old bureaucracy covering its ass, and an old man getting his rocks off. The thought pulled tight the knot in his stomach, and he suppressed the reflex to vomit.

Outside, thick gray clouds made the approaching dawn more a lessening of the dark than an arrival of light. Through a stand of elms planted back when Lyndon Johnson was vice president, a security guard raised the flag in front of the headquarters building to the top, then lowered it to half-staff. Santich turned from the window to compose his statement.

8

No matter how many glasses of water he drank, his throat remained parched. The pitcher the public affairs secretary had filled for the two men was almost empty, and they were still a few minutes from starting.

Many of the reporters who covered NASA usually approached the podium before the start of a briefing to chat, earn brownie points, and in the case of one or two, just be polite. There was none of that this morning. The reporters huddled among themselves in the audience, trading gossip, while Bruce and Santich sat silently at their seats, reading and rereading their prepared statements.

Bruce sifted through a dozen note cards while Santich rubbed and twisted a single sheet of computer paper. Only the top fourth had any writing. Beside them, Len Concord wore his earpiece, every so often glancing at Bruce as if to gauge whether he planned to walk out again.

Santich peeked over the reading glasses he wore largely to avoid eye contact and saw that the previous day's handful of reporters had swollen to five or six dozen, not including the public relations staffs from the shuttle's original builder, the manufacturer of the tires, and the maker of the fuel cells the shuttle used for generating electricity. Where was the flack for the space-suit maker? Santich wondered if he even knew that he was the one who *should* be there.

Santich fiddled with his sheet. What if they asked him

about 104's landing? What if they asked about Torrington? What was he going to tell them? Would he lie? What if he told the truth? Bruce couldn't stop him, not with so many reporters there. . . . But Bruce and Hooper were right. Such a revelation would destroy the program, and he would never fly. Maybe he could tell them what he and Grieve were talking about: that he recommended suspending flights pending a thorough investigation. He turned to sneak a glance at Bruce. No, it was too late for that. He'd forsaken that option when he'd climbed up on that podium with him. No, if they asked him about 104, or Torrington, he would do what Bruce knew he would do. He would lie.

After an interminable delay, Concord welcomed the other field centers to the briefing via satellite television, reminded them of the ground rules, and turned it over to Bruce, who surprised the room by apologizing for his previous day's behavior.

"We'd had a long night, but that's no excuse. I know that all of you who cover the program also had long nights. Anyway, water under the bridge. Let me start by answering Mr. Lawrence's question from yesterday, which at the time I didn't have the answer to.

"Yes, *Atlantis* did experience some off-nominal wear yesterday morning during its return to KSC. All six tires, the nose gear structural members, the nosewheel brakes, the left main brakes, and the drag chute suffered varying degrees of damage. And, yes, it will cost the program some money to get *Atlantis* ready to fly again. I don't have an estimate at this time, but I can assure you it won't be anywhere near the half billion or two hundred million I've seen in some of your dispatches. As Mark Twain might of said, the reports of 104's death have been greatly exaggerated."

One or two laughs answered. Santich kept his eyes glued to his printout.

"We haven't, of course, had time to thoroughly investigate the damage, but our preliminary assessment is that both the hardware and the computer software functioned nominally. We'll get more to you as we learn it."

Santich bit his tongue. Hooper had been right. By ruling out mechanical and computer failures, Bruce was leaving Banke to twist in the wind. He didn't come right out and say it was pilot error; that would have been unprecedented, even for Bruce. The papers and the TV, though, would pick up on what wasn't said. And his mere presence next to Bruce made him party to it.

"Another matter I'm sure you're interested in: We here in the program, and within NASA in general, were deeply shocked and saddened by the loss of one of our own, Samuel Torrington. Ask anyone here at Johnson, and they'll tell you: Sam was truly special and a credit to the corps. There will be a memorial service in the auditorium this afternoon for any of you who would like to attend, either personally or professionally.

"That, however, is as far as I can help you regarding Sam. The program is not investigating the car accident. That's a matter better left to the local authorities at Kennedy. It's a great loss and a tragedy for the office, but not really within our jurisdiction.

"Finally, as we told you yesterday, the GRO was left in a fully operational mode and is gathering volumes of useful science as we speak. However, we didn't accomplish one hundred percent of the mission objectives because of the newly discovered failure of the sun sensors. As it happens, we have two additional sensors on hand. They were built as test articles but were later certified for flight. I know you all are used to the occasional delays the program experiences; I can't help but notice the headlines on those stories, they're so big. So now is your chance to write a different kind of headline: NASA to finish GRO repairs next month."

Santich peeked over his glasses and saw the beat reporters look at one another skeptically. The others, those not familiar with NASA, didn't know enough to be skeptical.

"I can see some of you find that hard to swallow. Well, it's happened for a couple of reasons. The payload for STS-68 has slipped about two months. And since *Endeavour* comes back from its mods next week, it can do 68 and still be turned around for 76 in September. So that leaves *Columbia* available and ready to go next month with no primary payload. We've decided to take advantage of that by sending up a second GRO mission in early May.

"I'm sure all of you recognize the man on my left. For years, he's been in charge of safety and reliability for the center director here, but he's always remained a flight-ready pilot. And that makes him perfect to command STS-74A. In short, the shuttle program is demonstrating its flexibility and responsiveness as it approaches the space station era by designing, training and carrying out a mission all in one month.

"Granted, a bird was already in final processing at the Cape, or we couldn't have done it, but from a mission ops standpoint, I think it says quite a lot. Now, Santy, I believe you had something?"

Santich pushed the glasses up the bridge of his nose and licked his lips. They were dry, though the carafe of water was now empty.

"Good morning. It's been awhile since I've sat here, but I'm pleased to say that I'm very excited about mission STS-74 Alpha and that I'm certain we'll accomplish our objectives. The Gamma Ray Observatory is an important scientific instrument, and I look forward to making it even more capable and reliable than it is now."

The final sentence was Bruce's contribution. "I know the circumstances surrounding the return of STS-74 were somewhat off-nominal, but I can assure you in my Safety, Reliability and Quality Assurance capacity that these were isolated anomalies and won't affect the safe conduct of 74A." He glanced up, saw everyone looking at him. "Thank you."

After a moment Concord opened it up for questions, and the barrage began. Amazingly, all of them were directed at Bruce, and while a few were of the aren't-you-worried-how-this-will-play-in-Congress and is-this-a-desperate-gambit-to-save-Space-Station ilk, most were along the lines

Bruce had led them. How difficult was it to plan such a complex mission on such short notice? Would it set any records? Would it answer once and for all questions about NASA's ability to work quickly in space? In their rush to be first, they had ignored the important stuff—what the hell had happened to STS-74?—to focus on the sound bite of the day that Bruce had fed them.

Santich sat stony-faced, listening and trying to contain his disgust: with the media, with NASA, but mostly with STS-74A mission commander Santiago Santich.

The satellite was configured to take questions from Kennedy, and the nonsense continued. Until they got to Rob Lawrence.

"I guess it's just me, but I'm having a real tough time understanding how you guys can have the worst mission since *Challenger* and the next day be talking about flying again in five weeks, especially with a stickler for safety like Captain Santich in the left seat. Are you saying you've completely ruled out nonhuman factors in 104's problems? And if so, was the failure at Mission Control or in the cockpit? I mean, we've heard that you had a crosswind well over nighttime limits, and that's why *Atlantis* suffered so much damage. If so, why did you guys come to Florida in the first place? And finally, how can an astronaut die within hours of returning from orbit and you guys not be worried about it? Isn't there the remote chance that the car crash was caused by a medical condition associated with space-flight?"

This is it, Santich felt in his gut: the beginning of the end. He licked his lips, trying to arrange his response, as Bruce began.

"I'll take that one. First off, I already said up front: We have nothing further to say about Sam Torrington's death. We have no reason to believe his accident was in any way associated with the flight, and until we have cause to think otherwise, we're going to grieve his passing and move on.

"Second, I have to take issue with your description of STS-74 as the worst since 51-L. As I've stated repeatedly, we accomplished the primary objectives. An anomaly in the fuel cells forced us back early. It turns out the problem was instrumentation, not actually the fuel cell, but we couldn't know that at the time. Yes, we did suffer some minor damage at touchdown, but the crew arrived safe and sound. And not to belittle the damage or the dollar value it might come to, but we had a saying in the Air Force: Any landing you walk away from is a good landing.

"Now, about the winds. There may have been some gusts over the stated values in the guidelines, but the steady-state winds were within limits. You have to understand that the orbiter is not a Cessna. It isn't affected by brief gusts because it plows right through them. We've run tests in the simulators and in the wind tunnel at Ames proving that our limits are far too conservative. We could ease them thirty to forty percent and still maintain adequate safety margins."

Santich squirmed as Bruce lied, trying to keep a poker face. The orbiter *was* affected strongly by gusts, especially gusts right near the ground, and the decision to return to Florida had nearly gotten the rest of the crew killed. He bit his tongue and turned his eyes downward to stare at the podium.

"Finally," Bruce continued, "we've reviewed our data here, and the call to return to Florida was based on a green forecast, and conditions at the shuttle landing facility at touchdown were also green. If we weren't fully confident about this, we wouldn't be preparing to fly again in May."

Santich continued his intense study of the wood veneer covering the podium, noticed it was peeling around the edges. Bruce went on, taking the remainder of the questions, and Santich counted fifty-four staples that held the corner molding onto the podium top. No one else asked about the botched landing. No one else cared about Sam Torrington's fiery demise. Lawrence's was the only confrontational question; all the rest were softballs. In fifteen short minutes, he had become all he had fought against.

9

"I thought you considered Steve a friend."

Her call was among those Santich knew he would get. He didn't think she would be first, that she would, in fact, have called in the middle of the conference and have patiently held the line for twenty minutes until her husband finished and returned to his office.

"Honey?"

"Yes, I'm listening. And I like Steve. Believe me, it wasn't my idea to nail him to the cross."

"You know that doesn't matter. The two of you together like that. Anything he said, you may as well have said yourself."

Santich's stomach did a quarter turn. As always, Emily cut away artifice and went straight to the heart.

"Dear, you've given up too many of your best years, my best years, *your children's* best years, to get where you are. But at least where you are is a decent place. People look up to you."

"People don't care. Nobody cares," Santich said with irritation.

"It's talk like that that reminds me why I left. Okay, people don't hang on your every word and idolize you like some movie star. But is that what you want? The world needs good men. You are one of them. Don't throw it away."

68

Pity hadn't worked; maybe duty would. "I'm not throwing it away. But believe me, Emily, if this flight doesn't go off just right, that's the end of NASA."

"Oh, so now you're the only one who can fly the shuttle? 'This thing is so damned automated that a monkey could fly it.' Santiago Santich, 1979. And then, 'This agency is so full of inbred bootlickers, they ought to scrap it.' Santiago Santich, 1987."

Santich sighed. She knew him as well as he knew himself, maybe better. "I need to do this, baby. You know that. For ten years, all I've wanted was one more shot, and it's now or never." He paused, but the line stayed silent. "You won't believe me, but just yesterday morning I was writing my resignation letter to Bruce. I decided I'd waited long enough. That I'd kept you, Tony, Moira, and the grandkids waiting long enough. I was going to call it quits week after next: April twelfth." He thought about telling her Grieve's plan, decided against it. "Then this morning, Bruce walked in, told me he needed me to fly next month to clean up the mess they left with GRO. You *know* me, honey; this has been my life for thirty years. I couldn't turn it down."

The phone breathed Emily's sigh. "Yes, I guess I do know you. And I can see you couldn't turn it down. But that doesn't stop me from knowing you should have."

Again silence filled the air between Houston and Naples. "Well," Santich said finally. "I promise: This is it. This is the last one. Then I come home."

"Dear, you've said that when you were flying the A-6 in Maryland. You said it before Gemini; you said it before Apollo; you said it before STS-1. I didn't believe you then; why should I believe you now? The only difference is, I'm not waiting for you anymore. I haven't been for four years, and I'm not about to go back to that now."

"Meaning?"

"Meaning you do what you must, and so will I. Just remember, dear, the other lives you're affecting. I don't mean just your family. I mean the others there who count on you. I just find it a little strange that a man who dislikes you as much as Marty Bruce all of a sudden lets you fly again. There's something very fishy. Is there something you aren't telling me?''

Santich screwed up his courage to lie to his wife. ''No. There isn't.''

Another pause. ''Well, I'm not sure I believe that, either. I'm not sure I understand. You used to tell me all sorts of secrets: how fast the jets you tested could go, the types of weapons they had. . . . But anyway, I'm not really interested. So go on, go fly your spaceship. Have a good time.''

More than anyone, more than Air Force Lt. Anthony Santich, more than his mother, the rigid moralist, Emily could strike just the right chord to make him feel terrible. He cleared the lump in his throat. ''I love you.''

''You have a funny way of showing it.''

The line went dead, and Santich stared at the handset, as if holding it long enough might bring her back, before giving up and setting it back in the cradle. On cue, Grieve burst through the door, and Lynnette's voice crackled on the intercom. ''I told him you were talking to Emily. I kept him out as long as I could.''

''You son of a bitch!'' Grieve began, moving to the desk in two strides. ''You cocksucking son of a bitch!''

Santich couldn't think of a response.

''You son of a bitch!'' Grieve repeated. ''I thought, wrongly, I see, that we were friends. That I could count on you, if not to help me, then at least not to screw me.''

''How does this screw you?'' Santich asked shamefully, his face a deep scarlet.

''Don't yank my chain! Tell me, how long did it take you to agree? An hour? Thirty minutes?''

More like five, Santich thought, but said nothing. He deserved his lumps, and he would take them silently.

''So that's it, then? You guys hose Banke, Bruce stays where he is, and you get to fly. Is that it? Six months? You couldn't wait six rotten months to get back up there?''

Santich took a deep breath. ''Please, for a moment, put

yourself in my position, and be honest. What would you have done?''

Grieve didn't hesitate. "I wouldn't have screwed my friends.''

"If Bruce walked through the door right now and said, 'Butch, you can fly next month,' what would you say?''

"The man is destroying the program!''

"Be honest: That's not why you cooked up the plan to get rid of him. It was so you could get his job and maybe fly again.''

Grieve shook his head in disgust. "You said yesterday that this morning you would tell me whether you'd help me or retire. Right? Help me, or retire. You didn't mention a third option: making me bend over and take it up the ass!''

"This doesn't preclude you from going ahead with your thing," Santich said defensively. "In fact, I'd like you to put some heat on Bruce to prove the thing can fly safely.''

"Oh, please," Grieve scoffed. "You're one of the Gemini Nine, willing to climb on top of a fucking *Titan* to get into orbit. Besides, what are the odds of losing two fuel cells again?''

Santich wondered if the real story would ever get around Building 4. "I'm sorry," he said simply.

"You should be. I hope it's worth it. You've given up a lot, you know. Oh, you're doing okay on the TV—fucking Caesar, home from the wars," Grieve snorted. "But people around here, they all looked up to you. They might have been too afraid to say so, to avoid getting on the outs, but you were a hero. Now they know. You're no better than they are.''

He stalked out of the office, leaving Santich to wade through the new paperwork on his desk and watch himself on CNN. Grieve, for once, had not been exaggerating. The media lapped up the whole thing. One or two reports Santich read on the wires mentioned 104's questionable landing and the damage it suffered, but the rest of them and the television heralded the upcoming flight as a make-or-break mission for a troubled space agency. Self-proclaimed space experts from academia and Washington think tanks, those who were pro-NASA, said STS-74A would restore the luster the agency lost after Apollo. Other experts, anti-NASA, said, no, the whole thing was a publicity gimmick, and it wouldn't save the Space Station from near certain cancellation later in the year.

Many reports had long pieces about Santiago Santich's naval and NASA careers—using material saved for an obituary, he was sure—and about how he had remained an active astronaut while serving more than a decade in limbo at JSC Headquarters.

But as Grieve had predicted, the reaction on campus was far from adulatory. Throughout the day, everyone he ran into muttered congratulations and attaboys, but the good wishes had a pro forma, wooden quality. When he left Tim Garvey's office after discussing the official naming of the flight crew, the three other astronauts in the outer office immediately stopped their conversation and looked elsewhere. Santich walked past them with an awkward smile.

It was, he remembered bitterly, the same treatment they'd given him when he'd been removed from his post of chief astronaut. Well, if they wanted to be mean-spirited, let them. He hadn't needed them these past ten years, and he could certainly get by without them another five weeks.

The one reaction that surprised him, though, was his best friend's. He assumed, when he responded to the phone message to meet at the Outpost at six-thirty, that it would be a celebratory get-together. His only one, he thought. But at the bar, Hoop had his back turned, face toward the television, and when Santich came up from behind him with a pat on his shoulder, Hooper stared suspiciously, his pale skin reflecting the blue-green light from the set.

"What are you doing?" he hissed, eyes darting around the nearly empty barroom.

Santich blinked, spread his palms upward. "What?"

Hooper scanned the foursome shooting pool, a hand-holding couple in front of the jukebox and the three T-shirt-

and-shorts-clad tourists eating greasy cheeseburgers at a table near the entrance.

"Have you lost your mind?"

Santich dropped onto a stool. The barkeep was already on his way, Heineken in hand. "I've gotten this from *everybody* today, but *you*, I figured, would be different. See? I've gotten with the program. Sold out. I won't be making waves now, and your precious Space Station is safe. I thought you'd be thrilled."

Hooper shook his head, started to open his mouth, and shook his head some more. "You don't understand."

"What?" Santich asked, exasperated. "What don't I understand?"

Hooper sat silently, thought for a moment. "There's a lot more to this than you know."

Santich took a sip from the frosty bottle. "A lot more to what?" he asked slowly.

"To the whole thing. To why 104 came back like it did, to how Torrington died." Hooper seemed to weigh how much he should tell. "Something that was never supposed to happen happened night before last. Torrington died from explosive decompression. Out in the payload bay during the EVA."

Santich weighed how much he should let on. "How do you know this?"

"Believe me, it was a tough nut to crack. I don't think more than a couple dozen people know." He looked around nervously for eavesdroppers. "If this gets out, we're all fucked. The whole thing, I mean."

"I know," Santich admitted. "Bruce told me this morning."

Hooper looked up in alarm. "He *told* you?"

"Everything. The helmet seal failure, the cover-up, the faked car wreck, everything."

"They know why it failed?"

Santich shook his head.

"But they're sending you guys up anyway."

Santich nodded. "Bruce thinks they need to do something to make sure Station passes this summer.''

Hooper looked into his glass. "Of all the stupid, shit-for-brained . . ." He looked up and caught his friend's eyes. "Don't go, Santy. This is a serious failure. And if it happens again?"

"Come on, Hoop. If anything breaks this time, I'll guarantee it won't be a space suit. I'll bet Gates Rubber is putting a set together right now that wouldn't leak if you put a fire hose down the sleeve." He grinned. "The safest launch is right after the one that blows up."

"No! Not if Bruce wants to launch in five weeks!" Hooper shook his head. "Gates won't have more than a week or ten days to figure out what went wrong and fix it. I'll bet they won't have any idea what exactly happened. They'll just send up three more suits and cross their fingers."

"It's just the helmet seal! How many different things *could* have gone wrong with it? I mean, Gates has been making suits since . . . Apollo? And this is the first one that's ever had a problem."

Hooper studied the bubbles left at the bottom of his mug, turned it one way, then the other. "I asked about 2601. Did Bruce tell you about that, too?"

"No. Grieve did."

"Did he tell you about Option Zulu?"

Santich looked at him blankly.

Hooper stopped playing with his mug. "Option Zulu is for when Bruce isn't certain his flight crew will maintain the cover-up. So to make sure, the Shuttle Training Aircraft bringing them back from Florida blows up over the Gulf."

Santich felt his pulse race, then settle back down. "No. I can't believe that."

Hooper shrugged. "I'm just telling you what I was told. And I got that from the same guy who told me about Torrington, and he was right about that."

Santich twisted it, turned it over, rejected it. Cold-blooded murder seemed more than a bit far-fetched, even for a Machiavelle like Bruce. "How did this guy know? I mean about the STA?"

"That's what the flight crews believe, anyway. I'm surprised you haven't heard."

Santich finished his beer and counted out three dollar bills. "Yeah, well, maybe now that I'm back on the flight roster, Bruce will tell me about it."

As he got up to leave, Hooper grabbed his arm. "Yesterday, when I didn't want you to dig too deep, I was asking you, for the sake of the program. Today, I'm *telling* you, for your own good. There's something really wrong, okay? It's not safe to fly."

Santich nodded, shook his arm free. "Thanks. I'll be talking to you."

10

Photocopied flight plans, with their tiny lettering, often poorly reproduced, were never easy to read. Lack of sleep only made it worse. Hoop had never steered him wrong; why was he so adamant about not flying 74A? And that thing about the STA—would Bruce dare sabotage the Gulfstream? He couldn't possibly get away with it. Although he *had* stuck Torrington's corpse into a rented Chrysler and run it into a tanker full of jet fuel, and so far he'd gotten away with *that*.

The second cup of coffee churned inside Santich's empty stomach like battery acid. He had to stop worrying about this nonsense and get to the business at hand: a six-day flight, with possibly two extension days, plus two contingency days to allow for bad weather at the landing sites. Flight day one was launch and the first two rendezvous burns, day two was more burns, day three was rendezvous, day four the EVA to fix GRO, day five reboost, day six was entry prep, and day seven was entry and landing. If Orlov and O'Day had problems on the space walk, then a second, or even third, EVA could be inserted between day four and day five. As commander, his duties were simple: Make sure the computers handled the targeting burns properly, fly the final approach by hand until Anderson could grab the Gamma Ray Observatory with *Columbia*'s robot

doors, stowing the Ku antenna, and so forth. Any questions?''

Alexandra raised her hand shyly. "Um, I was wondering. There don't seem to be any secondary experiments."

"No, there aren't. I guess another advantage of a rushed mission. To put all the tool racks and so forth from *Atlantis* into *Columbia*'s payload bay, they had to remove the Get-Away-Special canisters *Columbia* originally was going to have in order to maintain center of gravity." Santich grinned. "In terms of crew cabin experiments, there wasn't enough time to integrate any of that make-work stuff into the flight plan."

"Oh, I don't think it's make-work stuff." Sincerity oozed from Alexandra's eyes. "Those GAS canisters had some neat satellites built by high-school classes from all over the country. I spoke to some of the kids a few months ago, and they were really excited about seeing their stuff fly. And those crew-cabin secondaries have some important science. It's a shame we can't help out."

Melanie rolled her eyes and crossed her arms, then sighed. "Oh, well. I guess there's always next flight."

Alexandra answered quietly. "I just think we have an obligation to perform as much science as we can on every mission, that's all."

Melanie suppressed a grin. "Well, I suppose, Alex Prime, that you could always tell Marty that you can't in good conscience fly on such a scientifically insignificant mission. That he'll have to pick someone else."

Alexandra paused a moment. "No. I don't think I'll do that. *I've* been in the pool three years before getting assigned."

Melanie's eyes blazed. It was something that everyone in the corps had thought, and no one had yet said aloud. *She* had been in pilot pool for only four months before getting assigned a flight, and she and everyone else knew why. "Dr. O'Day, is there something you'd like to say to me?''

Alexandra kept her eyes down, shuffled some papers. "I think I've said enough."

Orlov crossed his arms and turned his head toward Melanie for her reply, when Santich decided it had already gone too far. "Okay, Commander Anderson, Dr. O'Day. You'll have plenty of time to continue your discussion on orbit. The fact is, there are no secondaries on this flight, and I'm not prepared to waste any of our training time to memorize which switches need to be thrown when on the biomass—waste renewal generator, or whatever the hell they'd stick us with." Santich realized, too late, that he'd openly taken Melanie's side. "Anyway, we have a lot more important things to worry about."

He looked at the closed door, wondered whether anyone lurked behind it with an ear pressed. He lowered his voice. "Is everyone comfortable about how management is investigating the last flight?"

Orlov pursed his lips, Alexandra looked at Santich blankly and Melanie kept a cool, detached expression.

"You mean about the fuel cell issue and the landing?" Alexandra asked.

Santich nodded.

Alexandra looked around the table at the others. "What's there to investigate? I mean, didn't Marty say the fuel cell was an instrumentation problem? And the landing, I thought that was pilot error."

Orlov snorted, kept his arms folded.

"Alex?" Santich asked.

"I did not know that was a topic we were to discuss."

"Well, I'm old-fashioned Navy enough to believe that on my ship, my crew and I discuss anything we damn well please."

Orlov looked Santich over, made up his mind. "With the understanding, of course, that none of this leaves this room."

Santich nodded.

"Steve Banke saved my life the other morning. If not for his superb flying, we would have died in a hydrazine fire at the near end of KSC thirty-three. You see, we wound up low on energy on final, and the crosswind was much higher than forecast, as much as twenty or twenty-five knots.

"I could see the runway sliding away from us. Each time he moved us back over the strip, he had to give up altitude. Finally, we were so low and so far right, he did not have a choice. He rolled us left, bringing us down hard. Then, and I am certain this is not in any of the procedures manuals, he deployed the drag chute to yaw the nose back in line. If he had not, we would have gone into the ditch at two hundred knots.

"So to hear him criticized for violating flight rules by using the chute in too much wind, or for damaging the landing gear, is insulting."

Santich listened to the careful, precise English of someone who had learned it as a second tongue; watched closely the man who he knew had witnessed Torrington's helmet explode, had seen the remnants of his head burst outward, and then had the nerve to haul the body back into the air lock. After it was all over, he had to keep quiet about it. What kind of man could do that, Santich wondered. Bruce, for one. Probably a fair number of the shuttle pilots, who were, with one or two exceptions, drawn from the military. But Orlov wasn't military. He was a scientist, the son of the noted Soviet physicist, pacifist and, ultimately, defector, Leonid Orlov.

"Why were you low on energy?" Alexandra asked.

Alexis shrugged. "The wind. It was stronger than predicted all the way down, and until our final turn, it was a tailwind, stealing our altitude." He lifted his eyes toward Santich. "I think maybe in those conditions, Edwards might have been the better choice."

Santich looked back for a second, trying to determine whether the reference was innocent, respectful, or mocking. Edwards versus Kennedy landings, everyone at JSC knew quite well, had been the subject of one of the memos that had cost Santich so much. He had written a sharp critique of NASA's decision to land shuttles at Kennedy Space Center, which had a single strip surrounded by marsh, while Edwards Air Force Base's numerous runways on the hard-packed clay of the dry lake bed were, except for a brief rainy season, always available.

When written, the memo had been ignored, but when it was made public after *Challenger* exploded, it poured gas on the NASA-is-sacrificing-safety-to-meet-a-schedule fire consuming the media.

Santich knew exactly why *Atlantis* had come back to Florida in such miserable weather. He knew Orlov knew, and wondered whether Orlov hoped Santich would start asking difficult questions. If so, Santich knew he would disappoint yet another.

"Oh, well. I guess spaceflight is still a risky business," Alexandra said with a shake of her head.

"Oh, well," Melanie said with an innocent smile.

Santich pushed his reading glasses back on. "Okay. Then everyone's satisfied that the major anomalies will be closed by the time we launch?"

The women nodded. Orlov shrugged. Santich again wondered about him. How had Bruce made him fly again so soon? What was promised? Or was it the simple, mindless compulsion for as many flights as possible, even if it meant suppressing the trauma from the last one?

"In that case, let's wrap this up and get on with training. We've got a bundle to memorize, and just enough time to do it."

All four gathered piles of paperwork and made their way out into the sunshine. Alexandra, still grinning, went with Orlov toward the WET-F—the Weightless Environment Training Facility, JSC's giant swimming pool—to prepare for their first session, while Santich and Melanie turned toward Building 5, which housed the sophisticated simulators the astronauts used to commit each switch throw, every keyboard entry of their entire mission to memory. The last thing Santich heard as the pairs parted was Alexandra's schoolgirl whisper: "I can't believe this is happening!"

"Well," Santich said after the Alexes were out of earshot, "that makes two of us." At once he regretted it. He had grown so accustomed to treating his right-seat as a fellow fraternity member, an automatic ally against the non-pilot members of the corps, that he had forgotten Melanie was no ordinary pilot. By dint of her gender and skin color, she had already cut way ahead in line, past pilots much older and much more experienced, to get where she was. Her meteoric rise had not gone unresented.

Melanie smiled conspiratorially. "I guess NASA wants a good cross section in the corps: engineers, doctors, researchers, dingbats. . . ."

"Black women pilots," Santich finished, again regretting he'd said anything.

She stiffened, and for a moment they walked in silence. "You know, Captain Santich, I've listened to that crap for seven years, ever since Annapolis."

"Seven years? In and out of Miramar, Pax River, Atlantic Command. Not a bad seven years. Even without a single combat assignment, you'd have made admiral by the time you were thirty-five, if you hadn't stopped to play astronaut. Even here, there's no holding you back. In on your first try, flying pilot your first flight when male pilots in the class *before* yours are still going up as mission specialists. I wouldn't bet against you commanding your next mission."

"For the record, sir, and with all due respect: Women were not allowed combat roles aboard ship, and flying an F-18 is typically done off a ship. Regarding the male pilots here, sir, I've consistently beaten them in the simulators. I've even equalled your scores. Sir."

That, he knew, was true, though he had little faith in the simulators' scorekeeping. Again he wished he'd kept his mouth shut. "Listen, Melanie. First of all, call me Santy, okay? Second, I didn't mean to question your qualifications. Certainly you're more than qualified for everything you've done. All I meant is that you, personally, not your race, and not your gender, but you personally have been lucky to have been in the right place at the right time, with the right career goals. That's all.''

She began to open her mouth, and Santich preempted her. ''And I'm the first to admit that I've had more than my share of luck. And I also firmly believe that it's better to be mediocre and lucky than superb but unlucky.''

Melanie's elegant features softened, and the smile returned. ''Everyone said you were a character, the kind they don't let into the program anymore.''

''I'll take that as a compliment.'' He noticed, finally, that his copilot was strikingly attractive: long, slender figure, high cheekbones, and skin the color of rich cocoa. She wore no makeup. She didn't need to. He also noticed that she was as tall as he, and looked like she could be as strong. She certainly matched him stride for stride as they made their way along the well-kept lawns and little ponds that separated the buildings.

''Tell me,'' he said as they rounded the cafeteria, ''what did they tell you about this mission? I mean, didn't it seem a bit odd? How they put it together and everything?''

''The rumor started two nights ago that Headquarters wanted to send a second mission ASAP. Yesterday morning you and Bruce made it official, and he called me last night and told me I had an assignment if I wanted it.''

''And what did you say?''

Melanie smiled. ''What did you say when they offered *you* your first shot?''

The same thing I said when they offered me my seventh, Santich thought. ''You accepted on the spot.''

''Hell, yeah, I accepted on the spot! *My* momma didn't raise no fool! You think I gave up my captain's stripe so I could return letters to space cadets and talk to Rotary Clubs the rest of my life?''

Santich grinned. When an astronaut wasn't in his last months of training for a mission, those were the sorts of public relations tasks that occupied a good-size chunk of his time. Of course, Santich hadn't answered an autograph hound's request in years, and NASA had stopped sending him to Rotary and Kiwanis functions for fear of what he might say.

"Can I ask you something?"

"Hmmm?" Santich returned from his reverie. "What?"

"As you so gracefully pointed out, I *know* why *I* was picked for this flight. Why they'd want Alex also makes sense, because he's just been there and knows the GRO. The talented Dr. O'Day: Well, apparently she used to design widgets like the one they're going to replace on GRO, so she makes sense. The only thing I can't figure is you."

They arrived at Building 5. Santich produced his card key and inserted it into a slot next to the steel door, making it click open.

"Hendricks, Conner, Malley," Melanie continued, her voice hushed now in the narrow, fluorescent-lit corridor. "All three are in the rotation for another command. All three have done a rendezvous before. You haven't. Yet Bruce picks you. I'm not sure I get it."

"That makes two of us," Santich joked. "Maybe the political value? Polishing an old relic, the agency's safety nut to trot in front of Congress?"

Melanie shook her head. "I thought about that, but it doesn't make sense. To make Congress happy, all they've got to do is fix the damn satellite before June. Doesn't matter who gets it done. And if that's the case, then send Conner. He's done *two* rendezvous. He's the one who took GRO up there in the first place." She grinned. "Plus he's better behaved than you, wouldn't you agree?"

Again, she was right. Conner was on every feel-good-about-ourselves committee in the program. Every time they needed an articulate spokesman from the office, it was Conner at the National Press Club, Conner on Capitol Hill.

"Why did you ask me about whether I'd agreed to fly right away?" she asked suddenly.

Santich shrugged. "Curious, I guess."

"Because I figured maybe you had some reservations

about this flight, and thought maybe the rest of us did, too.''

Santich remembered again the shudder from the boost-ers, the heavy hand pushing down his chest, and recalled how the memories had intoxicated him when Bruce had made the offer. ''What kind of reservations?'' he asked cautiously.

''Well, I'm embarrassed to say I didn't think of them at the time. They only occurred to me after I'd already said yes.'' They were approaching the door where the simulator supervisor and his team were to greet them, and she hushed her voice even further. ''I mean, you have a reputation for sticking your nose into safety issues, right? So what if something *really* bad happened on 104? What better way to keep you quiet than to keep you too busy training to look into it?''

Santich gulped, but before he could think of a way to rationalize away her fear, the door ten yards away opened to let out a thick black mustache and some equally dark horn-rim glasses.

''Captain Santiago Santich, United States Navy, Retired! It's been too long!''

11

The bright orange explosions that pushed away the burned-out booster rockets had long since faded when the Klaxon sounded.

"Houston, *Columbia*. We have a cabin pressure warning. We're at thirteen-point-six psi, and falling."

"Roger, *Columbia*. We show a delta-P of one-point-five psi per minute, and at this time call for TAL."

"Roger, Houston, selecting TAL." With his left hand, Santich turned a round knob so the arrow pointed to the letters representing Transoceanic Abort Landing, one of four abort scenarios programmed into the flight software.

"*Columbia*, Houston, you have a go for a three-engine TAL."

"Roger, Houston." Santich flipped the plastic finger guard and pressed the red ABORT button. "TAL abort selected, MET five minutes, fifteen-decimal-eight seconds."

Simulator Supervisor Claude Musgrave was right. It had been a long time. Not since Santich had been in the simulators, but since he'd been there for a reason. Once a week Santich had come by and, with Musgrave's complicity, strapped himself into the machine to run a few abort landings: touchdowns in The Gambia, Morocco, or Spain, or some truly inventive U-turns back to Kennedy Space Center that stretched both imagination and engineering models.

That, in fact, was the ostensible justification of giving so much ten-thousand-dollars-an-hour time to a fifty-nine-year-old man with little chance of flying again: Musgrave, who'd been a simsup since the first serious simulator was installed for Apollo, would dutifully report that the machines were validating the new flight modes that were constantly cooked up by the eager engineers in the Orbiter Flight Project office. The new modes were basically stunts—rolls, split-S's—that could be used to escape outlandish problems that took a vivid imagination just to dream up. None, of course, had any real chance of acceptance by the program. The aerobatic stunts were far too risky and would occupy too much valuable space in the computers' limited memory banks.

Santich didn't care; he had fun flying them. Once he managed to pull *Atlantis* through an inside loop. He tried the trick with *Columbia* and *Discovery*, but the two older craft were too heavy and always stalled. Once in a while he'd take another astronaut into the simulator with him, usually a rookie awestruck at actually training with *the* Santy Santich, but typically he went alone.

On that morning Santich had climbed into the left-hand chair, legs up, back and head resting flat against the floor. The thrill of being in the machine *for a purpose*, the gentle, simulated rumble of liftoff—it all made him ignore the sliver of doubt that Melanie had pricked him with.

Of course they're keeping me from making a stew over something, Santich told himself. That something is Sam Torrington's in-orbit death. And they bought me off with a seventh trip into space.

"A cabin leak is an easy one," Santich told Melanie, who lay strapped in beside him. "We keep all three engines and make a nominal entry into Zaragoza. By the end of the week, we'll be losing engines, Auxiliary Power Units, Inertial Measurement Units, the works. All at the same time."

The computer reached the part of its program where it rolled the orbiter over, so that it rode on top of the great orange fuel tank instead of beneath it. To simulate this, the pod they lay in tilted upright, so that Santich and Melanie sat up.

"And all of them in the first two minutes and thirty seconds, so that we come back on a wing and a prayer?" Melanie asked.

That had been another of Santich's famous indiscretions. He'd told *Aviation Week and Space Technology* magazine that a crippled shuttle attempting a Return to Launch Site abort, an RTLS—its only option until it had enough momentum to cross the Atlantic for a TAL—would have but a wing and a prayer of making it back safely. He'd gone on to say that the only reason the program trained for RTLS was that it was too ashamed to admit that the astronauts were as good as dead if an engine failed in the first 150 seconds of flight.

But the Santich who had said those things was a grounded astronaut, and the Santich who replied to Melanie was a born-again flier. "I hope we never have to do it, but if we do, I think we could pull it off." He winked at her. "Anyway, better that than the fireman's pole."

Another object of Santich's public criticisms: a telescoping pole that emerged from the crew hatch that, in theory, would let the astronauts bail out of a doomed shuttle without mashing themselves on the port wing. The device had been invented during the *Challenger* hiatus. Almost every astronaut agreed the pole was not likely to work. All but one kept his mouth shut about it.

Melanie turned toward her displays and smiled to herself. In a few moments, the artificial horizon display slid downward while images of clouds and ocean were displayed on the "windows" in front of them. A dull thunk came over the loudspeakers. Almost immediately the "windows" pointed upward again as the shuttle raised its nose toward the sky.

"Houston, we have external tank jettison," Santich called.

"Roger, *Columbia*, ET jettison. FIDO sees a good separation and a good entry attitude."

Santich wondered whether he knew the FIDO, the flight dynamics officer, for his mission. He didn't think so. On his previous flights, he'd made a point of meeting each and every one of the ground controllers prior to launch. Yet another chore in the remaining month.

The controllers, he knew, were by and large kids Melanie's age or even younger, with secret, and sometimes not-so-secret, ambitions to someday be on the other end of the radio link. More than a few had joined NASA just to be at Johnson, to try to get an inside track at the astronaut selection process. He wondered whether his FIDO would be one of the numerous aspiring astronauts whose applications he had personally blackballed.

"*Columbia*, Houston. The Zaragoza weather is ten thousand scattered, thirty thousand scattered, with two-eighths cover. Surface winds zero-three-zero, ten knots."

"Roger, Houston. Copy all. Ten thousand scattered, thirty thousand scattered, two-eighths cover. Zero-three-zero at ten."

"Good copy."

God it was great! Once again in the left-hand seat, and going somewhere! He wondered what an actual TAL would be like: to bring this great big spaceship down onto some dust-blown air base, burn up the brakes stopping her on the short runway, walk down the ladder, give the tires a good kick and stomp off. He reminded himself to take a set of car keys with him, in case they did have a TAL, so he could toss them carelessly at the leader of the convoy team: "She's a piece of junk! You take her from here!"

So far a shuttle had never landed anywhere except the United States. Edwards Air Force Base in the Mojave Desert, the Kennedy Space Center, and, once, on the third shuttle flight, White Sands Missile Range when bad weather precluded the other two. That would, in fact, be a good way to mark his record seventh spaceflight: the shortest spaceflight since Project Mercury. A mere thirty minutes above the atmosphere in a long, high arc to Europe. Or maybe Africa! Wouldn't that be something: land in Ben

Guerir in the morning, catch the train in the afternoon, and by evening be in Marrakech or Casablanca. . . . What a way to leave NASA. He'd climb out of his pressure suit, past the flunkies waiting to debrief him, and go search for Rick's Café Américain.

"*Columbia*, take TACAN and air data," the headset squawked, but Santich was still in the Sahara. "*Columbia*, take TACAN and air data."

"Taking TACAN," Melanie finally answered, flipping a switch that let the computers use simulated tactical air navigation information from ground stations near their Spanish landing site. "You still on this spaceship, Captain?"

Santich allowed himself a wide smile, and Melanie smiled back. "We'll take turns. You can land the next one."

12

It may have been how the Bronco was parked: off to the side, more on lawn than asphalt, pulled close to the garage, as if trying to hide in its shadow. Right away, a week's worth of good feelings evaporated and were replaced with the fundamental *wrongness* of it all.

Santich drove his battered Buick past it and to the garage. He walked back to the driveway, and noticed there was no ticking from the Ford's engine. The man lying in the driver's seat, head back, mouth open, had been there for some time.

He knocked on the window, and Steve Banke snapped his eyes open, hands reaching for the wheel. Santich backed away, in case Banke meant to throw the car into gear and tear off, but slowly the hands eased their grip. With a gulp, Banke leaned across to unlock the passenger side door. Santich hesitated, then walked around to climb in.

The acrid smell of sweat struck him immediately, but it was more than that. It was the smell he'd noticed in his own cockpit as he'd climbed out, shaken after losing his second engine that dark night so long ago. The first engine had gone at the first turn in his routine pattern. No problem. Plenty of gas to get back. But there wasn't. Somewhere there had been a leak. By the time Santich isolated it, he had barely enough to reach the USS *Intrepid*. But a malfunctioning radar on the carrier and the rain and mist turned the seemingly easy task of finding a ship as large as a city block into a life-or-death challenge. Finally there was enough fuel left for one last turn on his search pattern: right or left. Santich picked left and guessed right. There it was, with ball and bar runway lights heaving and swinging wildly. And as Santich's tiny F7U Cutlass dropped below eight hundred feet, the last of the vapors passed through the remaining engine, and Santich began a dead-stick descent at the carrier. He was too low to bail out into the pitch-black Mediterranean, too low to circle and try again. He rolled his wings as he fell, trying to match the leftover storm swell that rocked his tiny runway to and fro. With a bone-jarring slam, Santich was home, the tail of his plane hooked securely onto a cable running across the flight deck.

As per the fighter pilot code, he never admitted he'd been afraid: not to his cohorts, not to his superiors, not even to his young wife. But he knew, and the flight deck crew that helped him out knew. He'd very nearly died, and after it was over, it scared him. He could smell it.

"Steve," Santich acknowledged, breaking the awkward silence.

"Santy," Banke said.

Santich gulped again, not knowing where to begin apologizing, or if that was even the purpose of the visit. "Listen, I've been meaning to call you about that landing. I heard you did quite a job."

Banke's eyes remained locked on the dashboard. "Nothing you wouldn't have done, I'm sure." He finally turned to face Santich. "Thanks for your support on that, by the way."

He deserved that, Santich knew. "Yeah. Listen, I'm really—"

"Save it. It doesn't matter." Banke's hazel eyes flickered to the rearview mirror as a car passed through the quiet suburb. "You can't change it now. And in all honesty, I don't know if I'd have behaved any different if it was me. I think sometimes this brings out the worst in us. Look what we've given up: career"—he turned toward Santich—

"wives, family, all so we can walk around with our dicks hanging out, tell people we've been in space. Matthew's almost twenty-four. How much time have I spent with him in the last dozen years? Six months? Seven?"

Santich sat quietly, rebuked.

"That's not why I'm here. I'm going away for a bit, and I needed to see you before I left." He paused, looked at the rearview mirror again.

Santich turned around to see another car pass the blind curve. He also noticed the two duffel bags, rolled up foul-weather gear and seaboots in the back of the Bronco.

"He works in EVA, and he came to my office this morning with a hell of a story. Said he was processing some paper on the tools for the next Hubble mission, and he realized he'd thrown away a spec sheet he needed. He went to the bin to see if he could find it.

"He couldn't. But he did find a torn-up problem report. It was for In-Flight Anomaly 74-11, logged on my flight. You want to guess what it was about?"

There it was, then. The big secret was out, and once the press got wind of it, Headquarters would put the brakes on his flight. Everything and everyone associated with the cover-up, including Santich, would be disgraced. "Torrington's helmet," he said flatly.

Banke's face went paler and his eyes widened again. "You know about it?" he whispered.

"That his helmet seal ruptured? Yeah. Bruce told me about it."

Banke shook his head. "No. Not just ruptured. That's the story they're going to tell each other. It didn't *just* rupture. These seals are supposed to be used only once, then replaced. That's because the thermal cycling of daylight and night makes the rubber brittle, or something like that. Anyway, this report says the serial number attached to this seal was wrong, and that the lab analysis says the seal either flew a couple of times before or went through at least a thousand cycles in the vacuum chamber."

Santich remembered the chamber; in the early days of

Gemini, *he* had gone through what seemed a thousand cycles: forty-five minutes of intense heat followed by forty-five minutes of bitter cold, all in a tiny hyperbaric chamber from which the air had been pumped out.

"They let a test article get installed in a suit?"

Banke shrugged, shook his head impatiently. "I have no idea. I'm just relaying what this guy told me. You'll have to talk to him yourself. That's why I'm here, to see if you're interested."

Santich's heart sank. Just twenty-two days away, and now this. Such mind-boggling incompetence *deserved* a grounding until they could verify how it happened, and guarantee that it wouldn't happen again. After all, every shuttle flight carried space suits, whether an EVA, or extra-vehicular activity, was planned or not, in case the crew had to close the cargo bay doors manually or perform some other critical repair. An investigation like that could take months, and, ultimately, the whole, ugly, venal truth would be revealed.

"Of course I'm interested," he said with a sigh.

"Try not to sound so enthusiastic. You'll get your precious flight. I'll bet heads are rolling at Gates Rubber, and they've gone over *Columbia*'s suits with a microscope. Just to make sure, though, you ought to stick your nose into it." Banke stared at the dark and leathery skin gripping the blood-red wheel. "Believe me. Watching a suit fail in orbit . . ." He shook his head. "You don't want to see it."

Santich groped for words. "Listen, Steve, I'm real sorry. . . . I should have done more to stick by you."

Banke waved a hand. "Forget it. *I'm* trying to."

"So that's it?" Santich asked cautiously. "You just want me to see what's going on? You don't want to tell the world what happened?"

"And throw the baby out with the bathwater? Plus, if I wanted that, I wouldn't have come to you. Anyway, it's not an option. *You* know that."

Santich wasn't sure he did, but nodded anyway, glancing back over his shoulder. "You taking Matt out on *Simoon*?"

Simoon was the twenty-four-foot sloop Banke kept in Galveston Bay. Santich had been on her once for a beer-and-chips party. He'd said he wanted to learn how to sail, someday, and Banke had offered to teach him, someday. Neither had followed up on the invitation.

"No. Classes go through the middle of next month. I'm going alone." Banke's eyes were glassy, like he hadn't slept in days.

"That should be nice," Santich offered. "Get some rest."

"We'll see," Banke shrugged. "I'm taking her to Key West."

"Key West? Like in Florida?"

"Are there others?"

Santich looked back at the gear again. "Isn't it early in the season to cross the Gulf? Especially for something so *small*?"

"It's been done in boats half *Simoon*'s size. Anyway, it's only the Gulf. It's not Cape Horn."

Santich shrugged. "Okay. So who's this guy in EVA?"

"Name's Kyle Hartsfield. He's NASA, not Gates Rubber. Don't call him at his office. Get him at home. It's in the center directory, but not the phone book."

"Paranoid?"

Banke went glassy-eyed again, and Santich thought about 2601 and its ominous Zulu Option.

"What's paranoid and what's careful? Anyway, he's got a lot to lose. Wife doesn't work. New baby."

Santich thought for a moment. "What's the IFA number again?"

"Seventy-four-dash-eleven. But don't bother. It doesn't exist. I mean, the *number's* there, but it references some other problem. The fan in the head, I think."

"What do you mean?"

"Just like I said. I went to the log, but 74-11 talks about a loose contact on the blower switch."

"So this guy could be full of it?" Santich said, immediately wishing he hadn't sounded so hopeful.

"Think about it. Our boss made me touch down in a fucking windstorm to keep this a secret. You think he wouldn't screw with the IFA log?"

"All right. Point made. I'll call him tomorrow." Santich got out of the car but walked around to the driver's window. "Listen. You ever heard of 2601? A Zulu Option?"

Banke's eyes danced toward the rearview mirror, across the dashboard, and finally back to Santich. He turned the ignition key and put the Bronco into reverse before answering. "The man is *fucking* crazy," he whispered hoarsely. The car slid backward into the street and was gone.

13

The sun had long since set, and the red and green flashes from channel markers were all that remained of Santich's view of Galveston Bay. After 30 years of living in Houston, and thousands of times driving over the Kemah Bridge, this was the first time he'd made his way to the run-down frame house set amid the marsh grass and the litter.

THE CRAB HOUSE a big pink sign announced. You can't miss it, Hartsfield had promised. But the young engineer was late, and Santich sat sipping a warm draft beer, breathing in the moist, salty air. Around him, families whacked at stone crab claws with mallets or dug into blue crabs with spice-stained fingers. Off across the water, tiny sets of lights bobbed toward the Gulf, and Santich wondered which might belong to Steve Banke and his little sloop.

It wasn't so much the parting words but the way he'd said them that had kept Santich up. *The man is fucking crazy*. What exactly was that supposed to mean? That Bruce didn't care how many people died in orbit, as long as they did so quietly? That a similar fate awaited anyone who couldn't keep that secret?

By 4:00 A.M. he'd decided that sleep wasn't going to return, and he rose to drive the eleven miles to the office. An hour later he'd fidgeted for as long as he could before dialing the number he'd looked up in the JSC directory.

"Kyle?"

Silence for a moment, until the voice decided there was no getting around who he was, in his own house, in the middle of the night. "Yeah," he answered warily.

"Santy Santich." More silence. "Steve Banke told me to call."

Santy heard faint banging and rustling, like the phone was being moved out of the bedroom, away from a still-sleeping wife, out into the hall.

"You at home?"

"Yes," Santich lied, dreading the thought of driving all the way home to continue this cloak-and-dagger nonsense.

"The Crab House. Under the Kemah Bridge. You can't miss it. Eight o'clock."

But forty minutes past the appointed hour, Santich was still alone, preparing to flag down his waiter for the tab, when a thin face with pale, nervous eyes hovered over the rough-hewn picnic table. Long, thin fingers clutched a manila envelope folded in half.

"Thank God you're still here," Kyle Hartsfield apologized, working his gangly limbs into the gap between table and bench across from Santich. The envelope disappeared under the table. "They had a problem with one of the torque drivers they're making for 84. The design review went three hours late."

"Don't sweat it."

"I would have come to you directly, but I'd never met you before. I *had* met Steve. Anyway, I wasn't sure you'd be interested."

"Why wouldn't I be interested?"

Hartsfield blushed. "With all due respect, you must admit, you *did* seem out of character, sitting there next to Bruce, doing this mission. I'd heard you were always the most conservative voice at the Flight Readiness Reviews, a pain in everybody's neck."

Santich half grinned. He'd heard himself described much

more unpleasantly. Then he realized the unspoken message: *I used to respect you; I don't anymore.*

"Kyle, I don't expect you to understand that. I'm not sure I understand it myself. But I can say without hesitation that I won't risk the lives of my crew. Period. And if what Steve said is true, then there needs to be some serious explaining before another shuttle leaves the pad. That kind of incompetence can't be tolerated."

The pale eyes blinked once. "Incompetence? Oh, no, sir. It's much beyond that. I thought I made that . . ."

Santich's waiter stood over the table, took Santich's order for another draft and an ice water for Hartsfield.

"I thought I made that clear to Steve," he continued, his voice barely above a whisper. "From what I can gather from the problem report, this had to be intentional."

Santich stared at the light brown curls, the barest hint of fuzz on the cheeks. It was a face typical at Johnson: a young, eager engineer, making a decent but not great salary, working long hours, all for the greater glory of men and women like Santich. And this particular earnest young face was telling him that NASA's worst accident since *Challenger* was no accident. Yet there was no shock. Only reluctant acceptance, as if somehow he'd known it would come to this.

"Sabotage?"

"That I can't tell you. Here."

Finally the envelope was placed on the table, opened, and a thin piece of rubber extracted. Great, Santich thought, another rubber ring. Just like *Challenger*. The press will love it.

"The helmet locking ring is held in with rubber?"

Hartsfield shook his head. "It's a polysulfide compound designed for minimal volume change in extreme temperature shifts. But you can call it rubber if you like. As you can feel, it's quite rubbery."

Santich rolled it over in his fingers. "This was on Torrington's helmet?"

"Oh, no. That's a new one. I brought it for comparison."

He pulled out a sealed Ziploc bag with a smaller segment in it. "This is from his helmet."

A dim yellow light escaped the restaurant's dining room onto its porch, where Santich studied the two samples, the one still in its protective plastic, side by side.

"This material works very well, but it has one serious flaw. It gets brittle with exposure to atomic oxygen."

"Like it would in low earth orbit," Santich murmured, stretching first one segment, then, by working the bag like a loose layer of skin, the other.

"Like it would in LEO," agreed Hartsfield. "Which is why at first I thought it was negligence. You know, a used seal, or maybe a test article accidentally misplaced, mistaken for a new one, gets installed, and so forth."

Santich handed the bits of rubber back to Hartsfield. "But you don't think that anymore?"

He shook his head. "The problem is the serial numbers. You see, the manufacturer can't stamp a serial number into the seal without deforming it. So the number is on paper, and it accompanies the rest of the documentation. That's why I thought it was a simple mistake: Two seals got mixed up.

"But with Sam's suit, we had to send the helmet back for adjustments, and while that was going on, the proper seal, serial number 0078-slash-3C404, was sent back because one of our guys noticed a flaw in it, a tiny nick. The maker sent us 0078-slash-3C577 as a replacement. They told us so in a memo. Anyway, I went back to look at the paper on Torrington's suit, and guess which seal had been installed? Four oh-four."

"But I thought you guys sent that back?"

"We did. And we got a failure analysis on it last week. A problem during the pouring. Wrong temperature or something. Anyway, we sent 404 back, they got 404, they *destroyed* 404 in the process of analyzing it. And so I checked to see whatever happened to 577; it came in two days after the suit was assembled and shipped to the Cape."

"And so, the seal that was installed in the suit *wasn't* 404—"

"And it *wasn't* 577, either. But it *did* have 404's documentation."

Hartsfield let Santich digest this. "In other words, somebody, somehow, installed a seal with 404's paper onto Torrington's suit, not realizing that 404 had already been sent back as damaged goods, and not realizing that 577 was supposed to be installed."

"And the seal that flew was bad."

"Look at it. It's got those cracks you can see with the naked eye."

Santich thought for a moment. "How did you get it? The bad seal?"

"Well, I happened on a lab report about 404, which I thought was strange, since I'd just a day or two earlier *gotten* the lab report on 404. I asked around, but no one seemed to know anything about it. No one had sent it to the lab; no one had seen the new report.

"Well, that didn't seem right. On a hunch, I went through the discard bin in the workshop." He smiled a timid smile. "The one advantage of all these budget cuts: The janitor doesn't come by every day anymore. That"—he nodded at the four-inch piece in the Ziploc bag—"was in there, just like that, with its lab tag still on it: 0078-slash-3C404."

Santich shook his head in disbelief, then nodded. "Okay, so you brought this to your supervisor, and what did he say?"

"Well, I went to *her* right after I found the report and the seal segment. She said drop it and get back on the Hubble tools, that Bruce's office was handling the suit issue. I tried to explain about the lab analysis, but she didn't want to hear it. I couldn't believe it. I tried to explain again, and she shut the door and asked if I was having trouble hearing. I was to drop it, and that's the last she wanted to hear of it. She asked me how Melissa and Julie Ann, that's my ten-month-old, were doing, and said that someone with so much depending on him had better do as he was told.

"Captain Santich, I was floored. I never imagined I would hear that kind of threat, not here in the *civilian* space program! I walked out of there pretty pissed off, if you'll excuse my language. So I called Colonel Banke. I met him once at an office function, and he seemed like a straight shooter. I figured if anyone knew about the suit problem, he would."

Santich nodded, wondering just how many people in EVA knew about this.

"Well, I talked to him yesterday morning. I tried to get hold of him again last night, but I kept getting his machine. I left a message, but he never got back to me."

"He went sailing. He's taking his boat down to Key West," Santich told him, trying to imagine the tiny sailboat in the big, wide Gulf.

"Oh, well. I guess it isn't important. Now that *you* know about it."

Yeah, Santich thought. Now that *I* know, that solves everything. Why would someone want to kill Torrington? But when he stopped to think about it, he could imagine dozens of men, the assorted husbands and lovers of Torrington's conquests, who would have loved to. But that didn't make sense. That kind of killing happened in the barrios and out in west Texas, not in the modern, divorce-sophisticated crowd around the space center. Plus, if you wanted to kill someone, there were shotguns, knives, poison, piano wire. Why go to the trouble of screwing around with flight hardware, getting your stuff past the contractors' inspectors, past NASA Safety?

Or maybe it wasn't someone who hated Torrington, but who hated the space program, and who figured that an orbital death would be a damaging black eye for the agency. But that didn't make sense either. People who *liked* the program tended to be fanatics, true believers. Those who disliked it did so the same way others disliked tobacco subsidies or welfare fraud: with little, if any, passion.

"It's too bad Torrington died so soon after landing,"

Hartsfield said. "There'd be *no* ignoring it if he were still alive. It's sad, but almost funny, isn't it? He escapes what could have been a catastrophic failure in orbit, only to die in a car wreck a few hours later."

For a few moments, Santich sat silently, stunned, as the realization sunk in. This poor kid had no idea what had really happened! Now what should he do? More to the point, what would Hartsfield do if *he* knew? Go above his boss's head? Go to the press? How much trouble would the guy get into? And how much trouble could he make?

"Listen. There's something I've got to tell you, but before I do, you've got to promise me something."

Hartsfield shrugged. "Okay," he said trustingly.

"You've got to promise me you won't repeat what I tell you. Not to a soul. Not to your friends, not to your wife, not anybody."

He thought for a moment. "Okay. I promise."

Santich licked his lips, bent his head across the table. "Sam Torrington *didn't* die in a car wreck. He died when his helmet blew out during that EVA. All that stuff about the fuel cells was a smoke screen to get 104 back to Kennedy as quickly and quietly as possible."

Hartsfield's shoulders sagged. His mouth fell open and stayed open. "Incredible, yet somehow it makes perfect sense," he said after a while. "No wonder Sally was so nervous when I asked her about the seal. God, I wonder! How many guys in my office know about this? 'Cause if they do, no one's said a word."

He ran both hands through his curls, pressing his skull, as if to keep it from exploding into nothingness. "My God! I can't believe they've kept it a secret! What about the other crew? Why haven't they said anything?"

Santich studied the bottom of his glass. What had he done? "Apparently Bruce extracts a vow of secrecy before he lets them fly now," he said carefully. "And look at the rest of the crew: Halvorson, who's dying for his first command, and two rookies, Habuda and Orlov, who both want to fly again. Orlov, of course, flies again next month."

Hartsfield shook his head. "These people would *lie* like that, just to fly again? I mean, aren't they *human*?"

Santich looked at his hands. "Sometimes I wonder," he mumbled.

"And what about Banke? After the treatment Bruce gave him, why doesn't he go straight to the *New York Times*?"

Santich shook his head slowly. "I have no idea, although he didn't seem himself when I saw him. He seemed, I don't know, jumpy." Santich thought about 2601 and Zulu Option, wondered whether to tell Hartsfield, decided against it. "Maybe he wants to fly again, too. After he's been rehabilitated, of course."

"He was murdered!" Hartsfield exclaimed, like the idea had just then struck him. "Someone, someone *within* the program, someone *I probably know* went out of their way to kill him!"

Santich hadn't thought of it like that, and for a moment, it froze him. Although he probably didn't know the killer personally. As a pilot, he had little reason to know the folks over in EVA, since only mission-specialist astronauts got to perform them. "That's what it seems like, doesn't it?" he said, trying to sound matter-of-fact about it.

"So what do we do? Go to Headquarters? The police?"

What now? How straitlaced was this kid? How much of a true believer was he?

"Kyle, there are other considerations we ought to discuss. For example, if we go to Headquarters, we might find the same reaction you've found here. They might back Bruce all the way." He paused, studied Hartsfield's reaction. "And if we go to the police, well, that's a whole different ball game."

Hartsfield sat, his face expressionless.

"First, they might not believe us. I mean, *why* kill somebody like that? Isn't there a risk that what you do won't work? Wouldn't it be easier just to follow 'em one night to a convenience store parking lot and put a bullet in their head?" He licked his lips. "And if they *do* believe us . . . Well, we need to consider the consequences. The program is finished. The fact you work here, at Johnson, rather than in the private sector making twice or three times as much money tells me you have some commitment to the space program. Am I right?''

Hartsfield said nothing, as if he sensed where Santich was going and didn't like it.

"If we go to the police, they'll ask a lot of questions, the *Houston Herald* will find out, and then it really hits the fan. The cover-up will come out, and everyone will know that we nearly wrecked a two-billion-dollar orbiter and killed four other astronauts just to keep one death—at the time, what seemed like one *accidental* death—a secret. Secret from the same public that pays the bills and deserves the truth, when you get down to it.''

"*We* didn't cover it up; Bruce did," Hartsfield protested.

"That distinction will get lost real quick. To the public, we're all the same NASA, screwing up again. No, if this comes out, we're all out on the street in a matter of months." He halted, realizing he'd just sounded like Hooper, or even Bruce. "Look," he said, softening his tone. "I'll be brutally honest here. I've had some real conflicts about doing this mission, but in the end, I decided to do it because *someone* was going to fly it. And I wanted one more. I know it's selfish, shortsighted, et cetera, et cetera.

"But if everything goes to hell, and if they dismantle the Space Transportation System, I can retire. I've got two pensions coming, and no expenses. Things are different for you. I mean, no doubt you're a very smart young man, and you'll eventually land on your feet. But you've got people counting on you, don't you?''

Again, Santich realized what he was doing, and why, and it sickened him. "Well, enough of that," he mumbled after a while. "You do what you think is right.''

Kyle Hartsfield looked out at the dark bay, and Santich wished he had the last ten days back to do over. He'd wake up, Grieve would come to him with one scheme, Bruce with another, and he'd tell them both to stick it. He'd hand in his resignation and be casting for snook by the weekend.

"I guess there isn't a single right answer, is there?" Hartsfield asked, still staring out over the water. "I mean, it's a typical design problem: every solution a compromise. Either Torrington's killer gets away, or manned spaceflight goes down the tubes. That's a heck of a choice."

Santich stared out at a green light that flashed every six seconds. Ever since *Challenger,* it seemed, he'd been one step behind. It took him too long to figure out what they were doing to him, and he realized too late that they'd succeeded. He was too long deciding to get out, and now, it seemed, he'd been had again.

"Captain Santich?"

"Hmmm?"

"What if we waited until after your flight before we went to the police? I mean, it's an image problem, not an engineering one, right? If we go public right now, with Torrington's death and the bad landing being the last things NASA's done, then we look incompetent. But say we wait until after your flight, and you guys successfully fix the GRO, and come back heroes, and *then* go to the police. . . ."

Santich sat silently, considering both the merits of the idea and the mettle of this young engineer. Yes, he thought, it might work. He could tell them that he'd only recently uncovered this monstrosity, and that it was his obligation to come forward. . . . He nodded slowly, trying to contain his growing enthusiasm. "I'm listening."

"Well, maybe we could ask around, quietly, to get as much information together as we can about what happened. I mean, my dad was a detective on the Des Moines PD for twenty-five years, and he told me that simple, dumb questions were all he ever had to ask ninety-nine percent of the time. And who better to ask basic questions about EVA equipment and astronauts than us?"

Santich smiled. "You want to catch the killer?"

Even in the dim light, Santich could see Hartsfield blush. "Well, not exactly. And I don't mean to make it sound easy. I mean, I'm not a cop. I'm not my dad. Even if I was, I don't think Des Moines ever had a''—he searched for the proper word—''*homicide* quite like this one in all the time I was growing up. Anyway, we wouldn't be catching him. We'd just gather all the relevant information the police will want to know.''

Santich recalled the two bar fights, one in Pensacola, the other in Norfolk, that marked his only experience with law enforcement. And he hadn't even been involved. Each time his role had been to convince the local police that the situation would be better handled by the military police. He suspected, though, that a murder within the astronaut corps would be juicy enough to interest policemen of all kinds: local, state, certainly federal. He could see their well-intentioned help getting badly misinterpreted.

''Did your dad the detective ever talk about obstruction of justice as a punishable crime? We *would* be keeping this under our hats for somewhat dubious motives, from their point of view.''

Hartsfield squinted one eye up at the flashing lights of a plane passing overhead. ''I guess I hadn't thought of that. But they wouldn't even know about it if not for us, right? And it's not like they'll miss anything by getting into it a month late; it's not like they can dust Torrington's suit for prints or anything.''

Santich again studied the young face in the Crab House's weak yellow light. This kid was serious. He was willing to do this.

''Okay, supposing we do this. Where do we start?''

Hartsfield rubbed his hands together and leaned forward. ''Okay. I'll keep looking into the technical stuff: how exactly it was done. I think learning that should narrow who *could* have done it. And maybe you could try to figure out who might have *wanted* to do it. Like who might have disliked him enough to kill him.''

Santich snorted. ''Well, that limits the field to about, oh, a few hundred jealous husbands and ex-girlfriends.''

''Really?'' Hartsfield's eyes widened. ''I had no idea he

was such a''—another search for the right word—''ladies' man. I must live under a rock.''

Santich nodded. ''Fact was that he had a number of people who thought he was a complete asshole. To be honest, I think there were as many smiles as there were tears the day he died.''

''He was in trouble with the feds, too, wasn't he? Something to do with fixing Station contracts?''

''That's right. See? You don't live under a rock after all. Sam had some buddies at the Kerro Group, and they wanted the truss assembly contract. Sam got himself on the Truss Assembly Working Group and steered the contract their way. I think basically he told them what bid they were looking for. You know, then Kerro would lowball it, win the contract, and make a killing on the overruns. Business as usual around here. Anyway, the feds found out about it, and they were getting ready to indict him. Next month, I think. Rumor was, ol' Sam was getting ready to turn state's evidence, as they say, and rat out his pals at Kerro.''

Hartsfield shook his head. ''I didn't realize he was in it so deeply. I figured he had some peripheral role.''

''No, sir. Sam Torrington was in the thick of that mess, no doubt about it. With him dead, I don't know where that leaves the U.S. attorney's investigation. Closed, I imagine.''

''You think maybe that stuff with Kerro was why he was killed? You know, to keep from testifying? I mean, someone went to a lot of trouble, arranged a lot of details to kill him this way. As you point out, wouldn't a jealous lover be more likely to shoot him? Or at least back over him with a pickup?''

Santich blinked. He knew a couple of the bigwigs at Kerro. He'd been at Pax River with them. That they were unethical, bending rules to win the game, was a given. But kill someone? To keep him quiet? He shuddered.

''No, I don't think so. It's not like anyone caught in this will do any hard time. We're not dealing with gangsters here. It's a bunch of ex-NASA officials who paid their dues and wanted to line their pockets a little. Anyway, I think we're getting off track. I think you were right earlier. We don't *have* to have all the details worked out and say, 'Book, 'em, Danny-boy.' ''

Hartsfield grinned. ''That's, 'Book 'em, Danno.' You don't watch a lot of TV, do you, Captain?''

Santich's ears burned. He hated when his once-in-a-blue-moon attempts at colloquial speech fell flat. ''Whatever. The point is, we only need to make a presentable effort, something to show we're on *their* side, not on Bruce's. And please, call me Santy. I've been retired long enough not to miss it.''

''Okay, Santy.''

Hartsfield grinned, looked down at his hands, and Santich wondered if this was where he would confess that Santich had been an idol of his growing up, an inspiration to study engineering or astronomy or underwater basket-weaving. He often wondered how he and his cohorts ever managed to get into space in the first place, not having had any astronauts to idolize in their formative years.

''You know, maybe afterward, if this works out, we can set up shop together: Hartsfield and Santich, P.I. Or Santich and Hartsfield. It doesn't matter to me.''

Santich relaxed, liking him more for not fawning. ''Well, let's just try to keep our butts out of the fire and see how this works out.''

Hartsfield bit his lower lip. ''You know, it just occurred to me. Whoever did this has already murdered someone. What if they find out we're asking questions?''

''I wouldn't worry,'' Santich said, for the first time worrying about this possibility. ''Like I said, this isn't the Mafia.''

''You're probably right. I guess I can't see old Dennis Young at Kerro putting a horse's head in my bed.''

Santich smiled, deduced he had once again missed some piece of popular culture. ''No, I guess not.''

''So how should we stay in touch? What's our plan?''

''The telephone?'' Santich shrugged. ''Learn as much as

we can in the next two weeks. I'll be really busy, but I'll
see what I can manage on my end. Then, after landing, we
go to the cops, explain what we've found, and let them run
it from there.''

"Sounds good to me," Hartsfield agreed. "Only I think
we should only call from our homes. I don't trust that Cen-
trex system. Sometimes I get the feeling there's a little
room somewhere, with a guy who does nothing all day but
eavesdrop on conversations, taping all the good ones.
Maybe I'm paranoid, but, like you said, I've got a family
now.''

The secretiveness did seem paranoid, but Santich said
nothing. "All right, then. We'll talk again in a few days?
Thursday, maybe? I'll call you, early in the morning. Five-
ish.''

Hartsfield nodded, looked around nervously. "I've never
seen NASA types around here. That's why I picked it. But
just the same, would you mind if we left separately? I'll go
now, and you wait ten minutes?''

Santich suppressed a grin, nodded, and held out his hand.
"I'm glad we talked.''

"Me, too.''

And he was gone, leaving Santich to study the completely dark bay.

14

Because the little boat had had a conservative designer, the string of nasty squalls the previous night hadn't knocked over the mast. They just blew out the big genoa and the mainsail. Their tattered remnants hung sadly from the triple-reinforced edges, flapping idly in the still air.

Because the little boat had had a conservative owner, she refused to sink, despite the wide-open seacocks that let the Gulf flood in. Hydrostatically triggered tanks of carbon dioxide automatically inflated a series of tough nylon bags in the main cabin, providing enough buoyancy to keep the top few inches of the hull above the waterline.

With no means of propulsion and invisible save from a short distance, she wallowed with the swell, drifting slowly eastward with the current.

From above a solitary gull swooped down and landed atop the lonely mast, cawing for attention. It rested a few minutes, flapped its wings and was gone.

15

Josephine Pointer picked at the slice of roast beef on her plate, peeling a vein of fat away with knife and fork, only to leave both remnants in a "discard" pile. Santich decided he hated women who picked at their food.

"So," she said between bites of kidney beans from her picked-over salad, "what's the big scoop you've got for me?"

In all his years at Johnson, Santich had both loved and hated the cafeteria across the walkway from Building 4. Loved it because it was the only place "on campus" that served a full meal, so management, engineers, accountants, astronauts and even tourists had to eat the same mediocre food, and no one was treated any better than anybody else. Hated it because it was the only place "on campus" to get a full meal, so that even when he was tired or irritated or pissed off, his choices remained taking a lot of time to drive into Clear Lake or becoming a walking tourist attraction in the cafeteria. Worse, the press covering NASA often hung around the cafeteria, hoping to corner somebody important for a quotation or sound bite. He hated the ambushes because they forced him to behave rudely, and he had taken to eating his lunch at odd hours, either late morning or midafternoon.

But on the afternoon after his meeting with the young engineer from the Extra-Vehicular Activities Office, he'd spent nearly two hours at a corner table in the huge, glass-walled building through prime lunch hours. In his hands was the detailed rocket-firing time line for catching the Gamma Ray Observatory. He hadn't even gotten through the first page, as he kept scanning entrances, the two cashiers' queues, and the walkways outside for his least favorite space reporter. It was her habit, ever since moving to Houston from Florida three years earlier, to prowl the cafeteria each breakfast and lunch, looking for victims.

The rookies were warned of the press in general, and advised not to wear their navy-blue flight suits unless they were actually on their way to Ellington to fly in something. But Space Slut was beyond mere flight-suit chasing. She collected each astronaut's portrait from the Public Affairs Office right after they were selected. She memorized faces, matching them with names and trivia from the bio sheets, in order to lure and flatter the receptive astronaut ego.

And sure enough, at a little after one, she'd strolled in beside two flight-suited rookies. As he'd hoped, all he had to do was make eye contact, and she'd come to him within minutes. He'd never returned her calls, never responded to her requests for interviews, which over the years had totaled in the dozens, never even said hello to her the few times he'd run into her.

"Some dark secret about Marty Bruce's sexual preferences?" she asked with characteristic sarcasm.

As he did about once every third time he saw her, Santich could understand how so many of his colleagues, if the boasting could be believed, had taken her to bed. True, her facial features were plain, with a squarish chin, thin lips and wan cheeks. But under some dirty-blond haircut in a tomboy style and behind some thin wire-rimmed glasses were the deepest Caribbean-blue eyes he'd ever seen. Her figure, though, was what the guys in the Ellington locker room all talked about. Thin, well-muscled limbs connected by a torso so slender the ribs stuck out, yet endowed with an enormous pair of breasts that stretched skin so white and so thin that each blue vein could be clearly traced. These

Jo Pointer used to great advantage, both by showcasing them in tight sweaters and blouses, and more directly by grabbing a victim's forearm and letting it graze across her chest.

The men's dressing room at Ellington for some months had a Jo Pointer scorecard posted on the wall, awarding points for "touch-and-go," "visual approach," "handing over the stick," and, finally, "hard landing and rollout." The sign was finally taken down when one of her few real friends in the corps hinted that under federal EEOC guidelines, it could constitute sexual harassment, possibly leading to loss of flight status.

Santich wondered whether she knew the astronaut corps' nickname for her, or whether she cared. "Well, Jo, it's nothing so sensational, I'm afraid. I just wanted to know whether you'd be interested in a human-interest type story about an aging astronaut. You see, this is my last flight. And when I get back, I'm hanging up my pressure suit."

"Oh, really?" Her eyes grew wide as she leaned forward, resting her bosom on the table.

Santich forced his eyes back upward. "I guess it's not that much of a surprise. Anyway, you and I both know that I'm not in the habit of chatting it up with the press."

"I'll say," Jo Pointer agreed, rolling the aquamarine eyes.

"I guess I ought to apologize for that, for maybe giving you and some of the others short shrift."

Jo shrugged, lifted her breasts off the table momentarily, only to plop them back down. "No big deal."

"Anyway. I got this call from an editor at Pantheon Publishing in New York the other day." Santich had rehearsed this part dozens of times, stealing the script from other Apollo-era astronauts who actually *had* been asked for their autobiographies. "They seem to think my life, or at least my time at NASA, would make a good book. I'm not sure I understand why, but they wanted to know if I was interested."

He could tell she was leaping ahead in anticipation. "I

told them I wasn't much of a writer. She said that's okay; most autobiographies weren't written by the person. She said she could find a ghostwriter for me, or if I knew a professional writer, that would be fine by them as well.''

Here was the tricky part, the one Santich hoped Jo's ego would let him sneak past. He licked his lips. ''So here I am. I've obviously read a lot of your stuff over the years.'' It was a bald-faced lie. He couldn't recall a single thing. ''And I've admired that of all the reporters covering this agency, you give us a fair shake most of the time.''

From what the others in the office had told him, she gave more than a fair shake. Her articles consistently defended the party line, always sucked up to program bigwigs.

''Well, I've always tried to be fair,'' she offered modestly. ''I think what y'all are doing is pretty difficult, pretty important stuff, and that's the way I present it. I think there are some in the press always looking for something negative. I think that does a great disservice to the program, as well as to the public.''

He waited, but she was finished. ''Anyway, I've started asking around to see who might be interested.''

She leaned further forward, pushing her tray out of the way. ''I'm always looking for offers,'' she said with a wink. ''I mean, what they pay at World News Service barely covers the rent. I like to have two or three other projects going all the time.''

Now came the touchiest moment, where he'd find out if he'd set the hook correctly. ''Now, I know this might be a bad time for you, with what happened to Sam and all.''

Jo Pointer leaned back, crossed her thin arms across her storied chest, which lifted several inches as she took a deep breath. Santich held his, knowing he'd gone too fast. He'd blown it.

She paused, bit her lower lip, then her upper one. ''I appreciate your concern, but believe me, it's not an issue. We were friends, close friends. And it was a terrible shock. But I'm over it.''

Santich paused. He needed more. He wished he knew where to prod.

"I guess, to be candid, we were perhaps more than close friends. At least for a while," she added.

It almost seemed she realized that in return for the chance to ghostwrite Santich's autobiography, she needed to tell him the dirt on herself.

"I don't know why I'm so surprised; I guess everybody knew," she explained.

He *hadn't* known, actually. It was only after overhearing Millie talking to Lynnette by the coffee machine that he figured Jo Pointer had been Sam Torrington's last conquest.

"I don't mean to pry," he muttered lamely, knowing that was *exactly* what he meant.

"No. It's no big deal. I know Sam had a reputation, as they used to say in school." She shrugged, twisting her lips a bit and glancing out through the plate glass at the sunlit courtyard. "Maybe if I had to do it over again, I wouldn't have let it happen. I mean, it was a lot of grief." She snorted a bitter laugh. "Even before he drove into a tanker truck."

Santich looked at his hands, ashamed. He had never liked this manipulative schemer, but was that an excuse to lie to her? He felt terrible; he wasn't even getting anything useful.

"I'm sorry," he said, with conviction this time.

"Not as sorry as I am. I guess the only silver lining is that Mrs. Torrington has finally stopped harassing me."

"*Mrs.* Torrington? Sam's mother?"

"Nooooo, not Sam's mother." She twisted her lips again, but this time crossed her eyes at him, too. "His ex-wife. He said it was because she was still jealous, even though they've been apart two years now. I don't know. Maybe he was late on child support. You know, one of those deadbeat dads? Now *there's* a story I bet the folks at Headquarters would mess their pants over: 'Space Couple's Spat, Tot's Trauma,' or something."

Santich's ears perked up. "Space *couple*?"

"Yeah. Trudy Cortain. You know her? She's a bitch."

The name vaguely rang a bell, but he'd been out of the loop for so long. The only ones he knew well were the simulator engineers. And Hoop. "No. She works out here? Who is she?"

"We haven't been formally introduced. I just know her voice, especially the raspy one she has at three in the morning."

"She would call you?"

"Every day. She'd call me names, bawl me out, then hang up."

Santich didn't particularly care if she'd gone to Jo's house and repeatedly slapped her. "What does she *do* here? Is she a secretary or something?"

Again Jo's lips contorted to register her displeasure. "Now *that's* pretty sexist. Is that all you think us chicks are good for? To type your letters and make your coffee? You better watch it, what with two women on your crew. Did you know that's another first? Not the two women; that's been done. But two women on such a small crew. This will be the first time that half of the crew is female."

"I didn't *mean* anything by it. I haven't heard of her, is all."

The apology seemed to work, and Jo calmed down. "She works in Mission Operations, I think in a back room. EVA, I'm pretty sure."

Santich suddenly felt a draft in the cafeteria, as if those three letters had chilled the air. His mind raced, considering and discarding the possibilities. Surely flight controllers wouldn't have access to space suits, would they? But would they be likely to befriend someone who did? But what did *that* prove? *Anybody* on campus was "likely" to befriend anybody else, regardless of where they worked. On the other hand, Trudy Cortain wasn't just anybody. She was apparently a very jealous ex–Mrs. Torrington. Was that enough for her to have done something about it? He would have to meet her, that much was certain. He'd lured Jo Pointer with the promise of some work; how would he lure *her*?

"Hellooooo! Is anyone there?"

"Yeah. Sorry. It's just strange, you know? The coincidence, I mean."

"What coincidence?"

His breath caught in his throat. *Of course* she couldn't see any coincidence. She thought he died in a car crash. "You know," he said lamely. "Him having finished his first space walk, just hours before dying. And her an EVA controller."

Jo shrugged. "I guess. It's not like she was on console that flight."

"She wasn't?" he asked timidly.

"No. Sam didn't want it, and I think MOD was sensitive to what was going on. Anyway, she's new to EVA, and hasn't moved into the front room yet. It's not like she *could* be on console."

How would he meet her? *Hi, I'm Santy Santich, and I think your ex-husband was murdered. Did you by chance do it?* Maybe he wouldn't have to meet her. Maybe just giving her name to the police next month would be enough. But what if she had nothing to do with it? That would be stupid, telling the police that a bitter ex-wife *might* be a suspect. Of course a bitter ex-wife was a suspect. Santich suddenly realized that Jo Pointer had decided they'd talked enough about Sam and Trudy Torrington, and was rambling on about herself: what a talented writer she was, all the profiles of famous astronauts she'd written for various magazines, how they didn't appreciate her at WNS, and how co-writing an autobiography would be the break she'd always needed. When would he decide?

"To tell you the truth," he began, embellishing his lie. "To tell you the truth, there are a lot of details I need to work out before I'd agree to do it."

Jo Pointer sat in stony-faced silence; pangs of guilt again struck at Santich. "I mean, I'm insisting on full control of what's in there and what's not, and they seemed touchy about it," he improvised. "Anyway, I just wanted to see if anybody would be interested."

"I take it I'm not the only writer you've asked?"

Behind the thin glasses, the blue-green eyes glazed over with a film of water. Santich looked down at his hands. "Like I said, I'm in the real early stages. I asked you first because I happened to see you here." He nodded toward the cash registers. "Plus with launch in less than three weeks, I don't have a whole lot of time to devote to this. In fact"—he checked his watch—"I really need to get back to the SMS. I need to be there in five minutes."

Jo stood, smoothed the wrinkles in her denim miniskirt. He glanced down, noticing the pale, smooth legs that led to skinny ankles above the dark-blue flats. How could ankles so frail support breasts so large?

"Well, let it never be said that I hindered the training of a space shuttle commander on the eve of an important mission." She forced a smile. "It was good finally talking to you. I hope we can work together."

Santich swallowed hard, waited until she had left before he returned his own tray and headed back toward his office.

16

"I've never dated a moonwalker before," Trudy Cortain said as she slurped the enormous frozen margarita before her.

Santich set down the Corona he'd settled for—they had no Heineken—and wondered how anyone could drink such swill. It was almost as bad as Coors. "Well, I hadn't really thought of it as a *date*."

The problem of how to meet the prime suspect had solved itself. He'd learned by leafing through the Mission Operations schedule that she was one of the back-room EVA controllers for his flight. He'd immediately arranged with the lead flight director to meet the entire flight control team that afternoon, just as he'd done prior to his previous six space missions.

The Orbit One team was working an air lock malfunction simulation when he arrived, but within minutes, Craig Varnes called for a break. Slowly, the back-room controllers filtered into the MOCR, the Mission Operations Control Room, each moving toward the console where his or her front-room counterpart sat. Halfway through this procession, a slender, ginger-haired woman wearing a white blouse and red skirt climbed the steps. Santich knew even before she edged toward the EVA station that she was the one.

As he'd gone around the room being introduced to every-

one individually, he'd noticed her chatting with her colleagues. As he'd neared her side of the room, he'd noticed
how much older she was than she'd first appeared.

He didn't dare say anything to her then, not in front of
Melanie, the two Alexes and the two hundred or so flight
controllers. But he called her office late that afternoon, and
somehow, amazingly, asked if he could see her that evening. Even more amazingly, he thought, she'd agreed, and
told him of a little Mexican restaurant next door to her
health club.

He wondered if she always carried a change of clothing
with her, because she'd implied she would go straight to
El Bandito after working out. The white ruffled blouse and
knee-length skirt were gone, replaced by a black wrap-
around dress that managed to bundle everything up and
thrust it forward at the same time. It was only spring, yet
she sported a late-summer tan. Santich decided she had a
naturally dark complexion.

"Okay. Suit yourself. It's not a date. Only I have to warn
you, my kids come back from my mother's after this mission, and then I'll be too tired for dates."

They sat in a corner booth, a bowl of slightly oily, just-
fried tortilla chips between them. She poked a tiny red
straw at the salt piled along the rim of the huge goblet, then
stuck it into the slush to draw a sip. Deep red lipstick darkened and exaggerated her mouth, while too much eyeshad-
ow hid and overwhelmed, rather than highlighted, a pair of
light brown eyes. Traces of small creases around lips and
eyes were visible despite the carefully applied makeup. An
attractive woman, an especially attractive woman, Santich
thought, trying desperately to be a young woman again.

"I don't know where to begin," he began. Over the edge
of the table, he watched her gently swinging a slender foot.
A black pump hung off her toes and a thin gold bracelet
lay over the ankle.

"Where would you like to begin?" she smiled.

At that tanned brown ankle and work his way up, he
thought. God! What was the matter with him? For years

he'd spent each night missing Emily, or denying to himself that he missed her. Now, with reconciliation only weeks away, he was lusting after a woman half his age. A woman, he reminded himself, who may have murdered her husband.

"You know I've had a quasi-official Safety and Quality assignment for the last eight years." He began the speech he'd rehearsed in the car. "And, of course, with the circumstances of 104's landing a few weeks ago, I wanted to talk to as many people in as many different offices as I could to see if they could shed any light on what may have led to that. Now, I realize that you're in EVA, and EVA doesn't have a direct connection with entry and landing. But nonetheless . . ."

He looked up to see her smiling coyly. She wasn't buying a word of it. Why should she? She knew his job title was a sham. It was all a come-on to get into that sexy little dress of hers. "It's about your husband," he said softly.

In seconds, Trudy Cortain aged a decade. The lips and eyes drooped; her shoulders fell. Even the dress seemed to give up and sag. Gamely, she continued poking at the salt on the rim, and Santich noticed the deep lines that ran across her hands.

"What would you like to know?" she asked.

"I, uh, only recently learned that his ex-wife, you, I mean, worked here at Johnson." Santich looked up to her confused stare, looked back at his tepid Corona. "What I mean is, that must have been hard for you."

She stirred the greenish slush slowly. "What part of it?" she sighed. "Him running around for three years and everyone looking at me like I'm a bitch? Or me having to track him down to make him raise his own children? Or then his killing himself and everyone looking at me like I'm a bitch?"

All he'd had to do was tell Bruce no, to go screw himself. Then he would have been done, and none of this would be happening. He looked again at the once confident, once proud woman across from him and wanted to kick himself. Yeah, *sure,* the ex-wife did it. This one, she was

a vicious killer. Suddenly, Kyle Hartsfield and his fantastic
theories seemed like a dream, a faraway, interesting, but
irrelevant dream. If somebody *had* murdered Sam Torrington, catching him and punishing him was not his problem.
And based on the former Mrs. Torrington, maybe that
somebody deserved a medal, not prison.

"Forgive me, ma'am." He wriggled sideways and got
ready to stand up. "I've made a terrible mistake here, and
the best I can do, I think, is just leave."

Trudy reached across the table and grabbed his wrist. A
spark he hadn't felt in years shot up his arm. "No, please.
I'm the one who should apologize. Please, sit down."

Santich hesitated. Her hand was still on his. Slowly he
sat.

"I'm sorry. I didn't mean to go off like that. It's just
that, well, you're right: It has been hard. I mean, for the
last five years he's been the most self-centered, egotistical
child I've ever known. It's taken me years to get my head
together about that, and now he's a hero because he's *dead*?
Jesus! He would have been in *jail* in another few months
if he'd stayed alive!" Her hands flew to her face; it took
Santich a few moments to realize she was sobbing quietly.
"Sorry. Again."

Santich looked around the restaurant, saw no one looking
at them, and awkwardly reached across the table to pat her
bare shoulder. "It's okay," he mumbled, immediately feeling like an idiot. *It's okay? How* was it *okay*? "It's okay,"
he repeated.

"Look," she said after a final sob. "I'm sorry. It won't
happen again. I promise." She sniffed at her paper napkin.
"What can I tell you about Sam?"

He suppressed a shrug, looked thoughtfully at the salsa
bowl. What *could* she tell him about Sam? If she didn't
somehow break into Building 7 and sabotage his space suit,
how the hell could she help him?

"Well, you know I'm flying 74A." *Brilliant*—of course
she knew he was doing 74A. So was she. "And I wanted
to find out more about Sam, because, you know, I just don't

want anything like that to happen with us.'' He remembered suddenly that she would know nothing about how he really died. Nor should she. ''Not that it would, of course, but I think it's a good idea to cover all the bases, you know. No stone left unturned, all the i's dotted, et cetera . . .''

At first her face was blank, but suddenly, her eyes widened, then narrowed. ''What do you know?'' she whispered, leaning across the table.

''Know?''

''You must know something, or suspect something. Or you wouldn't be asking questions. What do you suspect?''

Santich's mouth hung open as he searched for an answer to satisfy this poor woman and also keep his secret safe. ''I, uh,'' he stumbled, then realized he could turn things around. ''I came to ask you the same thing. What do you suspect?''

Trudy pursed her lips, tapping her long, thin fingers on the table. ''Okay. Not that I care, mind you, but the car accident seemed a little cozy.''

''Cozy?''

''Yeah. You know. Neat. Tidy. How come his body was flown back here so fast? How come the Brevard County medical examiner didn't do the autopsy? That's where he died, didn't he?''

Santich studied the caramel-colored eyes, noticing for the first time the darker brown flecks at the outside edge of each iris. ''I thought you weren't interested.''

''Believe me, I'm not. But Lone Star Mutual is *very* interested.''

''Lone Star. The insurance company?''

She nodded. ''Their adjusters have a major problem with the autopsy. They think the proper authorities should have handled it, not a NASA flight surgeon.''

Santich thought for a moment. ''You're a beneficiary?'' he asked incredulously.

''No, but my boys are. And I'm their legal guardian.''

''So they don't want to pay?''

She shrugged. ''My lawyer says they have to. Anyway,

like I said, I don't care. It's two hundred thousand each, and it all goes into a trust fund until they're eighteen. It's for their college education, so I've got plenty of time to wait on this."

"So it doesn't matter to you if there *is* something suspicious about the accident. You're pretty sure your kids will get their trust funds."

"That's right. Unless, of course, I can somehow prove Sam died in flight. In which case Chris and Jimmy each get seven hundred thousand. The two hundred thousand from the first policy, and a half million each from a spaceflight policy the office buys."

Santich nodded. It was a post-*Challenger* reform, designed to care for astronauts' dependents in the event of an accident. Management wanted to avoid the sort of lingering, bad-taste-in-the-mouth lawsuits that the *Challenger* families had brought against NASA.

"So can I?"

"Can you what?"

"You know." Trudy was done flirting, done pitying herself. Her eyes shone with intensity, the soft face had hardened. "Prove it? That Sam died in flight?"

"Is that what you think?" Santich asked carefully.

Trudy looked at him for what seemed a full minute, then let out a long sigh. "Okay. I understand what's going on. The only reason I'm not walking out is that I've always had a good feeling about you. I just hope, despite how things look, you're on the side of what's right around here."

Santich swallowed hard, studying her face. She wanted some encouragement, some acknowledgment that what she said was true. He fidgeted with a tortilla chip, spilling a glob of salsa onto his napkin. A small chunk of tomato seeped through the thin paper onto his trousers. Glad for the distraction, he wet the rest of the napkin in his water glass and dabbed at the stain.

"Yes, I think Sam died in flight," Trudy continued softly. "Because I know for a fact he wasn't driving drunk that morning. Sam stopped drinking a year ago. He was getting so bad that the office was about to pull him from the flight roster. They gave him two months to shape up. He did, and that's when he was assigned to STS-74.''

That Santich hadn't heard about. Not that it was surprising. Nowadays there was a lot going on that he didn't know about. Still, no one, officially, had said he *had* been drinking before the accident.

"Yes, but that's their implication," she answered. "Besides, the flight surgeon's autopsy lists a blood-alcohol level of point-oh-five percent. I have a copy at home. But I know for a fact that's wrong because he quit."

"Maybe he didn't quit," Santich said, continuing as devil's advocate. "Maybe the autopsy is the truth and what he told you was a lie."

She shook her head. "No. Believe me, Santy, he couldn't have faked all the crap he went through last year. You're probably wondering how I know. After all, I'm his *ex*-wife, right? Well, he'd come crawling back to me about a week after he was done with the Skirt-of-the-Month. You see, he was a bastard, but an insecure bastard."

Santich looked at her blankly. What could he add to that?

"Anyhow. There's more. Where did he get the car? The papers said it was a rental, right? The red Le Baron convertible he always got? All right. The fuel cell anomaly happened around two, right?"

"Something like that."

"They landed at about four-thirty, Florida time. It takes another hour to get out of the ship and back to the O and C Building. Then the crew had showers and breakfast until seven-thirty, and went into debriefings until nine-thirty. The autopsy gave the time of death as between nine-thirty-five, when a security patrol passed by the accident scene without seeing anything, and nine-fifty-three, when the fire was reported. Okay, nine-thirty to nine-fifty-three leaves twenty-three minutes for him to race out of the O and C, down to Cocoa Beach, rent the car, get plastered, *drive back* to KSC, and run it into a conveniently parked fuel truck. I mean, what's a truck full of jet fuel doing out by the beach road anyway? But that's not the point. The point is that he couldn't possibly have driven all that way in twenty minutes!''

Santich tried to disinterestedly analyze her argument, then caught himself: He knew damn well Sam Torrington *hadn't* driven to Cocoa Beach that morning, or anywhere else. ''Maybe he left it there before launch so he could use it afterward?'' he asked lamely.

''Why? You know the drill. Land, shower, eat, get on the STA back to Ellington. What would he need a car for? Besides. I know Sam. He was much too cheap to rent a car for nine days and not use it.''

Santich sighed deeply, wondering where it would end. ''You're right,'' he said softly.

''I am? You don't think he died in that car either?''

''No,'' he whispered. ''I know he didn't die in any car.''

And so, amid the canned fiesta music, the din of silver against ceramic and general after-work laughter, Santich in hushed tones told the former Mrs. Torrington how her womanizing, child-support-welshing ex-husband had really expired. The story didn't take long. In fact, the uneasy silence afterward was nearly twice as lengthy.

''I think I need another drink,'' Trudy whispered.

After the waitress returned with it, she took a long sip, not through the straw, but right from the glass. Santich finished the rest of his water and sat quietly. He realized he was starved. ''Shouldn't we eat something?''

Trudy nodded. ''But not here.'' She looked around nervously. ''All of a sudden I'm uncomfortable here.''

Santich nodded, left a twenty to cover the bill. Together they walked out into the quickly cooling evening.

17

In the four years since Emily had left, Santich hadn't been alone with many single women in their houses. In fact, he hadn't been with any, when he stopped to think about it. Nervously, with hands behind his back, he examined the mantelpiece decorations while awaiting her return.

It was a small house, in one of the older subdivisions in Clear Lake, and simply decorated: blue drapes, lighter blue carpet, worn green furniture. Framed Monet prints hung on the walls, while a small Little League trophy, presented to the Most Sportsmanlike Player, held center stage over the fireplace, surrounded by school portraits of each child in the cardboard frames provided by the studio.

On the coffee table lay the Taco Bell wrappers from dinner. It wasn't a conscious continuation of the Mexican theme. Taco Bell was just the first fast-food place on the way to Trudy's house. They had eaten in silence. He had chewed his food softly to be sure to hear the first word. There hadn't been one. Afterward she excused herself to get out of the suddenly awkward dress.

Santich studied the photos of the boys, noticed the older one's resemblance to his father. The younger favored Trudy. He wondered how long ago they had been taken. If they were recent, then they were almost the same age as his daughter's boys. On the other hand, Trudy was older

129

than Moira, at least seven or eight years. The Torringtons had obviously started their brood a lot later.

"They're what I live for, you know." She had returned, dressed in sweatshirt and jogging shorts. Just for a moment, Santich had worried she'd reappear in a negligee. "They have been, for the last eight years."

He recalled Torrington's biography sheet he had dug up early that morning. "Ever since Sam joined the corps?"

She nodded. "You got it. I've never completely understood it. He was such a mild-mannered guy before that. When we started dating, I was the one who kissed *him* first. He was still active Army, but he was working here through a fellowship from UA, Huntsville. We got married in eighty-five. I got pregnant right away, and when Chris was born, I left MOD."

"You were in EVA then?"

"Oh, no. I only started that when I went back to work two years ago, after Jimmy turned three. No, from eighty-two till eighty-five, I was in PROP." She smiled shyly. "Propellent was my life. Won't you sit down?"

Santich turned to find her curled in the corner of the green upholstered couch, her pretty brown feet tucked up beneath her. Was he supposed to sit on the couch next to her? Or on the love seat? To get there, though, he would have to squeeze between the coffee table and her knees. He would almost certainly brush against her as he passed. He settled for the opposite end of the couch.

"So Christopher was born in eighty-six?" he asked.

"February 28. A month to the day after *Challenger*. That really put us in a bind. Here we were, with all these new expenses, and we didn't know if his job was going to last another week. If the thing had been shut down then, Sam probably would have had to go back to Huntsville, or maybe even the Army." The brown eyes misted slightly, and she turned away. "Of course, if that had happened, Sam would still be alive, and we'd still be happily married."

He dropped his eyes to give her some privacy, reached

for his empty soft-drink cup and drained more of the melted ice. "You don't have to talk about this if you don't want to."

She sniffed and looked up with a tear-streaked smile. "God, you must think I'm a horrible wreck. How am I supposed to handle the pressure of the front room if I can't even talk about this?"

"I think I'd be more worried if you *could* talk about this calmly." A chill passed through him as he imagined her reaction if she'd been on console when her husband's head exploded. He shivered involuntarily.

"So to continue the soap opera, we had Jimmy in January eighty-nine, and Sam learned he made the corps about a week later. And that, as they say, was the beginning of the end."

Santich had heard *this* story before. Not about Sam Torrington, but about other men who'd made it.

"Santy, I don't know how to describe it. Even before he started astronaut-candidate training, he started getting cards and letters from all kinds of crazies. Sure, some of them were really sweet, but most were the sort who go to Star Trek conventions, you know?"

He smiled, trying to remember how many straight years he'd declined the Trekkies' invitations to speak at their events.

"Those were pretty harmless, though. What I thought were the funniest were these *women* who'd send long love letters to him, asking him to father their children. Some were *married*! They said their husbands would never find out, that the baby would be their *space* child! Some sent nude pictures of themselves, and one woman actually mailed him her panties, asking him to take them up with him, and then, when he returned, she'd give him a blow job to get them back.

"The sad part was, instead of laughing it off, Sam started to believe he *had* become a sex god, just by getting his stupid little wings. Whammo! Instant jerk! Tell me, was it just him? Or does it happen a lot?"

Santich thought of the other guys in the corps with reputations for parlaying their wings and flight suits for various goodies. There was their regular pay from NASA, flight pay from the Air Force or Navy, and pussy pay from all the teased-hair, miniskirted honeys.

"I guess it happens once in a while," he admitted. "I think, though, and I'm not trying to defend Sam or make excuses for him, but I think that the pilots are used to the female attention. I mean, right from flight school onward, you have the same thing. Go to any bar near any naval air station or Air Force base, and you'll find the pilot groupies.

"So by the time the pilots become astronauts, they've seen ten or fifteen years of this stuff. Even if they were inclined to take advantage of it, they've probably gotten it out of their systems." Yeah. Like the former chief astronaut had gotten it out of *his* system. He was caught taking a cocktail waitress up in a T-38 from Ellington. She was seventeen. He retired a year later, without a blemish on his record.

"Mission specialists, like Sam, rarely have been worshiped like that," he continued. "Until they get their wings. Now most of them couldn't care less. Their obsession with flying in space has made them pretty tunnel-visioned. They're not interested in sex. Others . . . Well, others kind of *like* being sex symbols. I guess Sam was one of those, although that's just hearsay. I have no way of knowing for sure."

Trudy scoffed, rolled her eyes. "Believe me. It wasn't just hearsay. The son of a bitch actually got the clap from one of them. Can you believe it? In this day and age, he caught the clap. He's lucky it wasn't AIDS."

And then she must have realized how silly that sounded, and the mistiness returned to her eyes. Santich glanced at the miniature grandfather clock in the hall, saw that it was already close to eleven. He had a sim that started at six the next morning, and he hadn't even glanced at the flight plan.

"Trudy, I know this will sound awful, but I have to ask

you. Do you know anyone who hated Sam so badly, that they might, you know . . .''

"Have tampered with his helmet so his head would explode?" she finished softly. "You mean other than me?"

The breath caught in his throat as he tried simultaneously to inhale and come up with a believable denial.

"Don't sweat it," she said with a wave of a hand. "But tell me, what were you going to do if I *had* done it? And how were you going to tell for sure?"

"Two very good questions," he admitted. "For which I haven't the foggiest answer. You see, that friend I told you about . . ."

"Your inside source?"

"Yes. Him."

"Or her."

"Right," he grinned. "Or her. That friend and I decided that to go public with this right now would likely have consequences that we'd hate to see."

"Station would get canceled."

"Right. And, given the way Bruce handled it, there's a better than even chance that shuttle would get canceled, too. So we thought we'd keep this under our hats until after I get back, then present the whole ball of wax to the police. We figured they'd be less angry at *us* if we had some solid information to give them, rather than just what we know right now."

"So you're playing Hardy boys."

"I guess we are. Believe me, I really don't have time for it. But I think it's the only way out of a bad situation."

Trudy sipped at the glass of zinfandel she'd brought with her when she changed and stretched her arms above her head. The sweatshirt pulled up over her midriff for an instant, revealing the once firm, then flabby, now firm again brown tummy.

"Sometimes I wonder if that would be such a bad thing."

Santich pulled his eyes back up to meet hers. "What would?"

"If all this weren't just up and canceled, once and for all. I could get a real job and not have to agonize over each year's Space Station vote. I mean—don't get me wrong— I'm not looking forward to starting my career all over again. But if I have to do it, I'd rather do it now than in another five or six or ten years."

Santich shrugged silently.

"You don't agree? You think there's some point to all this other than gratifiying the egos of the likes of my husband?"

"I don't know. I'm a pilot and an engineer. I'm not a scientist."

"Please. I won't write an article for the JSC newsletter calling you a heretic if you don't toe the company line. Surely *you* of all people have been around long enough to see what it's all about."

He shrugged again. He hated this discussion.

She turned her body to face him. "Can I ask you something? I've been curious about this for a long time. Why did you hang around after they screwed you so bad?"

Because I knew someday I'd get my chance to go back! "Because this agency doesn't belong just to Bruce and his buddies. It belongs to all of us. To leave would be to wave a white flag, tell them the program is theirs to do with as they please. I like to think that my carping about safety had *some* beneficial effect." He knew his piousness sounded a bit hollow. "Plus, I guess, I wanted to fly again. And, short of moving to Russia, this is the only game in town."

"Well, I figured *that* was at least part of it. But twelve years? Was it worth it? I mean, what kept you going on the average morning, say, three years ago, when no one paid any attention to a word you said?"

"You really want to know?" he asked with a sigh.

"I wouldn't have asked if I didn't."

"This is going to sound really dumb, really naive. But deep down, I guess I'm really an optimist, although sometimes I wonder. What kept me going was that, someday, if we as a species manage not to blow ourselves up, or poison ourselves, or turn ourselves into mutants, if someday we manage to get past all those things, we still have to leave here.''

"The old, sun's-going-nova, send-the-lifeboats theory.''

He shrugged defensively. "Like I said, it's awfully optimistic. But even a scientific illiterate like me knows that last part is true. An asteroid could hit the planet tomorrow. The interglacial could end in fifty years and bring a hundred thousand years of ice age. And if neither of those happens, the sun *will* become a red giant in another few billion years. Someday, we're going to have to leave. And if we don't leave, we die. Now, I suppose you could argue that a species that treats a home as beautiful as ours with such contempt *deserves* to die. And I don't think I would care to argue that point. On some days, I would even agree.''

Trudy pulled her sweatshirt over her knees, dug her toes under the cushion Santich sat upon. "Was it going to the moon? Was that what made you feel this way?''

"Partly,'' he nodded. "I know it's a cliché, but I personally have never truly appreciated a place until I've left it and missed it. And standing at the foot of those barren, gray mountains, looking out at such a little Earth, all blue and white, and with just that tiny lander to get us back . . .'' He remembered the tears that had come to his eyes as he watched. For a full five minutes they had stood and stared, until Houston had reminded them they had to get their rocks back aboard and get to sleep. "Yeah, I missed it.''

She bit her lip, like a schoolgirl deciding whether to reveal a crush. "You know, I applied to the corps, too. Three times.''

"Really? What years?''

"Before you were on the committee. I finally realized I didn't kiss enough ass to get picked.''

Santich wondered if he'd come along now instead of when he did, whether he would even have applied. "I guess there *is* a lot of ass to kiss nowadays.''

"Sam was rejected three times, too. But on the fourth try, he got in. He always said later, fourth time is a charm.

You should try once more. But after he made it, I really didn't want to. For one thing, I didn't want to be one of those astronaut couples. You know? They're such freaks. Anyway, I realized that the ass-kissing gets going in earnest *after* you make it in.''

He could occasionally feel her feet wiggling under his thigh. He shifted away uncomfortably. ''Was Sam's making it a sore point between you two?''

She shook her head. ''Not in the slightest, although, later, Sam assumed it was. That I was jealous. But it wasn't that way at all. I was so happy for him. Because I truly loved him. At the time, he was truly lovable.''

The word ''jealous'' rang a bell, and Santich remembered Jo Pointer's description of the late-night phone calls. Either the soft, gentle creature he'd befriended or Jo's portrait of a bitter hag was a phony.

''I don't mean to harp on this, but I guess I need to know who Sam was seeing when he died, and who he might have broken up with prior to that.'' Now *that* sounded terrible. ''If you know,'' he added weakly.

She snorted. ''Hah! That shows how little you know about women. Of *course* I know. And not because I wanted to find out, mind you. It's just that every woman I know at JSC went out of her way to tell me the latest gossip about Sam! Can you believe it? And I would tell them: He really isn't my concern anymore. But they'd go right ahead, with their little smirks, like they were telling me for my own good.'' She shook her head. ''Women are such miserable creatures. Anyway, yes. I do know that before he died he was seeing two women, actually. One of them you could probably guess. She's that reporter? The one with the great big boobs?''

''Jo Pointer,'' he said.

''Space Slut. Isn't that what you all call her? Anyway, he had just started with her a few months before launch. And he was breaking it off with some other woman. I don't really know who she was, other than that she was married. He let that slip once. Oh, and her name was Lana, Lena, something like that. I know because he has call-waiting on his phone? He was talking to her, and I called, and he switched back and forth, and got us confused.''

"Did you speak to him often?"

"As little as I could. He'd call every couple of weeks, complaining about some horrible thing or another they were doing to him in the office, or looking for a sympathy lay.''

Santich looked at his hands, blushed at what he was about to ask. "And would he get one?"

Trudy cupped the wineglass and looked into his eyes. "At first. During our first year apart, yes. But not since then. In fact, in the last year, I was probably calling him as often as he called me. See, he was *always* late with the child support. The amazing thing was, I think he truly loved the boys. So why it was such an effort to put that check in the mail, I'll never understand.''

"You called him at home?"

She nodded. "I didn't want to be one of those nags who calls at work so everyone in the office knows what's going on. I don't know why, but I was always pretty civil with him. I never called too late at night, except for once, when the bastard was two months late, winter tuition was due, and Jimmy's birthday was a week off.'' She paused, shook her head. "He had some woman over. I could tell. He kept breaking off in midsentence, and kept covering up the mouthpiece. What a jerk.''

"Do you know who it was?"

"Well, it was January, so it must have been either Lena-Lana or Space Slut. Not that I cared.''

"Have you ever met her?"

"Who? Space Slut?"

He nodded.

"At some awards dinner once. It was a pretty silly thing, really, and she was the only reporter there. I think she just likes hanging around astronauts. Anyway, all I remember was her tits. She was wearing this tight dress, with scooped-out armholes. And she kept rubbing them up against every guy she met!''

"Do you think maybe she was mad at him, these last couple of months?"

"Space Slut? Like in mad enough to kill him? No. For one thing, she's a nobody. How would she even begin?"

Santich shrugged. "Well, she *does* have those breasts. Maybe she rubbed them up against an engineer at Gates Rubber."

"Maybe, but if she did, she did it for the sheer pleasure of having them rubbed. No, as far as I know, she and Sam were a happy item. Anyway, if they were having a falling out, he wouldn't have had her bra with him."

He blinked. "Her bra?"

"You didn't see the inventory of his personal locker?"

"I didn't think to look."

"Well, both of his folks are dead, so they came to me with all his personal effects, since I guess they technically belong to Chris and Jimmy. Although what they'd want with a Maidenform size thirty-six-D underwire support, I really can't say."

"A bra," he marveled. "What did you do with it?"

"I mailed it back to her. I wrote a note saying I was sure Sam would have wanted her to have it."

That explains that, Santich thought. The lingering doubts about Trudy Cortain vanished, and he wondered how and where to find another suspect.

"So have I cleared my good name, Inspector Santich?" she teased. Deep dimples and the crinkles around her eyes, cleared of the earlier makeup, punctuated her smile.

He smiled back. "I'm sorry. I shouldn't have jumped to conclusions. But I guess I really haven't learned anything. Maybe this was a stupid idea. I should go to the police right now."

Something passed through her head, and the mistiness returned to her eyes. "You know, it really is terrible what happened. He treated me badly, but he was basically good at heart. Anyway, no one deserves *that*. I don't care what they've done."

Santich swallowed hard. Not once had he even stopped

to consider whether the murder had been right or wrong. Only how it might affect the shuttle program and, in particular, *his* flight.

She took his arm. "I want to help you. You and your friend."

"What?"

"Who knows more about Sam than I do?"

He gulped once, studying her earnest eyes. What would Kyle think about this? He'd started out suspecting the dead man's beautiful widow, and wound up taking her in their confidence.

"Please? It would mean a lot to me."

"Let me think about it, and talk to my friend." He glanced at the hall clock. It was nearing midnight. "I really have to go. I've got to be in the SMS in six hours."

Trudy arose and walked him to the front door. "I, uh, guess I should apologize for earlier. You know, that dress and all. I thought you were interested in something else." Even in the dim porch light, he could see she was blushing. "I mean, I heard you were divorced, and, well, anyway. Sorry."

He fumbled with the keys to the Buick. She *had* been interested in him! "No, nothing to be sorry for. Really. And you have nothing to apologize for about that dress."

"You're a sweetheart. Thank you." Before he could react, she had thrown her arms around his neck, stood on her toes, and kissed him on the lips. "Thank you for a wonderful evening. Let me know? About helping you?"

He nodded quickly, backing up to the driveway. "I will."

18

It was a ritual he'd learned forty years earlier in Pensacola: start at the cockpit and work clockwise, around the nose, the starboard wing, the tail, the port wing, and end where he began. Trainers, fighters, bombers, experimental aircraft, transports; thousands of circuits around hundreds of planes. He tried to remember how many times he'd circled the sleek Gulfstream business jet, how many times he'd nose-dived at the ground before pulling up and executing a light touch-and-go.

The Shuttle Training Aircraft, NASA called it. Modified to fly as poorly as the space shuttle so commanders and pilots could practice landings. The left seat was outfitted as if it were the left seat on the shuttle flight deck, with every switch and display an exact replica. Even the windows were fitted with partial coverings, to reduce the field of view to that of the shuttle.

Astronauts flew to White Sands Missile Range in New Mexico to practice rather than fly the terrifying-looking descent over metropolitan Houston with its two commercial airports. This would be the first of several such trips for Santich, Melanie, and Orlov, the crew's designated flight engineer.

Melanie was in the cockpit going through the preflight checklist while Santich did the visual once-over. He was just finishing when the recollection jolted him: NASA 946.

The same tail number Banke's crew had ridden home after their landing.

He walked back to the nose, bent over to peer up into the wheel well. If only he had a flashlight . . .

"It will not be there."

He whacked his head against the starboard landing gear door as he whirled around. It was Orlov.

"*What* will not be there?" he asked, rubbing his temple.

"You know," Orlov said softly. "What you are looking for. We looked also. It was not there."

Santich glanced at the two ground crews still at the fuel hose and motioned Orlov up the stairs. "Later. After we're up."

Orlov nodded and strapped himself into the jump seat. Santich fidgeted in the left seat; he let Melanie get aloft from the copilot's chair, the one with the better visibility. He waited until the jet climbed through twenty-five thousand feet and the takeoff chatter with the ground had finished before he moved back into the passenger compartment.

Within moments, his stocky, balding flight engineer joined him. "I do not think it is something that can be found easily," he began without prompting. "If it exists, it must be installed in a difficult-to-reach bay. It is probably removed for routine flights, yes?"

How much did he know? How much did he suspect? Santich couldn't bring himself to come straight with him. It was something about the cold, blank, gray eyes. His father was one of the leading theoretical physicists in the Soviet Union, an outspoken pacifist who finally left the country he loved three years after helping his wife and young son escape.

The young son grew up a mathematician and a tournament-caliber chess prodigy. He could have been good, *really* good, Santich had read somewhere. Instead he'd given it up to become a spaceman. The first Russian-born American to fly in space, the press had trumpeted. The press was always looking for "firsts" to trumpet. How about the first spacewalker to watch his partner explode? God! How could he possibly want to fly again, so soon after?

Santich stared silently; Orlov stared back. Through the windows, the hills and bluffs of the Edwards Plateau passed slowly backward. If he was willing to hint about Option Zulu, maybe he wanted to talk.

"Would you call this a routine flight? Two of the three people aboard know what happened."

Orlov shook his head quickly. "No. This must go smoothly. They cannot afford to have anything bad happen, not with the vote in just two months."

Warmer, but not quite. "We're not sure whether we can trust each other," Santich said slowly. "I think we should try."

Orlov shrugged slowly, sticking his lower lip out for emphasis. A Slavic expression, Santich guessed.

"We are colleagues, yes? But we have different motives. Perhaps we can find common ground."

"Common ground. Like, for example, not getting blown up in this plane?"

"That is the rumor." He sat by one of the windows to stare out. "It all looks so different, when you are outside. Not like this. Here, you are still inside, part of it. There, you look down, and there is nothing, nothing at all between your hand and . . . this." He spread his fingers on the pane of Plexiglas. "You can reach out and touch it."

The Gulfstream banked left, and the midday sun poured through the window, setting aglow the gold wings and gold lettering on Orlov's blue flight suit. O-R-L-O-V, Santich thought. Thirty years earlier, the name alone would have kept him out of the corps, kept him from even being considered. Now, in the post-Soviet era, the name was a plus. NASA needed all the astronauts it could find who spoke Russian, if the plan to build a joint station was ever going to fly.

Orlov turned his gaze back to Santich. "It is too bad you are a pilot astronaut and cannot spacewalk. It is an expe-

rience all astronauts should have, at least once, before . . ."
He trailed off.

"They die?" Santich asked.

Orlov grinned. "I was going to say, before they leave
NASA."

The gray eyes flashed, and Santich shivered. Cold as ice
they were, dirty river ice that every so often would flow
down the Patuxent River during a particularly nasty winter
freeze.

Santich sat across from his crewmate. "I know what happened," he said softly, slowly.

The gray eyes barely flickered. "I assumed so. Why else
would you be looking for . . . it."

Santich recalled the terror in Banke's voice. "Why were
you guys looking for it?"

Another shrug. "At the time, we did not know what the
official story would be. We feared they might think it safer
to silence us than worry about what we would say."

"They didn't have to worry, did they? You're not going
to say anything."

"No."

"Why?"

Orlov turned his head back to the window, slipped on
his gray-green Ray-Bans. "We all wish to fly again." He
looked at Santich and smiled. "Yes?"

"Some more than others," Santich answered evenly.

"Perhaps."

"Except, of course, for Steve."

Orlov nodded. "Except for Steve. They are not certain
about him. They fear he will say something."

He obviously hadn't talked to the man recently, Santich
thought. "I would think the one who actually saw it happen, who had to drag the bloody mess back inside, I would
think that *he* would be most likely to talk."

"Then you would be incorrect. Did Colonel Bruce tell
you that it was Steve and I who . . . disposed of Torrington?
We were supposed to be sleeping. Marty thought the fewer
people involved, the better. . . ." Orlov turned the Ray-

Bans at Santich. "Please do not think me a monster. After all, there are many who question *your* motivations."

Santich watched the eyes; they hadn't blinked once. *God!* No wonder Banke was such a wreck! A chill ran through Santich: If Orlov would do *this* for Bruce, what else would he do? "How *could* you?" Santich asked helplessly.

Again a shrug, this one quicker, more perfunctory. "If someone is in an automobile accident where someone dies, do we tell that person, no, you should never ride in a car again? We do not. So why should I not enjoy what I am trained for, and what I love? Why would it be okay for another man to perform EVA but not for me?"

Santich's jaw almost dropped. Could he really think it was an *accident*? Of *course*! Why wouldn't he? A good company boy would never snoop where he shouldn't. Santich swallowed hard, decided to back out. "Well, whether you're a monster or not doesn't change a damn thing. We're flying together, so let's make the best of it. Deal?"

Orlov nodded quickly. "Deal." He pulled out some schematic drawings of GRO's sun sensor and laid them across his lap. "By the way, about our earlier discussion? No, I do not believe there is an Option Zulu. If there were, I do not think I would be here right now."

Santich nodded and walked back into the cockpit.

19

The room and its occupants had frozen into a permanent tableau. No one had moved in the five minutes he was in the kitchen. As he recalled the silences between the whirring of the microwave and the clicking of the ice machine, he realized no one had even spoken.

In one corner sat Kyle Hartsfield, stiff in the reclining chair, arms crossed. Trudy Cortain sat on the couch, eyes cast downward into her lap. And Dusty Hooper stood by the fireplace, staring out the bay window. They had been there almost a half hour, and the ice was still midwinter thick. The distrust was as pungent as Trudy's spring-lilac perfume.

Santich set the tray on the coffee table and moved to the far end of the couch. He passed Trudy a glass of red wine while Hooper moved in to secure a beer.

"All right, people. Trudy and I have another sim in two hours, and I imagine you guys have things to do as well. Now, I'm sorry about bringing everyone together like this, but there wasn't time for individual consultation, not with just two and a half weeks left. So, any suggestions?"

Hooper snorted. "I got one. I suggest you all get your heads examined. Have you lost your minds? Has anyone thought this through? *Why,* for God's sake, would someone murder Sam like this? Doesn't it seem a bit far-fetched?

Doesn't a dumb, careless accident sound a lot more likely?''

Kyle cleared his throat. ''If I may, sir, I think I know why. The killer is using the siege mentality at this agency to help him get away.'' He looked up to find all eyes on him. ''If you kill someone in their house, or on the street, or pretty much anywhere, the police, the medical examiner, the district attorney, they all have routines they follow to find the killer and throw him in jail. That's their job. That's what they do.

''But when an *astronaut* dies on a shuttle, that's a whole different matter. Remember how NASA even kept the Florida medical examiner from looking at the *Challenger* bodies? The whole dynamic in this case is skewed. Instead of the primary focus being to find the killer, or see if there even *was* a killer, the goal—from the administrator on down—is to minimize the impact on the program, even if it means covering the whole thing up and letting a murderer go free. Look at us. We're living proof. If we weren't interested in protecting the agency's image, we'd have gone to the police long ago. It's this bizarre culture the murderer is taking advantage of.''

Hooper popped some peanuts into his mouth. ''Son, if we don't watch out for NASA, who the fuck will? You think the press will? You think Congress will?'' He turned toward Santich. ''I've told you before, Santy, I'll tell you now: Drop this. The NASA budget goes to House Appropriations next month. You guys unload this around then, and we're all fucked.''

''A man died here,'' Kyle said in a monotone, his eyes focused on the center of Santich's beige living-room carpet.

''I agree. That's awful,'' Hooper allowed. ''But we can't undo it. The question is: Is catching whoever did it worth torpedoing the program?''

''The man we're talking about,'' Trudy said softly, ''was someone I once loved.''

''Okay,'' Santich broke in. ''Dusty? I think the rest of us agree that Sam's murder will be reported. That's a given.

The issue now is how to make sure the guilty party gets punished without punishing the program. That's why I called you. Because if anybody is plugged into the system, you are. You can help us find who did it. Then it becomes a regular run-of-the-mill murder instead of Murder-at-NASA.''

Hooper shook his head violently. ''No! No matter what you guys come up with, it's *never* going to be anything other than Murder-at-NASA. Come on! It happened on a fucking space walk! Plus think about this: You aren't dealing with a guy who sticks up the 7-Eleven and shoots the cashier. Whoever did this is fucking smart, and fucking ruthless. Who's to say he won't come after you next?''

Kyle's eyes widened as he looked up at Santich, but he said nothing.

''I guess what you're missing, Mr. Hooper, is that this isn't a debatable point.'' Trudy's chin jutted aggressively. ''I frankly couldn't care less about your precious space station. But I have a job that puts food on the table for my boys, so I'll go along with Santy. But if I thought for one minute that y'all would sweep this thing under the rug, I'd march to the police station this instant.''

Hooper raised his arm as if to say something, stopped and shrugged. ''All right. For the record, as if anybody cares, I think this is crazy. We don't know the kind of people we're dealing with here, and this is likely to blow up in our faces. But, as a favor to Santy, you can count on my help.''

Trudy glared at him, and Santich jumped in to preserve the consensus. ''Great. So let's go over what we know: Sam was killed when his helmet gasket failed. The loss of pressure was instantaneous. And it seems the gasket was certain to fail, either because it had flown before, or was a test article. Right?''

Kyle nodded. ''At this point, I would have to say it was a test article. I've been asking around, and I don't think flight hardware would be lying around like that. Plus I don't think that a *dozen* EVAs would make the material that brittle."

"What about the flight history of that helmet?" Trudy waved a potato chip like a pointer. "Maybe there was a mix-up during an earlier flight? And maybe the helmet wasn't inspected properly?"

"I looked into that." Kyle lifted a manila folder out of his briefcase and shuffled through it. Three pairs of eyes craned forward to catch a peek. "The helmet itself was procured as part of an order in 1991. A dozen lower torsos, eighteen upper torsos, three dozen gloves, and twenty helmets. It flew only once before, in December 1993. The first Hubble servicing. The only anomaly reported was a piece of foam that came loose. The crew fixed it on-orbit with contact cement. Unauthorized. Apparently there was some question later about sublimation and fumes in low pressure, but there were no ill effects reported. When it was returned for this flight, of course, there was the bad seal, and EVA sent it back for a new one. That was how I figured out what had happened."

The room fell silent as Kyle sifted through his papers. Dusty Hooper tilted the bottle to finish his beer, then walked to the coffee table to set down the empty. He paused as he passed the easy chair, reading over Kyle's shoulder. "You've, uh, done quite a bit on this, huh?"

Hartsfield looked up nervously, shook his head. "No. Not that much. Just a little digging." His eyes shot to Santich's. "Nothing anybody would notice."

Hooper nodded, walked back to his place by the mantel.

"There's, uh, something I got here I found interesting," Kyle continued. "I looked up the qualification tables for the compound in the gasket, and that material should only have a one-in-one hundred failure rate given that level of deterioration."

Trudy blinked twice. "Whoa. Wait. So there was a ninety-nine percent chance Sam would have survived?"

"I knew it!" Hooper declared. "There you have it! What the hell kind of murder is it with those odds? I thought from the beginning this sounded far-fetched. So let me pose the question again: Do you guys want to destroy NASA over an *accident*?"

"It wasn't an accident." Kyle's eyes locked with Hooper's, then with Santich's. "You still have all the paperwork, the forged quality-control stamps, faked signatures. Somebody went to a lot of trouble to get this particular gasket on Sam Torrington's space suit."

"But you just said the failure rate for that kind of stuff was one percent! Hell, everyone in this room can account for the funny paperwork: It happens all the time. *We* know that! People covering their asses, cutting corners to meet deadlines, make incentives! Come on!"

Santich felt his stomach constricting. "Just one percent does sound low, Kyle. Are you sure about the tables?"

"They're from Gates Rubber's own analysis."

"Could they have padded them, to make it sound better than it was?" Santich asked.

"Maybe, but I doubt it. See, the table was put together back in seventy-seven, when Gates was still comparing different compounds. They'd already won the contract for the suits. Their engineers had nothing to gain by making one material seem better than another."

"The defense rests," Hooper said after a brief silence.

"I don't think so," Kyle said flatly. "Like I said, somebody went to a lot of trouble to get *this* particular seal on *this* particular helmet on *this* particular flight. If it was just CYA, the phony paper would have been jettisoned after the original seal was rejected by NASA."

Hooper nodded. "Okay," he challenged. "Then how did this somebody make sure the damn thing failed this one particular time, if the chances were so slim?"

Santich turned back to his new friend. He had nothing, other than the familiar, queasy feeling in his gut—*things had worked out so nicely for Sam's killer*—that could help him.

"I haven't gotten that far yet," Kyle admitted. "I just got this failure rate yesterday. But I'm certain there's something else. Maybe they tampered with something else in the suit, something that raised the odds from one percent to ninety percent. I don't know."

Santich winced, expecting Hooper to tear Kyle apart. Instead, though, he shook his head silently.

"Isn't the suit contract up for renewal?" Trudy stared into the fireplace next to Hooper. "Isn't Gates bidding against a couple of other companies?"

"Rochester Products so far. Maybe one or two others," Kyle said. "I guess it depends on whether this gets out. If it does, I'll bet everyone and his brother bids, why?" He blinked twice. "Oh."

"Exactly." Her eyes flashed on each of them in turn. "Maybe we're going after this all wrong. Maybe the point wasn't to kill Sam for the sake of killing Sam. Maybe they killed Sam to wreck Gates's chances of winning that contract again. Maybe this whole thing is just about money."

For a moment everybody looked at one another. Hooper coughed, shook his head again. "Come on, guys. I know contractors are ruthless, but isn't that a bit much?"

"How much is that contract worth?" Trudy persisted.

Kyle tilted back the sandy curls and stroked the intermittent fuzz on his chin. "It's for all the suits for Station. About four dozen sets, total, I think. About twenty million each, so, in round numbers, about one billion?"

Trudy nodded, looked at Hooper. "The prosecution rests."

"Oh come on!" he roared. "You have nothing! Not a shred of proof! You want to go to the cops with that?"

"We'll get it," she answered softly. "We'll get proof."

Headlights flashed through the window, and Santich saw his neighbor's car pull into his drive. He looked at his watch and saw it was well past six. "All right. We're going to have to break this up for now. Trudy and I have to get back to the center for more sims." He caught Hooper's eye. "So we agree to look into this as best we can? Hoop?"

Hooper uncrossed his arms and dug into his pants pocket for his car keys. "Yeah. Stupid idea, but you can count on me. I'll see what I can find out about Rochester Products and Gates. Maybe someone from Rochester infiltrated Gates or something. 'Astronaut Killed; Industrial Sabotage Suspected.' Great.''

Trudy brushed her off-white skirt flat as she stood. "I'll keep digging into who might have hated Sam enough to kill him. I don't know how much luck I'll have, though. I still can't figure out who this Lana woman is."

Santich walked his guests to the front door, flipped on the porch light, and locked the door behind him. Hooper, the first to arrive, was the last to leave.

"You're getting us into some serious shit, my friend," he said as he pushed the key into the ignition.

Santich nodded, leaned over the driver's window of the BMW. "I know. Listen, I owe you. Thanks."

Hooper stared at the dashboard, fiddled with the trip odometer knob. "Don't thank me. I haven't done anything yet. I can tell when you've made up your mind, so I know this is falling on deaf ears. But my best advice is still what it was two weeks ago. Leave this alone."

"I asked you for your help, as a friend."

Hooper's eyes stayed straight ahead. "And I'm giving it to you, as a friend. But my advice, as a friend, is to stay out of it." He turned the key and shifted into reverse. "I'll call you."

Santich watched him round the corner and walk into his garage, past the garbage bins and rakes and into the Buick. He'd begun to back out when he slammed on the brakes. Not five feet behind him was Kyle's Honda. In seconds he was at Santich's window.

"I doubled around the block and waited till they'd left."

Santich shifted into park and turned off the engine. "What happened?"

Kyle looked back into the empty street, and Santich remembered Steve Banke's nervous visit. "I've been getting calls. In the middle of the night."

"Phone calls?"

He gulped. "The first time, a voice said Kyle. That's it.

Just Kyle. I thought maybe it was you, so I said yes.''

''It wasn't me. Then what?''

''He hung up. That was it.''

''They called again?''

''Three more times. I'm certain it was the same one, because they called at the exact same time each night: three-thirty-three A.M. Four nights in a row.''

Kyle glanced back at the street again, and Santich noticed the beads of sweat on the forehead and upper lip. ''What did they say the next nights?''

''Nothing the second or third night. Just a hang-up. Then last night, he said something, just two words: Simon's gone.''

''Simon's gone?''

''I think so. Actually he pronounced it: 'Suh-moon.' It didn't make any sense.''

Santich's heart skipped. ''*Simoon*? He said *Simoon*'s gone?''

Kyle nodded. ''Yeah. Why? What's *Simoon*?''

Santich could feel the sweat beading on his brow as he wiped a clammy hand over his lips. ''Steve's boat.''

''*Simoon*'s gone? Steve's boat's gone?''

''How long ago did he leave?'' Santich counted the sims, the T-38 runs, and tried to calculate days. ''Have you talked to him since?''

Kyle shook his head. ''Do you think something's happened to him?''

Kyle's eyes had widened even further, and Santich saw his face lose its color. ''Listen. Someone's messing with you. Steve should be in Key West soon. I'll find out where tomorrow and get hold of him. In the meantime, why the hell is somebody calling you?''

''I don't know. It has to be this, what we're doing. Maybe your friend Hooper was right. Maybe we've underestimated the people we're dealing with. Maybe . . .''

''Stop.'' Santich's mind raced. Who? And how did they possibly know what Kyle was up to? ''Okay. How would someone know what you're doing?''

Kyle shook his head. "I've only asked for raw data, from people I've known for years. They haven't asked why I was asking, and I didn't volunteer."

"This stuff you asked for, any unusual requests? Anything out of the ordinary?"

"Nothing. The kind of information I've always asked for. Plus I'm on the bid evaluation team for the space-suit contract, perfect cover for nosing around about engineering properties and so forth."

Santich nodded. "Okay. How do we know this guy knows what we're doing? Could he be a random nut case? Have you had crank callers before?"

"Once. About a year ago. He would say rude things when Melissa answered, but would hang up whenever I picked up. That's why I always answer the phone after about ten o'clock." He took a deep breath, glancing again at the road. "But *Simoon*. That's not exactly a common name, is it?"

We don't know the kind of people we're dealing with, Hoop had warned. Santich tried to swallow, couldn't. "No. We should probably assume our caller knows what we're doing. How, I have no idea. Maybe someone at Gates put two and two together; I don't know. In any case, we've got to be more careful. Is there any way you can tape that guy if he calls back?"

"I think so. The answering machine has a feature where you can record a conversation. The booklet said it might be illegal, though."

Santich couldn't help a grin. "I think in this case, the FCC might cut you some slack."

Kyle smiled sheepishly. "Okay, if he calls back, I'll tape him. What else?"

He thought hard, gulped. "Given we've been found out, and given that someone is harassing you, I think we should consider dropping this."

Kyle blinked. "Dropping it? You mean giving up?"

"Not giving up. Just turning it over to the police right now."

"But we don't have anything. Hoop was right about that. Right now, the hard evidence says it was an accident."

"Kyle, let me be honest. If we go to the cops now, the next mission is postponed, indefinitely. And there's nothing I want more than to fly that next mission. But the more I think about it, the more I think we should drop it. I mean, some nut is calling you, not me. I'm leaving town in two weeks. You're not. Maybe this *is* out of our league."

Kyle stood straight, thrust his hands in his pockets, blew a breath out his mouth. "I think we're real close, Santy. I can't pin it down, but I just know there's some little thing that will make everything fall together."

Santich tapped his fingers on the wheel, his mind twisting and pulling two wildly opposed emotions. Half wanted to sigh with relief: His flight was a go! The other half wanted to grab this kid and beat some sense into him.

"How about this," Kyle continued. "You track down Steve Banke and ask him if anything unusual has happened to him or his boat. Then after you find him and he's okay, then I'll decide that the guy had actually said Simon, not *Simoon*, and was a crank, and I won't have to worry anymore."

Santich put on a smile, but he already had a bad feeling about what he'd find. "Deal. I'll call tomorrow. And it won't be at four A.M."

20

It wasn't 4:00 A.M., but it was close, when Santich coaxed Kyle to drive out to Johnson's rocket garden, a random halfway point between their homes. He arrived first, and walked the length of the huge Saturn 5 that lay on its side. He grinned; the rusting museum piece wasn't a model. It was the real thing, and once upon a time might have taken three men to the moon, if budget cuts hadn't killed Project Apollo's final three flights. Another one lay at Kennedy Space Center, surrounded by a fence and speakers broadcasting an informational tape. More than $350 million each, in 1970s dollars, all so tourists could take a neat picture.

"Reminiscing about old times?"

Kyle had walked up quietly, and Santich lost the grin. "I've been waiting six hours to talk to you. The sim computer went down twice, and we didn't finish until a half hour ago."

Kyle stopped, put his hands in his jacket pockets. "Bad news?"

"I think so. I asked around the office, told everyone I wanted to talk to Banke about the drag chute–induced yaw during his landing. No one has heard from him. He's on leave through next week, so no one misses him either.

"I tracked down his son. You know, I'd completely forgotten what an asshole I was a couple of weeks ago, sitting next to Bruce while he trashed Steve. Well, Matthew hadn't

155

forgotten. I had to apologize every way to Sunday before he calmed down.''

"Had he heard from him?''

Santich shook his head. "I didn't want to scare him for no reason, so I didn't tell him about your middle-of-the-night calls or what we're doing. Anyway, he said Steve was planning a landfall on Garden Key in the Dry Tortugas, about sixty miles from Key West. There's no marina or anything, just an old fort. He was going to stay anchored there until he ran out of water or was run out by bad weather. *Then* he was going to Key West.''

"So his family doesn't miss him either.''

"Exactly. The upshot is we can't be sure. The kid suggested calling the coastal VHF stations in Florida, so that in the off chance Steve listened to the traffic lists, he'd know I was looking for him. I went ahead and called the ones in Fort Myers, Key West and Marathon, but I'm not too hopeful. I mean, the man went sailing to get *away* from all this.''

Kyle sighed, let his eyes study the Saturn 5 from capsule to engine bells. "So we're no closer than we were yesterday.''

"You had no luck either?''

He shook his head slowly. "I can't figure it out. They must have found a way to make that gasket fail on the first try. Maybe they tampered with it some more, altered it chemically.''

"You mean dab on some oxidizer or hardener or something?''

"No. That would've been caught by NASA Safety. Something that wouldn't leave a trace, or maybe something that could be done *after* Safety was through with it.''

Santich whistled. "That last one, I don't know. That means recruiting a saboteur among the closeout crew at the Cape. I don't think there's any way. Those guys are like the palace guard. They'd rather chew off an arm than hurt the shuttle.''

"It's there. I'll find it.'' Kyle glanced at his watch.

"Damn! It's almost quarter past! I need to be home when my psycho calls. I don't want Melissa answering it. That's the *last* thing I need."

"All right. Get going. Call me in a half hour, either way, okay?"

Kyle was already trotting back to the visitor's lot as he spun in midstride, waved and spun back around. Santich grinned at the pirouette and, at a slower pace, followed his steps.

He pulled out the main gate, past the little wooden sign announcing how many days until the next launch. Right now it was still blank; the security staff wouldn't start counting down for another week. He didn't need any sign, though: twelve days, twenty hours and some odd minutes. His mental countdown had been accurate to the hour for the past week, although the Torrington thing had become a consuming distraction.

More than a few times, he'd lost his place in the time line during a sim, and Melanie had had to bail him out to keep the operators from sensing a problem. She hadn't said anything about the lapses, and he wondered whether she thought he was going senile. He knew she wouldn't tell anyone; that would only delay her own first trip into space or even cancel it.

He vowed to pay closer attention to the mission, not that it required much effort on his part. He could sleepwalk through the launch and landing, and the rendezvous burn profile was textbook stuff. It just wouldn't do for the Dean of American Astronauts to screw up his final moment of glory. At least the training for this had been quick and to the point, and for that he was grateful. Most of the public relations stuff had been nixed for lack of time, and for that he was extremely grateful. Only a single press event was scheduled, despite a torrent of media interview requests.

In two days he and his crew would fly to the Cape for a countdown dry run. On the second of their three days there, the KSC flacks would herd the press to the launch-pad, where he and the others would be subjected to the usual idiocy for ten or fifteen minutes. But that would be all: no interminable press conference, no afternoon-long series of interviews. He could already imagine the questions: How important is this mission to NASA's future? Was it hard to pack two years of training into one month? And, from the one or two nonsycophants in the bunch, why is NASA performing a flight that violates its own safety guidelines? To save Space Station?

He had to remember not to piss them off. He needed them to jump on the Torrington murder after he got back. He needed them to attack Bruce specifically, not the whole shuttle program, for the cover-up, or else the damage to manned spaceflight would be just as severe as if Banke had gone public right from the beginning.

The blue Regal swung onto Bay Street of its own volition, and Santich focused to find himself turning left onto Galveston and right onto Gulfbreeze. He drove into the open garage, turned off the engine, and heard the phone. Quickly he pulled himself out, fumbled with the keys, burst into the kitchen, and grabbed the handset as it vibrated from the last ring.

He half expected to be a moment too late, and held it silently to his ear.

"Santy?"

It wasn't Kyle. "Trudy?"

"Thank God! I've been trying to reach you for the past hour. Santy, something strange is going on. After the sim tonight, the lead flight director told me I had to move into the front room *on this mission*!"

He couldn't tell whether she meant it as good news or bad. "You're kidding," he said neutrally.

"Santy, this is *unheard* of! To get out in the front room in just two years? In EVA? It doesn't happen. So I asked what happened to Etheridge. They said he had to take leave and would miss this flight. So I asked if there wasn't someone else already qualified for the console that they could get, and they said no, no one else had the mission-specific training."

Santich held the line silently; the queasiness returned.

"Santy?"

"Yeah. I'm listening."

"Santy, Mike Etheridge did Sam's flight. He was on console when it happened. He *has* to know, right?"

Banke, Kyle, Etheridge ... Was this the murderer's doing? Or Bruce's? "Had you talked to him about Torrington? Either before or after we talked?"

"No. But it really changed him. He used to crack jokes, laugh all the time, you know? Right after 74 he became all serious. I'd tell him I was taking the coffee he'd brewed over to the propellant shop for analysis. He wouldn't even smile."

"You think his leaving has to do with Sam's death."

"I know it does. In the years I've known him, he's never taken a sick day. He'd hardly take vacation, and then only when he had a good three months until his next flight. He'd *never* abandon a mission two weeks from launch."

"Did they say why he left?"

"They said he didn't give a reason, that he filed for emergency leave yesterday afternoon and was gone two hours later."

Another pause as he thought it through.

"Santy, something's happened to him, hasn't it?"

That had been his gut reaction, too. He swallowed softly. "We don't know that," he said calmly. "For all we know, his mom's sick and he's taking care of her."

More silence. "You think I'm being silly? That there's nothing to worry about?"

He swallowed again. "No. I don't think you're silly, and maybe there *is* something to worry about. I think we all need to meet again. Tomorrow, or today, rather," he said, remembering the time. "Let's try for five o'clock. We have a two-hour break about then, right?"

"Yeah. Okay. The four of us? Including Dusty Hooper?"

"Yeah. Why?"

"Nothing. It's just . . . I don't know. He's so set against us, that's all."

"Hoop's a bit headstrong, a bit evangelical about manned flight," Santich said. "Trust me. If it came to it, he'd die for me. Plus he knows more about this place than anyone."

"I know you're right. I didn't mean to insult him. Five o'clock, then?"

"Five o'clock," he agreed, and hung up.

21

"He never called," Hartsfield explained. "I waited until six A.M., but nothing. I'd just nodded off when Santy called."

Again they had converged on Santich's small ranch-style house. This time there were no refreshments except for the beer Hooper had swiped from the fridge. This time Trudy shared Kyle's fearful look.

"I asked around about Mike Etheridge today," she began, then noticed Kyle's puzzled expression. "Lead EVA for 74? He up and disappeared yesterday afternoon. Told the office he was taking emergency leave. Well, it seems no one, I mean *no one*, has a clue about it. He's divorced, no kids, mom's dead, father in Maine, a sister in Colorado. I got hold of both father and sister, and neither had any idea where he was. His sister said he usually took some time off right after a mission. I guess she didn't realize he was also working 74A."

Hooper stroked his chin. "So what are you doing about it?"

Trudy threw her hands up. "What can I do? I'm moving into the front room. Two years ahead of schedule, not sure I know everything to do the job right, and worried as hell about Mike."

"Hoop? Do you have anything?" Santich asked.

Hooper nodded, set his beer on the coffee table, and

pulled out a folded sheet of paper from his back pocket. "Curtis Austin, systems integration manager for Allied Chemical, a subsidiary of Rochester Products. Has been with Rochester for three years. His last job: Space Systems Division at Gates Rubber." He looked up from the sheet and folded it neatly. "I called a buddy at Gates. Austin was canned by the home office. Embezzling through his expense account, he thought."

"He's here?" Trudy asked.

"Uh-huh." Hooper raised his silver eyebrows at her. "I guess maybe you were right. Allied has a subcontract for the foam insulation on orbiter wiring. He works right here in Building 9A."

"What else?" Kyle kept his gaze on the carpet. "I mean, does he have the expertise to sabotage a space suit? Could he get access to them?"

Hooper snorted. "What am I, Sherlock fucking Holmes? It was a lot of work just getting this!"

"So we go to the police and tell them Austin is their man, on the grounds that he works for a company that wants the space-suit contract and got fired from the one that holds it now? That's nothing!"

"My point exactly," Hooper nodded. "I don't know if this guy knows a space suit from his asshole."

"Well, how much space stuff does Gates make?" Santich asked. "I mean, he *was* with Space Systems Division, right? Do you think you can find out more about him?"

Hooper lifted his broad shoulders. "I suppose, but I'll tell you right now I can't devote all my time to this." He looked at Trudy. "I know you guys don't give a rat's ass about Station, but my bosses do. And I'm going to Washington tomorrow for a week on the Hill. But I'll see what more I can get on this guy, okay? I just can't promise it by the end of business tomorrow, that's all."

"That's fine," Santich interjected. "We still have a week and a half to launch, then another week in orbit before we take this to the cops."

"I can't wait," Hooper scoffed. " 'Hero Astronaut Saves

Satellite, Solves Murder.' Just what the program needs.''

Trudy rolled her eyes at Santich, making sure Hooper couldn't see. ''What about Mike Etheridge? And Kyle's phone creep?''

''Any word on Banke?'' Kyle asked.

Santich shook his head. ''Hoop? You heard anything about Banke? Anyone talk to him recently? Anyone worried about him?''

''Nada.'' Hooper spread his jeans-clad legs, crossed his arms and stared out the window. ''Personally, I think crossing the Gulf in a boat that size is plain stupid. No telling what sort of trouble you could get yourself into.''

''Well,'' Santich continued. ''Apparently he hasn't been out long enough for anyone to worry. I hear it could take a week, ten days, or even two weeks, depending on the weather. That's what a couple of guys in the office who sail told me, anyway.''

''Two weeks!'' Kyle's mouth hung open. ''I have to deal with this for another week?''

''Well, maybe he *is* a crank,'' Santich said. ''How could anyone connect *you* to Steve Banke?''

''Maybe someone saw me talking to him. You know, that day before he met you?''

''Santy's right. He's probably a crank,'' Hooper's voice boomed confidently.

Kyle turned a look of disbelief toward him. ''A couple days ago you said we didn't know the type of people we were dealing with. Well, now, two out of the *handful* of people who know what really happened have disappeared, and you can shrug it off?''

''Well,'' Hooper mumbled. ''Perhaps I said that last time to dissuade you guys from going ahead with this.''

Trudy gasped, shook her head slowly, this time making no effort to hide her disgust. ''I think we need to be careful, okay? And run straight to the police at the first sign of trouble.''

''Absolutely,'' Santich agreed. ''If any of you see, or even think you see, somebody suspicious hanging around your office, or your house, don't hesitate turning over the whole ball of wax to the cops. Let the psycho start calling *them* at three-thirty-three each morning. Let's see how far he gets."

"Let me give you all my pager number," Trudy said. "If you need to reach me in a hurry."

"Oh, yeah, I have a cell phone in my car," Kyle said, blushing immediately. "For when Melissa was expecting."

"I'll check out one of the office cell phones tomorrow and get you all that number," Santich said. "I think that reaches me even in Florida when I'm there later this week."

Hooper looked around the room. "I have a cell number, a pager and an answering service," he sighed. "All three reach me no matter where I am."

"Good," Santich said. "We'll keep at this as best we can. I'm afraid Trudy and I will be up to our necks for the next week with sims, but I can still squeeze a few minutes here and there to nose around."

"And I think I'm getting closer to the failure mechanism," Kyle said as they moved toward the door. "A rapid pressure change prior to the failure, I think. Maybe in the next couple of days I'll have more."

"A pressure change?" Hooper asked.

"Yeah. Like if somehow the helmet underwent a rapid pressurization or depressurization prior to use. That might have stressed the gasket enough to dislodge it or even break it."

Hooper stared at his door handle, pulled it open, and slid into the driver's seat. "I'll call you about Austin," he shouted as the 520i backed into the street.

"Sometimes," Trudy began as she watched the big black car turn the curve onto Galveston, "I wish you hadn't told him about this." She looked up at Santich. "Sorry."

"He'll pull through for us." He knew he hadn't convinced her. As he got into the Buick, he wondered why he couldn't quite convince himself either.

22

"NASA 914, NASA 911. Eleven more days, Mel."

In way of answer, the sleek jet on his wingtip started a roll to port. He nudged the stick gently to the left to follow.

"Ten days, four hours and . . . twenty-three minutes, you mean. You don't have to remind me," Melanie's voice crackled softly over the headset.

Of all training, flight time in the T-38s was Santich's favorite. Since the beginning of the space program, astronauts had been afforded some of the sweetest flying toys ever built. Officially, the fifteen hours per month each pilot spent at the stick was to maintain proficiency in high-performance aircraft. The peculiar logic of keeping a fleet of nimble little trainers for astronauts preparing to fly the aerodynamically cumbersome shuttle never bothered anyone at NASA, Santich included, and he savored each minute zipping along just under the speed of sound over the dazzlingly blue Gulf one hundred miles south of Galveston.

"Hey, keep an eye out for a little sailboat, would you?" he asked.

"Any one in particular?" she answered.

"Beige hull, blue trim. Small, twenty-four feet. Named *Simoon.*"

"Steve Banke's boat?"

"That's the one." Santich started the exchange as a joke but found himself looking anxiously around the horizon.

"If you see him, let's go down and call him on the VHF."

"Roger that."

Melanie dropped to five hundred feet, then three hundred, and sped westward over the whitecapped water. Santich followed, trying to guess the size of the waves. Five, maybe six feet, he figured. Nothing for an aircraft carrier but probably enough to make life on a twenty-four-footer more than a little uncomfortable. All night that two-word snippet, "*Simoon*'s gone," had run in and out of his dreams. Most unnerving was not being able to know. It seemed far-fetched that someone had learned what Kyle was doing and knew exactly what would scare him. Maybe it was a crank caller, and he *hadn't* really said *Simoon* after all. But on the other hand, what word sounded like *Simoon*? And the first time the man had called, he had asked for Kyle. That ruled out the possibility that it was a wrong number.

Simoon's gone. What was that supposed to mean? A warning? A threat? *This is what happens to people who mess with us.* But Steve hadn't messed with anyone. He hadn't protested his innocence about the landing. He hadn't gone to the press. Why would anyone harm him? Was he *about* to protest his innocence? Was he *about* to go to the press? The night he'd come by to pass the word about the young engineer in the EVA shop, he didn't seem like someone about to go public with anything. Quite the contrary.

"NASA 911, NASA 914. Shall we start heading back?"

Santich glanced at the fuel gauge, saw the needle sitting just over the halfway mark. "Roger, 914. Let's get on back and pretend to catch that satellite for the ten-thousandth time."

Melanie's nose pulled a little ahead and began a gentle starboard roll. She had led for the past half hour, and Santich hadn't tired of watching her fluid touch. Her background made her talent all the more amazing: the oldest of three daughters of a single mom in South Central Los Angeles, valedictorian of an inner-city high school while also holding down a full-time job to help raise her sisters, an appointment to Annapolis, and the rest was history. The best pure pilot to come along in decades. Her plane never jarred, never lurched; it just slid into whatever position Melanie wanted. He wasn't surprised—she'd been a candidate for the Blue Angels, the Navy's aerobatic team, when she became an instructor at Pax River instead.

Santich was trying to let his hand relax to match his right seat's grace when he noticed the faint beeping. Instantly he scanned the displays, but he knew from the sound it wasn't a warning tone. He began to wonder when he remembered: the cell phone! He had stowed it in a pocket of his flight suit, in case Kyle or Trudy needed to reach him.

It had already been ringing fifteen or twenty seconds, and he still couldn't get to it, not while he was following Melanie's wingtip.

"Nine-fourteen, 911," he called.

"Go ahead."

"Mel, let me lead for a bit."

"It's yours."

Santich rose to one thousand feet, got himself in trim and set the autopilot before twisting and stretching in the tiny canopy to reach his left sleeve. The phone was one of the latest on the market, a gadget no larger than his palm. He turned the microphone gain on his radio all the way down, unfolded the phone and fumbled with miniaturized keys before finding the power button.

"Hello," he grunted, struggling to hold the phone against his radio headset.

"Santy?" The voice faded, the static threatening to drown it out altogether. "Santy? Are you there?"

"Kyle?"

"Nine-eleven, 914." Melanie's voice came through loud and clear, and Santich reached for the volume button.

"Santy, I've been trying to reach you for the last half hour! Where have you been? I think I'm in real trouble."

"I've been up in the T-38. What's wrong?"

"Hold on!"

Santy heard the faint tinkle of glass, and a shout. "Kyle? Kyle!"

"Yeah," the voice quavered. "Santy, he's trying to kill me."

"Kill you? Who? Kyle!"

"I . . . I don't know. He's behind me. He's been following me for an hour, and just now he tried to knock me off the road."

"Jesus . . . Are you sure?"

"Christ's sake, Santy, he pulled up next to me and he hit me!"

"Fuck. Okay. Where are you?"

"God, Santy, I'm in trouble. . . . A couple of miles back I got off the main road going to the bridge. I'm heading west on Gulfshore and I'm running out of room. Plus the fog's rolled in—I can barely see in front of me and I'm doing eighty!"

"Jesus! What the fuck are you doing down there?"

"I . . . I don't know. I left the center to go home, and noticed this car turning each time I did. So I kept going. Next thing I knew, I was on I-45 toward Galveston!"

"Okay. Give me a minute."

Santich looked out from the canopy. To the right, the western tip of the long, thin barrier island was barely visible, the higher dunes poking through the late afternoon ground fog. He bit first the bottom lip, then the top. *Now what?* The cops couldn't possibly get there in time. . . . He hesitated a moment, then flicked the switch on the radio.

"Nine-fourteen, 911," he called.

"Nine-eleven, go."

"Mel, turn down your transmit power, would you? I'm getting some bad distortion."

"How far down?"

"As low as you can."

A pause. "Is that better?"

"Roger, stand by one. I'm still lead."

"I'm on your wingtip."

Santich pushed the stick away and eased it right, rolling

his little bird back toward the fuzzy shape of land. The two blue-and-white jets shrieked toward shore at four hundred knots, barely thirty feet over the wave tops, low enough to coat the canopies with salt spray.

"Kyle? You still with me?"

"Yes. Oh God, Santy, I should have called the cops when I first saw him. What am I going to do?"

"Kyle. Listen closely. How fast are you going?"

"About eighty, now."

"Okay. Is this guy still on your ass? Is he still trying to ram you?"

"I don't . . . I don't think so. He must know this is a dead end. He's about two hundred yards behind me."

"Okay. Is there any other traffic?"

"No. There's no one. I'm all alone out here, Santy!"

"Any houses?"

"A few, but I don't think anyone's there. It's mainly sand dunes."

It was the same as he remembered it from his last visit three years earlier. "Okay. I'm on my way. Slow down as much as you can without letting him get too close, okay?"

"Yeah, but . . . What do you mean, you're on your way?"

"Just what I said. My ETA is about . . . two minutes."

"Two minutes? Oh, Jesus! *You're still in the T-38!*"

"Now listen up. I need you to be calm, all right?"

"I'm trying."

"Okay. Now watch the road in front of you. Nothing else, okay?"

A long pause. "Okay."

"I mean it. This all depends on you."

Another pause, this one shorter. "Okay. Santy?"

"Yeah?"

"Be careful, all right?"

"No sweat," he said coolly. He could already feel the beads appearing on his forehead. He hadn't flown a plane in anger in decades, and he hoped he'd remember the nerve.

"Nine-eleven, 914."

"Go ahead, Mel."

"Santy, who are you talking to?"

He'd forgotten to turn off his microphone. No matter. There was no way he could hide this from her. In fact, he would need her help, both to make it happen and then to hide it from the rest of the world.

"Mel, I'm counting on you. I'm about to do something that's going to seem crazy. But you've got to trust me, okay?"

She didn't hesitate. "You got it. What are we doing?"

We doing, he thought with relief. "We're going in along the beach road. You stay on my starboard wing. At a certain moment, we're going to cross over. I'll lead. Then we get back out here and vector in toward Ellington."

A long pause; he'd lost her.

"You want to stay thirty feet off the deck the whole way?"

He breathed again. "Roger that."

"I take it you'll explain this to me back at the officer's club."

He couldn't help a grin. "Roger that also. Oh, and, Mel? Let's keep radio silence till we're back out here."

"Copy all."

Santich turned the transmitter off and wedged the phone between his headset and his ear. "How you doing, Kyle?"

"Not too good. I'm down to fifty, and I'm afraid he's about to try something."

"What's he driving?"

"A blue Chevy Beretta. Its front bumper's all smashed."

"Is he alone?"

"I . . . I think so. I haven't seen anybody else."

Ahead, Santich could see the low, dense blanket of fog hovering over the beach; he banked left until the two jets were at what he hoped was San Luis Pass, where West Bay opened into the Gulf. He eased ahead of Melanie and banked right. Blue-green water became brown-green and then nearly disappeared as the they roared into the coastal fog. He strained through the mist-covered canopy to see the breakers give way to weed-covered sand. Santich nudged the stick forward and back to hug the rolling dunes that popped out of the fog a fraction of a second before impact. Ahead of him lay a deserted circular parking lot, out of which ran two lanes of asphalt to the east.

"Santy, I just passed a dead-end sign!"

The cell-phone connection was crystal clear, now. "Okay, you've got at least a mile. Remember, keep your eyes on the road."

Santich checked his airspeed, saw he was doing 320 knots. Not a real smooth landing if he buried the nose into a dune. A few yards away, Melanie followed the south side of the road, hanging on Santich's wing as if connected with a steel rod.

Suddenly, out of the mist popped Kyle's Honda, coming straight down the center line of the road. Santich pushed the jet even lower, barely fifteen feet above the shoulder. The exhaust trails and the wingtip vortices churned sand, dust, and fog into three twirling streams behind each plane.

At the planes' speed, the whole thing took less than a fraction of a second, but to Santich, it played itself out in surreal, vivid slow motion.

The white Honda slipped between the T-38s just as the blue Beretta emerged from the fog. Santich pushed the stick ever so slightly, rolling the jet to the right. Almost simultaneously, Melanie rolled left, and the two forty-six-foot-long fighter trainers crisscrossed, barely thirty feet in front and five feet above the speeding car. Santich noticed only a pair of bulging eyes, and a tiny yellow Hertz sticker in the corner of the windshield before the Beretta blurred past him.

He straightened out of the roll and climbed to thirty feet, checking to make sure Melanie was all right before replacing the phone that had fallen into his lap.

"... Santy? Santy? Are you okay?"

"Fine. You?"

"I'm scared shitless, but okay. Jesus! Santy, I saw it in the rearview! I was afraid you lost your wing on his roof!"

"Where are you?"

"I stopped, and I'm heading back the other way. I thought I saw him go off the road, and . . . Oh, God . . ."

Santich waited an eternal second. "Kyle?"

"Yeah. Jesus, Santy, he landed upside down. The windows are gone, and . . . oh God, Santy, his head—it's all twisted. . . . I think he's dead. Should I check? I'll call an ambulance. . . ."

"Negative, no. Just keep driving. Don't speed. Don't run stop signs. Just get home. I'll call you in a few hours. We need to hang up now."

"Jesus Christ . . . Okay. I'm with you. Don't worry about me. I'll, uh, talk to you later. Good-bye."

Santich heard the click and the ready tone before he turned off the phone and rolled right, back out over the water and into the dying sunshine. He waited until they were a good twenty-five miles offshore before he switched his transmitter back on to the lowest power level.

"Mel?"

"Yeah?"

"You okay?"

"That guy . . . He's dead, isn't he, Santy?"

"Are you all right?"

"Yeah . . . I think so. I've never . . . I've never killed anyone before."

Santich thought about the first time he'd launched a missile at a Korean MiG that was attacking his cruiser. That was before flight school, before Annapolis, even. He didn't know whether the missile had destroyed the plane or if it was a round from the fifty-millimeter cannon blazing away at it. At the moment the plane exploded, he had felt euphoria. It wasn't until that night that he began feeling the emptiness. Later, after Annapolis and Pensacola, he'd always favored flight-test and teaching assignments above carrier duty.

"It's not easy, is it?"

"I don't know. I think it was *too* easy. And we don't even have any guns on these things."

"Okay. We'll have a few beers and talk about it later. If it's any consolation, the guy in the blue car was trying to kill the guy in the white car. And the guy in the white car is a good friend of mine."

Silence.

"I don't expect it to make sense right now. But it's important. Mel?"

"Yeah, I'm with you."

"This is critical: Did you see any other cars or any people back there?"

"Negative. But I could barely see a hundred feet in front of me. I still can't believe we flew like that! If it weren't all so automatic, I don't think I could have. Anyway, the beach looked empty; I guess it's still too cold. I couldn't see the bridge through the fog, and there were no other cars."

Santich checked the fuel gauge, saw it was below one-quarter. "All right, let's go home."

23

Ten minutes of this nonsense, fifteen tops. That's what the Kennedy public affairs officer promised when she explained the format of the press conference by the launchpad. He'd dreaded it for days, knowing he would have a hard time keeping his good humor. The events of the past thirty-six hours hadn't helped.

He and Melanie returned to Ellington Field, where a ground crew quietly and unquestioningly hosed the salt spray off the two trainers. Such antics were almost expected from astronauts about to go aloft, it seemed. One hurdle down, some unknown number to go.

That night, after another long-running malfunction simulation in Building 5, they had assembled again in his living room. Hooper, despite his boasts of accessibility, had been unreachable in Washington. In his stead sat Melanie, who, by virtue of her reluctant combat, became their fifth conspirator. They hashed and rehashed what it meant. They considered bailing out and going to the police, but decided that admitting to using the T-38s as ground attack fighters would prejudice things against them. He, Trudy and Melanie urged Kyle to take his family and hide, at least until launch day. Kyle didn't want to because that meant explaining to his wife about being chased for eighty miles instead of having called the police the moment he thought he was being followed. Plus he thought he was ever so close to solving the gasket problem. A rapid pressure change was the most likely means of weakening the seal to the point where failure was inevitable. Now all he had to do was discover the mechanism. They finally persuaded him to invent an excuse and take a couple of weeks off, go to his folks' place in Tennessee with the wife and baby.

Then there was the man in the rented Beretta: Who the hell was he? And what sort of connection did he have to Kyle or Torrington or even JSC for that matter? They watched the late news, flipping the dial from channel to channel, hoping to catch something. But there'd been nothing to catch. The next morning the only mention of it was in the *Herald,* a four-paragraph blurb about the Galveston County Sheriff's Office investigating a single-car accident out at the end of Gulfshore Drive. Mike Toner, age thirty-eight, a businessman from Chicago, apparently lost control of his rented car, swerved across the oncoming lane, went up and over a sand dune and landed upside down. He was declared dead at the scene, probably of a broken neck. He had no known survivors. Police didn't know what sort of "business" he was conducting on that stretch of empty beach. Nor did they know why he suddenly slammed on the brakes and lost control, but speculated that the coastal fog might have had something to do with it. There were no witnesses, and investigators asked anyone who might have seen anything to come forward.

Kyle's immediate response, one that he whispered over the phone early the following morning upon seeing the article, was "Mafia hit man." But that flew in the face of their whole premise: that Torrington was killed by someone at Johnson. What did the Mafia know or care about space?

Anyway, Santich had asked angrily, why was Kyle still in town? He then promised to leave by the end of the day, which, with Santich and Melanie flying out to the Cape later that morning, left only Trudy in Houston. She had said she would discreetly find out if Toner ever worked at JSC, or for a NASA contractor or subcontractor in Chicago.

The two-hour flight to KSC should have been a time to

sort things out, but instead it had been consumed with a pointless argument with Alexandra O'Day, who rode in the back seat of his T-38. It had started with a discussion of the value of the Terminal Countdown Demonstration Test. It was a dress rehearsal that all shuttle crews underwent a week or two before the real thing. Santich offhandedly called it a waste of time and money. After seventy launches, NASA shouldn't need any more expensive practice countdowns. She said she thought they were a good idea, and was really looking forward to it. He answered that all rookies creamed their jeans at the thought of sitting in a real live spaceship on a real live launchpad.

That shocked her into silence, but only for a half hour. When she found her voice, she revived her idea of somehow getting some secondary experiments aboard at the last minute, some that were already flight certified, or even those that had flown before. A scientist can never have too much data, she pointed out.

It was then that Santich simply turned off the intercom between him and the back seat. What he really wanted was to talk to Melanie, who, although just off his starboard wingtip, may as well have been on the moon. He knew she still hurt badly over scaring that man off the road. It was one thing to fire missiles capable of destroying a city block in a bombing range. It was quite another to see, and to have described to you in gory detail, the effects of your airmanship. Of course, they hadn't *known* he would die, hadn't *meant* for him to die. But his losing control of his car and wrecking was certainly a predictable outcome: one that, in his rush to protect Kyle and help him escape, was never fully considered. He wanted to console her, tell her that he, too, hated the feeling it gave him and that he understood exactly how she felt.

Why he wasn't as strongly affected by the experience he didn't wholly understand. He had risked quite a lot flying the way he did. He'd jeopardized not only the upcoming mission but the entire shuttle program, something he hadn't considered until he was in bed that night, wide-eyed and

staring at the ceiling. One beachgoer, that's all it would
have taken. One old man in long pants and a windbreaker,
one young mother taking her little boy to play in the damp,
mist-chilled sand. *Yes, sir, I'm positive. They were white
and blue, with that red NASA logo on the tail. . . .*

None of that had occurred to him as he brought the
trainer barreling down the highway. What if Kyle had been
mistaken? Would he have frightened an innocent man to
death? No, not for eighty miles could Kyle have been mistaken. Certainly not after he was rammed from behind. That
was no innocent man who flipped over and broke his neck.

A chill passed through him as he realized the man in the
car must have been the same one who'd called Kyle in the
middle of the night. And that meant the threat about *Simoon*
wasn't idle; something bad had probably happened to Steve
Banke. Everyone who knew what had occurred on STS-74,
it seemed, was in danger. So did Toner sabotage the helmet? That would be a tidy ending to everything. Somehow
he knew it wasn't that simple. There was an elegant pattern
to all of this, one he felt but couldn't yet see, and Toner
was just one thread. Each time he thought he was close to
understanding, the familiar uneasiness settled in his gut and
his mouth went dry.

He wondered how much a Chicago hit man cost, and
whether it was within the budget of a jealous spouse, or if
it was an expense only a large aerospace corporation could
justify. *You don't know the type of people you're dealing
with.* Hooper had been right after all.

Such were the goings-on in Santich's head as he, Melanie and the two Alexes toured first the launchpad, then an
armored personnel carrier that would let them escape the
hellish inferno the pad would become in a fire, and finally
the amusement-park-like baskets that would whisk them
from the top of the launch tower down to a concrete bunker
a quarter mile away along steel cables that ended in rows
of rope netting, optimistically designed to slow the baskets
to a gentle stop. Finally all that was over, and the four were
arranged like mannequins in a sand strip under one of the

slide wires, *Columbia* on the pad behind them, a grinning mob of photographers and reporters in front.

The Kennedy flack introduced them to the press, and before he'd realized it, she'd given him the microphone.

"Uh, good morning," he began. "It seems Lisa has done a more than adequate job with the introductions, so I'll open it up for questions."

A mistake, he realized immediately. He should have babbled and chewed up as much of the 15 minutes as possible. He thought about switching the mike back on and continuing, but it was too late. The first grinning idiot had stepped up to the media microphone.

"Hi. Bill Marks with *This Week in Space*. This is for Commander Santich. Did you realize that if you'd launched three weeks earlier, you would have gone up on the sixteenth anniversary of STS-1, also aboard *Columbia*? And that if you launch two weeks later, you'd go on the thirty-fourth anniversary of *Faith 7*, the final Mercury flight?"

Santich grimaced. This was why he hated these things, and the temper he swore he'd check suddenly escaped. "Right. First, my military rank is captain, more correctly, captain, United States Navy, retired. In that NASA is a civilian organization, the title 'commander' doesn't really mean anything. It's actually kind of silly. After all, I'm the pilot, *Lieutenant Commander* Melanie Anderson, United States Navy, is the copilot. But since we astronauts have such big egos, no one wants to be *co*-anything. So we're commander and pilot. Next question: Yes. Last question: No."

The grinning mob fell silent. He knew that even among his colleagues, Bill Marks was regarded as a doofus: an obese, unkempt Trekkie who wrote for a few newsletters to stay close to his heroes. But Santich's testy response to a silly but harmless question had, at least momentarily, subdued the throng that ordinarily used this event to kiss as much astronaut butt as possible. Finally one of them pushed through to the microphone.

"Robert Lawrence, *Cocoa Beach Today*. Captain Santich, if I remember correctly, you were to report to the Mission Management Team on the fuel cell anomaly before 74A's Flight Readiness Review. Well, that's on Monday, and so far I haven't been able to get word one about that report. Are you one hundred percent confident the problem was instrumentation? Was it a bad 'ducer? And what have y'all done to make sure it doesn't happen on *Columbia*?''

Damn! He'd forgotten all about the fuel cell report. Bruce hadn't mentioned it again, and with all Santich had learned afterward, the thought of pursuing a nonexistent flaw in the fuel cells had never crossed his mind.

"Since the MMT has been kept apprised as to my progress verbally, I didn't think I needed an interim report on the matter," he began, inventing as he went. "As far as I'm concerned, the fuel cell problem is a nonissue for 74A. The anomaly was traced using the standard troubleshooting procedures, and the most likely cause was a bad transistor between the input signal from the transducer and the multiplexer.''

Now, why did he say that? He should have kept it vague, something they wouldn't be able to check. God, he hoped Bruce hadn't released some contrary cover story he didn't know about! He decided to finish vaguely.

"I can tell you this much: I'm absolutely, one hundred percent certain that what happened to *Atlantis*'s fuel cells will not happen to *Columbia*'s. And I'll report that to the FRR without hesitation next week.''

Santich could tell from Lawrence's scowl that he wasn't satisfied, but fortunately, a smartly dressed blond had wedged herself between him and the mike.

"Julie Kensit from WFSH-TV in Orlando. This is for the two rookies: How does it feel to be making your first flight on such an important mission to both astronomy as well as the future of NASA?''

Never before had Santich so welcomed a softball. Alexandra looked questioningly at Santich, and he ceded her the microphone.

"Well, I, for one, couldn't be more excited. I think this

mission is just crucial, not just for high-energy physics and astronomy, even though if that were the only benefit, getting the Gamma Ray Observatory back to fully operational status, that would be . . .''

Santich tuned her out after the first thirty seconds, wondering instead about Lawrence. They were going to need someone in the press to tell their story. Maybe Bob Lawrence would be just the man. He didn't seem to like NASA very much; such a story would certainly appeal to him. And he did seem aggressive enough to root out those details that Santich wouldn't be able to provide. Yes, maybe he'd give Bob a call while he was in Florida. That would also serve the double purpose of keeping him from writing embarrassing articles about why *Columbia* was launching before *Atlantis*'s problems were fully understood. You could never tell when an article like that would fall on the desk of some influential anti-NASA congressman and spur him to start an annoying, fleet-grounding investigation.

''. . . with all the benefits this country sees from its space program, it would be *folly* not to continue investing in it. In fact, the average American spends more on potato chips each year than on his or her share of the space program. Surely new materials, more efficient manufacturing and drugs to cure horrible diseases like AIDS and cancer is worth what we spend on a high-fat junk food, isn't it?''

This once, Santich actually enjoyed Alexandra's sermon, for it chewed up the remainder of the question-and-answer period. Lisa Mulligan stepped in artfully, took the mike from Alexandra and ended the session. At once, the pack of photographers and reporters converged on the four flight-suited figures, taking pictures, shouting questions, even asking for autographs.

Santich smiled and nodded, but ignored the queries as he wandered back to the astronaut bus parked in front of the bunker. Through the government-issue Ray-Bans, he spotted Bob Lawrence still scowling at him and walking toward the media bus. Santich plotted an intercept course that would give him a quick word, maybe let him set up a phone call later. He got to within fifteen feet of his target when he felt warm softness against his right arm.

"We need to talk."

Jo Pointer had materialized out of the crowd and grabbed hold of his arm, pressing it against the side of her ample bosom. Santich hadn't even noticed her earlier. He tried to remember exactly what he had promised her.

"I'm sorry I haven't gotten back to you yet. I just got caught up with the mission, and have put the book off until . . ."

"You and I need to talk. Not about the book," she breathed in a conspiratorial whisper.

She leaned up to his ear. "A little bird told me that a pair of T-38s were kicking up beach sand a couple of days ago."

Santich froze. *How much did she know?* "Where and when?"

"Tonight. Eight o'clock. At a little Japanese steak house on Merritt Island, at State Road 3 and 520. It's called Tai-Ho. Don't be late."

With that, she faded back into the mob, leaving Santich staring.

"You okay? You look like you've seen a ghost," Melanie said as she sidled next to him.

"Yeah. I'm fine. Something's come up. I'll tell you later."

24

Santich kept studying well after he had already memorized it. It was the usual Japanese steak house fare: shrimp, chicken, steak, shrimp and chicken, shrimp and steak, chicken and steak.

"What's good here?"

Jo Pointer leaned forward over the shared menu, giving Santich a long look at her pale, blue-veined cleavage. She wore a green low-cut silk blouse and black stretch pants. He noticed when she walked in that she didn't seem to be wearing anything underneath the pants; he saw now that she wore nothing beneath the blouse either.

"It's all pretty good. I eat here every time I come to the Cape. I'm partial to the steak and shrimp, myself."

Santich looked up to find the kimono-clad waitress deliver two cups of sake and then stand expectantly for their order. "Two steak and shrimp," he said.

The waitress bowed and turned away, leaving Santich to resume his inspection of his dinner partner. The large table with the built-in grill was made to seat eight, but they had it, and half the dining room, to themselves. "So," he began.

"Sew. A needle pulling thread," she said, and laughed.

He forced a grin. Was he being seduced? Or coerced? "So what can I tell you about T-38s on the beach?"

"You can deny it."

182

"I don't know what I'm supposed to deny."

"You're supposed to deny that you were in NASA 911 as it and NASA 914 came screaming down the beach road west of Galveston two days ago, so low they were kicking up a sandstorm. You can deny they were covered with salt spray when they got back to Ellington, like they'd flown right at the wave tops, maybe to stay below air traffic control radar. And you can deny that about that same time, according to the Galveston County Sheriff's Office, a rental car driven by a Chicago businessman went off the road, killing him."

Santich looked for cracks he could try to widen. "Well, I can't help you with that last thing. I mean, if the police say a car accident happened the same time that you're telling me these T-38s were in the area, I have no way of knowing. . . ."

He sighed, knowing it was pointless. He took a sip from his cup; the warm liquid grew even warmer as it went down. "So what, if I may ask, are you planning to do about it?"

Her thin lips pulled into a smile. "My little bird never lies," she said smugly.

He put down the cup, stared at her wordlessly. She had him, and she knew it. What price would she exact, particularly after he'd so callously wrung her for information? For the umpteenth time since he'd walked in to Bruce sitting at his desk, he saw the whole thing falling apart. His only hope was that Jo Pointer was an unabashed NASA booster, and she might not want to write anything that would hurt her beloved program.

"Forgive me if I take some pleasure in this. The mighty Dean of American Astronauts: felled by a mere journalist, and a woman at that!"

Surely she wanted something, needed something. Otherwise she wouldn't be here. Otherwise he would have already awakened one morning to her article reprinted in every newspaper in the country, accompanied by a blurb reporting that in light of recent developments, NASA Headquarters had delayed STS-74A indefinitely, and would likely change the crew before launch.

He balled his napkin and dropped it on the table. "I'll borrow a line from Bruce here. If you kids will excuse me, I have a busy day tomorrow."

She grabbed his arm and pulled him down. "You can't leave! You haven't eaten! No shuttle commander should start a practice countdown on an empty stomach." She gingerly replaced the napkin on his lap; he was repelled but couldn't help feeling a twinge of excitement. "Okay. I'm finished gloating. I apologize, but you had it coming, with that come-on about an autobiography. I should have known better than to believe, even for a minute, that Santiago Santich cared enough of what people thought of him to do an autobiography."

She sipped her sake. He sat stone-faced, watching her. He would give her nothing until he knew what she was up to.

"Anyway, of *course* I asked my publishing friends what they'd heard about a project on you at Pantheon, and they hadn't. Period. So I got to thinking: If that wasn't the point of that lunch, something else was. Like maybe, Sam Torrington? Like maybe, his ex-wife? A few discreet questions and, sure enough, my little bird tells me you're *dating* Trudy Torrington!" She smiled slyly. "Does Emily know?"

A Japanese man outfitted in white chef's garb and pushing a trolley of ingredients approached with a cheery "Herrooo!" and began smearing butter over the stainless steel grill top.

Jo leaned over, pushing her silk-covered breast against his bare forearm. He could feel the erect nipple underneath, and again felt the funny warm feeling all over. Again he felt ashamed of himself. "We'll have to continue this discussion later," she whispered.

A half hour of corny jokes about Japanese french fries, Japanese hot dogs and Japanese hamburgers ensued. Jo laughed and applauded enthusiastically while Santich smiled politely. Unlike before, when she strove to make a good impression and had eaten sparingly, she all but inhaled her dinner, devouring each dish before the next was finished. In short order their plates were cleared and Santich awaited the return of his Amex card.

"I suppose it's time to finish our, uh, discussion?" he asked.

She shook her head. "Not here."

He looked around. Only two of the other tables were occupied. "Why not? This place is deserted."

"I need something to write with!" She crossed her eyes at him and made a face; he wondered whether other men found that endearing.

"You didn't bring them with you?"

She spread her arms, inviting him to frisk her. "I don't carry a purse, and does it look like I have any place to keep a notebook?"

He looked over her outfit again, signed the credit-card voucher and stood. She rose also, leading him out to the parking lot, from where she led him a few blocks to the Holiday Inn on Route 520's commercial strip. They parked their respective rentals, and he followed her to her second-floor room.

"I hope you don't mind talking in here," she said as she flicked on the lights. "There's a bunch of reporters staying here, and the last thing I need is for them to see us at the bar and horn in on my scoop."

He glanced around the standard room: two double beds, a nineteen-inch color RCA, beige carpeting, a small round table by the windows, with two stuffed chairs pushed beside it. The nearer of the beds was littered with panty hose, bras and various clothing spilling from an overnight bag that Jo hastened to refill and slide onto the floor.

"What scoop might that be, exactly?" he asked, walking to one of the seats before the table.

"You know, exactly." She kicked off the black high heels, picked up a notebook from the dresser and sat cross-legged before him on the bed next to the table. "You want anything? Wine? Beer? Water?"

"No, thank you. I'm fine. I'd appreciate it if you got to the point."

Jo sighed, then crossed her arms and leaned a little forward, giving him a clear view down the canyon again. He wondered if she knew what effects her movements had on her anatomy, quickly decided she knew *exactly* what she was doing.

"You don't know what it's like to be a reporter. You work your whole life for small-minded idiots who think they know your beat better than you do. You write for a public that really couldn't care less. You get to see really neat stuff from the sideline, but you're not part of them. You just write about them. Take the moon landings: an incredible, important part of human history! But could I take part? No! The best available to *me* was to say how wonderful it was for people like *you*, who actually *did* take part."

He stared at the unlined face, the smooth, fresh skin. No way was she old enough to have written about Apollo. "I didn't realize you worked for World News Service in the third grade."

Again she flashed the crossed eyes. "You know what I mean."

This was becoming tiresome, but he knew he didn't have a choice. She had played her trump, and it was a doozy. "We make our decisions, and we have to live by them. If you really wanted, you could've become a scientist, worked hard, and then kissed NASA's ass to be a mission specialist. Look at Alex O'Day."

She sat straight up, taking away his view. "Maybe I should have. But there are other ways." She arched her eyebrows. "I hear that Headquarters wants to send a public affairs officer up to sell the program to Joe Six-Pack. I hear they're waiting to see what the White House thinks."

He'd never heard such a stupid thing; knowing Headquarters, that probably meant it was true. "Please," he sighed. "Can we please get to the point? What do you want from me?"

She leaned forward again, her eyes locked on his. "I want the full story on Sam Torrington and STS-74. It wasn't like they said, was it?"

So she had guessed. Or was starting to guess along the right track. Wearily he played dumb. "What about Torrington?"

She slapped her notebook with an open hand. "You *know* what about Torrington!" She took a deep breath. "Okay. I know something is up, and I know it's tied in with your buzzing that guy off the beach road the other day." She paused for a moment, continued. "Look, if a reporter is lucky in their career, they get one shot at something *really* big, like a Pulitzer. This is my shot. Do you know what it would mean to win that? I could write my own ticket, do anything, work anywhere I wanted. All those highbrow assholes I deal with from other papers, the other wires: 'Oh there's Jo, polishing NASA's knob again.' I'd give anything to see the looks on their faces when my name's announced."

Slowly, the idea began buzzing. . . . Why couldn't Jo Pointer write the article they needed? She seemed hungry enough, plus she was *right here,* in his hair, and was going to write *something.* He may as well get her to write what he wanted.

"So, I know I have a great story here, with what I've already got. But I bet I'd have an even better one if you talk to me."

He sat quietly, feigning great reluctance. "Well, you're absolutely right: It is an even better story."

She smiled, pushed her shoulders back and her chest out. "I knew it!"

"But," he began. "But I'll only tell it to you on certain conditions."

He waited for her reaction. As he expected, she grew defensive, crossing her arms. Her smile disappeared.

"I would think that *I* should be the one offering conditions, not you."

He stood as if to leave. "Okay. You go right ahead with your article. Tell the world that Melanie and I flew too low near the beach. I'll bet the tower at Ellington will say we never went below three hundred feet, and that was when we were well offshore. I'll find a half-dozen astronauts who'll swear they routinely fly low, at five hundred feet, near the beach. It's good training for contingency abort scenarios. Now. You want to hear the conditions? Or do I walk out the door?"

"Such as?"

"Right," he nodded. "First, your article *must* appear immediately after we land. It can appear no earlier than that. That's not negotiable. Agreed?"

"Now, wait. I can't control when something runs. If my editor wants to go with something, I can't really hold her back."

Santich stood again, and her eyes widened in alarm.

"But I suppose she doesn't have to *know* about the story until *Columbia* lands," she conceded.

"Good. Second, not one word about that car accident on the beach, or any T-38s near the coast. Okay?"

She swallowed, pursed her lips, seemed to weigh what she was about to hear against what she already knew. "Okay."

He allowed himself a smile; it had gone easier than he'd thought. "Okay. Get your pencil ready: Sam Torrington didn't die in a car wreck, he died on orbit, during that EVA. STS-74's emergency landing was based on his death, and the story about the fuel cells was a cover-up. Any questions?"

Her pen had frozen over the pad, and for a minute she was speechless. When she recovered her voice, the questions were rapid-fire, one after the other, until finally he began a step-by-step narrative of his role in the matter, leaving out the names of his cohorts, and also deleting his and Melanie's dune-top run down the beach. At first she scribbled furiously, but later she sat mute and motionless, her shoulders sagging, the bright blue eyes unable even to blink.

When he finished, they both sat silently for a while. "I don't know what to say," she began. "I can barely believe it, except that it ties up all the loose ends floating around for the last month." She fell silent again, blinked. "So someone actually killed him. Frankly, I wouldn't be surprised if it was his ex-wife, or maybe some other ex-lover."

Inwardly he flinched, but managed to hold his stony expression.

"So who do you think did it?"

He shrugged. "I don't know, yet. I may soon, though."

"You'll tell me when you do?"

"Absolutely."

She went quiet again. "God, you know, when this gets out, Marty Bruce is finished. Maybe even the whole shuttle program. I wonder if it wouldn't be better just to let it go?"

Klaxons went off in his head, and he fought to keep his voice even. "Yes, Bruce is gone. But frankly, that's what he deserves. And no one will question the shuttle program. After all, the commander of the most recent, gloriously successful mission will have told the story, right? That proves the program is self-policing and can be trusted." He watched her expression carefully, but the eyes were focused on another, inner world, and gave away nothing. "Besides, do you want to win that Pulitzer or don't you?"

"Hmmmm? Oh no, I'm not saying I won't write it. It's just that, I guess I need to be careful *how* I write it. You know. I'd hate to cut off my nose to spite my face. Anyway, it's a fantastic story, especially the cover-up." She paused, thought for a moment. "It's hard to believe that someone I slept with was actually murdered. In orbit no less."

Santich tried to detect sorrow in the statement but couldn't. There was almost a sense of accomplishment that he found unnerving. Finally, it seemed, she had taken part in space history. He stood up, went through the ritual pat down of wallet in back pocket, keys in hip pocket. "I'll leave you to your grief. I've got to get up early to pretend like I'm lifting off.''

''Wait.'' She scrambled up from the bed and grabbed his elbow. ''You don't have to leave just yet, do you?''

She had edged closer, so that with each inhaled breath, the silk of her blouse grazed the hairs on his forearms.

''You have more questions? I thought we covered everything.''

''For the story, yes. I mean, we're both adults. I mean, come on, Santy, I dressed like this for a reason!''

He gulped softly, thought for a moment how easy it would be, but immediately chided himself. If he was going to cheat on his wife, he should at least have the courage to do it with someone decent, like Trudy Cortain.

''Come on, Santy. I promise I won't bite. And if I do, I promise you won't mind.'' She winked and allowed herself to press more firmly against his arm. ''From what I've heard of the reviews, I'm not half bad.''

He'd heard the reviews, too. He remembered something to the effect that the visuals were the best part. ''Please, Jo.'' He struggled to find some kind way out. ''I can't say I'm not flattered, but really. Emily and I are getting back together after four years, and I just couldn't.''

''What she doesn't know can't hurt her. Or you.'' She winked again. ''Anyway, don't you want to feel some firm young flesh again for a change?''

That got his hackles up. Who was this tramp to insult someone she'd never met? ''The way five dozen other male astronauts have felt it?''

She drew back half an inch. ''They weren't all males. Besides, there haven't been *that* many.'' She pushed closer again. ''You'd be the first moonwalker.''

He laughed, pulled free. ''So that's the attraction! Now I get it.'' He laughed again, thinking of her bra in Torrington's personal locker. ''Sorry. There are eleven others, though. You can give them a try.''

He made his way to the door, turned. ''Let's keep this on a professional level, okay? I'm sure you have my home number. Call me if you think of anything else."

As he walked down the hallway toward the stairs, he heard her voice from the doorway. "I'm a persistent woman, Santy. And I'm used to getting what I want." He grinned to himself and kept walking.

25

For a split second, Santich had a frightening moment of déja vù. It was 4:30 A.M., with a full day of simulations to start in an hour. He'd gone to Building 4 to grab a procedures handbook. There, sitting at his desk, leafing through the papers on the desktop, was a nattily suited, wide-awake, clean-shaven Marty Bruce.

"I've taken the liberty to make some coffee." He nodded to the half-full pot on the machine behind him. "Would you like a cup?"

"You're too kind," Santich said dryly. "Don't you ever sleep?"

"The luxuries of the carefree. Someday, Captain Santich, when you have my job, you won't have time to sleep either."

Santich hesitated, then continued hanging up his raincoat. "What makes you think I want your job?"

"Don't you? Why else would you knock yourself out on a problem that I specifically told you not to worry about?"

The beady eyes stared intently, the jaw set aggressively. Santich wondered how he'd found out, and whether he knew how far Santich planned to go.

"Somebody had to." He sat down on the visitor's side of the desk, picked up the procedures manual he had come for. "If you'd done some of the work you said you'd do, maybe I could have gone on with mine."

"Maybe I've done exactly what I said I would: made sure that what happened on 74 absolutely can't happen on 74 Alpha."

Santich scoffed. "He was murdered, you son of a bitch!"

Bruce tilted his head ever so slightly, his version of a shrug. "Most likely, yes. The helmet seal does appear to have been tampered with. As to who and why: a jealous lover, perhaps, or a colleague worried about his relationship with the authorities in that bid-rigging investigation. In either event, you must agree that this killer or killers have a certain level of sophistication, no? To be able to kill a man as he orbits one hundred eighty miles overhead. And if so, you will agree that they're probably not the sort to stick up a convenience store and shoot the clerk. Hence, they are not a real threat to society, are they? And if that's the case, then we as members of that society certainly have lost the public-safety component for our traditional desire to find and imprison them. Which leaves only the punishment component. And when I weigh the need to punish the guilty versus the continuation of the program, I unequivocally come down on the side of the program. Besides, you have nothing to fear on your flight. Surely his murderer or murderers had reason to kill him. And surely they can't have reason to kill you, correct?"

Santich tried to digest this. "So you've finished your investigation, and the killers get to go free?"

Bruce sighed. "In this case, yes. Unless, of course, you personally are willing to mete out justice without adversely affecting the program."

"You mean kill them myself?" Santich blinked, then snorted. "You're mad. I could tell you to kiss my ass right now, and refuse to fly."

The thin face broke into a sly smile. "Yes, but you won't. You want it too much. That eight-minute joyride. A week of playtime. You're so close, you wouldn't dare risk losing it." He paused, looked at the ceiling. "Can you imagine what a dangerous fellow that would be? An astronaut with enough moral fiber to do the right thing, even if it meant never flying again? You were a little like that once, weren't you?''

His belly constricted. Why was Bruce goading him? He thought again of Option Zulu, tried to read in Bruce's face whether he was actually capable of it.

''Anyway, I have nothing to fear,'' Bruce continued, standing. ''You and I are basically the same. We know we have a mission, and that it's too important to let it slip away over petty details.'' He smiled the jackal's smile again. ''Don't be so insulted, Santy: I said *basically* the same. You're a lot more sensitive than I am. Who knows? Maybe that's a good thing. Maybe on my deathbed I'll regret not having been more like you.''

He walked to the door, stopped short. ''This wasn't entirely a social call: I've invested too much of my life in this to let you piss it away. Don't fuck with me in orbit, Santich. I used 2601 once; I won't hesitate to use it again.''

The terse warning echoed through Santich's head as the door clicked shut, kept echoing through that morning's rendezvous simulation, that afternoon's runs in the T-38s, that evening's contingency abort scenarios.

It wasn't until late that night before he could call Trudy and arrange to meet her at his house.

''Kyle finally left town,'' he explained. ''He's at his parents' place in Knoxville. Hoop's still in D.C. We traded phone messages a couple of times, but that's it. I don't even know if he knows about Toner yet.''

Trudy sat down in the love seat, the one he and Emily used to share, and pulled off her shoes. She massaged one foot, then the other. She, like Santich, had been working all day.

''Is Melanie okay about the other day?''

Santich sat on the sofa and laid his head back. ''I think so. It wasn't much fun.'' He remembered again the momentary glimpse of Toner's eyes. ''We didn't mean to kill him, you know. What am I saying; Melanie didn't mean to do anything. *I* didn't mean to kill him.''

''I know,'' Trudy said quickly, reassuringly.

"Just needed to scare him enough to let Kyle escape. Though having two fighter jets screaming straight at you, it's a wonder he didn't have a heart attack."

Neither spoke for a minute. "He would have killed Kyle," Trudy said finally. "Like he probably killed Steve Banke. As far as we know, he might have even killed Mike Etheridge. I still haven't been able to find him."

"I know. Which is why I think Mel will put it behind her, eventually. But now Bruce is threatening me, telling me not to fuck with his program. Or else."

"Meaning what?" Trudy asked. "He won't assign you any more flights?"

He shrugged. "I have no idea. He knows I don't want any more flights." Maybe Option Zulu was alive and well, and their Shuttle Training Aircraft flight back to Houston would simply disappear over the Gulf, just like Banke had disappeared. "Maybe the bastard plans to kill the whole crew after we get back."

Trudy's eyes widened. "You really don't think so, do you? I mean, that doesn't make sense! It would devastate the program!"

"You're right. Losing a whole crew, even in an STA, makes NASA look like a bunch of idiots, even if it *was* right after a successful mission. No, I can't believe he'd take such drastic measures to cover up what looked like an accident, and then turn around and do something that would bring even worse publicity." He paused, remembered the thin smile, the unblinking eyes. "Still and all, that guy makes me nervous. Maybe we're missing something." He lifted his head. "Maybe you ought to leave town, too."

Trudy shook her head. "I can't. There's no one left to work console on EVA. If I disappear, the mission is shot."

Santich shrugged. "Maybe that wouldn't be such a bad thing. I think Hooper was right: We're in way over our heads. I still have no idea who Toner was, or why he was killing everyone who knew what happened."

"Not everyone," Trudy interjected. "Halvorson, Habuda, Orlov. Even Bruce. They all know what happened, but they seem to be okay.''

''Seem to be. I guess we can't know for sure unless we ask them. And even *then* we might not know for sure. So it looks like Toner was only after those people he thought—''

''Or somebody thought.''

''Or somebody thought,'' Santich agreed, ''were likely to talk. On the other hand, I haven't gotten any midnight phone calls; I haven't been chased a hundred miles.''

''You're a celebrity, Santy. No one would dare. It would be counterproductive.''

''But you're not a celebrity. That's why you should go hide for a couple of weeks.'' He found her looking into his eyes, and he looked back. ''I'd feel awful if something happened. I mean, I'm the one who dragged you into this.''

''You didn't drag me; I *wanted* to get involved. Remember?'' She got out of the love seat and moved next to him on the couch, nestling her head against his shoulder. ''Just another week, Santy. Then we tell the world.''

He fidgeted uncomfortably. Why, after four years of celibacy, were the younger women coming out of the woodwork *now,* just as he and Emily were talking again? Where were they three years earlier, in his hour of need? Just that morning he had called and promised to take her to Captiva Island for their anniversary, on May 18, come hell or high water. He'd promised to take her and the grandkids fishing, that he'd teach them how to catch the Big One. She'd laughed, not believing *Columbia* would even lift off by May 18, and asked him how he planned to teach *anyone* how to catch fish. Was he bringing a guide?

Happy domesticity, his golden years just two weeks away, and suddenly he was fighting them off with a stick. He blinked, remembering Jo Pointer. ''I told Space Slut all about it when I was at the Cape.''

Trudy's jaw dropped. ''Why?''

''I had no choice. She had me by the . . . uh, she had me trapped. Somehow she found out about the flight over the beach. She said either I told her what was going on or she'd print that article.''

"That little bitch," Trudy breathed. "Santy, I don't like this. I don't trust her. You know she used to call my house and hang up? I didn't know it was her until Sam told me. She was afraid he was coming around my place. Cheating on her.''

Santich smiled; the last bit of *that* puzzle had fallen into place. "Well, we had to tell someone in the press, right? I'll admit my first choice was that Bob Lawrence guy at the Cocoa Beach paper. But Jo forced my hand." He could see Trudy was unconvinced. "Anyway, we'll be fine. She promised to write up what I told her the day after *Columbia* lands. If she doesn't follow through, we go to the cops and call a press conference to announce what we've done. Assuming Toner was working with somebody, that should get them off our backs, once and for all.''

Trudy thought for a moment. "But we still don't know who killed Sam, unless it was Toner.''

Santich sighed. "No. We don't. That's a problem, with launch in five days. But I don't think it's catastrophic. I think we have enough now to make a respectable presentation to the police. By then, *Columbia* will be home safely, the GRO will be saved, and everyone will see that Bruce and his circle of evil, not the rest of us, are the problem at NASA, and everyone else will live happily ever after.''

Trudy sat up, smiling. "And you'll have gotten your seventh flight.''

Santich blushed. "And I'll have gotten my seventh flight.''

She poked him in the ribs, tickling him until he flinched. "You're like a little boy who can't wait for Christmas, aren't you?" She smiled, leaning back against his shoulder. "I wish I were going with you.''

"Really? Emily never did. She couldn't see the point of it. But then, she never liked roller coasters either." He felt strangely guilty for mentioning his wife to Trudy. But the more he thought about it, the more guilty he felt for *not* mentioning her more often.

"Well, I see the point in it. Maybe Sam was right. Maybe I *was* just jealous about him making it and me not. God! Seeing the planet turn under you, that's got to be incredible!"

"Boy, you're not kidding!" he answered giddily. "You climb up and up and up, and soon the main engines tail off, and the blue sky gets blacker and blacker, and eventually you're in night, while it's still daylight under you. You cross the Atlantic, then Africa, the Indian Ocean. . . . I just can't get tired of it." He thought again about free-floating above it all, something he'd never experience. "I guess the only thing I wish I'd done that I won't is an orbital space walk."

"Sam finally got to do one," she answered quietly.

"I'm sorry. That was thoughtless." He paused. "I don't mean to make this sound like the end-all of existence. Like Emily used to say, all the wonders you can see from up there are all down here. We should appreciate that."

She lay against him quietly in silence. "You've mentioned her twice now in the last five minutes," she said softly.

He swallowed. "I know. It's to remind myself not to get carried away by the moment. I can't tell you how nice it feels to have you lying here like this. I think it would be very easy for something to happen that we'd both regret later."

She remained still. Even her breathing seemed to have stopped. "Do you love her?"

He wondered. Did he? Or had he just grown accustomed to having her around for thirty-six years, and was ready to return to that after four years alone? Maybe there was no difference; maybe after all the angst and passion and longing was through, maybe *that* was what was left, and *that* was love.

From the kitchen, the phone began its self-centered

clamor, and Santich extricated himself. "Saved by the bell," he murmured.

Trudy released her hold and let him pass. He glanced at his watch, saw it was nearly 1:00 A.M., and grabbed the receiver by the fourth ring.

"Guess what I'm wearing."

He blinked. He thought only men made obscene calls. He tried to place the voice but couldn't. "Who is this?"

"Jo!" the voice answered merrily. "Guess what I'm wearing!"

"A pressure suit. Do you realize it's one in the morning?"

"Nope. I'm wearing absolutely nothing. Except a smile." She paused for a reaction, got none. "I just got out of the bath, and my skin is all pink and warm. You want to come over?"

In spite of himself, Santich imagined her stepping out of a tub, the water slipping down the soapy flesh. "You know, I'm old enough to be your father."

"Ah, but you're not! A crucial distinction!"

"Did you call for a reason?"

"I asked around our Chicago bureau about our friend Toner, which, by the way, is one of several aliases. His real name was Martin. He's been arrested eleven times and convicted four, all for relatively minor stuff. Extortion. Threatening a witness. Assault. He did eighteen months in state prison for the assault. That was five years ago. He's stayed out of trouble since."

Santich's heart skipped a beat. Kyle had been right; there was no way he was an employee of an aerospace company, not with a felony record. "Meaning?" he asked, though he already knew.

"Meaning, according to the boys in the bureau, that he's either what's known as a soldier in one of the organized crime families, or he's a small-time hood." She paused. "Are you sure this guy was involved with NASA? Maybe your buddy is a compulsive gambler and owes money to people he shouldn't owe money to."

He tried to imagine Kyle gambling, or doing anything compulsively. "Like I said, a person called my friend nightly. On the final call he told him that *Simoon* was missing. *Simoon* is Steve Banke's boat, which, by the way, is now officially overdue in Key West. And within two days, my friend is getting chased down Galveston Island. Now, either Toner made those phone calls, and knew something about *Simoon,* or we have two unrelated crazies out there whose stories just happen to mesh. Which makes more sense?''

"Well, I don't know. . . ."

"Anyway, it doesn't matter, because your article isn't going to mention Galveston. Right?"

For a few seconds, all he could hear on the line was her breathing. He wondered again if she was really naked. "Is there anything else?" he asked finally.

"No. Except I haven't given up on you yet."

"Jo, launch is in five days. I'm already in health stabilization. Plus I'm happily married, thank you."

"You're happily married because Emily is in another state, and you're boinking Trudy Cortain to your heart's content. Don't deny it; isn't that her car out front?"

Santich could feel his ears growing hot. "Who I choose to 'boink' is none of your business. Anyway, we're just chatting about the mission. And your bra size. And whether you're going to want any more lingerie sent up this flight."

A long silence answered him, and he knew he had won the last word. "Good-bye, Jo," he said, and hung up.

He chuckled to himself as he walked back to the living room, where he found Trudy looking at the wedding photographs on the mantelpiece. Two were of his son and daughter and their spouses. The third showed a very young Navy flier in full dress uniform and a slim, auburn-haired beauty on his arm wearing a form-fitting white dress.

"She was very beautiful," Trudy said, still looking at the photo.

"She still is," Santich answered. He sat down on the

love seat. "Does the word 'boink' mean what I think it does?"

Trudy turned with a smile, sat on the sofa. "I think so. Why? Who was that?"

"Jo Pointer."

Trudy laughed out loud. "I should have known. Did she tell you she was naked? If she did, I'm sorry to burst your bubble. She says that to every man. Sam told me."

Santich felt himself blush and wondered if it was visible. "She wanted to know how come I could boink you but not her. I asked her what underwear she wanted me to take up for her."

"You didn't!" she laughed. "Good for you! She called at this hour to flirt?"

"No, not entirely." He remembered Kyle's voice describing the upside-down Beretta, the twisted neck, and grew somber. "She said she was able to check out this Toner. He was either a small-time hood or a small-time mafioso. Which means my theory that he worked for Gates Rubber or Rochester Products or Kerro Group is pretty much shot."

"Not necessarily. Maybe someone from one of those companies hired him."

"Yeah, maybe. But that doesn't help us. With him dead, there's no way to find out who hired him. Well, maybe there is, with bank records and such, but that's not the sort of thing we can get."

"Oh, well. Like you said earlier: This doesn't change our plan, right? We still go public after the flight."

He bit his lip and shook his head. "If they can hire one hit man, why can't they hire another? I don't like it. Listen, if you won't go disappear for a while, then would you at least stay somewhere else during the mission? With a friend, maybe?"

"God, Santy, if I'm really in danger, I wouldn't feel right dragging someone else into it. Besides, I'll be fine. The boys are at my mom's, and I'll be in Mission Control six-

teen or twenty hours a day anyway. I'll just duck out for a
few hours for some sleep once in a while.''

Santich thought for a moment. "How about here? It's
closer to the center than your place. And nobody would
think of looking here.''

She looked around the room. "Do you really think I need
to?''

"I'm hoping no, you don't need to. I'm hoping Toner
did this alone, and that if he *did* have accomplices, his death
scared them off. But I don't think we should rely on that.
You stay here until landing, deal?''

"Okay. Deal. But what if they follow me, like they followed Kyle?''

He nodded. "Good point. Is there someone who could
give you a ride? Someone you trust not to ask questions?''

She smiled. "As a matter of fact, there's this guy in the
back room who's like ten years younger than me. He's been
chatting me up for two years, and I'd bet he'd fall all over
himself for the chance to give me a ride.''

"Great. Just watch the road, make sure you're not being
followed, okay? I can't come swooping in to the rescue
with *Columbia*." He went through a mental checklist. "I'll
get you a key tomorrow. In fact, I think me, you and Hoop
should meet, just to get everything squared away before I
leave. Can you think of anything we're forgetting?''

Trudy shook her head slowly. "I just wish there was
some way we could talk to each other during the mission.
I mean, it's crazy that even though I'm on console, I might
as well be on a desert island.''

"Even if we could talk, the whole planet would be listening in." He smiled. "I know: We'll get on Air-to-
Ground Two and talk in pig latin.''

Trudy bit her lower lip and absently teased her hair.
"What if you took a cell phone with you? Like you had
the other day?''

"No, I think you have to be within a few miles of a
repeater. We'll be two hundred nautical miles up when we
pass overhead." He thought a moment. "But if we had real

UHF radios, we could communicate whenever *Columbia* is over the horizon. You don't know any hams, do you?"

She turned with a smile. "Like in SAREX? Shuttle Amateur Radio Experiment, where these nerdy guys with all the radio gear go to the schools so kids can ask you what it feels like to be in space? Guess who's a charter member of the local outfit? That back-room guy!"

"That would be great, if he's got something." Santich rested his face in his hands, looked up to find Trudy's eyes closed and head back. "I guess we've worried about this as much as we can for one night."

Trudy opened her eyes, looked at her watch, and jumped up. "My God! I had no idea! Santy, we have that final sim in less than four hours."

He nodded, stood to walk her out. "About earlier," he began. "I think I . . ."

"Don't," she interrupted. "It's over and done." She walked through the open door and turned back. "When this is finished, Santy, I want to be your friend. Yours and Emily's friend, both. If anything had happened earlier, it would have made that impossible."

She got into her Volvo station wagon. "See you tomorrow."

26

Hooper stared uncomprehendingly at the cassette-player-size gadget in one hand, then at the squarish object in the other before returning both to the Bacardi Rum carton on Santich's coffee table.

"This is as complicated as what we had in the military," he said.

"This *is* what they have in the military," Santich said, looking up at Trudy. "This is the same stuff they had us test on that DoD mission, 51-C, back in eighty-five. Military-Man-in-Space, they called it. They wanted to see if a guy in a spaceship could sit there with Zeiss binoculars and a UHF radio and tell people on the ground where the enemy tanks were. Where did your friend get it?"

Trudy shrugged. "I thought it was regular ham radio equipment. I told him I wanted to talk to a crewmember on the next flight without being overheard. He gave me three sets."

"Somehow I doubt these operate on FCC-approved amateur frequencies. But I guess that's all the better for our purposes. No one to overhear us." Santich picked up the radio and plugged in the squarish box with an attached cable. "This is the antenna, I take it?"

Trudy nodded. "You point it in the direction you want to talk. Those suction cups will stick to windows. And then"— she slipped on the headset—"this plugs in here. . . . And you're all set."

"What's the range?" Hooper asked, fiddling with the buttons on his set.

"Line-of-sight," Trudy answered. "If you can't see it, you can't talk with it."

"So just watch the tracking chart in Mission Control to see where we are," Santich said. "We ought to be able to talk whenever we're within about a thousand miles of Houston. That gives us two or three passes each day, with as much as ten minutes per pass."

"Should we contact each other on each pass?" Trudy turned her set on, checked the battery level, and turned it back off. "He said the batteries would last for an hour of transmitting, or twenty hours of receiving. He set each one to the same frequency. He said it would work best with the tuner."

Santich opened the back of his unit, looking for factory specifications. He found a sticky square where a label had been removed. "Well, I have no idea how much these have been modified. If they use frequencies the military also uses, we could be overheard. And if they overhear us, they might try to track you down. We better talk as little as possible. Maybe turn the sets on at each pass, but only transmit if there's something important."

"Like if a killer is chasing us through the JSC parking lot?" Trudy asked with a half smile.

Santich looked over at Hooper, noticing how quiet he had been. He had finally caught him at home early that morning to arrange the meeting. He'd agreed docilely. There had been none of the earlier pleas to abandon their scheme, to give up before it was too late.

"I guess I owe you an apology, Hoop. Remember? You warned us about the kind of people we're dealing with? You were right."

Hooper shrugged weakly. His eyes were puffy, with nearly black circles beneath. "I know we're close enough to launch now that you can taste it. Otherwise I'd try to talk you out of it.''

"Talk us out of? You mean our little inquiry?" Santich asked.

"The whole thing," Hooper replied. "My gut instinct on this, way back in the Outpost, the day of Banke's landing, was my best: Leave this alone; stay the hell out. Look what's happened. If someone's gone to the trouble of finding a professional killer, for God's sake, you know they're playing hardball. They're not going to let some amateur private eyes fuck with them.''

Santich watched his friend sit down, rub his eyeballs with his palms. "Hard trip to D.C.?"

Another shrug. "No worse than normal. I'm still kissing Congress's ass over the seventy-eight million it's costing to fix *Atlantis*. Wait till they get a load of *your* story."

Santich waited past a heavy pause. "Were you able to find out anything about Gates Rubber?"

"It's a dead end. Our man Austin was on a business trip to Tokyo for the two weeks prior to 74's launch. I guess Rochester Products is selling the Japanese their space suits, too.''

"So if he did tamper with Sam's suit, he must have done it before going to Japan," Trudy said.

"Which means Gates and NASA would have had two weeks to notice the problem and fix it," Santich finished.

He and Trudy looked at each other, then at Hooper, who had lain his head back on the easy chair and seemed asleep.

"You heard from Kyle?" she asked finally.

"No. Not in a few days. He's still with his folks. He's staying there until landing day.''

"Is that when you want to do the press conference?" she asked.

"Yeah. Except not here." He thought about Bruce's last words to him. "We'll do it at the Cape. You and Kyle should fly out there for landing. We'll talk to the cops in the morning, do the press conference that afternoon. That okay with you, Hoop?''

"Just fucking grand. Have fun." He lifted his eyelids. "Why not hold it here, in Houston?"

"Better safe than sorry," he said, thinking about Bruce's diabolical Option Zulu. "I don't even want to set foot in the STA."

"And if you land at Edwards?" Hooper asked.

"Then we'll do it out in California. As far as I'm concerned, the instant *Columbia*'s wheels stop, I'm finished with NASA."

"Will the press let you? Won't they hound you until the whole thing is resolved?" Trudy asked.

"They might try, for a few days," he conceded. "But they have such tiny attention spans, that a week of 'no comment' will discourage them into finding something else."

Trudy turned to Hooper. "Are you sure you won't join us at the press conference?"

He guffawed, his most visible sign of life all evening. "Thanks, but I'd rather chew asbestos." He opened his eyes and sat up straight. "Please, guys, and I mean this: Think about what you're doing. If Toner killed Sam, he's already dead. There's no point in dragging the program through the mud over that. And if you really believe Bruce is the wrong person to head Shuttle Ops, I'm sure you could find a discreet way of getting him out. All you'd have to do is go to the administrator with what you've got. Marty would resign within forty-eight hours. Shit, Santy, you could have his job if you wanted. What do you say?"

Santich turned to Trudy, found she was already looking his way. They both dropped their eyes. Hooper broke the awkward silence. "I had to give it a shot. I wish I could have persuaded you." He stood quickly, slinging his jacket over his shoulder. "Trudy, I'm sure I'll be seeing more of you." He nodded at her, then walked over to Santich, holding out his hand. "Santy, good luck, and have a safe flight. Enjoy number seven for me."

It was the phrase he'd used before each of Santich's flights, even the Gemini flight that launched just days after

Hooper was medically grounded. "Enjoy it for me." He turned, scooping up a radio, headset and antenna before making for the door.

Santich and Trudy watched him climb into the BMW and, with a final wave, drive off. "He was sure weird," she said as they went back inside.

"Things are different for him. I guess he never fit in with you and Kyle, huh?"

She shrugged. "It's not his fault. We have very different outlooks on this."

He thought for a moment, shook his head to clear his mind. "Right. Three days and two hours to go," he said with a grin. "Are you ready for your big debut? Lead EVA?"

"Some debut," she smiled. "I don't think it will be that hard. God knows we've gone over the mal procedures enough times. Leak in an Oh-Two tank, low batteries, air lock handle stuck open, air lock handle stuck closed, suit pressure too high, suit pressure too low, et cetera, et cetera, et cetera." The smile went away. "Santy, are you sure you guys are going to be all right? You really scared me with this Option Zulu thing."

Santich felt a twinge of unease, swallowed it quietly. "I'm sure it'll be fine. I was mainly joking about Option Zulu. I'm ninety-nine percent sure that Bruce is bluffing. The last thing he needs is more dead astronauts. Anyway, the safest launch is the one right after a failure, right?"

She smiled at the peculiar NASA logic behind the saying. "Okay. Be careful, all right?"

"Count on it. I'll see you at the Cape after landing?"

"Count on it."

She held out her hand. Santich took it and pulled her close for a hug. She returned it, stretching it for a few seconds longer than customary between friends, and pulled away, turning quickly to walk to her car.

"Do you have the key?" he shouted.

She held it up between thumb and forefinger before slipping it into her purse and pulling away.

27

It was not a normal working hour, but that was easily explained, if it had to be. When a mission draws near, work absolutely has to get done, regardless of the time of day. Just the same, the overhead light remained off. The computer monitor would provide all the light that was needed.

A few taps at the keyboard, and the little personal computer masqueraded as one of the giant mainframes in the Shuttle Avionics Integration Laboratory, a two-story, detailed, electrical mock-up of the space shuttle, down to the hundreds of miles of wire running the sixty-foot length of a make-pretend cargo bay.

The keyboard clattered in spurts, and a few phrases of code were entered among the hundreds of thousands of lines already there. Quickly, the database was exited, the computer switched off. The entire thing had taken less than seven minutes.

Fifteen hundred miles away, on Launchpad 39B, Orbiter Vehicle 102's fate was sealed.

28

Over three decades, much had changed at the Cape. Launch towers had grown to match the rockets, and had spread north from the Air Force Station up into the civilian space center. The tourists who were once content to watch the action from across the Banana and Indian Rivers now took tour buses into the hangars and right up to the launch-pads. Cocoa Beach's small-town tackiness had sprawled, like most places, into a modern, homogenized bustle of fast food and strip malls.

One thing hadn't changed, though, and for that Santich was thankful: the beach. So near the launchpads, the sea-shore to the east was too dangerous for houses. That had kept the grassy dunes and miles of tan sand just as they were when he'd first come to ride a two-man capsule bolted atop a converted ICBM.

As had become astronaut tradition in the two days prior to a launch, that's where Santich found himself: sitting on a threadbare blanket, watching the endless march of break-ers collapsing on the shore, and every so often peeking at the winged spaceship a mile behind his left shoulder. It was one of the few astronaut traditions that he liked, and he'd fully expected to enjoy his last visit to the little beach house out on Cape Road.

What he hadn't expected was his companion on the blan-ket beside him. She wore a maroon one-piece bathing suit that clung to her slim waist and bosom, although in the past hour, with the sun falling behind them, she had slipped on a light sweatshirt. Her hands looked just as they had two decades earlier, as did her face: angular but delicate; chin, cheekbones, and nose covered by still-tight skin. Only the hair, a mixture of gray and the original auburn and cut medium short, gave away her age. The years had been kind to her, Santich decided, as he watched her burrow her toes in the sand.

"That's quite a story," she said, looking out at the gibbous moon that had just poked over the eastern horizon.

"Yup. Lust, greed, jealousy, murder; it's all there."

"It won't make the agency look very good." It wasn't a warning, Santich knew, just an observation. She hadn't liked NASA much for years.

"No, I expect not."

He turned again to glance at *Columbia*. They had already pulled back the Rotating Service Structure, the protective housing that allowed technicians to prepare the shuttle for launch while keeping the delicate innards out of the rain and wind. But the edginess, the gnawing tension he'd always felt before a flight wasn't there. How could it be? Given the secret he planned to unload on the world upon his return.

"You don't seem concerned by that," she said. "I thought that was why you were going up: to put a better face on things when the truth came out."

He shrugged, a tired-of-trying-to-convince-himself shrug. "You know the real reason I'm going."

She slid her hand up his bare thigh, under his swim trunks, and grabbed him. "Because *that*"—she nodded at *Columbia*—"gives you a bigger thrill than I ever could."

He looked at her, startled. "When did you become so . . . forward?"

"Since I went four years without a man." She pulled her hand out, slipped it around his neck. "I've missed you."

He put his arm around her waist and drew next to her.

"I've missed you, too." He wondered what his face must have looked like when he opened the door to the beach house to find her standing there, looking up at the launch-pad, holding a wide straw hat to her head against the sea breeze. "I'm, uh, glad you came out. You surprised me."

"You sounded so uneasy on the phone the other day. It was unlike you, so close to a launch. Usually you're so upbeat by this time."

"Now you know why. I'm sorry I didn't tell you earlier. I don't know why I didn't." The first star was visible, about fifteen degrees south of the moon. Regulus, he guessed. "This sounds so weak, but I've been looking forward to this for years. One last shot. I don't know why, but I built it up in my head. And now I can't really feel anything. And look at what I've given up to get here."

She hugged him tighter, leaned her head on his shoulder, but didn't contradict him. "At least you've recognized your obsession. Others can't even do that."

Again they sat in silence. Other stars came out: Pollux, Spica, Arcturus. In another twenty-four hours, he'd use them to calibrate the shuttle's gyroscopes with a high-tech sextant. In its peculiar wisdom, NASA had given them all alphanumeric designations. To take the romance out of the Greek and Arabic names, he supposed. It pleased him that an instrument invented by Sir Isaac Newton still could guide his spaceship. He wondered if Banke had had a sextant aboard *Simoon*.

"I'm glad you're coming forward with it, even if it means the whole country is going to camp outside our door the day after you come home."

"They won't find us. Remember that place we went in the Ten Thousand Islands? We'll hide out there."

"That old shack? It was a wreck forty years ago! What makes you think it's even there? You're dreaming if you think you're dragging me out there. It's bad enough we did it once."

"You didn't have fun? I thought it was a great honey-moon."

She laughed, a clean wholesome laugh. *That* hadn't changed in decades either.

"Yes, it was wonderful. My honeymoon, by Emily Santich: We went to a swamp, stayed in a hut with no water or electricity, and ate canned food for five days. Dear, I'm *still* embarrassed to tell people." She smiled at the memory. "I guess it would have been okay if we'd actually caught fish."

"We caught a couple," he protested.

"I'm sorry; I meant to say caught fish large enough to eat. Large enough to fillet properly so there weren't scales and skin in every bite." She brushed some stray hairs off his forehead. "Has it occurred to you that you're the world's worst fisherman?"

"For eighty-four days, Emily, I have gone out and returned without catching a fish, but I can feel my luck is about to change. I will go far out, leave the smell of land behind, and catch the Big One."

She rolled her eyes at him. "Listen to you. It wasn't called *The Old Pilot Who Was the World's Worst Fisherman and the Sea,* was it?"

"You mock me, don't you?" He laughed and kissed her cheek. "Anyway, we had fun. You got to drive the boat. And you drove it well."

"Yeah, it really made the honeymoon."

Santich glanced backward, saw that some pale orange streaks were all that was left of the sun. He also saw *Columbia,* stark white against the darkening sky, lit by powerful floodlights. The sight sent a shiver down his spine. The following afternoon, when he would walk into the launch tower's elevator to climb up to the hatch, she would be filled with a half-million gallons of liquid hydrogen and oxygen, puffing boiled-off gas like a sleeping dragon.

"I see they've already rolled back the RSS," Emily noted, the NASA lexicon rolling off her tongue. "I'll admit, she's a beautiful sight."

He turned to her and smiled wide. "Not half as beautiful as the one next to me."

"Boy!" she laughed. "You must be horny!"

"Not at all. Just stating a fact. And let me promise you here and now: Our second honeymoon will make you forget the first. Our own cottage on Captiva, room service, quiet beach, eating fish that professional fishermen have caught . . ."

"Okay, you've sold me. When?"

"We're currently at Second Honeymoon minus nineteen days and counting. I promise. In fact, we'll even move it up. Landing day, I go rat out Marty Bruce. At landing plus one day, we're outta there. Captiva, here we come!"

"Oh, wonderful," she teased. "Once again, my life revolves around when that *machine* chooses to fly. First you'll break a computer, then lose a hydraulic pump, then a pressure transducer. . . . I could be waiting all summer."

He shook his head. "No ma'am, not this time. I absolutely guarantee it: We launch tomorrow, on time, under budget," he grinned.

Another roll of the eyes. "Anyway, even if you do launch on time, how do you plan to escape the press after you unload your story on them? They're not going to let you go so easily."

"How's that?" he scoffed. "Unless suddenly they've got the right to keep people under house arrest. In the middle of the night, we pack the car, check in under a fake name. Mr. and Mrs. Hemingway." He thought of the deal he'd cut with Jo Pointer. "Plus I've already given all the information to Jo Pointer, that World News Service reporter. She found out about that beach road thing in Galveston, and sort of blackmailed me."

Emily tilted her head in thought. "Jo Pointer, Jo Pointer . . . Why does that name ring a bell? Wait. Is she the one with the . . ."

"Boobs. Yes, that's her."

Emily nodded. "And doesn't she . . ."

"Sleep with all of them, too. Yes. That's her." He turned to her proudly. "She wanted to sleep with me."

"She hadn't had a moonwalker yet, huh?" Emily

laughed, then hugged him as he deflated. "I'm only teasing, honey. What woman in her right mind *wouldn't* want to sleep with you?"

He smiled, remembering the previous night, their first together in four years. "That was nice. Last night, I mean."

She leaned her head against his chest. "It sure was. There's a lot more where that came from, you know." She sat up and kissed him. "I'm glad I have my old Santy back. That other one, the one who'd forgotten how to laugh, I couldn't bear to see him. I guess I'm glad you're flying this mission, because it made him go away." She kissed him again. "Hopefully for good."

They kissed again, a long, slow one like the ones they shared as youths, parked near the runway in Pensacola where Santy was learning to land fast jets on dark, pitching ships. They were interrupted by the murmur of voices drawing near, separated to find Alexis Orlov walking south along the beach, arm in arm with a fine-featured blonde.

"We did not mean to interrupt," Orlov began, pointing toward the encroaching waves. "The tide has risen; there was nowhere else to walk."

"Quite all right," Santich said. "This is America, after all. You can walk anywhere you want. Except across that street," he joked, nodding over his shoulder toward the launchpad. "Or the rent-a-cops will open up on you with their M-16s."

"In Russia it was the same," Orlov said. "Except there they use Kalashnikovs. A much better weapon."

Santich looked at the woman on his arm. She stood demurely, wearing a half smile that said she was secure enough not to need introducing if no one wanted to talk to her.

"I don't think we've all met," Santich said. "I'm Santiago Santich, this is my wife Emily. Emily, this is Dr. Alexis Orlov, one of the lucky spacewalkers on our crew."

Orlov smiled at Emily, then remembered. "Of course. And this is my wife, Olena."

"I'm very pleased to meet you both," she said politely.

Santich tried to place the accent, decided that a finishing school had successfully obliterated it. "Beautiful night," he said finally.

"Yes. Yes, it is," Orlov answered. "On an evening as perfect as this, one wonders why anyone should want to leave this planet, hmmmm?"

Santich and Emily traded glances. "I've often said the same thing," she said. "In fact, we were just planning a little vacation after y'all come home. Enjoy some of this beautiful world while we can."

"An excellent idea," Orlov said. "Olena and I will also take a trip after our return. A second honeymoon of sorts. In the mountains, yes?"

Olena smiled at him but said nothing.

"Yes," he continued, "tomorrow is a big day. It looks as if we should have fine weather." He nodded at Emily. "It was a pleasure to meet you."

The pair continued toward the beach house. Santich waited until they were out of earshot. "Talk about obsession: That guy is pure machine."

"Alexis? He seemed pleasant enough."

"Sure. As polite as can be. He actually saw it happen, when Sam died. He was out there with him in the cargo bay."

Emily watched the two shadows melting into the gloom. "And he wants to fly again?"

"My thoughts exactly. I think if I saw a man's head explode, I'd stay the hell out of space pretty much for good. But Bruce had him signed up within days." He shook his head. "Amazing, huh?"

She shivered and zipped the sweatshirt. "Like I said, obsession." She kept looking down the beach, though nothing was visible. "I remember reading about him. Wasn't he a math professor? A chess player?"

"That's him."

"No wonder, then. Cold, calculating, logical. I bet for him, *not* flying again wasn't even an option." She turned toward him. "He'll make a good Dr. Spock for you."

Santich laughed. "I think that's *Mr.* Spock."

"I know, dear. I just like teasing you."

He smiled. "The other mission specialist, she's a real doozy, too. Now *there's* a space cadet. She probably has all the *Star Trek* episodes on tape."

"That O'Day woman?"

He nodded. "A blithering idiot. She's one of these who tells *other astronauts* that building a space station will cure cancer and end poverty. She asked me the other day why I hated her. I told her because she didn't have the intellectual honesty to admit that the reason she wanted to fly in space was because it was there, and instead had to make up these ridiculous, self-serving excuses to justify it."

"Ouch. That was a bit severe, wasn't it, dear? I'm sure you could say that about ninety percent of the corps, couldn't you? Maybe even a hundred percent?"

He was about to respond when he remembered the look of terror on Banke's face when he came to tell him about Kyle. How his main concern was that Banke not tell the press, for fear of ruining *his* flight. "I guess you're right. I suppose my reasons for keeping this secret until after the flight were pretty weak, huh?"

Emily shrugged, stroked his arm.

"God, Banke might be around today if I'd gone public with this thing a month ago."

They sat in silence for a while, long enough for him to realize that she considered this a possibility.

"No, you can't beat yourself up over that," she said finally. "What's done is done. The best you can do is go fly your mission, get everyone home safe and sound, and then deal with fixing NASA. Plus, you don't *know* he's dead, do you? Perhaps he just got caught in some bad weather. He'll turn up."

He put his arm around her and pulled her tight, kissing the top of her head. "You're a sweetheart, you know that?"

"You're just saying that because you want to get laid."

He drew away a bit to look at her face. "Why, Emily

Pembroke! I'm shocked. Shocked and appalled. That's not the *only* reason I said it.''

She laughed aloud and stood, dusting sand off her swimsuit. ''Shall we?''

He looked around, noticed the last traces of the sun were long gone, meaning it was after 8:00 P.M. ''I guess we'd better. I need to be at a weather briefing at ten at the O and C.''

She looked at him suspiciously. ''You don't have to spend the night there, do you?''

Because most launches were scheduled for early morning, astronauts typically spent the night before in the crew dormitory at the Operations and Checkout building near KSC Headquarters.

''Nope. Because of the evening launch, we were given a papal dispensation to stay at the beach house. Everyone's staying there tonight. Except for Dr. O'Day. She wanted to stay in the O and C. Like a *real* astronaut.''

Emily rolled her eyes. ''Tell her we're watching *Star Trek* videos all night.''

He took her arm and began the walk back to the beach house. ''I've got your *Star Trek* videos,'' he said, grabbing his crotch.

''Where did you learn that?'' she asked.

''Hoop. He says it all the time.'' He pinched her bottom. ''I'm getting out more, you know.''

29

For reasons he'd never understood, the commander always suited up first. Meaning he had to sweat the longest in the bulky orange pressure suit that the cheerful technicians helped him into. As if his getting dressed first would allow him to respond promptly should some space-shuttle flying emergency arise in the Operations and Checkout Building.

"Bet this feels a lot more comfortable in zero G, huh?" the tech asked. GREENE said the name tag on his white Lockheed coveralls. L. GREENE, according to the KSC badge pinned to his belt.

"Larry? Leonard?" Santich asked.

"Louis," the tech answered with a grin. "This is quite an honor, you know. I remember watching you on the moon when I was six years old. Then I finally met you six years ago, at the tenth anniversary of STS-1. You probably don't remember."

"Vaguely," Santich lied over the pressure suit's high collar. "The face sticks in my mind; I'm not so good with names."

Louis Greene finished stuffing Santich into the suit, zippered him shut, and started on the right boot. "That's nice of you to say, sir. Maybe when we're through, you wouldn't mind signing an autograph? For my little girl."

There were two knocks on the door before a rookie astronaut assigned as their gofer stuck his thin face into the room. "Hey, I'm really sorry to bother you, Captain Santich, but you have a phone call. It's from your son-in-law, Kyle. I told him you're suiting up and asked if it couldn't wait, but he says it's a matter of life and death."

Santich traded a glance with Melanie, who sat a few feet away being ministered to by A. ROSE. "Excuse me," he told Louis, struggling out of the chair in his stockinged feet.

He followed the flight-suited rookie out the door and down the hall. "I hope everything is okay, sir," he said as he showed Santich into a small office. "It's that first line. I'll be waiting outside."

Santich waited for the door to close before picking up the handset and pressing the flashing button. "Kyle?"

"Thank God I got you. I thought I'd be too late."

"What is it? Where are you?"

"I'm back in Houston. I got a break on that pressure problem. I started thinking that if something unusual happened to that helmet, maybe it was logged somewhere. I started by looking for processing paper. Nothing."

"Go on," Santich breathed.

"So I went to the IFA log. Bingo. In-Flight Anomaly number 74-09, two before the helmet seal failure, was an overpressurization of the air lock during air lock depress. The air lock pressure went *up* to twenty-point-three psi in a matter of two seconds, instead of going *down* to four-point-one."

"And the cabin was already at ten-point-two."

"Exactly. It doubled, and held there for forty-five seconds before it was lowered to four-point-one, and finally to zero."

"You think that was enough to do it?"

"Santy, I *know* it was. This is exactly what I was looking for, except I was looking for a four- or five-psi change, not ten!"

"Okay," Santich whispered. "Who did it?"

"The *crew*, Santy! It had to have been someone on 74!"

"Holy Mary, mother of God," Santich swore. "Are you

sure? It couldn't have been a ground command?''

"Negative. Absolutely certain. A ground command would have been logged, either by the mechanical systems officer or by EVA. Nothing. And anyway, air lock depress has always been a crew function. Always. It *can* be done from the ground, but it only exists in the mal books.''

Santich's mind raced: Banke, Halvorson, Habuda, Orlov. One of them had flipped the switches that an hour later killed Torrington. "Could it have been an accident?'' he asked, seeing a neat way out.

"Uh-uh. Possible, I guess, but extremely unlikely. Someone went out of their way to sabotage that helmet, right? Made it so a rapid pressure change would weaken or destroy the seal? That raised the odds of failure from one in a hundred to ninety-five in a hundred. What are the chances that the two events are unrelated?''

Which one? he wondered. Probably not Banke, given his reaction to it. Or perhaps that look in his eyes that night was actually guilt. Halvorson? Habuda? *Orlov?* "Can it be done from inside the air lock, or does it have to be done from the outside?''

The line went silent. "I'm not positive. I think it can be done from both, the air lock and the middeck. In fact, I think it can even be done from the flight deck, called up on the CRT.'' Another pause. "I know. That doesn't help narrow it down.''

Santich glanced at the clock on the wall, saw the shadow of his gofer through the frosted glass door. "Listen, I'm in the middle of suiting up, and I've got to go. You need to get the hell out of Houston, all right?''

"I'm okay,'' Kyle answered coolly. "I'll go, Santy, but I have to try to find how the pressurization command was sent. It might be on the data tapes, if they haven't expunged them.''

"Expunged them?''

"Yeah. Like they did the IFA log. In the current version, neither the overpressure nor the helmet seal are in there. I only found out because I kept the printout I made a month ago."

"Kyle, if they expunged the log, then they know that someone on 74's crew killed Torrington!"

"I know. I thought of that. That's why I called you." A brief pause. "Santy, what if it's Orlov?"

The thought had been lurking uneasily in Santich's mind. "I know. Do I want to go up with a killer? But listen, Bruce went out of his way to cover up the Torrington thing, right? It's obvious he needs a successful mission, right? So why risk that by sending up Orlov again if Orlov is the killer?"

"True, *if* they found out about 74-09 early enough. But if they only found it recently . . ."

"Then Bruce might have decided the bad publicity of a late crew change outweighed the risk of letting him fly."

"Exactly."

"And if we assume Orlov did it, we have to assume he did it for a reason, right? Unless he's a homicidal maniac, which I doubt. So my flight should be safe, right? I mean, why would he kill me or Melanie or Alexandra?"

Another pause. "What if he knows that you're onto him?" Kyle asked.

A cold flash zipped down, then back up, his spine. *What if he hired Toner? What if he knows that Melanie and I killed him?* His mind raced, interrupted by a knock on the frosted glass.

"Kyle, I've got to go. . . ."

"Santy, I had an idea. If I go through the current IFA log, I might be able to figure out when 74-09 was changed from the overpressurization to whatever it is now. But it'll take me a couple of hours. . . ."

Another knock, this one louder. "Captain Santich, sir," the voice called.

"Just a minute. I'll be right out," he shouted. "Okay. You can't get ahold of me from here on out," he whispered into the phone, pausing for a moment to think. "But Trudy can. Call her on console! If the log was changed early, before Orlov was named to the crew, then have her tell the flight director she noticed a voltage transient on EMU number 1.''

"Right! Good! And if the log was changed just recently, then I'll have her tell Flight that she noticed a *pressure* transient in the space suit's Oh-Two tank. How's that? Voltage is good news, pressure is bad."

"Good. I've got to run. If it's bad news, I'll screw up a switch throw and abort the count. Listen, keep a low profile! Don't go to your house!"

"You have my word," Kyle said, and hung up.

Santich replaced the receiver and waddled to the door, hitting the light switch as he left. The flight-suited rookie, Ken Boothe, had been pacing nervously, as if *he* would be held accountable if Santich delayed the count.

"Everything all right, sir?"

Santich smiled. "Yeah. That was my son-in-law," he explained, remembering too late that Boothe had told *him* that just a few minutes earlier. "It's my daughter. Her, uh, tests came back negative. It's quite a relief. But I want her to make sure, get a third opinion."

Boothe nodded knowingly.

"You have kids, Ken?"

"No, sir. Not yet."

"When you do, you'll understand better what I mean," he said with a smile.

Boothe nodded again and led him back to the dressing room, where technicians were installing the two Alexes into their suits. Santich sat back down before Louis to get into his boots.

"Everything all right?" Melanie asked nervously.

"Fine," Santich smiled. "The tests came back negative." He peeked over at Orlov, watched him smile and nod as he listened to a stream of babble from Alexandra. Surely it couldn't have been *him*; how could *anyone* be so casual after having killed in such a gruesome manner?

All day he'd been more cheerful and convivial than Santich had ever seen him, from the steak-and-eggs brunch through the enormous, space-shuttle-shaped sheet cake and the weather briefing and now through suit-up. Most of it under the ever present eye of the NASA Select television camera, which would follow their every move until they climbed aboard.

Then again, why should today be any different for him than yesterday, or the day before? *He* had no idea Santich knew his secret; in fact, the more time passed after Torrington's death, the safer he would feel. . . .

Louis finished with the boots and held out a wallet-size photo of a first- or second-grader and a pen. "Her name is Rachel," he said. "Rachel Anne."

Santich managed a smile and signed the back of the photo, all the while keeping one eye on Orlov. Now he was joking with the technician working on him, making the tech laugh heartily. Santich finished the autograph and sidled over to Melanie.

"It was someone on the crew," he mumbled when they were reasonably alone in the crowded room. "Someone pressurized the air lock to twice cabin pressure. That weakened the gasket enough to make it fail later."

The television cameraman moved in front of them. They smiled and waved weakly, then, at his prompting, gave him a thumbs-up. That satisfied him, and he wandered over to the Alexes.

"Who?" Melanie hissed.

"Don't know. Kyle's trying to find out."

That was all the privacy the two would get, as the KSC crew liaison entered the room, cell phone and radio in hand. It was time to go. Santich nodded at Melanie, trying to signal that he would explain when he could.

The four orange-suited astronauts and their entourage moved into the hallway and to the elevator. No one spoke, except for Alexandra O'Day.

"This is it," she half whispered, half squealed. "Sorry," she added with a smile.

Chief astronaut Tim Garvey smiled back at her. "This is the big day. Looks like we've got good weather, too."

The elevator doors opened, and the astronauts along with

about half of the support personnel stepped in, rode the elevator to the ground floor. The doors opened to whistles and applause, as O&C Building employees gave them the traditional send-off. The ovation was repeated as they stepped out into the sunlight, only this time press photographers were among the throng, snapping away at the four, hoping for the prize-winning last-shot-of-them-alive frame that would set them up for life.

Santich, leading his crew out the doorway and into the waiting van, smiled the obligatory smiles and waved the obligatory waves, every so often sneaking a sidelong glance at Orlov.

How the hell could he tell if he was the one? What mannerism would betray him? Santich scoffed to himself; there would be no such clue. He didn't know the man well enough to pick up on anything subtle, and he doubted Orlov would suddenly fall apart, confessing in the final minutes of the countdown. No, he would sit there quietly in the number-three seat, his head just inches behind Santich's on the flight deck. Any move Santich or Melanie made out of the ordinary, Orlov would notice.

The van slowed and stopped in front of the gargantuan Vehicle Assembly Building, letting out Garvey. He was on his way to KSC's three-mile-long runway to fly weather reconnaissance in a T-38 and then in an STA, looking for thick clouds, bad winds, rain, drizzle, hail, or any of the dozens of weather conditions that would make either the launch itself or an emergency landing back at Kennedy too risky. That was in theory, Santich knew. In practice, the powers who gave the final go for launch had become ever more liberal in their interpretations of the flight rules, allowing liftoff in such supposedly no-go conditions as extensive cloud cover or high crosswinds.

He wondered if he might use that as an excuse to delay the launch for a day, if he had to. After all, he *was* the most conservative voice in the program. Surely he could quibble about too high a wind or too thick a cloud deck and not arouse suspicion. One day might make a big difference for Kyle; he might be able to find out exactly who on 74 pressurized the air lock instead of depressurizing it.

But a glance through the van's windows showed only the darkening blue sky of a perfect midspring Florida afternoon, confirming what the Air Force forecasters had said an hour earlier: Weather wouldn't be an issue. How, then, to stop the count, short of blurting over the radio that he had to scrub because the man sitting behind him might be a murderer?

He mentally ran through the checklist he and Melanie would follow prior to launch, looking for someplace where a minor mistake would force the computers to break out. But the more he thought, the more he realized how redundant his very presence aboard the machine was. Every crew function in the checklist could easily be performed by ground command! What the hell was he going to do if Trudy gave the pressure transient warning? There *had* to be a wrench he could throw into the works. . . . Yes! The APUs!

Melanie had to switch the Auxiliary Power Units to the prestart position within a second of the correct moment. Too early or too late would force the Ground Launch Sequencer to stop the count. That was it: He had to get to her, alone, for a minute, tell her to delay throwing the APU switch just a second, *if* he gave the word.

"Is she as beautiful as the first time?"

It was Orlov. They had arrived at the security gate just outside the launchpad. The guard asked the driver if there were any matches or lighters in the vehicle: a formality, stretched to the edge of absurdity. The so-called Astro-van was the *last* place to find someone careless enough to bring flame near liquid hydrogen and oxygen rocket fuel. The guard waved the van through and gave the crew a thumbs-up, letting the driver slowly ascend the concrete ramp to the base of the launch platform.

Getting so close to a fully fueled rocket always put a lump in Santich's throat, and he momentarily forgot his worries as he craned his neck upward. They climbed out of the van and walked slowly toward the elevator, not bothering to hide their awe. Above them towered the eighteen-story spaceship, bolted to the pad by her twin twelve-foot-diameter booster rockets. Between them, thirty feet up, was the big orange tank, already filled with half a million gallons of fuels so cold that a finger placed in them would shatter like glass. Astride the tank was *Columbia,* a weather-beaten white on top, dull black beneath.

Santich stared at the puffs of boiled-off oxygen escaping from the top of the orange tank, the streams of nitrogen venting through the three eight-foot-tall engine nozzles. That it flew at all was testament to engineering tenacity, proof that given enough money, even an overweight, technologically impractical machine like the shuttle could be made to work. The Rube Goldberg plumbing in the main engines let explosive superhot hydrogen gas mix with equally hot pure oxygen at nearly a thousand gallons per second, with high-pressure helium blowing through the guts of the works to flush away the leaks that were never quite solved.

As powerful as *Columbia*'s engines were, they weren't a match for the massive boosters that straddled her. Each fifteen stories tall, together they accounted for 85 percent of the shuttle's power at liftoff. Burning solid fuel, these behemoths were as simple as the main engines were complex: light them and stand back. Two minutes later, if everything worked right, they would have pushed *Columbia* through the thickest part of the atmosphere, from where the main engines had enough oomph to get the ship into orbit. If everything didn't work right. . . . Well, everything hadn't worked right on *Challenger.*

High above, Santich saw the dirty spots on *Columbia*'s tiles: the singe marks of nearly two dozen fiery returns through Earth's atmosphere. He remembered standing there sixteen years earlier, awaiting her maiden flight. Launch day had been pushed back repeatedly as engineers and technicians worked around the clock, tackling one glitch after another, the most irritating being the twenty-five thousand ceramic tiles that refused to stick to the aluminum skin. Finally, two years late, he and Joe Forrester had ridden her up, a shiny, gleaming white bird ascending on a tail of yellow fire. On that first flight, the orange tank had been painted white, to match the orbiter and the boosters. Some engineer pointed out that painting it served no useful purpose, and that leaving it orange would save four hundred pounds in paint that could instead go toward shuttle payload. Starting with STS-3, every launch had used a plain orange tank.

Santich pulled his gaze back to Earth and noticed Orlov beside him, staring intently up into the engine nozzles. Santich shivered as he watched the unblinking gray eyes, shark eyes. Did a shark know beauty? Or only hunger?

"She's even more beautiful now," he answered Orlov, wondering why he needed to. "She has character now. Sixteen years ago, she was just the newest thing on the block."

Orlov pulled his pale lips into his imitation of a smile. "You defend her honor well, as if she were a woman. Few men today care about such things. Divorce is easier than honor." He arched his eyebrows. "You and I, we are of the old school."

Santich had just begun to wonder what Orlov was talking about when the white-overall-clad chief of the closeout crew appeared in the open elevator. "Excuse me. Don't mean to rush anyone, but are we flying today or not?"

"Come on!" Alexandra hissed, and led the way.

Santich hung back, and soon Melanie dropped behind Orlov and edged closer.

"What in God's name is going on?" she breathed.

"Kyle's trying to figure out who on 74 overpressed the air lock."

"How's that help us now?"

Santich guessed they had another twenty feet before they'd be within earshot of the crowd assembled by the elevator. "When you strap in, switch to intercom."

She had time for a quick nod before they rejoined their

colleagues. The four astronauts, looking like bright orange Michelin men, clambered into the elevator, followed by the closeout chief and two of his crew. The doors shut, and the car began its ascent.

What in God's name was Orlov talking about? What old school? He'd said it so knowingly, as if he and Santich were bonded by some common, searing pain that others simply wouldn't understand. *Divorce is easier than honor.*

"End of the line, folks," the closeout chief sang, leading his charges out of the elevator and onto the catwalk connecting the launch tower with the clean-air-flushed cubicle that sealed against the orbiter's hatch.

From 150 feet up, the western horizon was clearly visible. A setting sun painted the sky a brilliant blue-streaked pink, a pastel backdrop to the stark white, black and orange of the shuttle as it stood bathed in the million-candlepower xenon floodlights. A gentle breeze floated in off the sea that, even as they walked, grew darker with the approaching dusk.

This was a moment to savor, but Santich barely noticed it. *Old school?* And how the hell had he started talking about beauty and honor with that psycho, anyway?

The closeout chief stopped halfway across the catwalk and turned. "Y'all know the drill. The white room's only big enough for two, so if Doctors O'Day and Orlov could wait here, we'll take the commander and pilot first."

"Take your time," Alexandra grinned. "We'll enjoy the view."

Melanie and Santich continued down the walk, stepping into the white room. There, overall-clad technicians helped them into their parachute packs, complete with life raft, flares, and rations. Santich barely noticed the chitchat as he donned his helmet and sealed it to the collar of the pressure suit.

Was Orlov being eccentric, or were his words some convoluted confession? Surely it wasn't *that,* not from a tunnel-visioned chess champ. He would be the last person to confess to anything.

One of the Lockheed techs motioned toward the NASA Select camera mounted in the corner. Mechanically, Santich waved at it. *God, let Kyle find that someone other than Orlov did it.* He shook hands with the four techs, returned the salute of the closeout crew chief, who he knew had been a petty officer in the Navy, and walked over to the doormat that lay before the open hatch. He removed the galoshes they'd slipped over his boots back in the O & C to avoid tracking dust and dirt into the orbiter, where such contaminants clogged air filters and overheated sensitive electronics.

Next came the most strenuous part of any shuttle flight: crawling, in a heavy pressure suit, across a metal ladder into the flight deck. Getting from the downstairs middeck to the upstairs flight deck was no trouble in orbit and, with the ladder, fairly easy once back down on the runway. But with the shuttle vertical on the launchpad, the rear walls of the crew compartment became the floors, and the ladder became a narrow catwalk the crew had to crawl across to reach their seats.

Santich clambered across the rungs and into the left-hand seat, lying back to rest for a moment. The seats had been designed to be lain in wearing a lightweight flight suit, not a pressure suit and parachute pack. Indeed, after the first few test flights, shuttle crews had forsaken the pressure suits for the lighter, cooler blue jumpsuits. NASA had gone back to the pressure suits after *Challenger*, giving astronauts the dubious option of bailing out of a crippled shuttle at high altitudes over the often stormy North Atlantic.

After a brief feeling of comfort, Santich began to feel the awkward lump in his back from his parachute. Within moments, though, the more pressing problem chased the discomfort from his mind. He peered through the windows at the horizon, looking for clouds he could use to argue for a weather scrub. There were none. He plugged the jack from his headset into the junction box and switched the selector to Air-to-Ground 1.

"CDR, OTC. How copy?"

It was Alfie Miles, one of the controllers in the Launch Control Center three miles away, with the title "orbiter test conductor."

"OTC, CDR. I read you loud and clear. How me?"

"Loud and clear, Santy. Good evening. It's looking like a beautiful night for a launch. Weather's good and we're working no issues."

Terrific. The one time when he'd kill for an extra day, NASA would pull off a once-in-a-blue-moon on-time launch.

"Roger that, Alfie. Glad to hear it," he lied. "Can't wait to get back up there."

"Well, we're doing all we can to get you out of here A-S-A-P."

"Thanks for the good words," he said, and pulled out the prelaunch checklist to make sure all the switches were in their proper positions.

What if it was Orlov? What was he going to do? He would have to scrub; he would tell the launch director that the crew had a serious medical problem or something. And then? Go public with circumstantial evidence that pointed at Orlov? Or confront him first, detective-novel style, and hope for a confession?

Behind him, he heard Melanie bump the back of his seat, and he turned to watch her climb into the chair beside him. Soon she had plugged herself in and was checking with launch control.

"OTC, PLT, comm check."

"Good evening, Melanie. Read you loud and clear. How me?"

"Loud and clear, Alfie."

"Great. As I told Santy, we're green for the opening of the launch window."

"Roger that. Really looking forward to it."

"Understand. We'll get you out of here."

She waited a moment to see if there was more, then quickly switched the radio to intercom. Santich switched himself over to meet her.

"What's going on?" she asked without preface, her voice a hoarse whisper even over the headset.

"Kyle's trying to find out who overpressed the air lock. We figure whoever did murdered Torrington."

"Jesus Christ," she whispered.

"Mel, I need your help. Kyle's going to call Trudy with what he finds out. We're interested in one thing: Did Orlov do it? If it looks like he did, then she'll tell Flight she saw a pressure transient in one of the space suits. If he didn't do it, she'll report a voltage spike."

"Jesus," she said again.

"If she calls pressure, I need your help."

Brief silence. "Go on."

Thank you. "I need you to be a half second late with APU prestart."

Another pause. "So the Ground Launch Sequencer breaks out and stops the count."

"Exactly. With any luck, it'll take them long enough to figure out what went wrong that we won't be able to recycle for tonight."

"Then what?"

"I'm not sure. I *am* sure I don't want to lift off if Orlov was the one."

More silence, this time a long pause. "We should scrub right now, shouldn't we? I mean, this is insane, this last-minute shit."

It was a thought he had consciously avoided. "Truth be told, Mel," he said with a sigh. "Truth be told, we shouldn't have taken it this far. But we did."

She fell silent. Santich knew she would be thinking of the years dreaming about this moment, of the years of training, of missed promotions in the Navy, of time not spent with family. "This means a lot to me, Santy," she said softly.

"I know it does. It does for me, too." *More than it should.* "And that other, less selfish reason behind all this is still there. If we scrub now and Orlov is innocent, or if

Kyle is wrong, and *everyone* on 74 is innocent, than we've ruined the program. Maybe for good.''

The words left an unpleasant taste in his mouth, but he'd said them, and he left them out there.

"Okay, let's go ahead. If I hear a pressure transient call, I go late on APU prestart.''

"Right.''

"If I hear voltage transient, we do the nominal check-list.''

"Right.''

"What if we don't hear either?''

Another thought he'd avoided. "We'll cross that bridge. . . .''

Behind them, they heard a clattering on the ladder and quietly switched back to Air-to-Ground 1 as Mission Specialist Alexis Orlov moved into his seat behind them

"OTC, MS1. How copy?'' Orlov said after settling in.

Santich half listened to the banter as he skimmed through the cue cards in the three-ring flight data file. Mainly he worried about Melanie's unsettling scenario. What *was* he going to do if Kyle couldn't learn anything by launch time? What if tomorrow he found out Orlov *had* flipped those switches? Land on the next orbit? Call down for a Minimum Duration Flight on the grounds that his flight engineer should be in jail?

He tried to think positive: Kyle *would* find out in time, one way or the other. After all, he only had to search the computer to see when the IFA log was modified to alter the 74-09 entry. Kyle could do that in his sleep.

But as the little red numbers on the timer in front of him continued backing through the minutes, he worried more and more about what he hadn't heard over the loop. Alexandra climbed into her seat beside Orlov, and he listened to her titter her way through her radio check. He and Melanie flipped through their checklist, page by page, and still no word from Houston about the space suits, or Extravehicular Mobility Units, as they were called.

The clock ticked downward, down under an hour, until

the closeout crew finished buttoning up the orbiter hatch and evacuated the launchpad. Through the cockpit windows, the sky darkened through blue, darker blue, and finally black, and still capcom Mitch Dalke had nothing to say about EMUs.

As the clock drifted back into, then out of the ten-minute hold at the T-minus-twenty-minute mark, Santich started looking for something, anything, with which to argue for a scrub. But the skies around the Cape stayed clear and the winds remained under five knots. Throughout the count the only nonstandard item was a loose bolt on a handrail leading down from the launch platform. Even that was promptly tightened.

Sooner than seemed possible, the count was in the ten-minute hold at the T-minus-nine-minute point, and the NASA test director geared up for his final, go/no-go poll prior to launch.

Now what? Santich wondered as it became clear that Kyle hadn't found out what he needed. He would get no help, would have to decide blindly.

Over the radio, NTD Loren Wright's mechanical voice began the last formality before the launch, the last chance for Santich to stop the launch with the simple truth, for all the world to hear.

"Safety?"

"Safety is go."

"Range?"

"The range is clear to launch."

"Thank you. Launch weather?"

"Launch weather is go."

"Roger. Houston Flight?"

"Standby one."

Santich held his breath; Trudy had just told the ascent flight director about something she'd seen.

"Yeah, Loren, sorry for the delay. Just spilled a bit of coffee on the good-luck tie. Houston Flight is go."

Damn, this was it. He was next.

"Thank you. CDR?"

Commander is no-go because Mission Specialist 1 is a cold-blooded killer.

"CDR?"

"Standby one," Santich said finally. He turned to catch Melanie's eyes and switched his radio to intercom mode.

He watched her switch over, and for a moment studied her face through the helmet. He had seen that look before, in the faces of all the rookies he had flown with, and he knew that if he advocated a scrub, he would do so alone.

"What do you think?" he asked.

"Let's do it!" came Alexandra's shrill reply. She had switched over to intercom also.

If she had seen him adjust his radio, then Orlov must have, too, and in a moment his flat voice confirmed it.

"Is there a problem? Everything is green," he said. "We should go, Santy, unless you have good reason why we should not."

Santich ignored the backseat voices and watched Melanie. Her eyes were wide and animated; he knew from his own first ride on a rocket that her mouth would be parched. The nearness to launch began to weigh into the decision making. Orlov was right: There was no predicting what might happen during a countdown tomorrow or next week. A transistor that worked perfectly today could crap out at the T-minus-thirty-minute mark tomorrow. The Cape might have miserable weather for a week.

He was only nine minutes from *it,* what his past twelve years had revolved around; to throw it away now, without any real evidence, was criminal. After all, there were three suspects on STS-74 other than Orlov, and what if, God forbid, the whole thing *was* a freak accident? What if the switched helmet seal was an unfortunate mix-up and the air lock pressurization was a pure, doubly unfortunate accident? Whatever had happened, the police could sort it out later. There was no need for a monstrous scene that would ruin careers and set back manned space flight a dozen years.

When Melanie finally nodded, hesitantly at first, then

with conviction, Santich needed little encouragement. *The hell with it! Let's go for it!*

"NTD, CDR. The crew of STS-74 Alpha is go, Loren."

"Thank you, Santy. Launch director, NTD. You have a final go for launch."

"Roger, Loren," answered Bob Simon's monotone. "Thanks to everyone for getting us this far. It reminds us that a good count is a team effort, so let's stick together here for another seventeen and a half minutes and get this bird into orbit where she belongs. Santy, it was a pleasure working with you and your crew, and we wish you a safe trip and Godspeed. Y'all are a shining example to the world what we can do when we put our minds to it."

Yeah, right. Restart the count already. "Thanks for the good words, Bob," Santich began, continuing the genteel charade that he knew would find its way into the newspapers the next day. "We're looking forward to getting on orbit and getting the job done."

"Roger that. NTD, launch director."

"Go ahead."

"Pick up the count on schedule."

"Understand. Pick up the count at zero-one-hours, fourteen minutes, Zulu."

There. It was done. In just a few minutes, they would be on their way, and it would be too late for anyone to do anything about it. Eleven years, eight months of scut work, but it was about to pay off. The world would continue to turn below, billions would go about their everyday lives, just as they had for years too many to count. But of all the people who had ever lived, only six hundred had done what they were about to, and none had done it as often as he.

From behind, he felt a tap and saw Orlov's thin smile through the helmet's visor. He switched his radio to intercom.

"I paid a nonrefundable deposit for a week in the Smoky Mountains. I would have hated to tell Lena that I lost it."

Santich nodded and turned back to the console, flipping his radio back to the loop in time to hear Loren Wright resume the count. Good. With each passing milestone, a technical scrub became less and less likely.

T-minus seven minutes and thirty seconds. The orbiter access arm swung away from the ship, leaving her standing free on the launch tower. Santich savored the moment, relaxed as he monitored the caution and warning lights on the panel. NASA doctors had always marveled at his ability to stay physiologically calm, despite the circumstances. During *Columbia*'s maiden liftoff, his copilot's heart had raced to one-hundred thirty beats per minute. Santich's had stayed at sixty, just five over his rest rate.

T-minus six minutes, and the last critical crew-performed event was upon them.

"PLT, perform APU prestart."

Melanie's fingers had hovered over the switches, and at the correct moment, they moved a fraction of an inch downward.

"APU prestart complete," she answered. Silently she turned to him, and they shared a quick smile.

Far below him he heard the faint whine of the pumps that fed the Auxiliary Power Units their toxic diet of hydrazine and nitrogen tetroxide, both so deadly that breathing one part in a million was enough to kill a man.

At T-minus five minutes, the APUs ignited, giving *Columbia* the hydraulic power she needed to pivot her wing flaps and gimbal her main engines.

T-minus three minutes, fifty seconds. The ground power cables were disconnected, and *Columbia* switched to her internal fuel cells, which created electricity by chemically combining hydrogen with oxygen. The crew used the by-product, water, for cooking, cleaning and washing. Just like a ship leaving port, Santich thought, remembering his days aboard cruisers and carriers. Complete self-sufficiency: That was the dictum. Although if a ship got into trouble, there was the chance, a good chance, actually, of rescue. In orbit, there would be no help.

T-minus two minutes, thirty seconds. The metal beanie cap on top of the orange fuel tank that drew off the oxygen that kept boiling away was retracted, and the liquid fuels were allowed to come up to flight pressure.

T-minus one minute, fifteen seconds. The electrical circuits that would trigger a torrent of water to flow into the flame trench beneath the shuttle were armed. The water would absorb the tremendous vibration from the rocket engines, which might otherwise reverberate off the concrete and damage the ship.

So far, so good! Although the most critical operations were left until the final seconds before launch. After a month of agonizing, Santich felt strangely serene as the moment approached. True, there was still the matter of sorting it out. But that could wait, without ill consequence to anyone.

T-minus thirty-one seconds, and control of the countdown passed from the Ground Launch Sequencer computer in the Launch Control Center to the Redundant Set Launch Sequencer—the string of four IBM computers within *Columbia* that checked one another for errors a thousand times a second. If even one mismatch was detected, the countdown would stop automatically.

T-minus ten seconds. Santich heard the go for main engine start. *This was it. . . .*

T-minus 6.6 seconds, and Santich felt a gentle rumble as the three high-energy rocket engines ten stories below came alive, burning with their bluish, nearly transparent flames.

The seconds took forever now; any malfunction detected by the computers would result in an engine shutdown, leaving him and his crew stuck atop an armed bomb, with tons of volatile hydrogen wafting free near the engines, waiting for the single errant spark.

Four . . . three . . . two . . . one . . . and   the   ground snapped loose with a bang, as the giant booster rockets spewed their wicked orange flames, tearing *Columbia* free of her launchpad and, slowly at first, began pushing her skyward.

''Roll program initiated,'' came the voice from Houston,

which took command of the ship the moment the boosters ignited.

Columbia rolled gently to starboard as she rose. Quickly she picked up speed and began pitching over, so that she flew an upside-down trajectory toward Bermuda.

Above him, the ocean glowed unnaturally, as the bright orange glare from the boosters overpowered the gentle silver moonlight on the breakers. *God, what a glorious sight!* And he'd almost forsaken it on the groundless suspicion of a crewmate. After all, what possible motive could Orlov have had for killing Sam Torrington?

He felt a minute lessening in the acceleration as *Columbia's* computers throttled down the main engines to allow the ship to ease through the sound barrier's jarring turbulence without shaking herself to pieces.

The more he considered it, the sillier it seemed: Orlov wanting to murder Torrington. *But someone did it, someone on STS-74. . . .* Time slowed as he chewed on the unbidden and unwelcome thought. Yes, someone on 74 *had* done it, and none of the others had any obvious motive either.

Images flashed in his mind. Torrington's publicity photo, the dark curly hair and boyish grin. Trudy's olive complexion and pretty smile. Jo Pointer's generous, too obvious figure. The teary-eyed, miniskirted secretary at the Outpost. What could Orlov have had to do with any of this? He thought of the serene, classical features chiseled out of white marble. *This is my wife, Olena.*

Jesus, God! What had he done—Olena! Torrington's other girlfriend, *Lana, Lena, something like that,* Trudy had said. Olena. . . . Of course. *I would have hated telling Lena that I lost it!* All that rambling about honor, the "old school." . . . Maybe he'd believed the rumor that had gone around Building 4 that Santich and Emily had parted because of another man!

"*Columbia*, go at throttle-up," came the call on the radio.

"Roger, go at throttle-up," Melanie answered.

What now? God, it was right there in front of his face!

He'd heard Millie gossip about Orlov's troubled marriage not three months earlier. All he'd needed to do was ask someone what Orlov's wife's name was and it would have fallen together! And now, did Orlov think Santich knew? Was that bit about honor a twisted confession after all? Or just camaraderie, one cuckolded-husband-made-good to another?

Again *Columbia*'s acceleration slowed, this time more noticeably, and Santich saw the message flash on the CRT display that booster chamber pressure had fallen below fifty psi. The night sky in front of the windows flashed a bright red as small explosives shattered the bolts holding the boosters to *Columbia*'s fuel tank, letting the rockets tumble back toward Earth. The shuddering was replaced with a gentle rumble, and *Columbia*, now weighing a small fraction of what she had two minutes earlier on the ground, began accelerating again, the thickest part of the atmosphere beneath her.

"Houston, we have booster sep," Melanie reported.

"Roger, *Columbia*, we show a clean sep down here."

Okay. He still had some options: an abort landing. No way could Orlov interfere with that, not without getting himself killed. But what if he preferred that to losing his honor? *We are of the old school.* . . . It would take one good yank on Santich's arm at the right moment and *Columbia* would career off the runway. No one would survive the toxic fire. Without turning, he tried to gauge how far Orlov could reach from his seat. Far enough, Santich decided, especially if he unstrapped his restraining belts.

He could land her left-handed and use his right arm to fend Orlov off. . . . Or Melanie could land her, and he would keep Orlov out of the way. Still too risky: There were dozens of switches he could flip within easy reach that would ensure a wreck.

Or perhaps Orlov already believed his secret was out. That would explain his earlier remarks. If so, maybe he'd already decided to defend his name by sabotaging *Columbia* on orbit! God. . . . The shuttle was designed against every conceivable contingency, from computer failure to weightless astronauts bumping against switches. But there was *no* protection against intentional malice. A couple of cabin pressure valves, or the commands to ignite the big maneuvering engines, or the relief valves on the fuel cells—the list was endless.

"*Columbia,* Houston, two-engine Ben Guerir," capcom Mitch Dalke told them, announcing that the shuttle now had enough speed and altitude to reach Morocco even if one engine failed.

If only he knew Orlov better; right now, the man was a wild card, completely unpredictable. For the first time in his thirty-year career in space, Santich began to panic. Should he bring her home now and hope Orlov would be taken by surprise and accept his return docilely? Or should he make orbit, try to gauge him a little better, and then decide?

"*Columbia,* Houston. Negative return."

They were now going too fast to let Santich turn around and fly back to Kennedy. Just as well. He'd have needed a miracle to pull it off, even without a homicidal, possibly suicidal, maniac sitting inches behind him. But the call reminded him that one by one his options were closing behind him. Another four minutes and they would be in orbit.

As casually as he could against the mounting G-forces, he moved his left arm out beyond the rotary abort selector switch and the single red button that would irreversibly initiate an abort. A TAL, a Transoceanic Abort Landing, would be the fastest and safest, but it would bring Orlov back on foreign soil. An AOA, an Abort-Once-Around, would put them back at either Edwards or Kennedy, where he could hand Orlov to the police. But it would give Orlov a full hour and a half to realize his fate and act on it.

A turn of the knob and a push of the button. That's all it would take. He glanced beside him and saw Melanie staring at him, wide-eyed. He turned his helmet slightly and saw Orlov out of the corner of his eye. He seemed engrossed in the panel directly ahead of him. Quickly Santich returned his arm to his side.

"*Columbia,* Houston, single-engine ATO."

Only a couple of minutes left. They were already moving fast enough to reach a lower-than-planned orbit, an Abort-to-Orbit, even if two of the three engines failed. He glanced again at Melanie, who raised her eyebrows at him.

What was he missing? Why couldn't he push the button? Someone killed Torrington; one of his crewmates had done it; Torrington was screwing a woman named Lana or Lena; Orlov's wife's name was Lena. *Quod erat demonstrandum.* But was it? What if it wasn't. . . .

"*Columbia,* Houston, press to MECO."

The ship could now make the planned orbit with two failed engines. If he didn't decide now, the mission timer would decide for him. He could still select an AOA, although a TAL would mean an untested, steeper-than-normal reentry. Was it worth it?

Without warning, the gentle roar disappeared, replaced by a steady hum from all the fans and motors. He floated to the front of his pressure suit, which in turn nudged forward against the five-point restraint. It was too late. The computers had sensed they were in the correct orbit. They had Main Engine Cutoff.

"Houston, *Columbia.* We have MECO," he radioed down.

"Roger, *Columbia.* We show an early cutoff. Eight minutes and twenty-seven seconds. Looks like a little better performance than expected."

A sharp jolt shook the ship; explosive bolts had fired to blow the spent fuel tank away from *Columbia* and back down into the atmosphere. From behind him, Alexandra let out an unrestrained "Yippee!" into the radio.

"Roger that, Alex Prime," Dalke radioed. "Congratulations. You made it."

Yeah, they had made it, Santich thought. What a mess! His preparations were shot to hell; no way could he use the UHF radio to talk to Trudy, not with Orlov certain to see him. And if the man had sabotage in mind? How would he keep an eye on him twenty-four hours a day?

Cautiously he turned and looked back at Orlov, only to find Alexis's gray eyes already fixed on his.

30

"Alex?" He started in his normal speaking voice, gradually got louder. "Alex? Alex!"

"He can't hear you in that helmet," Alexandra told him.

Santich satisfied himself that she was right, and turned his attention toward the wide brown eyes, set in a face whose already soft features were rounded further by the lack of gravity.

Where to begin? He'd considered just telling her that, as commander, he had already decided, and that's the way it was going to be. But what if she didn't accept that? After all, she'd never been in the military, and probably wouldn't appreciate that type of logic.

For two days he'd gone through the motions of the spaceflight—the unbolting and stowing of the now useless chairs on the flight deck; the pleasant banter with ground controllers in Houston; the cooking, eating and cleaning that took up hours each day. All the while he'd teased and pulled and worked it over in his head, finally settling on a plan that, though risky, offered the best chance of success.

That shadow of doubt that prevented him from aborting the launch continued to nag him; the only sure way was to confront Orlov. But how? What if, in the panic of exposure, he decided to destroy *Columbia?* Santich had sorted the ways to undo whatever damage Orlov tried, but a saboteur on the flight deck, unless physically restrained, would easily stay two or three steps ahead of the repairmen.

Unless Orlov were so isolated and vulnerable that he couldn't possibly hurt the ship—like during the space walk. Someone had to confront him outside, in the cargo bay. Alexandra O'Day was out of the question. Melanie had trained twenty hours to perform an emergency space walk for things like closing the cargo bay doors and stowing the dish antenna by hand in case the electric motors failed. But despite her whispered protestations on the flight deck while the Alexes worked below, he wasn't about to make Melanie do his dirty work.

So it had come to this: He would tell Alexandra that she wouldn't walk in space like she'd dreamed about all these years. He would go out in her place. He, with absolutely no training for the satellite repair, with no more than two dozen water-tank hours in nearly twenty years with the shuttle program, was going to tell Dr. O'Day and Mission Control why *he* had to go out with Orlov to fix the Gamma Ray Observatory.

For the past day, he'd anticipated and dreaded this moment. He'd listened faithfully for the EMU code from Trudy and Kyle, but had heard nothing. He hadn't dared to take out the UHF radio to ask Trudy directly, for fear Orlov would overhear. Indeed, he and Melanie had passed the first two "nights"—each punctuated with five sunrises and sunsets—napping in two-and-a-half-hour watches on the flight deck to make sure Orlov didn't wreck *Columbia* while everyone slept. Finally, on flight day three there came his first opportunity. Orlov had begun four hours of "prebreathing": sitting in his space suit in the middeck breathing pure oxygen to prevent nitrogen bubbles from forming in his blood—the scuba-diving disease known as the bends—during the next day's space walk.

As the "intravehicular" crew, Melanie was below, helping Orlov in and out of his suit and monitoring his vital signs. Alexandra was already half-dressed for her own four-hour prebreathe as she hung suspended in front of Santich in her clingy white underwear. The thin fabric clearly showed the electrodes and wires taped to her breasts that would monitor her heartbeat and skin temperature. Santich noticed idly that zero gravity had modified her long, lithe figure into that of a top-heavy Barbie doll, as blood that ordinarily pooled in her legs instead swelled her upper torso.

"What's on your mind? I've got to start my prebreathe in another"—she glanced at the digital mission-elapsed timer on the cockpit console—"seven minutes."

He decided to reason with her first, and order her as a fallback. "That's what we need to discuss," he began. "I need you to call down and tell them you're sick."

Her jaw fell. "What? Why? I know I was sick the first day or so." She had been. After her first euphoric half hour in orbit, she'd proceeded to vomit almost hourly the rest of the day, that despite oral and intramuscular drugs designed to avert spacesickness. "It's not fair! Seventy percent of all astronauts get sick! Besides, I'm fine, now!"

It was true. She'd found her "space legs" after two days and now moved about the cabin without any ill effects.

"Not that kind of sick." He shook his head, turned to the cockpit windows. They were flying upside down and sideways to their direction of travel. He watched the sun sink and suddenly disappear over the western horizon. The thin slice of atmosphere above the edge of Earth turned orange, then red, and finally glowed bluish white. "I mean some other kind of sick."

He turned back to her and saw her eyes well with tears. Beneath the long black ponytail that at the moment stuck straight upward from her head, the effect was sadly comical. "There's something about this mission you don't know. Something important."

The tears welled even further, one huge tear over each eye, growing larger and larger as it stayed whole, the water's surface tension unmolested by gravity.

"I knew it would end like this," she sobbed. "I should never have gone along."

She knew? "Agreed to what?" he asked cautiously.

"The whole thing. It's a fake. There's nothing wrong with the sun sensors on GRO. I'm supposed to reinstall the same units I pull out."

He looked at her quizzically.

"You don't know? You must know; they had a major mal on *Atlantis*. They wouldn't tell me what. But the fuel cell anomaly, the sun sensor thing, it was all a fake. Made up to cover up whatever really happened. There *are* no spare sun sensors. I'm supposed to take the ones out of GRO, move them to the spares locker in the payload bay, pretend I'm switching them for the new ones, and then reinstall the same ones I took out."

She wasn't so pure after all. "When did they tell you?"

"A week after I was assigned. They originally thought there *were* some spares they could send up. Then they wouldn't have had to tell me anything. When they found out there weren't, they needed my cooperation." She lowered her eyes. "They said it wasn't too late to find someone else to fly."

So she was as venal as he. Somehow, he felt sorry for her, sorry for her shame. "Let me explain the major malfunction on the last flight," he said softly.

Her expression went from interest to revulsion to shock to sadness as he recounted the tale once more. When he finished, she floated limply, her hands clasped over her mouth, her face pale. Behind her, the sunrise burst through the pilot's window, throwing everything in the cockpit into either stark white glare or equally stark dark shadow.

"I can't believe it's Alexis. It can't be." She shook her head slowly.

He sighed. "I can't be positive. Not yet. That's why I need to do this."

"He's so . . . calm, so composed. He *couldn't* have done this."

"Maybe. You have to admit, it was carried out in a calm, composed way."

She paused, watched the blue-and-white morning Earth turn slowly beneath them. On the horizon were the jagged peaks of the Andes, sharp and brown behind the bright-blue Pacific. "*They* won't let you go out, you know."

He grinned. "How, exactly, will *they* stop me?" He remembered the glitch-plagued Apollo 14, when Houston was on the brink of telling Alan Shepard to abort the moon landing and turn back. He could tell from the Icy Commander's tone over the radio that he was getting ready to tell Houston to screw themselves and was going to land anyway. Santich had always wished *he* had been in that lunar module, and that Mission Control hadn't ultimately given the go for landing.

He watched Alexandra stare at the South Atlantic appearing behind the mountains. "I could do it," she said decisively. "Whatever you need me to do, *I* can do it!"

"You could kill him?" he asked softly. "If you had to? You could lock him out of the air lock? You could smash his helmet with a wrench?"

She shuddered involuntarily, remained silent.

"I didn't think so. Now, please. Get on the radio and ask for a PMC."

With a sigh, she picked the microphone off its Velcro mount on the metal bulkhead and called Mission Control for a private medical conference with the flight surgeon. With patient detail, she described the symptoms of an acute inner-ear infection: pain, loss of hearing, everything the medical book described.

He prescribed a series of antibiotics and told her to stay out of the air lock until the infection cleared up. Within minutes came the expected call from capcom Jules Carreau.

"*Columbia,* Houston, for Santy."

"Go ahead Jules," Santy answered.

"Yeah, Santy. We've just gotten word that Alex Prime is no-go for EVA, for at least three days. We've talked it over down here, and everyone agrees that puts us too far behind the time line."

Santich nodded, knowing what they would say next.

"Our options are: hope she has a speedy recovery, or do some heavy replanning and get Melanie out there to help

Alex,'' Carreau continued. ''Right now the flight surgeon's prognosis is pretty bleak for her getting better inside three or four days.''

This is where Mission Control goes apeshit, Santich thought. ''Copy that, Jules. We've been talking about it up here, too, and concur with everything except the personnel. We thought it would be better if Melanie stayed inside and I went out with Alex.''

He released the microphone button and let the slender, Magic Marker–size device hover in front of him, bobbing slightly in the air currents. He'd already turned off the flight deck TV cameras to make sure they couldn't watch his reaction during the exchange. Beside him, Alexandra watched the Falkland Islands pass from view.

''*Columbia*, Houston,'' Carreau said after a long pause. ''We're trying to make sure we copy correctly: Y'all think Melanie should continue as intravehicular crew, and you would go out to assist Alex?''

Santich wished he could listen in on the Mission Control room between transmissions. ''That's a roger. You copy all.''

''Standby one.''

Santich released the mike again, arched his eyebrows at Melanie as she drifted upward into the flight deck. She stopped her movement on the steel ladder so she could keep an eye on Orlov, who was still in his space suit.

''*Columbia*, Houston, for Santy. We're discussing it down here, and the way we see it, there are a number of advantages to sending Melanie outside: She's had some EVA training for this mission, it allows Alex Prime to take over as IV crew, which lets you fly the ship, preserving the option of jettisoning GRO and backing out in a hurry if we have to.''

He was doing an admirable job of translating what must have been a blue streak coming out of Lead Flight Director Craig Varnes's mouth into a remarkably civil conversation, Santich thought.

''We're curious,'' Carreau continued after Santich didn't

respond, "what you all think of that, and what the pros and cons are of keeping Melanie in and sending you out."

Santich licked his lips. "Right. Well, our way still allows Alexandra to jump in as IV if Melanie needs to fly the ship. We think our way is a better allocation of our resources," he said vaguely, wondering how hard a fight they would muster, given that anyone of importance in the Mission Control room must have known that the repair was a charade, a performance for the public's benefit.

"Standby one."

Again a long pause, during which Alexandra turned her gaze from the pilot's windows to the overhead windows, through which the Gamma Ray Observatory slowly grew from a point of light into a small square box. Capture was set for later that day.

"*Columbia,* Houston. Santy, we think Melanie might be a better choice to go outside, given her hours in the water tank in the past month, as opposed to your last run, which was in 1984, according to the logs."

All right, this nonsense had gone on long enough. "Understand, but I think we'll go ahead our way. After all, I do have *some* EVA time myself. More than anyone in the office, if I remember right."

"Roger that, Santy. Our point was merely that there might be a qualitative difference between a lunar EVA in one-sixth gravity and an orbital EVA in zero-G."

Perhaps a slightly more acid tone might end the discussion sooner. "Copy that. Thanks for the words. But we're not talking rocket science here. I mean, all I have to do is get in the space suit and hand Alex some tools, right? I'm very confident I can handle that."

Another pause. "Uh, yes, we're also confident you could perform the EVA if you needed to. It's just that—"

"Houston, *Columbia.* We're starting to get behind on the time line. I need to start my prebreathe. If you'd like, you can continue with Melanie or wait until I get in the middeck."

"Standby one." A brief pause. "Negative. We'll get

started on a new EVA time line. The big picture is that Alex will handle the critical tasks, and you'll assist as much as possible. We're going to try to keep it to six hours.''

And the argument was over. Santich started toward the ladder leading to the middeck. Now all that was left was the hard part.

31

Dawn was still an hour away when the big BMW pulled into the three-car driveway, waited a few moments as the white garage door rose in its tracks, and slowly pulled forward. The taillights flashed through white, became bright red and then disappeared. The garage door came down, and all was as it had been.

Crickets chirped in the quiet upscale subdivision. Most of the residents were senior contractor executives. Few civil servants could afford Briarwood Estates.

A light went on briefly in the room overlooking the street, giving a vague outline of movement through the filmy curtains, and then went out again. Overhead, a white satellite appeared as it caught the morning sun from its high perch, growing brighter as it slid from northwest to southeast. No one on Coventry Circle had bothered awakening early to watch it. They had all seen the shuttle fly overhead plenty of times before.

Without warning, a single shot rang out from the darkened house. There was no echo.

32

For two hours now, his field of view had been filled by Orlov's round face. Usually the cold gray eyes stared past him, almost through him; every once in a while they'd flash to attention, and Santich would know Orlov was awake.

He'd held his breath, waiting for Orlov's reaction to his gambit. Amazingly, there hadn't been one, although he'd monitored the conversation between Santich and the ground during his prebreathe. He consoled Alexandra on her ear infection, told her there was always next time. He told Santich not to worry, there wasn't very much to do, and that he could walk Santich through it, beginning to end.

Santich breathed the thinning air deeply as he rehearsed what he must do. He'd slept poorly the first two nights, and not at all that last night, and the strain was starting to show. He'd shouted at Melanie as she helped him into the too tight liquid-cooled underwear he'd borrowed from her—*Columbia* wasn't equipped with a set for him—when she pinched his skin between one of the snaps. He'd apologized immediately, but it was a loss of composure he would rather Orlov hadn't seen.

For the thousandth time, he studied Orlov's face: pale gray eyes, thick lips, straight, dark brown hair, thinning rapidly above the temples. . . . The face of a murderer? What if he confessed, then became unreasonable? Could he kill him? Smashing a wrench through his helmet and watching his life boil out the hole would be somewhat different from shooting a rocket at a plane miles away, or even buzzing an unsuspecting car. How hard would he have to hit the glass? What if it didn't shatter? He didn't even know what the helmet was made of. What if it was shatterproof Lexan?

With crossed eyes, he studied the insides of his own helmet, looking for an etched logo or trademark, then remembered: He hadn't inspected the helmet he was wearing! What if Orlov had guessed what Santich was doing, and had sabotaged the helmet he would use, Melanie's helmet, that past night?

"*Columbia,* Houston, ten seconds from Loss-of-Signal, we'll reacquire you on TDRS West in seven minutes."

The voice startled him, coming as it did after nearly a half hour of silence, but not nearly as much as Orlov did seconds after *Columbia* passed into the thin slice of its orbit, the Zone of Exclusion, where it was out of range of both of NASA's Tracking and Data Relay Satellites.

"There is nothing wrong with your helmet," Orlov said, his voice cartoonlike because of the space suit's low-pressure oxygen supply. "These are the best, most thoroughly inspected Extravehicular Mobility Units in the history of this agency. They do not wish to hide another body."

Santich willed his heart to slow down. Orlov must have seen him trying to study the inside of his helmet. "It's just been a few years since I've been in a real space suit, in a real air lock."

Orlov shrugged, or imitated a shrug as best he could confined in a rigid suit, packed with Santich into a cylinder about twice as wide as a phone booth. "Enjoy it. There is no real work to do. You must know that already."

It was a statement, not a question. Santich wondered what Orlov thought was his real motive for taking Alexandra's place. "You don't think I'd have bumped Dr. O'Day if there really was a repair needed?"

Again the imitation shrug. "It is the captain's prerogative. I have no complaint. You did not bump me."

They fell silent for a few minutes as *Columbia* drifted east, crossed the meridian over the Indian Ocean that marked AOS: Acquisition of Signal.

"*Columbia*, Houston, back with you on TDRS West," came Carreau's voice. Their precious minutes of privacy were up. During a space walk, the radios in the space suits were on "hot mike," so that every word each astronaut uttered was broadcast to Houston, and from there to the world.

"Roger, Houston. Air lock pressure at zero, and we have completed air lock depress. We are ready to proceed with the checklist," Orlov reported.

With that, he, Melanie and Carreau began a long list of switches, valves and space-suit functions that had to be checked, then rechecked before they could step outside. Santich sat and listened, occasionally peeking toward the bottom of the cylinder where the hatch would be pulled open. He steeled himself against what he had to do, yet couldn't suppress a giddiness about finally doing an orbital EVA.

The last time he'd been outside a spaceship, he'd been on a different world, and Earth was a quarter million miles away. How different it would feel to float free, hurtling noiselessly over his blue planet at five miles a second!

"EV2?" The voice tried again before it registered in Santich's mind. "EV2?"

"Houston, EV2, go ahead," he sputtered.

"Okay, Santy, ready for your suit levels."

"Roger. I have four-point-one psi, oxygen at ninety-eight percent, battery at ninety-eight percent."

"Looks good, Santy, and Alex, you have a go to open the hatch."

"All right," Orlov replied. "I am opening the hatch."

Orlov had already twisted himself so his torso was even with the handle. He turned it and pulled inward.

"Hatch open. Now I will open the thermal cover."

He unsnapped a series of fasteners that held the insulated blanket in place and pushed it outward on its hinge. The electric lights in the air lock suddenly were overpowered by the direct sunlight pouring in. Orlov reached out the hatch and snapped a carabiner onto an attachment point just outside on the cargo bay's forward bulkhead.

"I have secured my tether reel assembly and am disconnecting my umbilical. Time: Three days, two hours, twenty-seven minutes."

With that, Orlov slid out the open hatch, and Santich edged downward. He stuck his head out in time to see San Francisco Bay slide into view overhead. God, what a sight! Offshore, the ever present fog bank had already begun its daily creep toward the Golden Gate, which stood out dark blue against the jutting brown-and-green fingers of land on either side.

"Houston, I can almost see the morning traffic on the Golden Gate Bridge!" he said, the built-up years of cynicism gone without a trace.

"Roger, Santy. We're all envious down here. They tell us you've made more NASA history: the first astronaut ever to perform both a lunar and a space shuttle EVA."

The Bay area spun slowly out of view, replaced by the Central Valley, then the foothills of the Sierra Nevada, then the mountains themselves, still a stark white from their winter's snow.

"*Columbia,* Houston for EV2?"

"Right. Houston, EV2, go ahead."

"Roger, Santy, we can't really tell from Charlie camera if you've attached your tether reel."

Hurriedly he snapped the carabiner in place. "Uh, Roger, Houston. Done. And I'm ready to disconnect the umbilical. Time: Three days, two hours, thirty-three minutes."

With both hands he braced himself in the open hatch and gently pushed down. It was still too hard, and he flew out the hatch much faster than he'd intended. He compounded the mistake by twisting for a handhold, transforming his motion into a complex somersault, checked only by the tether reel assembly, which eventually stopped his outward movement and gradually reeled him back to the bulkhead.

He landed with a thump that only he and those inside *Columbia* could hear.

"Slow and easy," Melanie advised from her view at the flight deck's aft window.

"Roger," Santich answered, unhurt save for his ego.

With exaggerated slowness he turned around and for the first time truly appreciated the space shuttle's enormity. There before him, at the end of *Columbia*'s robot arm like a giant insect on a pin, was the GRO—the Gamma Ray Observatory, seventy feet across its thin solar panels. Beneath it was the vast cargo bay, sixty feet long and fifteen across, and largely empty except for a few tool and spare-parts lockers mounted against the walls. In front of one of these hung Orlov, wearing the red stripes on his legs marking him as EV1, slowly removing wrenches for the "repair" he and Santich would perform.

Overhead, the desert in Nevada gave way to the mountains of Utah, and Santich collected himself against the bulkhead. The grandeur of the view was gradually replaced by fear of what he needed to do: How in hell was he going to sneak up on Orlov and overpower him? He couldn't even maneuver from point A to point B, while Orlov moved about in complete control.

"Slow and easy," Melanie advised again.

He detected an edge to her voice, as if she were pondering the same problem. Well, he didn't have much time. It had to happen as soon as *Columbia* went Loss-of-Signal with Houston on this orbit, which took them far enough south to make contact even with the ground station on Diego Garcia in the Indian Ocean impossible.

Overhead were the Colorado Rockies; he had about an hour to get accustomed to the new environment and pick his ambush spot.

"Okay, Houston, I'm going to translate over to the port sill," he announced as he began pulling himself hand over hand. But with each pull of his arm, his legs swung out in the opposite direction, with increasing violence, until he could barely hold onto the grab rail.

"Slowly, Santy," came Orlov's voice over the headset. "Rotate your wrists slightly to dampen the torque."

Santich stopped, took a deep breath, and began again, as Orlov had advised, twisting his wrist each time he reached for a new handhold. The trick worked, and his legs stayed in control beneath him.

"Thank you, Alex," he said after he'd reached the port sill, ashamed of his debt to a man he was preparing to bludgeon or suffocate, whichever proved easier. He hooked a second tether onto a long wire that ran the length of the cargo bay just under the sill, allowing him to move back to where the tool lockers were mounted.

"*Columbia,* Houston. Handing over to TDRS East."

Already! Sure enough, *Columbia* had silently passed over the continental United States, and was out over the equatorial Atlantic. Half an orbit to go. Less than forty-five minutes.

Orlov was making his way to the GRO, which Melanie was lowering, using the robot arm, onto some support stands in the rear of the cargo bay.

"Soft dock," Orlov announced as a pin on the satellite slipped into a groove on the forward support. "I am moving forward to lock the pin."

Santich turned his attention back to the tool locker just to his left. Slowly, tentatively, he slid each boot into restraints mounted on a platform in front of the locker. "Houston, EV2. Retrieving my tools."

Orlov had left the doors open, and he reached in for a seven-sixteenths-inch wrench, a power wrench fitted with a seven-sixteenths-inch socket and a long, thin torque wrench calibrated to measure forces in tenths of an inch-pound. He weighed the last one in the stiff palm of his gloved hand, trying to determine its balance point if it were to come crashing down in a long, overhand swing. Which way would his legs move in response? God, he hoped it didn't come to that.

"Houston, *Columbia,* I'm moving on to Step 17 Alpha," Melanie announced.

"Roger, Mel. We concur."

Santich watched the roundwormlike end effector on the robot arm release the satellite and, guided by Melanie's touch in the flight deck, move toward a small platform mounted next to the tool locker. The end effector slid over a foot-long metal finger, then locked onto it with a series of crisscrossing metal wires that pulled tight.

"Have secured foot restraint," Melanie said. "Moving it over to Alex."

The triple-jointed arm lifted the platform out of its latches and slowly twisted and pivoted it to the cargo bay floor, where Alex waited to step in. *So far, so good,* Santich thought, and reminded himself he had to be on the other side of the cargo bay. Above him, he could already see the fuzzy line between day and night on the Earth's surface, just east of southern Africa's Atlantic coast. With tools clipped to his chest, he spun over and reached for handholds mounted down the side of the cargo bay to a two-inch pole that ran across to the starboard side. He clipped a tether to a thin wire that ran parallel to the pole and began his traverse, markedly less awkward now that he had some practice.

By the time *Columbia* had raced into nighttime and cargo bay floodlights had replaced sunshine, Santich was at the starboard side and clipping onto the safety wire that ran the length of the bay on that side.

"*Columbia,* Houston, twelve minutes to LOS, and be advised we'll have no comm out of Diego. You're on your own."

"Roger that, Jules. I think we can manage," Orlov replied.

"We're all sure you can. Great job so far, guys. Craig wants me to congratulate you on your work. You're about ten minutes ahead of the time line."

"Roger that," Orlov answered. "Thank you," he added, as if suddenly remembering that wholesome, public relations–oriented chitchat was more a part of this mission than "fixing" the satellite was.

Another twelve minutes. Then he would confront the man who'd murdered his wife's lover in outer space, then had set his body on fire in a staged car accident. If he was lucky, he would be able to trap him in the air lock and bring him home. If he wasn't lucky, another man would die in orbit. Santich wondered how NASA's crack PR staff would put a happy face on *that*.

"Also, *Columbia,* FYI, no action required. EVA reported a momentary voltage spike on Alex's power supply. Apparently saw something similar during ascent, too. We're pretty sure it's bad instrumentation down here."

Voltage spike! Jesus . . . Trudy's message! Was that good or bad? Christ, what a time to find out! Voltage was good, pressure was bad, Santich remembered. Voltage meant they had expunged the IFA log before the crew had been named. Which, according to his and Kyle's logic, meant that they knew who had overpressurized the air lock, and had assigned Orlov to the flight anyway.

Santich tried to think and move in the cumbersome suit at the same time, a challenge that slowed him further. Did their launch-day logic make any sense? What if Bruce wasn't sure who had overpressed the air lock, or worse, didn't care, so long as his big cover-up remained intact?

He had to slow things down, but a glance at his timer told him *Columbia* would lose signal in exactly four minutes, forty-three seconds. If only there was a way to question Orlov without the baseball-bat-over-the-head approach.

Santich saw that Orlov had already clamped his boots into the end-effector foot restraint, and was snapping his safety tether onto a metal ring beside his left boot. *Of course!* Once he was in that foot restraint, he was at Melanie's mercy.

"I am secure. Hoist me to the Bravo position," he told Melanie.

"Roger, Alex," she replied, gently moving a little joystick upward, then slightly to the right. In the cargo bay, Orlov moved correspondingly: upward and slightly right, until he was positioned directly in front of the bolts that held a large metal panel in place over the sun sensors.

"*Columbia,* Houston, one minute to LOS," Carreau announced. "We'll pick you back up on the other side in eleven minutes."

Santich's mind raced: If he gave a sharp command, could Melanie move Orlov before he could grab hold of the satellite? He watched Orlov take his power socket wrench off the tool caddy on his chest. Yes—the wrench required both hands to operate; it would probably give them the time they needed. But what about friction between the socket and the bolt head? Could that do anything? Like hold Orlov just long enough for him to grab GRO's long antenna boom over his head?

"Ten seconds to LOS."

Santich watched the wide cone of light from the work lamp on Orlov's helmet reflect off the gold foil wrapping much of the enormous spacecraft. Flashes of heat lightning over the Indian Ocean lit up the clouds in the background.

Abruptly, some of the static in his ears disappeared. They were alone, for nine minutes and forty seconds. He held his breath and listened, heard only the faint reverberations of his own heart, tripping along at nearly twice its normal rate.

"Fifteen turns, fifteen more to go," Orlov said, mainly to himself, concentrating on the first of four bolts he would have to remove to open the hinged panel.

Santich turned his head as little as possible to the right, and at the edge of the helmet's field of view saw Melanie standing at the controls of the robot arm, staring at him, eyes wide. He flicked his eyes back to Orlov, saw him still engrossed in the first bolt, and turned back to Melanie. He raised his right arm slowly, pointing his fingers at the satellite, and, making sure Orlov wasn't watching, suddenly jerked it to the right. Through the window, Melanie nodded.

Without warning, the robot arm pulled away from the satellite, yanking the power wrench out of Orlov's hands as he swayed back and forth at the end of the arm.

"Break! Break!" he shouted. "Melanie, I have translated forward five meters!" He turned toward Melanie, saw her staring at him, saw Santich against the starboard sill, the torque wrench in his hands like a club. "Oh."

He was indeed about fifteen feet ahead of the satellite, twenty feet from the cargo bay's forward bulkhead, and twenty feet from the cargo bay floor: stranded until Melanie freed him. Santich realized he'd held his breath since LOS and breathed deeply.

"What is this?" Orlov demanded.

Santich swallowed, took another deep breath. "You tell us. Why did you kill Torrington?" he blurted.

Even from twenty feet away, Santich saw the gray eyes blink twice, in seemingly genuine surprise.

"That is what you think? That I killed Sam?"

Yes? Or no? How the hell would he know for sure? "Stop fucking around, Alex. Three switch throws. That's all we need to jettison you and back *Columbia* away. Why did you kill him?"

Orlov shook his head slowly. "Listen to me. I did not murder Sam Torrington. I am not sure why you think I did, but I swear to you, I did not."

"Seven minutes to AOS, Santy."

Great. Seven minutes to force a confession. "Because he was screwing your wife," Santich accused. "You did the honorable thing, and you made an honest woman out of Olena again."

Again Orlov blinked and shook his head. "Captain Santich, you are making a terrible mistake. Yes, I believe Olena was having an affair with Sam, although she has never admitted it." He paused. "Is that what you thought I meant when I said you were an honorable man? I meant only that I admired how you returned to your wife, despite whatever may have happened. That is all. It is what I am trying to do with Lena."

That single cell of doubt in his mind at launch began to multiply rapidly. Like a cancer. He resisted, held his ground: *Someone* on 74 had killed Torrington; who had more reason than a jealous husband?

"Okay," Santich began. "Give me a good reason, any reason, why Banke or Halvorson or Habuda would want to kill him."

Orlov gave the barely noticeable shrug. "Why do you believe someone on *Atlantis* did it?"

"Five minutes, Santy."

Could he not know? He was in the damn air lock; he *had* to know. "IFA 74-11 was the failure of the helmet gasket on Sam's helmet. IFA 74-09 was what made it happen."

"Seventy-four-zero-nine," Orlov said slowly. "That must have been the air lock press." His eyes looked up suddenly. "How, Santy? How did 74-09 cause 74-11?"

The look was of alarm, not resignation; Santich felt a twinge of foreboding. "Torrington's helmet had been tampered with. The helmet seal was weakened on the ground. All it needed was a mild shock to jiggle it a bit and make its subsequent failure almost certain. IFA 74-09 was that jiggle. I know someone on *Atlantis* did it because I know there was no ground command."

Orlov shook his head slowly. "Oh, no, no, no, no!"

Santich watched him silently. *Was this it?* Was this the confession?

"No, no, no!" Orlov continued. "Santy, we are in trouble!"

Santich said nothing; the foreboding turned to dread.

"Santy, no one on 74 killed Sam. The command to overpressurize the air lock was in the automatic software."

Santich considered this a moment. "*Atlantis* killed Sam?"

"Someone wrote that command into the software, Santy. It did not write itself."

Was he telling the truth? How could he possibly check? Kyle knew computers, but he couldn't talk to him until he got back inside. That meant either letting Orlov back in, with the risk that he'd run amok and destroy the ship, or lock him out until he could talk with Trudy and Kyle. But when would that be? Would this next orbit come close enough to Houston? He tried to remember, instead thought again about what Orlov had said.

"What did you mean, *we* are in trouble?" he asked suddenly.

"Santy, someone has tampered with *Columbia*'s flight software. I am certain of it now."

"*What?*"

"Two minutes to AOS!" Melanie warned from her post.

"Someone has altered PASS. I saw the hydraulics low pressure message flicker twice on the way up, but it did not trigger the caution and warning system. I did not even suspect it could have been a deliberate change until you told me that 74-09 was the mechanism for the gasket failure."

Santich's head swam with the new information: Orlov didn't kill Sam; someone on the ground did? And whoever did also tampered with 102's PASS, its Primary Avionics Shuttle Software? Jesus God, if that was true, they *were* as good as dead! But what if this was bullshit, a story Orlov invented on the spot? He looked at Melanie, still at the controls of the robot arm, with Alexandra standing behind her, hands over her mouth. Orlov swayed slightly at the tip of the arm, suspended high above the cargo bay. Heat lightning still sparked behind his head.

"One minute to AOS!"

"Santy, I cannot prove to you in the next sixty seconds what I have said. You have to trust me."

The cold gray eyes stared at him unblinkingly. *How the hell could he stay so cool?* Santich felt his gut twist inside him, and consciously slowed his heart again. Slowly at first, then more quickly, he nodded his head. "Okay. I trust you. Can you figure out what's been done to the software without telling Houston?"

Orlov nodded. "I think so. But we need to lose contact with the ground. And I need more time than the ZOE can give us."

"Thirty seconds!"

"How?"

"We do not have time right now. At the next LOS. Now we must pretend nothing has happened. Melanie, move me back to the satellite."

Santich nodded at her, and she began moving Orlov back to his power wrench, still stuck to the half-removed bolt head. With a lurch, she stopped him, and he grabbed for the tool.

"*Columbia*, Houston, we're back with you on TDRS West."

"Roger, Houston," Orlov answered. "I had to change out the battery on the power wrench, so I am still on bolt number one."

"Roger, Alex. In that case, we take back our congratulations for getting ahead of the time line."

Santich waited for them to ask why it took ten minutes to replace a battery, but they never did. He cleared his mind and climbed to the spot where Alex was to hand him the old sun sensors. He would take them to the parts locker just aft of him, and then trot them right back out so Alex could reinstall them. It was a pointless exercise, inflicting the dangers of a space walk—micrometeoroids, cosmic rays, and solar flares—on two crews just to preserve a cover-up. If they were going to lie, they should have just faked a video problem at the TDRS ground station at the start of the space walk and restored the television link five hours later to find that—presto!—*Columbia*'s gallant crew had "fixed" GRO without any help from the ground.

Just like they would have to figure out their software problem without help from the ground.

God, he hoped Orlov was wrong about that. If the software had really been tampered with, it could prove impossible to fix in orbit, and would certainly be something they would need Houston's help with. But asking for assistance meant alerting the saboteur, and forcing him to desperate measures. And what if it was the mechanical systems officer, who could command the cargo bay doors to swing open during re-entry?

Santich shuddered. *Columbia* wouldn't have a chance. The doors would tear away in seconds. Within minutes, the searing heat would burn through the cargo bay floor and bulkheads. Very little wreckage would make it to Earth. Why would someone mess with *Columbia*'s software? Maybe their whole premise was wrong. Maybe it wasn't someone who wanted Sam Torrington dead; maybe it was a sociopath whose inner voice had decreed that someone should die on each space shuttle flight.

"Houston, *Columbia,* I have lost another battery. I will install my last spare."

"Go ahead, Alex."

Why was he stalling? They were more than an hour into the space walk, and they hadn't even taken the access panel off yet. Perhaps his initial suspicion was correct, and Orlov was merely buying time, plotting as Santy dithered. After all, he had only Orlov's word about the warning message. Neither he nor Melanie had noticed it. Maybe Orlov was a better liar than he thought, and had made it up on the spot. . . .

Above, the south Texas coastline rose over the horizon and turned slowly toward him. If only he had the UHF. He would ask Kyle exactly what he'd found in the previous versions of the IFA log. He'd ask Hoop if Celestial Data Systems had been given any last-minute software changes to put through SAIL, and he'd make sure Trudy was all right. The only comfort if Orlov was the villain was that it meant Trudy and Kyle were safe. But if it wasn't Orlov, then they were back where they started, and Trudy and Kyle had to be on their guard.

As Santich watched and waited, Orlov again complained about his wrench, and this time asked Melanie to take him to the tool locker so he could get a new one, and then to the air lock for some new batteries. This exercise ate another twenty minutes, and still only two of the four bolts were out.

Twenty-two minutes to go. The South Atlantic spun in and out of view, and with the African coast came nightfall. Santich turned on the helmet lamp and lifted the dark visor on his helmet up and out of the way. Now he wished he'd paid more attention to computers. It was another of the generational phenomena that had passed him by, like compact discs and videocassettes. Did Melanie know computers? He hoped so. He could trust her, and she could warn him if Orlov was lying.

"*Columbia,* Houston, ten minutes to LOS. This time it's only for seven minutes, but we still won't have comm through the ground stations. You're on your own again."

Orlov would need more than seven minutes to figure out what was wrong. They would have to extend the loss-of-signal period, perhaps indefinitely. That meant disrupting the Ku-band microwave antenna in the forward, starboard corner of the cargo bay. But that still left S-band radio communication possible. And those antennas were buried within *Columbia,* inaccessible to the crew.

"One more battery," Orlov announced. "We should find a new supplier, I think."

"Maybe we'll send up the Energizer bunny next time."

"It would be an improvement," Orlov said crossly.

He actually sounded irritated, Santich noticed. *He's a pretty good liar after all.* He turned toward the three-foot-diameter dish in the corner and wondered how best to disable it. It was mounted on a pivot that let it stow inside the cargo bay during liftoff and entry, and up and outboard while in orbit. They could swing the antenna into the stowed position and then jam it there with a screwdriver. But that left the chance that a particular flight orientation might point it in the general direction of a TDRS satellite, giving Houston a television peek at the goings-on. He looked at the stiff cables that passed the volumes of data running through the antenna. Yes . . . that would work. They fed into the wall through a quick-disconnect fitting that simply unplugged.

They would disconnect those and have Melanie disable the S-band radio from inside. That would leave only the shuttle's built-in UHF radio that would be useful only during the infrequent passes over a ground station.

"*Columbia,* Houston, ten seconds to LOS. We'll pick you back up on the other side."

Santich held his breath, waited for the static to go away. Finally, it did, and he pulled himself arm over arm, legs swinging, toward the Ku antenna.

"Melanie, disable the S-band. Make sure it can't be overridden from the ground. I'm gonna unplug the Ku."

"A good idea," Orlov said. "I will replace these bolts."

Santich knocked his legs against the wall as he moved, mentally counting down the time left. A long minute later, he arrived, breathing hard from the exertion, and yanked at the rubber plug holding the cables in the wall. Without resistance, a thin boot slid off, revealing the quick-disconnect fitting underneath. It was held in place with two tiny screws.

"Christ! There are goddamn screws on this thing!"

"The tool locker," Orlov suggested. "There are screwdrivers in the tool locker."

Santich stared at the screw heads, recalled the sizes and shapes of what was in the locker. "No way. We need an eyeglass-size flathead. There's nothing that small in there."

"We have that in here," Alexandra said over the radio. "I know we have it. I used it the other day to change out a filter element."

"There is no way," Orlov said as he worked. He was already tightening his third bolt and had one more to go. "We cannot possibly get into the air lock, repress, open it up, depress, and get out in time."

Santich looked down at the tools hanging from his chest. Big and clumsy, all of them. "We need a dime, that's what we need."

"I am finished. Alex Prime, take me to the Ku-antenna."

Alexandra stepped up to the controls and gingerly began pulling Orlov away from the GRO. Slowly she rotated him around to face the starboard wall.

"Today, Alexandra," Orlov said. "I must get there today."

"I don't want to rush and slam you into the bulkhead."

As he glided through space on his giant cherry picker, Orlov pulled apart his power tool and removed the battery.

"Could you slide over, Santy?" he asked. "Thank you. Alexandra, how much time until AOS?"

She kept her eyes focused on the controls and out the aft window. "Just a moment. I can only do one thing at a time," she muttered.

"Four minutes," Melanie grunted, "and fifteen seconds."

Santich watched as Orlov reached his gloved pinky into the recessed battery holder, dug around, and slowly pulled out the end of the copper flange that pressed against the battery's negative terminal.

"This may be too thin, but it is all I can think of." Orlov slowly slid the copper strip into the groove on one of the screws. With one hand he held it against the screw; with the other, he spun the power wrench counterclockwise. "Is it turning?"

Santich bent closer. "You're getting it. Can I help?"

"No. It is very awkward, and there is only room for one man."

"Time, Alexandra!" Santich shouted into the radio.

"Three minutes, twenty-seven seconds," Alexandra answered. "Can I ask what we're doing?" she added tentatively.

"Melanie, how are you doing?" Santich asked.

"Almost there," she answered, her breath still strained. "I'm in avionics bay three-A, and I'm disconnecting the power leads to the receiver. They can still send ground commands through UHF."

"I know. We can deal with that next. Thank God for budget cuts, eh?" The tracking station in the Australian Outback that had been there from the days of John Glenn aboard *Friendship 7* was gone, as were most of the dozens of stations NASA once maintained. "We have until Maui to disable UHF."

"There. It is out," Orlov announced.

Santich looked down in time to see the half-inch screw

escape from the tip of Orlov's makeshift screwdriver and start spinning upward. Santich moved his hand around it and closed his fingers.

"Good catch. Now the other." Orlov had already lined the copper strip into the groove and positioned his hands on the wrench. "How much time?"

"One minute, fifty-one seconds."

It was going to be close. They couldn't pull the plug after reacquiring signal because then Houston could re-create what had happened. On the other hand, there wasn't enough time to put everything back the way it was, either.

"Alexandra, turn off all the TV cameras, please." That would buy them at least a few extra seconds. Houston never turned on a camera before asking, not since the middeck camera on STS-53 caught a female astronaut, a physician with a doctorate in astrophysics and a mother of two, buck naked and sponging herself off, taking the space shuttle's equivalent of a shower. Still, Mission Control might make an exception during a space walk.

"One minute," Alexandra reported. "All the TV cameras are off."

"Almost there," Orlov grunted. Beads of sweat grew larger on his brow and nose. "A few more turns."

The screw popped out of the hole, and Santich bent over to catch it also. Orlov let the power wrench drift against his stomach as he reached for the fitting with both hands.

"It is stuck."

"What?"

"I am pulling as hard as I can; it will not budge."

"Thirty seconds." Alexandra's voice had risen a full octave.

Santich bent down, studied the fitting closely and finally saw the tiny arrow inscribed in the plastic. "It's threaded. Turn it counterclockwise."

Orlov turned, and within two revolutions, the outer collar came free, revealing the pin connectors underneath. He grabbed the plug and started pulling. "Still stuck. Must be the thermal cycling."

The fitting never saw temperatures in the hangar like it saw in orbit. It had probably swelled in the previous day-time pass and just hadn't cooled down yet. Santich reached behind Orlov and grabbed the thick cable to help him pull.

"Ten seconds!"

"It is coming," Orlov said. "I shall wiggle it; you pull."

They wiggled and pulled, Santich idly wondering how much high-energy radiation would jolt through him if *Columbia* automatically started transmitting data at AOS.

"Five!"

"It is coming."

Santich strained backward, his legs pushing against the cargo bay wall. Overhead he saw the twinkle of lights amid the lightning flashes. The Maldives, no doubt.

"Col—"

The plug popped free, sending Santich flying backward until a pull from Orlov, still planted on the end of the robot arm, brought him crashing back.

"Did you hear that?" He breathed deeply to slow down. "We were too late."

"I heard. I do not think they had enough to interpret correctly. Remember, it takes them a few seconds to fine tune the signal whenever they switch satellites."

"We didn't downlink anything." It was Melanie. "I barely heard Jules's first syllable."

The inside of Orlov's helmet was beaded with droplets of sweat. Santich squinted, saw that his was, too. "I was certain we were going to charbroil ourselves when the Ku came back on-line and started downlinking."

"No, there was never that risk. Our EMUs are completely insulated. We cannot form an electrical ground."

Orlov smiled, and for the first time, Santich thought, it wasn't the smile of a predator. "Okay. Now what?"

"Will someone please tell me what's going on?" Alexandra whined.

"I'll start on the UHF," Melanie said. "It shouldn't take long."

"I have buttoned up GRO. When we reestablish comm,

we can tell them we took out the modules and put in the so-called spares while Alex Prime worked the comm problem.''

"How long will it take to figure out the software?"

Orlov shrugged his space-suit shrug. "I do not know. If the new lines are flagged, then not long. If they are not, it could take days, even weeks."

Santich shook his head. "We don't have weeks. We don't even have days."

"I only tell you the problem as I see it. We may get lucky." He twisted back toward the giant satellite hovering over the cargo bay, panels outstretched. "I shall stow the tools, and then we can go inside."

Santich handed Orlov his wrenches, and Alexandra ferried him to the tool locker on the robot arm. He replaced each one into its specially fitted slot, then shut and latched the doors. Santich was already at the hatch when Orlov joined him. They took a final look at the Earth overhead, now back in daylight, before sliding into the air lock and closing the hatch.

33

Orlov pushed the switches that started repressurization while Santich plugged air and power umbilicals into the control units on their chests. "Why the rush to button up GRO?"

Orlov unfastened his helmet as the pressure inside the airlock climbed to 4.1 psi, the same as their suits. "Gamma Ray Observatory is a perfectly healthy scientific instrument. Our present difficulty is no reason to degrade it."

Santich watched Orlov, amazed, and more than a little frightened. They might all die in orbit if *Columbia* had indeed been booby-trapped, and Orlov was worried about a science research satellite. A creature of pure reason, driven by single-minded ambition. He wondered again if they were really on the same side.

With a heavy clank, the hatch into the middeck swung open, and Alexandra helped first Santich, then Orlov out of the air lock. Santich saw that her eyes were even wider than normal, her skin pale and clammy. She was scared. Good. So was he.

"The UHF radio is disabled. Houston cannot communicate with us," Melanie reported, her head poking downward from the flight deck.

Orlov pulled himself free from the legs portion of his suit and propelled himself across the middeck to the stor-

273

age lockers. "I need both notebook computers, and one of the GPCs."

They had turned off one of *Columbia*'s four General Purpose Computers upon reaching orbit to save electricity. The other three continued checking one another for errors.

"Can you power up GPC 4 and leave it off-line?" Santich asked.

"I know it can be done. Let me check the manuals to see how. Alex Prime, your undergraduate major was computer science. You will help me."

"That was years ago!" Alexandra complained. "FORTRAN, PASCAL, COBOL, stuff like that."

Melanie shrugged. "It's all Greek to me."

"I hate computers," Santich said flatly.

Orlov gathered both notebooks, a bundle of cable and some connectors and glided "up" the ladder into the flight deck. "Come," he ordered Alexandra.

Melanie sidled beside Santich and helped stow the stiff, still-damp space-suit torsos, legs, arms and helmets. "It looks like we bit off more than we can chew," she said quietly.

Santich closed the air lock hatch, pulled off the tops of his liquid-cooled long underwear, and started ripping off the electrodes taped to his chest. He winced as the one over his heart took four gray hairs with it.

"We did that when we agreed to fly this damned mission." He started pulling off his long johns, remembered Melanie was there, and went ahead anyway. "Which is worse: a murderer on the crew, or a murderer writing flight software?"

She averted her eyes, blindly held out for him some sweatpants and a blue golf shirt emblazoned with the STS-74A logo—four stars around a sketch of a space shuttle grabbing the GRO with its robot arm. "I think I'd rather have the killer on board. By the way, you're pretty cute in your birthday suit. Legs are a little skinny, though."

He climbed into his clothes. "Thanks. Now I'm gonna sue you for sexual harassment when we get home. And

Emily will hunt you down and beat the crap out of you.''

She smiled, but only for a moment. "Jesus, Santy, what if it *is* the flight software? How do we get home?''

The question scared him each time he thought about it. The computer programs that ran the shuttle were all-important, all-powerful and thoroughly undecipherable. "Well,'' he began, "we've got a couple of options. One, we call down, tell them the problem, have them work out a new package, and uplink it.''

"A whole package? It'll take them weeks to test it.''

"We don't need the whole thing. All we need is entry and landing stuff. Major modes 301 through 305.''

Melanie shook her head. "If we're going to ask for help, then why have we broken off comm?''

"I'd like to know who's out to get us. Alex thinks he can figure that out by looking at the coding on the software change.''

"*If* he can find it,'' she reminded him.

"If he can find it,'' he agreed. "Anyway, if the whole world knows we're in trouble and asking Houston for help, I think we'll get clean software, no matter *who* tampered with what we've got now.''

Melanie paused, stared off at the storage lockers. "Your radio!'' she exclaimed.

"Right!'' He floated toward one of the two lockers assigned for his personal gear. He pulled out a thick sweatshirt and carefully unwrapped the components. "Do we pass near Houston this rev?''

She bit her lower lip. "I think so. We passed a little to the north on the last orbit, so we should be a little south this time. I'd need to look at the ground-track program on the notebook to be sure.''

"Yeah. I doubt Alex will be done with it yet, though. Well, we can look out the windows and see where we are.''

He started drifting toward the flight deck with the radio in his hands when Melanie grabbed an elbow.

"Santy,'' she whispered. "Can we trust him?''

Santich listened to the two Alexes' voices on the flight

deck. "I don't know," he whispered back. "Did you see any funnies in the hydraulics on the ride up?"

Melanie shook her head.

"Neither did I. On the other hand, I wasn't paying as close attention as I should have. All we can do is play this by ear. For now, let's keep an eye on Orlov and try to call Trudy."

They floated into the flight deck, where Orlov was emerging from an open panel in front of Melanie's seat, his fingers gingerly surrounding a gray cable.

"Okay," he told Alexandra. "Try to load it now."

Her fingers typed out a command on the keyboard. "It's working."

Orlov nodded. "Good."

"Have you got it?" Santich asked.

"We have solved the hardware interface problem. There is no easy way to make the notebook talk to the GPC. I had to rig this cable. We just pulled a small subroutine to make sure the connection worked. Now we will start loading PASS."

Santich watched as Orlov typed out a brief command into the miniature keyboard. A small alarm clock appeared in the upper left-hand corner of the display. The four astronauts hovered overhead, waiting, as the tiny computer began loading the entire quarter-million-line Primary Avionics Shuttle Software program into its memory.

"You're going to fit all of PASS onto that tiny thing?" Santich had learned enough about the GPCs to know the working memory on each IBM AP-101 was not enough to handle the entire program, only the portion needed for a particular part of the mission.

"My friend, this chip is ten times faster with ten times as much memory as those four monsters put together," Orlov said, patting the notebook gently.

Santich nodded, looked out the overhead windows to see the blue Pacific scrolling out of view, replaced with the clouds and forests of British Columbia. "Will UHF transmissions interfere with your work?" he asked.

Orlov shook his head. "But I thought you had disabled the UHF."

"Different UHF," Santich said as he pressed the suction cups on the underside of the antenna to the triple-layered, two-and-a-half-inch-thick glass. "A good captain never leaves port without a spare."

He connected the radio to the antenna, plugged in the earphones and tested the batteries before leaving the assembled unit to float near the window.

Overhead, forests, mountains and deserts spun slowly beneath them, until Santich figured they were close enough to Texas. "We never talked about call signs," he said wistfully, turning the radio on. "Here goes: Trudy, Trudy, Trudy, *Columbia*." A pause. "Trudy, Trudy, Trudy, *Columbia*."

In response he got only static. He tried again, then again, until *Columbia* was well out over the Gulf of Mexico. He thought a moment, blinked, and shut off the radio. "I don't know what I was thinking. They're going apeshit down there. They've lost contact with us in the middle of an EVA. There's no way Trudy's going to get out of the control room, not even for a minute. We'll try again later."

Alexandra turned from the aft windows to face him. "Okay. I've been more than patient. Will someone please explain to me what's going on?"

Santich looked up at her with a sigh. "I told you all about Torrington. And you heard me and Alex talking outside."

"Why did we cut off communication with Houston?" Her eyes were moist, on the verge of enormous, weightless tears. "If someone has tampered with PASS, we're going to need their help!"

So young, so naive. And just now, so tiresome. "Probably, yes. But just remember the help 74 got when they were in a bind. They had to land in the middle of the night in a gale, just for appearance' sake. Hell, they even risked *your* neck on a completely unnecessary space walk, just to save face." He saw the tears ready to erupt and scolded himself. "Once we know what the problem is," he said gently, "we'll be a lot smarter about who in Mission Control we can trust."

She blotted her eyes with the sleeve of her green golf shirt and took a deep breath. "I'm sorry. I guess I just can't believe this is happening. I know it happens all the time, on the outside, on the news, in the papers." She inhaled sharply to clear her nose. "I never thought it would happen within the agency, you know? Everyone working for a common goal, pulling together?"

Santich felt the queasiness return to his stomach. *Within the agency*... Who? Who within the agency would sabotage his flight? He was still missing something, something critical. He shook his head and peered down over Orlov's shoulder at the columns of letters and numbers.

"Any luck?" he finally asked.

"I have the entry and landing portion right here, but it will take forever scrolling through it. This column right here?" He fingered the right-hand portion of the screen. "This is the documentation. That tells you in plain language what that particular line does in the program. And this column? This is the flag. These six numerals are the day, month and year that line was written. And this alphanumeric combination tells where the line originated. See? The AR prefix stands for Advanced Research Corp, the CD for Celestial Data Systems, SL for the SAIL lab, and so on."

"And the last two digits?"

"They supposedly tell you exactly *who* wrote the change, based on the password of the user. In practice, I am not sure how well that worked. I know passwords were a nuisance to some programmers, and they would walk away from the machines leaving them logged on and so forth."

Santich stared at the program code itself: the peculiar words, the strange symbols. The documentation he could understand: body flap up, body flap down, left rudder, right rudder; Orlov was scrolling through the flight control surfaces portion of the program. Each subroutine heading was followed by hundreds of lines of code, and each line had a date and origination flag.

"So you're looking at the last column, for recent changes? In the last month or two?" Santich's eyes were already swimming, giving him a slight sense of vertigo. "Even if the four of us sat here for hours, days, we would *still* probably miss it!"

"Yes, I agree," Orlov nodded. "I must write a program that searches that particular field, looking for lines written between last October and this May."

The numbers scrolled downward in a blur. Santich saw that most of the code was written in the late seventies, the original software, or in 1987, after *Challenger* blew up, killed a civilian schoolteacher and forced the agency to take up much of the slack it had given itself.

"Is it possible," he asked, "is it possible to write some code with the wrong date? So that it looks like it was old code instead of new code?"

Orlov shook his head. "It should not be possible. Because the date comes not from when it is written but when it is integrated into PASS at JSC. That is a real-time mainframe that date-stamps things as they come in. In theory it is possible, by resetting the date on the mainframe, adding the change, and resetting it back. But I do not think it likely. Too many people use the computer, day and night. It would be noticed."

Santich forced himself to look away from the blue-and-white screen. It was starting to give him a dull headache. He knew he hated computers for a reason; maybe this was it. Maybe for twenty-five years he subconsciously knew the machines could be easily subverted, more thoroughly and more dishonestly than a snipped hydraulic line or a loosened landing gear nut. Since the day he had first climbed into a Gemini capsule, he had suppressed that fear, knowing that man would never get into orbit without computers making the thousands of simultaneous calculations necessary to get up and back safely.

But with Gemini and Apollo, it was theoretically possible, given a loss of communication with Houston and computer failure aboard, to turn the capsule to the correct attitude, give or take a few degrees, fire the retrorockets the prescribed amount of time, and get home in one piece. Neil Armstrong had proven it on Gemini 8. With the space shuttle, that was out of the question. Just a degree or two off the correct attitude at the wrong moment could throw the vehicle into an unrecoverable stall or spin. The airframe would either tear apart or plummet like a rock. Either way, the crew would be doomed.

"Alex Prime, come write this program," Orlov commanded. "I will take the second notebook and load the BFS."

The BFS! He'd almost forgotten. The Backup Flight Software was just that: programs only for launch and landing, written and verified by completely different companies than those that produced the Primary Avionics Shuttle Software. Of course, he realized gloomily, why would a saboteur ruin PASS but leave BFS untouched?

"Wouldn't our saboteur have gone after BFS as well?" he asked.

"Not necessarily," Orlov replied, his head and shoulders stuck beneath the pilot's console again. "You see, the GPCs check for errors in the code by comparing with one another, not with some objective standard. If the code is the same on all four computers, then the GPC sees no error."

"So the GPCs could fly us into the side of Mount McKinley, if all four were seeing and saying the same thing."

"Yes."

Santich nodded, shrugged at Melanie, who answered with a sigh. "Mel, why don't you go ahead and get GRO into the release position. No matter what else we do, we have to get rid of that thing."

She nodded and eased over to the aft windows, where she activated the robot arm and began unberthing it from its cradle along the port sill.

Alexandra joined her at the windows. She had regained her composure, and now looked out at the satellite, its gold foil gleaming in the sunlight, the Amazon delta passing 205 nautical miles below as a backdrop. "Don't we have to reboost it before release?" she asked finally.

"That was the plan B.C.," Santich answered when no one else would. "Before crisis. I don't want to burn an extra ounce of gas until I figure out what we need to get home."

No one said anything for a while as Melanie and Orlov worked at their tasks. Only an occasional clacking of a keyboard or the whir of a motor broke the hum of cooling fans that, after four days, the astronauts had come to accept as silence.

"How much propellant would we need to reboost?" Alexandra asked.

Christ. "I'd have to look in the flight data file. A lot, though, given the weight of that satellite. Off the top of my head, I'd say a couple of hundred pounds."

Another pause. "Don't we carry a lot more than that for contingencies?"

Santich sighed. "Yes. For contingencies. Which, correct me if I'm wrong, we seem to be having."

This time there was no pause. "Shouldn't we at least accomplish the mission objective? I mean, I think the agency would look a lot better if—"

"Alex Prime, have you finished the search program I asked you to write?" Orlov interrupted.

"Uh, yes. I wrote it. I think. I wasn't sure if I did it right, so I wanted you to look at it before I started it."

"Run it," Orlov ordered.

"Yes, but it's been so long since—"

"Run it," he said. "I am busy right now and cannot watch over your shoulder. The faster we know what is wrong with PASS, the faster Santy can decide how to handle this. If you fuck it up, dump it and start all over."

The combination of his deference to Santich and his profanity seemed to shock her into submission, and she moved back to the notebook computer floating above Alex's head, typed a command, and pressed ENTER.

"It's going."

Orlov gently floated the second notebook up toward her. "Good. Now write the same program for the BFS."

Santich and Orlov moved back to the aft station, watched Melanie lift the massive satellite up and out of the cargo bay with the flick of a finger-size joystick. Soon the enormous bird was safely above the orbiter's tail, and Melanie locked the Remote Manipulator System's controls and turned off the power. "Okay. She's all set. All we need to do is let go and back away."

"Better it than me," Orlov said.

Santich turned to Orlov and found Alexis's eyes already locked on his. "I'm sorry. It's not something I enjoyed. I had to know."

Orlov jerked his shoulders and tilted his chin, his Slavic shrug free of the constraining space suit. "It was nothing personal. In your position, I would have done the same."

Melanie suddenly turned toward him. "Santy, what are we going to tell Houston about the comm failure?"

Santich thought for a moment. "I suppose if we think the software problem is something they'll help us with, we can tell them the truth. That we found something and needed time alone to diagnose it."

"And if we think they won't help us?"

"I don't know. I guess they probably won't believe that three separate radios all failed in a matter of minutes. Alex?"

Orlov scratched the top of his thinning hair; unconsciously, uselessly, in the lack of gravity, slid it forward onto his expanding forehead. "We can tell them we do not know why the Ku went down. Just that it did. We probably do not want them spying on us with television, anyway."

Santich nodded. Only the Ku-band antenna had the data capacity to transmit television pictures.

"As to the S-band and the UHF. We have not used UHF since ascent, and we had not used S-band for the last forty minutes before LOS. Maybe we can attribute them to separate, discrete failures?''

Melanie shook her head. ''Two radios go dead, that's already stretching it. Possible, but unlikely. All three? No way.''

''Are there any common elements to the two systems? S-band and UHF?'' Santich asked.

''No,'' Orlov said with a frown. ''That is the whole point of redundant systems. However''—he scratched his head some more, smoothing the hair forward—''some of the wiring runs close together where it enters the console.''

''Close enough to short them both out?'' Melanie asked.

''I will need to take a look, but yes, I think so. A paper clip perhaps, or a small screw . . .''

Melanie thought for a moment. ''It would take a lot of chafing to get through the insulation. I don't know. It doesn't sound very likely.''

''Likely, no. Possible? Certainly. Particularly if the foreign object had been there for more than one flight.''

''And whether it's likely or not, it's a sound, logical explanation for the simultaneous radio failures,'' Santich said. ''We'll tell them the circuit breakers kept tripping, we kept resetting them, and they kept tripping again. We'll tell them we found a loose screw under there, taped up the bare wires and fixed it. The worst they can do is doubt us.''

''And I do not think they will say anything even if they do not believe us,'' Orlov added. ''They will not want a public fuss, especially after their argument yesterday with Santy. Plus, I think they will be grateful to learn we have not been destroyed by a meteor.''

Santich imagined the hysteria on the ground as *Columbia* finished an entire orbit without a word or a single bit of data. The press would be all over them, especially since it happened in the middle of a space walk—a space walk commandeered by an untrained pilot. He hoped Marty Bruce was sweating bullets over it.

''The PASS search program is finished,'' Alexandra announced, staring at the computer's display. "Seventeen hits."

Orlov pushed off the aft console with an index finger and floated back to the front of the cockpit. "Let me see. Yes," he said, taking the computer from her. "Okay. The first five change the initialization tables. Weight, center of mass, et cetera. That is standard for each flight. They were inputted . . . last month at JSC. Very good. The next six are the DOLILOs, the Day of Launch I-Loads. Wind velocities, propellant temperatures, et cetera. They were, of course, inputted a few hours prior to T-zero. Okay."

The others squeezed around Orlov, hanging on every mumbled word as he decoded each entry.

"That leaves six lines," he continued. "These two are a change made back in November in the descent profile. It seems they have something to do with the alpha angle. Does anyone know anything about that?"

Santich nodded. "I remember. It was because of the density shears we'd seen on STS-63, 58 and 76. We were finding abnormally dense pockets of air and burning too much gas on the way down. The new software adjusts the flight attitude instead, whenever it infers a density shear."

Orlov arched his eyebrows. "Okay. That leaves us with four." He studied the coding silently for a minute. "I think we have found our culprit." He studied some more and shook his head slowly. "This is not good."

"What is it?" Melanie asked.

"This is not good. Alex Prime, let me see the BFS." He took the second computer, scrolled down several pages, and shook his head. "This is not good," Orlov repeated. He sighed deeply, blowing out the breath between spread lips. "My friends, we are in serious trouble."

No one said a word.

"Someone, on April twenty-seventh, a week ago, made a small change to Major Mode 305, our landing program. See here." He pointed a pudgy little finger at the middle of the screen. "This line is part of the sequence to open the landing gear doors. Normally, when the pilot throws the switch for 'gear down,' a series of charges is detonated that let the wheels swing down and lock into place. An electronic pulse sets off a charged capacitor, which blows the detonator, which lets the doors fall open, and so forth.''

He licked his lips. ''The problem is this: These next two lines, they create an infinite loop. They continually send the computer to the hydraulics systems subroutine, to check the operating pressure.''

''But dropping the gear has nothing to do with hydraulics!'' Melanie protested. ''It's gravity operated! The gear falls into place because it's heavy!''

''True,'' Orlov nodded. ''But the computer does not know that, and it does not care. It does as it is told. Each time it returns from the hydraulics check, it returns to this line. When it gets to this line, it goes back to check the hydraulics again. The Backup Flight Software has been tampered with the same way.''

''Can't you just delete that line? Or change it to the way it's supposed to be?'' Santich asked.

''There is the problem,'' Orlov said. ''Those lines once served a useful purpose in the program. Only I do not know what that purpose was. I *assume* they send a signal to the proper multiplexer-demultiplexer to charge that capacitor, but I do not know how to write that properly. You see, this software is extremely touchy. Any change can have unintended effects on other parts of the program that sometimes take hundreds or even thousands of simulation runs to understand fully. Do you remember that hydraulics warning message I saw during ascent?''

Santich and Melanie nodded.

''That is an example of an unintended effect. I have no idea why the new line caused the message to flicker, and I am certain that whoever wrote that new line did not mean for it to flicker either.''

Alexandra finally spoke up. ''So basically, the landing gear doors won't open when they're supposed to.''

''They will not open at all,'' Orlov said.

"Can't we land without the gear?" Alexandra asked. "Come in on the belly?"

Santich shook his head. "The hypergol tanks would rupture." It was a scenario he'd had nightmares over: hundreds of pounds of deadly hydrazine and nitrogen tetroxide spreading outward in a lethal orange cloud. "Even if we *could* purge the tanks on the way down, we still have some in the APUs. No, we'd all die, and we'd take the entire convoy crew with us."

Alexandra nodded and fell silent. For several minutes the three of them watched Orlov study the two computer screens, waiting for him to find a miracle in the glowing blue rectangles.

Santich cleared his throat. "Okay. We need their help. Is that a roger?"

"Unfortunately," Orlov said. "Unless we can get one of my programming friends at SAIL to write the new code and dictate it to me over that spy radio of yours."

"Hooper!" Santich exclaimed suddenly.

"Hooper. Dusty Hooper?" Orlov asked.

"The same. My best friend for the last, oh, thirty years. He runs the Johnson office of Celestial Data. They *wrote* PASS in the first place. He's become quite a programmer himself these last dozen years. Plus, he has one of these radios!"

Orlov glanced up at the set, its antenna still clinging to the overhead window with its suction cups. "How many of these are there?"

"Just three. I have one; Trudy, the lead EVA controller, has the second; and Hoop has the third."

Orlov nodded, frowned. "Celestial Data. Celestial. Wait one moment." He scrolled up a page on the PASS computer, then the one loaded with BFS. "Yes. I was right. Santy, the alterations in both of the programs were made at Celestial Data Systems."

"What? Are you sure?"

"See? The coding: CD. That line came from Celestial. If anyone downstream, at SAIL, for example, had modified it, it would have acquired that code instead.''

Santich shook his head. *Right under Hoop's nose!* ''Can you tell who, exactly?''

Orlov's stubby fingers flew over the keyboard. The file scrolled quickly upward. ''There is an appendix that translates the coding. Okay, there it is. We're looking for programmer thirty-seven at Celestial. . . . Here he is: Rudy McMahon.''

Santich blinked. *There he was.* The man who killed Torrington, who had tried to kill them. Finally, they had him.

''Remember what I said? That the code would not necessarily give us a name? This is an example.'' Orlov explained.

''How so?'' Melanie asked. ''You just gave us one.''

''Yes. And Dr. McMahon died of congestive heart failure three years ago.''

Santich deflated momentarily, remembering again his gut feeling about the killer: *Things had gone so well for him. . . .* And now, his luck was continuing. He had killed Torrington, he had learned that, despite Bruce's cover-up, Santich was on his trail, and he had rigged *Columbia* to crash on landing. He had known there would be a cover-up if Torrington died, and he had known what Santich was doing. *How* had he known?

Well, they weren't beaten. Hooper would find him out, and his only hope would be that the police were there to protect him from Hoop's wrath. Santich sighed. ''At least we're making progress.'' He smiled at Melanie. ''We're going to get out of this okay. Alex, when's our next pass over Houston?''

Fingers flew over the keyboard, called up the ground-track program. The screen displayed a miniature version of the electronic tracking map on the Mission Control–room wall, with the sinusoid path of *Columbia*'s next three orbits a white line crisscrossing the globe. ''Not for three hours. Then you have two orbits with an ascending node. Then in another three hours, you have a single, descending-node pass, but it's a nice long one that goes right overhead.''

Santich looked around, saw only anxious faces. "Cheer up, guys; we're going to make it. Tell you what, let's go ahead and reboost GRO while we're waiting for that first Houston pass."

Alexandra's lips curled into a smile, and Orlov nodded. Melanie's brow kept its furrows. "Are you sure you want to do that? We still haven't fixed the software problem."

"Sure. Why not? That software thing can't really hurt us unless we try to land. And we have to reboost GRO sometime. I mean, if we don't, we'll have done absolutely diddly-squat on this mission, other than nearly get smeared all over the runway." He smiled, but only Alexandra found it infectious.

"Thank you," she said quietly.

"It's nothing," he said as he slid into his seat and started calculating burn times.

34

With a final second thought, Santich nodded at Melanie, who ducked her head and torso into the console to reconnect the radio receivers she had earlier disconnected.

The last four hours had not been good. Santich tried and failed to raise Trudy or Hooper on the UHF. His mood, cheery as he fired *Columbia*'s twin maneuvering engines to raise their orbit thirty miles, had darkened considerably.

It had been nearly twelve hours since they'd broken contact with Houston, and nearly fourteen since he and Orlov had begun their space walk. He finally decided that no matter how much time passed, Trudy would not be able to leave her console and talk to him on the UHF until Lead Flight was satisfied the EVA team was safely inside. They wouldn't, *couldn't*, know that until *Columbia*'s crew told them so.

"Okay," Melanie said, her head emerging from the opening. "I've reattached everything."

Santich nodded at Orlov, who simultaneously reset the circuit breakers for both the S-band and *Columbia*'s UHF. Immediately, the ship was filled with the voice of Jules Carreau.

"*Columbia*, Houston. *Columbia*, Houston. Any copy?"

Santich subconsciously felt a wave of relief. For three decades, that single word—"Houston"—had been synonymous with safety and support. They had talked Pete Con-

289

rad's crew through a lightning strike during launch. They had, against all odds, brought Jim Lovell's crew back from the moon in a spaceship so crippled they had to turn it off and crawl into the tiny lunar lander for the long, cold trip home.

"Good . . . evening," Santich remembered, trying to force some enthusiasm. "Boy, are we glad to talk to you guys!"

"Santy! Are you guys alright? We've been calling for twelve hours now."

Right, Santich remembered. Carreau should have gone off-console nine hours ago. They must have kept the whole Orbit One team on duty until they reestablished contact. "Roger, Jules. We're fine. It took us this long to figure out what was wrong. We came out of the Zone-of-Exclusion, but never found you guys. We figured the Ku-system was down. Then we saw that S-band wasn't working either. The breaker had tripped. We reset it. It tripped right back. Same with the UHF. After Alex and I finished the EVA and came back in, we were able to get serious about the radios. We pulled the panels off and found a one-inch, number eight sheet metal screw wedged against wires from both radios. It had shorted them both. We removed it, taped up the insulation, and here we are. We still don't know what's wrong with the Ku."

Santich took a long breath and bit his lip, waiting for the reaction.

"Stand by . . . Okay, you found a screw had shorted out the S-band and the UHF? And you did an IFM to restore both radios?"

"Good copy, Houston. Actually it was Melanie who did the IFM: Lieutenant Commander In-Flight-Maintenance herself."

No one on the flight deck moved. Santich waited through an interminable silence, until he couldn't bear it anymore.

"Houston, *Columbia*. So the upshot is the vehicle is healthy, the crew is healthy and everything is fine. Alex and I finished the EVA about an hour early, we proceeded with the reboost, and we're now in a two thirty-seven-by-two thirty-six nautical mile orbit. We're waiting for the GRO people to check out their baby so we can set it free.''

"Roger, *Columbia*," Carreau answered slowly. "Copy all. We're going to want a detailed debrief, but as it's getting late, and you guys are already into your twenty-fifth hour this workday, we can wait on that till tomorrow. The folks here are downlinking data dumps to make sure *Columbia* didn't have any hiccups you all might not have noticed. It sounds so far, though, that everything is nominal, except for the Ku failure, and there's no reason to declare an MDF."

The flight deck let out a collective sigh. A Minimum Duration Flight meant going home at the first opportunity, which meant bringing the software problem to a head immediately. Or else flat-out refusing to return.

They're buying it, Santich thought, winking at Melanie. "Houston, *Columbia*. We're a tired crew here, and we'd like to start on presleep activities, if that's all right."

"Standby one."

Santich stared out the window, counting seconds. Below him, lightning flashed like fireflies, this time over the equatorial Atlantic, the so-called Inter-Tropical Convergence Zone. He tried to remember crossing the equator at night and *not* seeing lightning. He couldn't, not in any of his six, no, correction, seven flights.

Well, he got what he wanted, he thought. *Some flight.* Where would he be if Bruce hadn't been there that dark morning? In Florida with Emily? Happy after finally abandoning an unreasonable and unrealistic dream? Or still in Houston, brooding, bitter, waiting for an ungrateful agency to give him his due? *What the hell was going on down there?*

"*Columbia*, Houston," Carreau finally called.

"Go ahead, Jules."

"Yeah, Santy, we've been talking about it down here, and we think we need to go ahead and tell you right now. There's no reason to hold this from you."

Santich felt his heart skip, then accelerate. *What?* What had happened? Behind him, he heard the text and graphics printer—an overpriced, breakdown-prone fax machine—start humming. Whatever it was, they wanted him to see it in writing. The machine stopped, spit out a few inches of blank paper, and started humming again.

"*Columbia,* Houston. We've uplinked a couple of announcements we had to make today. Down here, we're all grieving their loss...."

Santich stopped listening and floated over to Melanie, who had torn the pages off the roll and was reading them silently, the Alexes over her shoulder. She shook her head and handed Santich the first one. It was an Associated Press rewrite of a NASA press release. Jesus God! He'd anticipated it, but seeing it on paper still shocked him:

PANAMA CITY, FLA. (AP)—VETERAN NASA ASTRONAUT STEVEN BANKE IS PRESUMED DROWNED AFTER HIS SAILBOAT WAS FOUND ADRIFT AND BARELY AFLOAT EARLY THIS MORNING. THE 24-FOOT SAILBOAT, *SIMOON*, WAS FOUND NEARLY FILLED WITH WATER, FLOATING WITH BARELY A FOOT OF HER CABIN ABOVE THE WAVES, DRIFTING SLOWLY SOUTHEAST, JUST SOUTH OF CAPE SAN BLAS. COAST GUARD OFFICIALS INVESTIGATING FOUND NO SIGN OF BANKE, A COLONEL IN THE UNITED STATES AIR FORCE. "A SAD DAY FOR NASA, AND A SAD DAY FOR AMERICA," SAID SHUTTLE PROGRAM CHIEF MARTIN BRUCE. "HE SEEMED IN GOOD SPIRITS WHEN HE CALLED FROM KEY WEST, SAID HE WAS LOOKING FORWARD TO ANOTHER MISSION. IT'S A TRUE TRAGEDY."

He looked up to see Melanie's eyes wide in alarm. She passed him the second sheet:

CLEAR LAKE, TEXAS (AP)—FORMER NASA ASTRONAUT DERMOTT "DUSTY" HOOPER WAS FOUND DEAD IN HIS HOME EARLY TODAY, APPARENTLY THE VICTIM OF A

GUNSHOT WOUND. CLEAR LAKE POLICE OFFICIALS DE-
CLINED TO PROVIDE FURTHER DETAILS, CITING THE ON-
GOING INVESTIGATION. BUT NEIGHBORS REPORTED
HEARING SHOTS AT ABOUT 6 A.M., CDT. ONE WOMAN,
WHO ASKED THAT HER NAME BE WITHHELD, SAID SHE
HEARD WHAT SOUNDED LIKE A SERIES OF FIRECRACKERS,
"MAYBE THREE OR FOUR," WHILE ANOTHER NEIGHBOR,
WHO ALSO ASKED TO REMAIN ANONYMOUS, SAID HE
HEARD ONLY A SINGLE SHOT. HOOPER, 58, WAS
AMONG THE NINE ASTRONAUTS CHOSEN FOR PROJECT
GEMINI, BUT WAS NEVER ABLE TO FLY BECAUSE OF AN
INNER-EAR MALADY.

They murdered him! They figured out he was working
with us, and they killed him. . . . Jesus Christ, Trudy! And
Kyle! His mouth went dry as he wondered how to warn
them. That was stupid; surely they knew what had happened and would take precautions. But would those be
enough? They had killed Hoop *in his own house!* He had
to talk to her! He turned back to the radio, realized Carreau
was still prattling on, struggling to fill the silence.

". . . has to be one of the saddest days we've ever had
around here. As you all know, these were just super, first-
class guys, and to lose them both like that, in a matter of
a few hours; well, it's quite a shock."

Santich licked his lips, found he had no saliva left.
"Houston, *Columbia*," he croaked. "We've just read these
and we, uh, agree. I guess it reminds us how precious these
moments really are." He groped for the appropriate response. What the hell did you say when your best friend
was murdered, because of something *you* did? It was his
cajoling that involved Hoop in any of this. And if he'd been
openly outraged from the beginning, no one—not Banke,
not that Toner thug, and certainly not his best friend—
would be dead now. When was the last time he'd even
visited Hoop's house? Not in more than two years, he remembered. Not since Iona died. He felt even more guilty.

He looked back at the article about Banke and shook his

head slowly. He'd expected to see this for some time, yet when he finally did, the anger and guilt tore at him anew. As if seeing it in print made it true. He read through a third time, noted disgustedly that Bruce had taken the opportunity to make points with the press. "Sad day for NASA, sad day for America." He'd thought so much of Banke that just a month earlier, he'd publicly humiliated him when he should've given him a medal. He looked at the next sentence and blinked. No, it hadn't seemed right the first time either.

"Jules, we're at a loss up here. We're just thinking out loud, but is there any chance Steve might still be out there? The boat was found afloat; maybe he took to the life raft . . . ?"

"All of us had prayed for that, too," Carreau answered. "The life raft was found behind the mast, undeployed. The Coast Guard officially terminated the search this afternoon. With the water as cold as it is in the Gulf . . ."

"Yeah, understand. It's such a shame. I guess he'd bounced back from 74 and was ready to go on?" Santich asked as casually as he could manage.

"Roger, Santy. He called Marty last week, said he was refreshed, and on his way home the next morning, looking forward to getting back to the office and training for another mission."

Santich let out his breath. That's what he'd been afraid of. "Right, well, that's the Steve we all knew and loved. It goes without saying that everyone up here sends out their hearts to their families, to Steve's kids and Hoop's daughter. We want to remind them that they're in our prayers tonight."

A longish pause. "We'll be sure to pass along those good words." Another pause. "*Columbia,* Houston, you can start on an accelerated presleep time line at your convenience. We think, given all your hard work today and in light of the things that have happened down here, we'll forego the wake-up call tomorrow morning. You guys just sleep until you wake up. You have a light day, just the release of GRO, so why don't y'all get a good night's sleep?''

"Thanks guys. I think we can all use it." Santich stuck the mike to its Velcro pad and stared out the window. Overhead, the Torres Strait slid from view, through which Bligh had successfully taken his tiny open boat after being thrown off the *Bounty* by Fletcher Christian. A desperate voyage, with terrible odds, but the man had made it. Testament to his seamanship, and his good luck.

"God, Santy," Melanie whispered, taking his arm. "I'm so sorry about Dusty. I know you two were close."

The Alexes also mumbled their condolences and patted Santich's shoulder. He stood impassively, watching the Pacific pass overhead. Tonga to Timor. Four thousand miles. It had taken Bligh forty-eight days. They had just done the reverse route in fourteen minutes. But without help from the ground, their chances of making it home made Bligh's trip look easy. And chances for getting that help had perished in a pool of blood with his friend.

"What are you thinking, Santy?" Orlov asked.

The strange uneasiness in his gut was gone, replaced with a quiet clarity. "I know who did it."

"What?" Alexandra asked.

He turned to face his crew. "There's no way in hell Steve Banke called Bruce a week ago. Back two weeks ago, my friend Kyle, the one who figured out how Torrington was murdered, was getting threatening phone calls. They said: '*Simoon* is gone.' By then Steve had already been at sea for six or seven days, and, based on that phone call, I'll bet he was already dead.

"Second, Steve did not want to come back to the office. He'd finished his three flights, and he'd been planning to leave for a while. And I think if he had made it to Key West, the *last* person on the planet he'd talk to would be Marty Bruce. He *hated* Bruce, and he was afraid of him." Again Santich remembered the wide, darting eyes. "I think, now, I'm afraid of him, too."

"Why?" Alexandra asked. "Why would Marty lie about talking with him?"

Santich sighed, a long weary sigh. "All along, I've looked at this and seen two unrelated circumstances. One, Bruce invents this 2601 cover-up plan. And two, Sam's murder escapes notice outside a tiny circle within the shuttle program. That circle, because of its ideologies and cliquishness, goes out of its way to cover it up.

"All this time, I've assumed that Sam's killer serendipitously escaped because of Bruce's 2601 cover-up." Santich paused, caught Melanie's eye, then Orlov's. "Now I think luck had nothing to do with it. When Toner went after Kyle, I kept asking myself, Is he protecting the murderer? Or Bruce's cover-up? I think the answer is yes, to both. That explains why our software was sabotaged last week. Somehow he found out how close we were getting. The only thing I can't figure is why he killed Sam in the first place."

Orlov took it all in, nodding slowly. "A frightening analysis."

Santich turned to him. "I know you logicians don't have much use for intuition, but I've got a bad feeling about this."

Orlov shook his head. "No, no. Quite the contrary. What we call intuition is actually a careful judgment, based on the sum of our experiences. In this case, your conjecture is most likely accurate."

"Hold on! The head of the shuttle program is murdering his own astronauts?" Alexandra looked at them in turn. "Has everyone lost their mind?"

Santich ignored her. If Bruce was behind the software change, then any hope of help from the ground was gone. He tried to estimate how much supercold cryogenic oxygen and hydrogen they had left, how many days of electricity they could make before, one way or another, they had to deorbit.

"Please, can't we at least call down, explain to them that we found a software glitch, and see what they say?" Alexandra pleaded.

Santich and Orlov traded glances. Orlov slowly shook

his head. Santich shrugged. "It may come to that. We can't land with this software load. That's the bad news. The good news is that Bruce, or whoever our enemies are down there, don't know we're onto them. We're safe here, and we have three, four, maybe five days of cryo left. So we have a little time."

Melanie nodded. "Right, and we can get hold of Trudy. . . ."

"Exactly. Trudy is the key. She's right in the control room; she knows what's going on. And she can talk to people on the telephone, tell them things."

"Yes," Orlov agreed. "Of course. The media."

Alexandra looked up in alarm. "The media? You can't mean you want to get all this in the newspapers! It would . . . it would end everything: Space Station, shuttle, everything."

Santich nodded. "I don't see a way around that. Not after this. Before we launched, I thought we could hand all the stuff about Sam to the police after we landed, and that would keep us in business, in the wake of a successful mission and all. Now I don't know if we can save it."

"Of course we can! We just keep quiet, and that's the end of it."

Santich wondered how far she would go, whether she would accept martyrdom for her cause. "And Bruce?"

"We could get him out," Alexandra said. "If he's actually guilty, of course. We could pressure him to leave." Her big brown eyes begged him. "You of all people, Santy. This agency has given you so much! How could you betray it? With all the benefits spaceflight has brought us, and will bring us, how can you even contemplate throwing it away?"

Yes, Santich thought, she'd burn at the stake. Quietly and without hesitation. "Sorry," he said softly. "It's a moot point, I'm afraid. I gave the story to a reporter before we left. She's going to print it the day we land."

Alexandra's face fell, and she drifted wordlessly to the aft window. Santich sighed, glanced at the timer on the cockpit console and powered up the UHF set to talk with Trudy. In the same instant, the radio crackled to life. Four bodies swung to it simultaneously.

"*Columbia,* Houston, for Santy."

35

The voice wasn't Jules Carreau's, the capcom for Orbit One. Nor was it Jim Eisenbach's, the rookie who'd been doing Orbit Three, the graveyard shift.

"Houston, *Columbia*," Santich answered carefully. "Robbie?"

"Roger that, Santy. Good ears."

Santich cast a worried look at the faces surrounding him. Rob Lynam was Bruce's protégé. In just his third year in the program, he'd already flown once and was scheduled for a second flight later in the year. In return, he had become Bruce's devoted errand boy and spy.

"Listen, sorry to bug you guys again, especially after such a long day and all. But if you could give us just another ten minutes or so, we have a special visitor here in Mission Control who wants to say hello. Mr. Vice President?"

Vice president? Of course! The joint, space-exploration, nuclear-reduction treaty with Russia went to the Senate in another week. Santich's mind raced: The vice president meant even the big national papers and TV networks would listen to every word. Bruce would go out of his way to avoid making a scene. Okay, what? What could he say? And to whom?

"Captain Santich? Can you hear me up they-uh?"

This was the break they needed; careful, now.

"Yes sir, loud and clear, sir. How do you read me?"

"Loud and cle-ah," came the southern drawl, stretched out a bit for Texan consumption. "Ah can never git over this! Where in the world are y'all?"

"Well, sir," Santich began. "We're currently about five hundred miles southeast of our launch site in Florida, starting our sixty-seventh orbit of Earth. In another few minutes, we'll cross the equator, and by the end of the conversation, we might be over southern Africa, or even the Indian Ocean."

"How about that?" the politician chortled. "Well, I know y'all have had quite a day already, so I promise to keep this brief."

Same as always, the vice president would make a speech; then the shuttle commander would kiss his ass.

"Fuhst, let me offer my condolences on the untimely passing of your colleagues, Colonel Steve Banke and former astronaut Dermott Hooper. I speak for the president and all the American people when I say that America is lesser today for their loss. Hah'evuh, I know that they both would be as proud of y'all as we are, and of the job you and your crew are doing. That telescope you fixed will help us see the fuh-thest stars, giving us new and impoh-tant scientific data to keep our scientists busy for yee-ahs."

Yeah, Santich thought. It seemed Mr. Vice President's staff hadn't bothered explaining to him that the "telescope" counted gamma ray blips and couldn't "see" a damned thing.

"And as you know, the president and I have worked hard to make sure you guys and gals get the funding you need to continue your outstanding work up they-ah, with robust space shuttle and space station programs, so that today's young people will get they-ah well-deserved chance to make they-ah own contribution in the years and decades to come. Our treaty with the Russian Republic only enhances that, with cooperation instead of competition, and a better future for all."

Santich waited a moment to make sure he was finished.

Okay, this is it: Don't blow it. "On behalf of Commander Anderson, and Drs. O'Day and Orlov, sir, I thank you for the kind words. We've worked hard these last days, but we enjoy it. Of course, we're just the tip of the iceberg of all the work that goes into a successful shuttle mission. Thousands of men and women out at the Cape, in Huntsville, at the various contractor locations and, of course, right there at the Johnson Space Center. People working above and beyond the call of duty to get the job, whatever the job, done."

Santich wetted his lips. It was now or never. "And it's not just those of us who work in the program directly. I think every one of us who works here at NASA can thank a father, mother, husband or wife for the support and encouragement we all need to do something like this." He affected a down-home chuckle. "I know in my case, my own gal has put up with all kinds of BS, if you'll pardon my French, for forty years. Why she practically raised little Kyle and Trudy all by herself, keeping them out of the trouble that little ones always seem to look for. I suppose with the work schedules we in the space business keep, sometimes we make sacrifices, but it's the folks at home that *really* make the sacrifices. So I just want to let her know that I'll be home sooner than she knows, and I'll make it up to her." He wiped the beads of sweat off his upper lip. He was rambling; he had to take a chance. "But really, this is something everyone at JSC knows, from our program director Marty Bruce, right on down to the newest trainees in the back rooms. Without the support from home, we're nothing. So Mr. Vice President, if you would be so kind to pass along a message to Mrs. Emily Santich, for all the times I've neglected to say it myself: Thanks."

Did they hear it? Would they understand?

"I'll thank her personally," the vice president said, a bit put out that Santich had hogged so much airtime. "Well, they tell me we ah almost out of time, so again, let me thank you and the rest of the crew, and after the mission, why, we'd love to see you in Washington."

"Thank you for the invite, sir. We'll take you up on it."

"Take cay-uh, now, and have a safe return."

A brief pause before Lynam's voice returned. "*Columbia*, Houston. Very nice. Thanks for the time. We're going to hand over to TDRS East, and then we have a couple of changes to the deploy time line. And then we promise to let you guys go to bed."

Santich hadn't even replaced the microphone before he began second-guessing himself. Should he have tried for more? Maybe with the vice president in the control room, he could have blurted it all out, at least enough to make it clear that they were in danger. He shook his head in frustration.

Orlov patted him on the shoulder. "No, Santy, you did the right thing. If you had said anything, they would have broken radio contact immediately. Do you think Bruce will realize that your children are not named Kyle and Trudy?"

Santich shook his head. "So long as they understand they're in danger." He looked up at Orlov. "They might be able to help us with a software patch, if we can get hold of them. Either way, we can't go back to KSC. Or Edwards."

Orlov nodded his head. "I was thinking the same thing: We should not land at a NASA site. If Bruce sabotaged the landing software, he may also have planted a radio-controlled explosive device, such as the one rumored to have been in the STA. Where were you thinking?"

"Homestead. If I remember right, it's got a longer strip than either Cecil Field or Pensacola. We have more than enough cross-range from a KSC deorbit. McDill's too close to Tampa, and Patrick's too close to KSC. The commercial fields are out of the question, not if there's the chance of a hydrazine fire." He tried to remember how long the former Air Force base's runway was. Two, two and a half miles. It would have to do.

"What are you thinking about the software?" Orlov asked.

"I don't know if we have much of a choice," Santich

said with a sigh. "If we can't call for help, that leaves us
with three options, all lousy. If we ditch in shallow water,
we'll rip her to pieces. We could bail out at twenty thousand feet, but that means relying on that damn pole to keep
the wing from cutting us in half. No, we need to set her
down. That means trying to raise Trudy again on the next
rev. Hopefully, now she knows how badly we need to talk
to her. Another half hour, and we get another pass—"

"*Columbia,* Houston, for Santy." It was Lynam. "We
have the GRO deploy time line if you're ready to copy."

36

"Santy? Santy? Is that you?"

Finally. It seemed he'd listened to static for hours, though a look at the clock showed he'd only been at it fifteen minutes. "Roger, Trudy. How copy?" Santich heard a broken sob. "Trudy? Are you all right?"

"Yes." A brief pause. "But I've got the most awful news. I got out when I heard your call with the vice president and I—"

"I know. It sounds incredible, but I'm almost certain of it. Everything points to him: He certainly had access; we *know* he's got the temperament for it. I know it's hard to believe. I'm sorry I got so hung up on Alex; I convinced myself he was the one. That's why I did the space walk. But when he told me that the overpress command came from the software, and then that stuff about Banke, I just knew it had—"

"Yes, I know! Santy!" Another sob. "I . . . I have something you need to read. I only got it a little while ago. Oh, Santy! Hooper . . ."

"Trudy, please." He glanced at the timer. Orlov held up seven fingers. "Trudy, we only have seven minutes left on this pass. Yes, I know about Hoop. I think I'm still too wound up to feel anything yet, but I know when we get back home, I'll hurt as much as you do now. Don't worry; we'll get that bastard Bruce and whoever else—"

304

"No! Santy! That's what I'm trying to tell you! Dusty shot *himself*!"

Santich's stomach tied itself in a knot, as did his lungs. The flight deck—it was spinning. . . . He struggled to draw a deep breath.

"It's in this letter. He sent it e-mail yesterday, and I didn't see it until today. God, Santy, if I'd only checked in from home, I . . . I could have stopped him! Jesus, Santy, I'm so sorry!"

Orlov tugged at his sleeve, held up six fingers. Santich took several deep breaths; the flight deck slowly stopped its rotation. "Okay, Trudy. We have to hurry. You have to read me the letter. You only have a few minutes."

He heard the tapping of keys through the headset. He motioned for Orlov to join him, pulled off the earphones and twisted them so each could listen to one.

"I'm going to start reading. It was sent to my e-mail address here in the office. 'Dear Trudy, I wish there was a way to make this sound excusable. But try as I might, I can't. I write to you to salve my conscience. If you get out of this unhurt, then what I did won't have been quite so evil.

" 'I never dreamed it would get to this point. How could it have? A cocktail party in Washington. I was there, some of the other lobbyists and Marty Bruce. I don't know how many drinks we had, but it was enough for me to talk candidly. Too candidly. We'd been griping about the latest round of budget cuts Congress was planning, and I suggested we needed another *Challenger*. The room fell silent, but I went on: NASA's highest budgets in two decades came right after the damn thing blew up. Americans were perverse: If the program went quietly along, no one noticed or cared. But if it looked like it was about to fail, they would throw good money after bad.

" 'I must have planted a seed in Bruce's mind; he called me in a few weeks later. He was blunt. He told me he needed to get into PASS and BFS undetected so he could make a minor software change that would let NASA win

America's sympathy. I thought he was joking, but as I sat there, I realized he wasn't. His idea was to get one of the shuttles into a minor but dramatic scrape, with the heroic crew escaping unhurt. Sort of stage an Apollo 13–type crisis. Something the press would eat up. To be honest, it didn't sound half bad. It was, after all, originally my idea. I agreed and taught him how to get in using the password of one of our programmers who died a couple of years ago. I asked him if he needed any help writing the code. He said he could manage. He used to run SAIL, remember.

" 'I don't know why I trusted him. I started wondering about things when 74 landed at KSC. I assumed the software change involved the fuel cell problem, but learned soon enough there was no fuel cell problem.

" 'I wondered about that, and grew disgusted at the way the plan had backfired. It was only at Santy's house, when Kyle mentioned the gasket on Sam's helmet, when I realized how it had been done, and how I had helped. Please believe me when I say I was devastated. I nearly drove into a tree that night. I wish now that I had. When later Kyle told us about the phone calls, I worked up the courage to confront him. Bruce told me it was none of my concern. That he could handle it. He told me about Toner, an acquaintance of a friend of a friend. I tried to steer him away from you all. For a while I thought I was succeeding. And after Toner died in that wreck, I thought Bruce would give up. No such luck. He was busy, it turns out, with something far worse.

" 'Looking back, I feel like I knew all along, and just pretended not to see. Why cover up Torrington's death, if the whole point was to create a tragic figure for the public? It was something you said that led me to it. That rumor about Sam was right. He was talking with the feds. It took some digging to find out, but I finally got it. He was about to give the FBI what they wanted: the big name, the one taking five- and six-figure kickbacks for favorable contracts.

" 'I guess I've always known. I never even told Santy

this, but five years ago, when Bruce was still overseeing the software program, he got in a bind. Made some sloppy investments, needed a loan. I, the head of Celestial Data's shuttle avionics office, gave him one. Neither of us has asked about paying it back. So it wasn't really a surprise when I found out that he was calling the shots, and Sam was just his liaison with Kerro. Why else go to the trouble to kill Sam in space, then make it look like he'd died on the ground?

" 'Why else kill Steve, the only one of the 74 crew who suspected Sam's death wasn't an accident? Poor guy. Toner followed him in a rented ski boat the morning he left Galveston. Steve was unarmed. He didn't have a chance. And then Mike Etheridge. God, I'm so sorry, Trudy. I know he was a friend. Toner drove him off the road into a ravine near Colorado Springs. I don't think they've even found his body yet.

" 'Fortunately, Toner died without having told him Kyle's name, or yours, or Santy's. But last week, Bruce somehow found out about Santy, and now, four more people are as good as dead. There are two critical software changes in *Columbia*'s computers. I finally found them last night. If nobody does anything, she'll crash at touchdown. But if anything the least bit unusual happens, Bruce can destroy her in midflight, and there won't be a shred of evidence. It would be our word against his. He would go free, and manned spaceflight would disappear. Maybe forever. I've worked too hard, Santy worked too hard, to let that happen.

" 'Believe me, there's no reasoning with him. I've tried, and now I have blood on my hands, that of three people already, and, by the time you read this, maybe another four; among them, my only real friend in the world.

" 'Please, Trudy, listen to what I say. He doesn't know you. He doesn't know Kyle. Use this advantage while you can. Go home; never come back. Tell Kyle. I wish it could be done over. But it can't, and I don't have the courage to accept the consequences. So please, Trudy: Get out. Tell

Kyle. I'm sorry.' Santy? Are you still there?''

He struggled for words. *No wonder he was adamant about me not flying, poor soul....* "Yeah, Trudy," he croaked. "We're out of time. Do as he said: Get out; go to your mom's. Tell Kyle to get back to Tennessee. Okay?''

"Yes, Santy, I—"

"Once you're safe, call Jo Pointer. Her number's in the Clear Lake book. Tell her what's happened. Tell her she's got to go ahead and print her story immediately. We're going to need new landing software and new targets for Homestead, and we only have five days cryo, max—"

"Santy, I already called her. That's what I'm trying to tell you. She left World News Service. Three days ago she became Marty Bruce's executive assistant for public affairs. She must have told Marty everything. He must know...."

Her voice faded as *Columbia* flew beyond Houston's horizon, until only static was left.

37

"Here it is. I do not know how I overlooked it," Orlov apologized.

"We all did," Santich murmured, unconsciously keeping his voice low, as if normal tones would somehow be overheard by Mission Control.

Once again, everyone crowded about the tiny computer screen, hovering as a group to and fro with the air currents. They had turned off the cabin lights, as if they were sleeping, so as not to alert the Electrical Generation and Illumination controller on console that somebody was awake. Trudy's call had left everyone silent and immobile for nearly a minute. Orlov had snapped to first and had set to work to find the second software change, the one Bruce could use to destroy *Columbia* whenever he pleased.

"It is just a one-line change," Orlov said slowly, pinching and twisting his lower lip. "It is very complicated, though. See? It checks the values of these two parameters. And if they are such, it goes on this subroutine, returning to this line."

"What's it do?" Santich asked, unable to make any sense out of the arcane coding.

"I do not know." Orlov studied it some more, then shook his head. "There are a number of problems. As you can see by the line number, this line is not an insertion. It replaced an existing line. I have no idea what the existing line did, but, presumably, it did something. That is the first problem. The second is that this line by itself tells me nothing. It seems to create an infinite loop. Maybe that is the point: to tie up the computer with this needless task, and slow it enough to degrade flight-critical performance.''

"You think that's it?" Melanie asked. She hovered upside down, her eyes just about even with everyone else's.

"No. These computers are ancient, but they can still multiplex one additional subroutine without difficulty. No, my guess is that the subroutine actually does something bad." He tapped his fingers against the gray plastic between the keyboard and the display. "It will take some time. At least an hour, maybe several, depending on how well documented everything is.''

Santich nodded, took a deep breath. It was hard to believe it hadn't even been a full twenty-four hours since he'd started his space walk. Time had compressed. A day earlier he had gone to bed thinking he would have to bring *Columbia* home with Orlov in the air lock, or perhaps dead in the cargo bay. Instead, the chess-playing mathematician was innocent, and his best friend had become his Judas. And for what? He thought of the house in Briarwood Estates, the BMW, and wondered whether Hooper had left anything out of his letter, whether he'd partnered with Bruce in bribery and kickbacks as well as sabotage and murder.

Poor man, Santich thought. For twenty years he'd waited, hoping someday, somehow, his medical grounding would go away. He'd taken medication, even had two separate operations. The blackouts and vertigo had abated but not disappeared. It wasn't good enough. For the last decade he had been with Celestial Data, staying in the thick of the program, becoming one of its most outspoken defenders on Capitol Hill. How much had been ideology, and how much greed?

"We can't get rid of GRO without them knowing, can we?" Melanie asked unnecessarily. She, too, was whispering.

Santich shook his head. "How quickly can you release it, stow the arm and shut the bay doors?"

"Five, then another ten. Maybe fifteen minutes, total."

He nodded, wondering how much time they would have, if the worst came. "I should never have told Jo Pointer anything. What the hell could she have done with that T-38 stuff without proof? Nothing."

"It's not your fault," Melanie said. "We can assume that Bruce knows everything you told her?"

"She probably typed out her notes for him. Put them in a three-ring binder," he said bitterly. "The only consolation is that we didn't have any idea who we were after back then."

"So he might not know we're onto him."

"Right. Not that it makes much difference. I mean, if he thinks we know about him, then he can't let us get back alive. Period. But even if he *doesn't* think we know about him, he still knows that I plan to tell the world everything I know after I get home. Pointer told him so. He must assume that a police investigation would eventually nail him."

"So he can't let us get home alive in any case," Melanie finished for him. "You know, you learn to put an F-18 onto the deck in the middle of a rainstorm. You never once worry that the guys on the ship might not get the cables up for you."

"No." Santich glanced up at Orlov, who typed a key here and there, but mainly just stared. The forty-five minute nighttime had fallen again, and the only lights visible were the blue computer screen, some monitor lights on the cockpit consoles, and the occasional bluish green curtains, the *aurora borealis*, that shimmered across the sky as *Columbia* arced over Hudson Bay. Alexandra hovered between the two seats, staring out mutely.

"You should get some sleep," Melanie suggested.

"So should you." He wondered if Emily were sleeping. Would she have been following the flight? Surely she would have. He recalled the two nights they'd had together in the beach house. Two nights after four years. It wasn't enough.

"Aha!" Orlov shouted, drawing Melanie and Santich to his computer. "Here! See? This command brings up the temperature of the cryogenic hydrogen, and then this one closes all the valves."

Santich's eyes went wide. "But that—"

"Yes," Orlov said. "The pressure builds explosively, too much for the relief valves, and ruptures the tanks. Then the next electrical relay that opens or closes—a spark, and a catastrophic explosion. If somehow we survive the fire, we have no electrical generating capacity."

Melanie shook her head. "No way is anyone from EGIL going to send commands that obviously would kill us!"

"There is the beauty. The two fatal commands are issued by the computer only if two unrelated, harmless and quite common commands are sent from the ground simultaneously. If a command to dump the backup data recorders is sent within ten milliseconds of a command to reset the payload interrogator, that automatically triggers the fuel cell tank subroutine, and we die." Orlov nodded in admiration. "Bruce did good work."

"Yeah, great work," Santich said. "Can you disable it?"

Orlov thought for a moment. "I do not think so. Not without accidentally introducing some terrible error. You see, this line of code has been inserted in all the major modes, not just those for ascent and entry. Assuming I can substitute safe lines for the altered ones, and that, I think, is a dangerous assumption, we then have to erase PASS and BFS—all of our flight software—from the GPCs and reload the programs, portion by portion, off the notebook. Such a thing has never been done. I can think of a dozen things to go wrong."

He paused a moment. "I suggest, instead, we switch off the backup data recorders and the payload interrogator. That way, the GPCs will reject both the dump command and the reset command until the equipment is first turned on. One of us watches the monitor at all times. If the equipment is activated, then we break radio link.''

Santich nodded. "Right. I see. We make the computers block out the two bad commands. And if they try to get around it, we have time to bail out. Good. Let's start immediately. Half-hour watches."

"I'll take the first one," Melanie offered, gliding to the console.

"Can't Houston reestablish radio link without our help?" Santich asked.

"Of course," Orlov shrugged. "But it will take a few seconds. And in that time, we must physically disable the radios, like last time. We cannot climb in, get at the proper wires and disconnect them in just a few seconds, so we will have to run some shunts out and onto the console, so the person on watch can disconnect them instantly."

Alexandra turned and raised her hand to volunteer. She disappeared into the middeck and returned with the electrical tool kit.

"We still have the fundamental problem of getting home," Orlov reminded.

"I know. I've been thinking about it. I don't know if I'm any closer to an answer," Santich admitted. "But we need to act fast. The longer we wait, the longer Bruce has to take the initiative."

One of the few things he'd disliked about spaceflight was the near total dependency upon the ground. If only space travel could be more like single-engine airplane travel, he'd thought: hop in, take off, go somewhere, and land, all by yourself. Finally, he was getting his wish. "I think we're on our own on this one."

"Won't you consider just openly calling for help?" Alexandra said, pulling a handful of wires out with her as she emerged from the access panel. "If everyone in Mission Control hears we're in trouble, they *have* to help."

Orlov looked up from his computer. He'd been studying the ground-track program. "She may have a point," he said. "On the other hand, if Bruce is desperate, such a call might be the trigger to push him over the edge. He must have at least one of the Data Processing System controllers under his thumb. What if he has more?''

Santich thought of the havoc even one or two flight controllers could play. The crew would never be able to keep up with the bad ground commands. No, they needed inside information; they needed to talk to Trudy again.

Outside, the sun began its meteoric ascent as they passed southeastward over the Florida-Georgia border. The next pass would bring them close enough to Houston. He would call her then.

38

Santich could not remember another ninety-one-minute period of his life that passed so excruciatingly slowly. Melanie stood at the aft station, ready to release the Gamma Ray Observatory at the proper word from the ground or a shout from Santich. Alexandra stood watch over the displays for the backup data recorders and the payload interrogator, ready to shut down the radios if she saw either instrument activated by ground command.

Orlov and Santich studied the ground-track program. "To come down here"—Santich touched his finger to the LCD screen—"we have to deorbit right about here?"

Orlov nodded. "I believe so. You know, if Trudy doesn't tell them, they will have no way of knowing we are coming. We have no way of calling them."

Santich looked down at the screen. The resolution wasn't high enough to see any distinguishing features of the coastline. "I know. The whole thing is a gamble, but it's the best shot we got."

"Okay," Orlov said with a nod. "I think that is a good choice. The weather looked clear all the way across the Gulf."

Santich turned to Melanie. "Mel? This sound okay?"

"I suppose it's the best we can hope for."

Santich nodded. "Alexandra?"

"Can't we talk to Bruce? Before we commit to this,

315

shouldn't we at least talk to him? Maybe, *just maybe,* he had nothing to do with it, and will be as surprised as we are.''

''Alexandra, one way or the other, everyone on the planet is going to know what happened on STS-74 and 74-Alpha. There's no way around that,'' Santich sighed. ''If the American people want shuttles to fly badly enough, then they'll fly. If not, then they won't.''

''There is one way,'' Alexandra said. ''If we tell them we had a system failure, and then keep quiet about everything else. Go right to Washington, straight to Administrator Silver's office and lay it all out. Bruce, if it was Bruce, and everyone who had anything to do with it will be gone, and the program can continue.''

She looked at Melanie and Orlov for support. ''Please. Think about the future? Please?'' Her eyes moistened. ''Okay, I'll grant you ninety-eight percent of the science we do up here could probably be done on the ground or on unmanned satellites. I'll even grant that two-thirds of *that* science is pure bullshit. But what about the spaceflights themselves? We absolutely need them. If we ever hope to get to other worlds, we need to learn how to get there—now. Before we spend years in space, we need to spend months, and before we can spend months, we need to spend weeks.''

It was Melanie's turn to sigh. ''Please, Alexandra. . . .''

''I'm thirty-four years old. I'm not married; I don't even have a boyfriend; my entire professional life has revolved around zero-gravity manufacturing, one of those bullshit sciences. Melanie can go back to flying her F-18s, Alex will find a nice mathematics professorship somewhere and Santy's going to retire anyway. What the fuck am I going to do when this is canceled?'' She looked around. ''Ever since I was four years old I wanted to be an astronaut! Santy, you were one of my idols! Please, can't we talk to Bruce?''

Orlov kept his gaze on the computer screen. ''Alex Prime, the matter is closed. Captain Santich has made up his mind. Now, please.'' He checked his watch. ''It is almost time, Santy.''

''Right.'' He moved toward the little UHF dangling from the overhead window. ''Can you enter the new targets?''

''Yes.'' Orlov stretched his arms over his head. ''That is only a matter of inputting new coordinates. The GPCs will do the necessary calculations: alpha angle, the number and timing of S-rolls, et cetera. I'll have it in within twenty minutes. The new software is another matter. It will take an hour to write, and many more to check. But please understand, I cannot do the certification work they do at SAIL. I can only do basic debugging. I am reasonably certain I can make the landing gear doors open. I am not at all certain what else might happen.''

''That's a chance we have to take.'' Santich pulled on the headset. He had some questions for Trudy and a message for the Homestead Air Reserve Base commander. ''Trudy? Trudy? Are you there?''

There was only static. ''Trudy? Trudy?'' He turned to Orlov. ''Are we in range?''

''Yes. Two minutes over the horizon, eight minutes to go.''

Santich closed his eyes to concentrate on the static. Maybe she'd decided her mom's place wasn't far enough, and had left the area entirely. Good for her. Still, if he could reach her, she might know something crucial, something about the software changes. Who could tell? Maybe she and Kyle had done their own search of the PASS system and had found the correct coding to fix the problems. ''Trudy, Trudy, Trudy. Any copy, Trudy?''

Santich had the volume turned up so high that when the clear voice broke through the white noise, it boomed into his ears. The surprise helped him manage the icy panic that clutched his gut.

''Trudy's not here right now. Can I take a message for her? Or perhaps you'd like to talk with Kyle Hartsfield instead?''

Santich forced himself to breathe, counted to ten in his

head. There was no mistaking the controlled, slightly nasal, slightly too-high-pitched tones. *He knew! The son of a bitch knew about Trudy and Kyle!* He nodded at Orlov, mouthing the name for him before remembering the radio wouldn't transmit unless he keyed the mike. "It's him!" he shouted at Orlov. "Break radio link at my signal!"

Orlov scrambled to the console as Santich composed himself.

"It's nice to hear your voice, Marty," he managed finally.

Bruce laughed. "I'm glad to see I at least provoked a reaction." A brief pause. "Like I said, Mrs. Torrington doesn't seem to be around at the moment. Is there anything I can do for you?"

Santich could just picture the partially raised eyebrow, the sharklike half smile, the perfectly creased suit. How had he gotten the radio? Had he gone to Hoop's house? Maybe Hooper *hadn't* killed himself. *That murdering son of a bitch!*

"Where'd you get the radio, Marty?" he asked sharply.

Another laugh. "Take it easy, Santy. I should have known this would get your conspiracy-theory juices flowing. The police have closed their investigation. It was a suicide, open and shut. For whatever reason, they returned this radio to JSC, along with the personal computer he'd checked out. A stroke of luck, that's all, that we get to chat like this."

Where was Trudy? God, that cocksucker had done something to her. . . .

"Well it's been nice, Marty, but I really need to speak with Trudy."

"Like I said, Santy, she hasn't been around. She didn't come in for her shift today. I could call her for you. Let her know you're looking for her."

Good. He doesn't know where she is. Or, maybe he's just saying that to make me think she's safe. . . . Santich wiped away the droplets of sweat from his upper lip. He stared wide-eyed at Orlov, who flashed one open hand at him: five minutes left. God, what the hell was he supposed to say? Should he try to bargain with him for that software patch? He thought again of Alexandra's insistence that they talk to him. Why? Maybe she . . . No, it couldn't be. In a flash of inspiration, he motioned her to join him, turned the headphones apart so each could listen to one, and moved the mouthpiece into the middle. She looked at him with half fear, half puzzlement, but held the offered headphone to her ear.

"Santy? Santy, are you still there?"

Alexandra hesitated, then spoke. "Hi, Marty, it's me. Alex." She added a nervous titter.

"Well, hello there, young lady. And how has your first spaceflight been treating you?" he asked.

"Oh, it's been really neat. I was a little sick for the first couple of days, but then I got better." She half smiled, then frowned. "But then I got that ear infection."

"Yes, I'm sorry to hear that. It's a shame you couldn't do your EVA."

"Yes, I know." She gulped softly. "Captain Santich thought that Alex, that is, Dr. Orlov, might have had something to do with Sam Torrington's death," she said carefully.

Santich moved his hand to the mouthpiece microphone, then checked himself.

"I had a feeling that's what it was about. Everyone down here thought it was just the Dean of American Astronauts pulling rank to fulfill his dream, the one thing he hadn't done. But I had a feeling it had to do with his detective game."

Alexandra thought for a moment. "I'm afraid he's still convinced Sam was murdered, and now he thinks whoever killed Sam also rigged *Columbia* to kill us as well."

Bruce laughed heartily. "Isn't that something? And how does he think this is to occur?"

Santich's right hand reached for the microphone, but Alexandra pushed it away. "He doesn't know. But he says he has four more days to find it."

Bruce laughed again, this time more of a chuckle. "Actually, four days, eighteen hours, is what EGIL was saying this morning. But seriously, Alex, and you, too, Santy, this is becoming ridiculous. That was cute with the radios, but I'm not going to cover for you guys much longer. I want you guys to deploy that satellite and get your butts down here day after tomorrow. You'll return to a hero's welcome. You've already got an invitation to the White House."

Alexandra caught Santich's eyes. "Marty, he's convinced there's a problem. I keep telling them that they're wrong, that you would never let something like that happen. You wouldn't, would you? To me?"

A long pause hung in the flight deck. Three pairs of eyes kept their lock on Alexandra. She shut hers.

"Of course not, Alex. You know I couldn't. Now let me talk to Santy."

Tears welled in her eyes, swelling until they threatened to float off like bubbles before she blotted them on her sleeve. "You know, because he actually got me worried. I mean, all the different things that could go wrong: the hydraulics, the fuel cells, the nav aids, the software—so many things! We can't possibly check them all!"

"I assure you that—"

"I mean," Alexandra continued, "just a small amount of contaminant added to the fuel cells would destroy them. Just a single coding error in the software could—"

"Alex, please. That's what we have Mission Control for. We're down here monitoring all that stuff so you don't have to. Okay? Regardless of what Santy tells you. Example: When you guys broke contact, we had double shifts in here. The back rooms went through every possible scenario we could think of. We pulled out the flight software, both PASS and BFS, and ran them through the simulators, each major mode, one at a time, right through landing, to make sure there were no errors we'd somehow missed before launch."

Alexandra took a sharp breath, then let it out slowly,

quietly. On her face, resignation replaced fear. "Really?" she asked.

"Promise." Bruce answered.

Alexandra released the headphone, drifted toward the aft windows. Orlov flashed three fingers.

"Okay, Marty, you're talking to me again," Santich said.

"Well, isn't this my lucky day. I'm sure you heard everything I said. So quit fucking around. Get the job done and come home."

Santich thought a moment. What could he learn from this? "What about your pep talk a couple of weeks ago: 'Don't fuck with me.' What happens now?"

"What happens now? Nothing happens now. What can I do to you? Not assign you to any more flights?" A brief pause. "Santy, I needed you. I needed a hero to bail the program out of a tough spot. And, to the world, that's what you've done. Yes. They think you're a hero for filling in for Alexandra and saving the mission. So come on home. You've had a good career."

"And if I think it's in the program's best interest to tell the world what I know about Torrington?"

"I would hope, in the best interest of the program, that you won't."

You murdering cocksucker! All this high-and-mighty talk about mankind's destiny, sacred mission, safeguarding the faith! It was only about money. Nothing but a thief, and an extortionist, and now a murderer.

Santich struggled to control his anger. No need to tell Bruce all he knew. Not yet. "And suppose I've already told my story to a member of the press, who promised to run it the day after we land? Or, in the event that some unfortunate catastrophe strikes, and we don't land, then as soon after the unfortunate catastrophe as possible?"

Go on: Brag about how you've already taken care of that. . . .

Bruce sighed a long sigh. "Then, I guess, there's not much I can do. You've taken it upon yourself to destroy forty years of hard work by many hundreds of thousands of people. You'll probably cause a twenty-year hiatus in human space exploration, and when it resumes, it will probably be the Japanese. You'll put tens of thousands of people out of work. Again, for the sake of the program, I hope you haven't done that.''

Orlov flashed two fingers at him; he nodded in response. ''All right, Marty, I've listened to your bullshit long enough. You're a menace to the program. It's *you* who's compounded the problems caused by Sam's murder, not me. So don't lay that guilt trip on us.

''We'll be down day after tomorrow, and you just be ready to do some explaining to the administrator, to Congress, to the president, to fucking Dan Rather, about your idea of an open, civilian space program.''

Santich waited for a response, heard none. He looked up at Orlov, who was watching the computer screen running the ground-track program.

''You should have comm for another forty-five seconds,'' Orlov said. ''Maybe he does not wish to talk to you anymore.'' He looked up from the screen. ''Surely you were not serious about staying up another two days?''

Santich shook his head. ''We go in tomorrow, as planned. Can you get the software ready in time?''

''I will start on it right away. As I said earlier, the first part is easy. The second part . . .'' He shook his head and turned to the notebook computer hovering near the ceiling.

Santich floated back to the aft windows, where Melanie had an arm around Alexandra's shoulder. Santich came up to her from the other side, and she laid her head against his shoulder.

''When?'' he asked softly.

She sobbed twice. ''Five years ago. I . . . I'm so ashamed of myself. We got to talking at a party. He seemed really nice. Some of the girls in the office suggested it wouldn't hurt my chances to pursue it. So . . . I never thought it would end up, like, you know . . .'' She dried her eyes, took a deep breath. "It only lasted about a week. It was enough, though, I guess. Here I am."

Santich shared a quick glance at Melanie and tightened his hold around Alexandra's shoulders. For long minutes they stood there, watching the panorama of gold-foiled satellite passing before blue Earth and black heavens. Soon the sun passed into their view, between the cargo bay sill and Earth, and plunged suddenly below the fuzzy horizon, again painting the rim of the planet a series of oranges and purples as it disappeared. Within moments, what had been a perfect, matte-black sky was dotted with thousands, tens of thousands, of cold, unblinking lights.

Alexandra sighed heavily, the breath still broken with the remnants of a sob. "It is so beautiful up here." She looked up at Santich. "I guess it must get old for you, huh, after six flights."

Santich looked out at the Pleiades approach the horizon, then drop down into the soft blanket of air that distorted the brilliant blue points and made them twinkle. "No. It doesn't."

Below them a meteor blazed through the upper atmosphere, leaving a bright yellow streak that was immediately answered by a flash of lightning over the Indian Ocean. It struck him that she had been right: They would be the last Americans for some time, maybe even forever, to stare down like this. What would it take to change that? They would need to convince enough people in Mission Control that they were telling the truth, that to save four lives, they must accept that their boss was a sociopath. Would they? Santich snorted. If he were in their position, would he? Still, the *real* software was their best chance of making it down in one piece.

"Okay. We'll try it your way," he said, looking down at Alexandra.

"No! I mean, you were right, Santy. The man is a maniac. He'll—"

Santich put a hand on her shoulder to quiet her. "Yes. I know. We'll try asking for help, and we'll break contact at

the first hint of trouble.'' He glanced around the flight deck.
''After all, I guess we owe it to the taxpayers to try to save
two billion dollars' worth of their hardware. Plus, they've
rigged it so we can't land, so they can blow us up in seconds. What more could they do?''

One by one, they drifted away from the aft window.

39

In a fraction of a second, the commands went from fingertips to keyboard to computer to radio to satellite and finally to the orbiting ship. The command was complicated, using a strange, convoluted pathway and bypassing the normal precautionary self-checks. No matter. The commands didn't violate the computer's internal logic, and that, ultimately, was the sole arbiter of right and wrong.

The bits of electrical impulses translated themselves into ones and zeros, delivering the command to the linked series of computers, where, as in the crowded and tense Control Room, they bypassed normal paths and went directly to a multiplexer-demultiplexer beneath the cargo bay.

There the computer signals were converted to electrical impulses that energized a small solenoid valve, which, in turn, pressurized a larger tank valve. The end result was a small jet of white gas that appeared on the port side of the ship, a few feet below the cargo bay sill.

Space shuttle *Columbia* began bleeding to death.

40

"Okay? Are we set?" Santich asked.

Three heads nodded. Melanie sat with each hand on a thin electrical wire, each thumb ready to flick open a quick-disconnect fitting Alexandra had crimped into place. The two Alexes watched the switches for the backup data recorders and the payload interrogator. They were both off, and their job was to make sure they stayed that way.

"Alex, how close are you?"

He shrugged. "I have loaded the coordinates for Home-stead. I have written substitute lines for the landing gear subroutine, but I have not done even a cursory debugging. I need to go back through, line by line, and look for errors. It would be better to put it through the simulator, but . . ."

Santich nodded. "Well, if this works, we may not need to." He took a deep breath. "Okay. Here goes. Houston, *Columbia*."

The ground hadn't disturbed them for nearly three hours, giving them a leisurely lunch break before the scheduled release of the Gamma Ray Observatory satellite.

"Go ahead, Santy." It was still Lynam.

"Yeah, I guess Jules is still out with a cold?" He would rather have talked to Carreau.

"Roger that, Santy. It turns out it's a flu bug. I guess you have me for the duration."

Santich bit his lip. Was it worth it? After all, what more

326

could they do? At the first sign of trouble, Melanie would break the wires, killing the radios. And it was late morning in Houston, the time of day when the maximum number of people would be in their offices. They only needed a few to hear him—and one to act.

Another deep breath. "All right, I want everyone down there to listen closely. We have a potential catastrophe on our hands: *Columbia*'s software has been booby-trapped by Marty Bruce. Two unrelated commands sent from the ground will make the fuel cells explode, and the landing gear doors have been programmed not to open. Repeat, we need software patches to land, but most important, *we need to arrest Marty Bruce*! Torrington was about to name him to the feds for bribery! He killed Sam Torrington, he killed Steve Banke, he killed Mike Etheridge, and he may have killed Dusty Hooper! Please, down there: *We need help!*"

Santich wiped the sweat off his brow and his lip. The radio was silent. What did he expect? "Houston, how copy?" Still no answer. "Houston!"

"We copy five by five, Santy. Stand by one."

Stand by? Were they kidding?

"Hello, Santy, this is Jon Sorenson." It was the flight surgeon, the one who'd been on console when Torrington's head exploded. "Santy, I'd like to reconfigure comm for a PMC. Can you do that for me?"

A private medical conference . . . That was it, then. Bruce had already laid the groundwork: Poor old Santiago, he finally snapped. First he goes EVA without a lick of training. Now everyone's out to kill him.

"Santy, you've been under a lot of strain, and I just want to talk to you, okay?"

"*No, goddamn it!* Look at the PASS and BFS we've got, and run them through the simulator. Listen, he's already killed! Torrington was about to name him in Operation Bedbug. That's what it's all about! That son of a bitch didn't want to go to jail, so he murdered four people, and now he wants to murder four more!"

Santy looked at Orlov, Melanie, turned his eyes toward

Alexandra just in time to see hers bulge wide.

"Look!" She pointed through the aft windows.

Outside, the cargo bay was filled with a thin, pale cloud that obscured the GRO. Santich pushed himself out of the seat and flung himself to the aft windows. "The cryo tanks."

Orlov twisted over to the fuel cell switches, flipped through them one after the other. "We have lost most of the oxygen," he said calmly.

That was when Melanie screamed, her eyes glued to the back up data recorder panel. The red light over them had just blinked on. With two flicks of her thumbs, she popped open the quick disconnect fittings that kept the radio power leads intact. She grabbed the ends of the fittings, making sure they wouldn't accidentally float back together. "They tried to kill us, Santy! They actually tried."

"How much left?" Santich asked.

Orlov shook his head grimly. "Less than ten pounds. Somehow they disengaged the caution and warning system and sent those commands up, overriding all the safeguards. We are in serious trouble: Ten pounds is enough for one hour, more or less."

An hour! Sixty minutes. Maybe less. A nominal deorbit and entry took longer than that.

"Alexandra! Jettison the GRO the instant we get into a bay-upward attitude. Mel, configure for deorbit burn. Time of ignition: three minutes." He climbed forward into the left seat. "Alex, I hope you loaded those targets right."

He disengaged the digital autopilot that had kept *Columbia* in the same, cargo-bay-toward-Earth attitude for days, rolled *Columbia* into a right-side-up position, and prepared the upward firing thrusters.

"GRO is away," Alexandra announced. "Shall I stow the arm?"

"How quickly can you do it?" He gave a five-second burst on the thrusters, sliding *Columbia* downward, away from the satellite and toward Earth.

"Two minutes."

Santich shook his head. "Too long. Jettison it."

Orlov looked up from his computer. "No! The program accounts for the arm's mass. If we lose it, that will upset the calculations."

"We don't have time. As it is, we're cutting it close on cryo." When the cryogenic oxygen ran out, the fuel cells that fed *Columbia* her electricity would shut down. The spaceship would die instantly. "Alexandra, jettison the arm . . . now."

With the flick of a switch, a small guillotine chopped through the bundle of wires connecting the Canadian-built Remote Manipulator System to the port sill. Mechanical clamps released their grip, and Santich again fired the thrusters. Within a few seconds, the fifty-foot-long, triple-joined arm was safely above the cargo bay. Its red maple leaf caught the new dawn's first light.

"RMS is clear," she said.

"Close the doors," Santich said, reaching for the yaw-axis thrusters to spin *Columbia* around so her twin Orbital Maneuvering System engines pointed in the direction of travel.

"Two minutes to ignition," Melanie said quietly.

Santich turned around to watch the sixty-foot-long, seven-and-a-half-foot-wide port door start its painfully slow swing downward. He held his breath as it finally rested against the bulkheads and covered the left-hand side of the cargo bay. Okay, one more . . . This is where the mission could end, he knew. The shuttle would burn to a crisp if it tried to re-enter the atmosphere with one of its long, floppy doors not properly latched. The turbulence of re-entry would pull it open, yank it off, and allow superhot plasma to scorch through the unprotected cargo bay floor. If the right-hand door didn't shut, they didn't have time to go out and close it manually. Slowly, finally, the starboard door came down, bounced twice, and pulled itself against the port door.

"Centerline latches secure," Alexandra said. "Bulkhead latches . . . Santy, we have a problem with one of the aft bulkhead latches! I'm not getting a closed reading!''

"Thirty seconds to ignition," Melanie said. "Should I abort?''

"Negative," Santich said, pushing off toward the aft windows. Sure enough, the microswitch for the aft starboard latch still read OPEN. Orlov flipped on the cargo bay lights and Santich stared out with a pair of binoculars. "There. I see it. Looks like some of the weather seal has torn free and folded back between the door and bulkhead.''

"Are we going to be okay?" Alexandra asked.

Santich shook his head. "I don't like it. The gap's about two inches. But we don't have a lot of options—''

All three were shoved against the aft console as *Columbia*'s OMS engines rumbled to life, spewing flame to drop *Columbia* out of orbit and back to Earth.

"Two engines up and burning," Melanie said.

The slight thrust continued, enough to let Santich spin around and stand up on the aft wall. "Like I was saying. We didn't have time to go out and fix it. We could try to recycle the doors after the burn, but I'm afraid it might stick even further open.''

He saw Orlov raise the Zeiss binoculars against the window, lower them quietly. He flicked off the cargo bay lights, reached for the cabin light switch. "We need to save every milliamp," he said.

Santich looked at the cluttered flight deck. "We also need to clean up. And get the chairs installed, and suit up. And we have exactly . . . thirty-five minutes until entry interface.''

The crew separated to gather the necessary equipment, leaving Santich to pick up the loose pens, notebooks, hand microphones and other bits of hardware that had collected on the aft bulkhead. He took a quick glance through the aft windows into the now pitch-black cargo bay. For a decade, he'd made safety his first concern. He'd dreamed up outlandish failure scenarios and then invented procedures to get out of them alive. In all those years, he had never thought of circumstances quite this grim.

In less than an hour, *Columbia* would run out of electricity, her life-giving elixir. Without it, the computers wouldn't work, and without computers to make the continuous, mind-boggling number of flight dynamics calculations every second, the hundred-ton ship would fly like a refrigerator. And for that hour, the crew would rely on a suspect computer program, modified in flight, and never debugged.

The crisis's only positive aspect was that it happened at a point that let them reach their new destination, Santich thought. After the deorbit burn, *Columbia* could not make any significant changes to her trajectory. She would be out of gas, able to maneuver, at most, about a thousand miles right or left of the point that gravity would bring her down.

"I would like to keep this one plugged in, to monitor our progress," Orlov said, lifting one of the notebook computers over the commander's seat so the slight artificial gravity pushed it against the backrest.

Santich nodded, pushed himself out of the way so Orlov and Alexandra could bolt onto the flight deck the two additional seats that they had stowed in the first hours of the mission.

Within minutes the seats were in place, and the crew helped one another into the bright orange launch-and-entry suits. They worked quietly, and Santich wondered what thoughts ran through their heads. Fear, certainly, though probably not panic. Melanie's fighter pilot training prepared her for a wide variety of unpleasant scenarios. Even the basic astronaut training included some survival skills.

"When did we last update our state vector?" Melanie asked.

Santich blinked, stopped fussing with the unwieldy jacket he had been struggling with. He had forgotten all about that. Normally the shuttle received updated positions from the ground, based on radar tracking, to correct the errors that crept into the inertial navigation position based on the shuttle's gyroscopes. "This morning," he said finally. "Right after the vice president's call."

"I do not think we will be more than a few miles off by the time we reach our target," Orlov said. "With good weather, you should be able to correct that visually."

He was right, Santich thought, attaching the helmet to his collar. He turned to help Alexandra with hers and then glanced around. "Are we ready?" he asked. Three helmets nodded quickly. "Let's do it."

41

Even with the visor down, the sun was blinding, and Santich closed one eye, then the other for some relief. Just a few more minutes . . . Outside, the occasional flash of orange flame still licked the windows as *Columbia* plunged through the atmosphere, her nose pointed upward to let the heat-resistant belly bear the brunt. Behind them, the occasional flame licked down through the gap in the cargo bay doors, giving them a flash of red from the aft windows, too. He had already seen the rubber weather stripping burst into bright yellow fire. He finally had to tell Alexandra to stop turning around and looking. If the door ripped open, they were finished. There was nothing they could do.

Sweat dribbled freely down his nose, off his jaw and pooled down by the pressure suit's collar, the result of an electricity-saving measure Orlov had recommended ten minutes earlier. All the interior lights, all the extraneous equipment had been turned off, and it still wasn't enough. Orlov predicted *Columbia* would run out of juice at 150,000 feet, more than 120 miles northwest of Tampa. Santich had reluctantly agreed to turn off the shuttle's biggest power hog: the air-conditioning. Keeping the humans cool, of course, was merely a secondary benefit. The system was designed to prevent all the sensitive electronic equipment from overheating.

"How hot is it, Alex?"

"I show ninety-four degrees," Orlov answered. "The electronics boxes are supposed to be rated for one hundred twenty."

Supposed to be. Great. "How are we doing, power-wise?"

"We have between twenty-five and thirty minutes, at this rate."

Barely enough. So much for turning the air-conditioning back on. *Come on ... one more minute.* Then *Columbia,* still traveling twenty times the speed of sound, would race out of the eastern Pacific's morning and into British Columbia's early afternoon. That would put the sun higher overhead and out of their eyes.

"How we doing, Mel?"

"Close to nominal," she answered. "But I think we're a few miles downrange of where we should be."

Santich thought a moment. "Yeah. It makes sense. We're about nine hundred pounds lighter without the robot arm. You better add a half degree to our alpha angle."

Melanie leaned forward and typed into the keyboard at her left hand. "Done."

Columbia responded imperceptibly, tilting her nose up another half degree, increasing the aerodynamic drag and slowing down a bit more. She continued on this course for another five minutes, when her port wing dropped suddenly, bringing her course from southeast to just north of east. This attitude was held for a few minutes, followed by a dip in the right wing and a new course just east of south.

"First roll reversal," Melanie announced. "We're down to Mach 18."

The series of rolls further killed their speed, with the aim of giving Santich ten thousand feet of altitude and four hundred knots of speed when the computers reached the latitude and longitude that Orlov had given them earlier that morning.

Outside the starboard-side windows, the snow-covered Canadian Rockies passed forty miles beneath them, followed in a few minutes by the northern Great Plains.

His last view. Never again would he be this high. Never again would the planet rush before him so fast, giving him the entire world in ninety minutes. *Columbia* started rolling back to port, giving Santich a dark, almost indigo Lake Superior. *Never again.*

"Guys, I'm sorry it turned out this way," he said quietly.

No one said anything for a moment. "It's not your fault, Santy," Melanie answered.

"Well, it is. I knew what was going on. I had the least to lose. I could have stopped this back in March. The program, your careers, everything, would have been much better off."

Again a brief silence. "No, Santy," Alexandra said. "Any one of us could have stopped this. We all knew there was something fishy, but we went along anyway. Whatever happens to the program, to manned spaceflight, I think there's enough blame to go around."

The Great Lakes gave way to the Mississippi Valley, surrounded by lush green farmland. They would be there soon. Thirty years, he'd given to this. *For what?* Was it all just ego gratification? Maybe someday someone would be able to build on what they'd started, someone not interested in keeping alive a bloated bureaucracy, a giant cold war industry, an elite cadre of the nation's brightest and most egotistical. Some other time, and definitely some other person. That much he knew.

Thirty miles below, the Delta spread into the Gulf. *Columbia* banked to the east again, flying just off the coast. The crew watched through the downhill window as the harbor cities slipped past: Biloxi, Mobile, Pensacola.

Santich watched the artificial horizon and rate of descent displays closely, ready to grab the stick away at a moment's notice. But the GPCs were having no problem with the new target they'd been given, and rolled *Columbia* again to the south.

"Three hundred miles, one hundred fifty thousand feet," Melanie said.

The northwest Florida coast: the last undeveloped stretch

left. Maybe he and Emily could find a little place there. Maybe he would finally learn how to sail. He sighed, thinking again of Banke, and then Hooper. *For what?* He shook his head, trying to free himself from the cloud that threatened to fog his concentration. He couldn't allow that.

"Santy, we have a problem," Orlov said flatly.

"What?"

"Something . . . We just had a burp. I show less than three minutes of cryo left."

Three minutes!

"Two hundred miles, one hundred twenty thousand feet," Melanie said.

"How the—"

"I do not know. Perhaps the gauge is wrong. Perhaps it was wrong earlier."

Christ. Santich bit his lip, recalled his written appraisal of the telescoping escape pole seven years earlier. He'd called it a $75 million public relations gimmick. But was there a choice? He grabbed the stick and disengaged the autopilot. "Okay. Everyone unstrap. Alex, blow the hatch on my command. Then bail out. Mel, you first, then Alexandra, then you, Alex. I'll bring up the rear."

"Can't we try for McDill Air Force—" Alexandra began.

"No. We might make it down, or we might fall onto downtown Saint Pete. We can't risk that. *Come on: Go, go, go!*"

42

Keener ears heard the sonic boom way up the Gulf coast, but even the hard of hearing noticed it along Tampa Bay. Cars stopped on the Sunshine Skyway, drivers searching first their cars, then the bridge and finally, the sky for the source.

There, way off in the distance, barely a speck . . .

About ten miles up and twenty miles southwest, the black-and-white delta shape began a dive down, down, down, toward the pale green water before finally leveling off. With a puff of smoke, a round metal plug blew off the port forward side. From the hole extended a metal pole that grew to ten feet, drooping downward slightly from its own weight.

Suddenly a bright orange figure slid feet first off and down the pole, and plunged head over heels toward the water for a few seconds before a thin white stream of nylon erupted from its backpack, seemingly yanking the orange shape upward. The process repeated twice more, until three white blossoms floated gently toward the sea.

Above, a fourth orange figure appeared at the hole, then disappeared as the spaceship suddenly pointed her nose downward. In a few seconds, the ship leveled off, but a moment later began diving again. Again she leveled off, but only for a second, as once more she pitched downward, this time rolling to starboard as well. By the time he reap-

337

peared at the opening, the craft was nose down, rolling twice a minute.

He grabbed the pole, waited for the downward roll and flung himself out the hatch. His legs barely missed the tip of the huge delta wing, but his backpack didn't, taking a clip that sent him spinning as wildly as the out-of-control ship that passed him in its reckless plummet.

The white bloom popped free as humankind's most traveled spaceship began a yaw that, for a final fatal moment, turned the craft broadside to her fall. The wings first cracked, then sheared off, followed by the tail assembly. Bright orange smoke spewed from torn hypergolic tanks before the lethal gases found each other. The blast tore apart the rear of the fuselage and finally triggered another explosion that destroyed the nose.

The space shuttle *Columbia* was no longer.

43

The late afternoon sun felt good on his chest, and he wondered whether it would be warm enough, long enough, for another swim. He decided against it. He had no towel, and the night might get chilly.

He looked up again at the mangrove swamp slowly getting closer, now barely a half mile to the east. A sea breeze, he knew, pushing gently against the raft's half-erected canopy. A sea breeze that would die as the sun sank. He sighed, looking at the mess he'd made in the tiny life raft. The various pieces of his pressure suit, the sweaty clothes he'd put on—when? yesterday, right after the space walk—the balled-up, still-wet parachute. There wasn't even room to lie down. Come nightfall, some of this was going to have to go, he decided, wondering if the pressure suit would sink.

He shook his head, remembering the escape. Just another ten seconds, that's all he would have needed, when the nose dropped out from under him. He'd scrambled up the stairs into the flight deck, and realized he shouldn't have. The fuel cells were down to their last gulp of oxygen, and the voltage supply had already become erratic. He turned off three of the GPCs, but that gave him only another few seconds.

That he got out alive was a minor miracle, especially given the blow he'd taken from the wing. The soreness in his back was only now setting in; he lifted his left arm to stretch things out again. Luckily, the only thing broken had been the emergency radio beacon, which took a dent in the metal casing and now refused to turn on. Well, they'd find him eventually.

It was a shame, of course, that the Homestead thing hadn't worked. That would have been a kick. He could have made his statement to a couple of wire-service reporters and snuck out before the rest of the pack even figured out what was happening. Oh, well. It had turned out all right, considering.

The transistor radio from the life raft kit told him that Coast Guard units from all over the state, Air Force planes from McDill and Homestead and Navy planes from Key West, Mayport and Pensacola were converging on a strip of water from Tampa Bay down to the Dry Tortugas.

A news station from Tampa had had the most detailed reports, including the fact that Colonel Martin Bruce, United States Air Force, was now a fugitive, last seen walking out of the Mission Control room, ostensibly to get a cup of coffee. It was still unclear what, exactly, he had done—the FBI agents and U.S. attorney's lawyers staking out Johnson weren't talking. It *was* clear, though, that Trudy Cortain, Kyle Hartsfield, Emily Pembroke Santich and *Columbia* commander Santiago Santich were heroes.

Trudy and Kyle, according to the Tampa station, had stormed into the federal building with a laptop and had insisted on seeing the prosecutors who had pursued her husband before his death. She had shown them the suicide note from Hooper, and when NASA Select once again went off the air without explanation, she'd convinced them that they had to get Bruce out of the control room.

Emily, according to a Top 40 station in Sarasota, had been calling Homestead Air Reserve Base all morning, trying to convince them her husband was bringing the shuttle their way. It was only after it was obvious that *Columbia* had indeed deorbited, and that NASA's Mission Control was in chaos, that the commander scrambled the base and left the main runway free and clear.

And a country-western station in Fort Myers had "scooped" the world, interviewing Orlov, Melanie and Alex as they stepped off a Coast Guard launch. They had also found Emily at home in Naples; she'd asked fishermen to look out for her husband. He couldn't fish to save his life, she explained, and would starve if they didn't find him soon.

He tugged on the cardboard spool again. Still nothing. How long had he been at it? He checked his watch. Two hours. Maybe using part of his rations for bait had been a dumb idea. He looked back over his shoulder. A quarter mile off now. Close enough to row the rest of the way. That's what he would do: row in, tie to a mangrove branch to stay put for the night and then strike out across the swamp at first light.

Couldn't fish to save his life. The nerve of the woman. Not long after that remark, just as the Tampa station had found some pundits to yammer on about What This Meant for NASA's Future, the battery faded, then died. And that, he decided, would be the subject of his first memo as a part-time NASA consultant: spare batteries for radios in life raft packs.

He picked up the plastic radio, flicked the power dial. Nope, nothing. A hero, they had called him. He knew better. A *real* hero would have gone forward immediately, the same morning he heard Bruce get up and lie about the landing. A real hero wouldn't let one, two, three innocent men, his best friend included, die just to satisfy an urge, an addiction. A real hero knew when it was time to go home.

Santich looked out at the horizon, at the gentle swell rolling in across the Gulf, and sighed.

He began reeling in the line when the sharp tug nearly yanked the spool out of his hands. He had something! Quickly he grabbed the spool with both hands, gave a little line as the fish started a run. Suddenly the surface broke fifty yards away, and a brown torpedo rose, then fell back with a splash.

A snook! At least fifteen, maybe twenty pounds! The world's worst fisherman, Emily had called him. *Couldn't fish to save his life.*

At the edge of his consciousness, he heard a low drone. *No!* Not now! *Come back in an hour!* He turned around and saw the dark shape approaching from the south. A P-3 Orion, he knew instantly. He held the spool with his left hand, reached for the flare pistol with his right. No, there was no way to load, cock and fire with just one hand.

Gingerly he tied the line to a stainless steel ring on the raft's upper tube and started on the flare gun. The line was only eight-pound test, so the fish would only have to run to . . .

SNAP! And the line went slack. He was gone. Santich clicked the pistol shut, pulled back the hammer and aimed straight upward. With a bang, a ball of yellow streaked upward, then floated down at the end of a tiny parachute. Still a mile away, the P-3 turned toward the flare, then wagged its wings before climbing slightly and starting a station-keeping circle.

Santich sat back down and started reeling in the line. At least it had broken near the leader. That would be the subject of the second memo: stronger fishing line in the life raft kit. He tied on his second, and last, braided stainless leader and hook, baited it with another piece of hot dog and tossed it overboard.

It would be another hour before the boat arrived, he knew. Maybe the fish was still hungry.

For four years, S.V. DÁTE covered NASA for the *Orlando Sentinel* in Cape Canaveral. He wrote *Final Orbit* during a year he spent sailing across the Atlantic and back with his wife aboard *Sounion,* their thirty-one-foot cutter. He now writes for the *Palm Beach Post*'s statehouse bureau in Tallahassee, where he and his wife have a one-year-old son. *Final Orbit* is his first novel.

EXPERIENCE THE PULSE-POUNDING EXCITEMENT OF

RICHARD HERMAN, JR.

CALL TO DUTY
71831-6/ $6.50 US/ $8.50 Can
"One of the best adventure writers around"
Clive Cussler, author of *Sahara*

FIREBREAK
71655-0/ $6.50 US/ $8.50 Can
"A thrilling military adventure story ...
on a par with Tom Clancy"
Denver Post

FORCE OF EAGLES
71102-8/ $6.99 US / $8.99 Can
"Breathtakingly realistic and truly
edge of the seat exciting ... a fantastic story"
Dale Brown

THE WARBIRDS
70838-8/ $4.95 US/ $5.95 Can
"Truly hair-raising ... thoroughly believable"
Kirkus Reviews

Buy these books at your local bookstore or use this coupon for ordering:

Mail to: Avon Books, Dept BP, Box 767, Rte 2, Dresden, TN 38225   G
Please send me the book(s) I have checked above.
❑ My check or money order—no cash or CODs please—for $_____is enclosed (please add $1.50 per order to cover postage and handling—Canadian residents add 7% GST). U.S. residents make checks payable to Avon Books; Canada residents make checks payable to Hearst Book Group of Canada.
❑ Charge my VISA/MC Acct#_____Exp Date_____
Minimum credit card order is two books or $7.50 (please add postage and handling charge of $1.50 per order—Canadian residents add 7% GST). For faster service, call 1-800-762-0779. Prices and numbers are subject to change without notice. Please allow six to eight weeks for delivery.
Name_____
Address_____
City_____State/Zip_____
Telephone No._____
                                                            RHJ 0897